W9-BNJ-776

ALSO BY ELIZABETH GRAVER

Have You Seen Me?

Unravelling

The Honey Thief

Awake

The End of the Point

Kantika

Kantika

A Novel

ELIZABETH GRAVER

METROPOLITAN BOOKS
Henry Holt and Company
New York

Metropolitan Books
Henry Holt and Company
Publishers since 1866
120 Broadway
New York, New York 10271
www.henryholt.com

Metropolitan Books® and m® are registered trademarks of
Macmillan Publishing Group, LLC.

Copyright © 2023 by Elizabeth Graver
All rights reserved.
Distributed in Canada by Raincoast Book Distribution Limited

All photographs courtesy of the author from her family archives, with the exception of the two photographs on page 124, which are reprinted with permission of the National Center for Jewish Film. Page 288 photograph by Jack Levy.

The Library of Congress Cataloging-in-Publication data is available.

ISBN: 9781250869845

Our books may be purchased in bulk for promotional, educational, or business use. Please contact your local bookseller or the Macmillan Corporate and Premium Sales Department at (800) 221-7945, extension 5442, or by email at MacmillanSpecialMarkets@macmillan.com.

First Edition 2023

Designed by Kelly S. Too

Printed in the United States of America

1 3 5 7 9 10 8 6 4 2

For my mother
Suzanne Levy Graver
& in memory of my grandmother
Rebecca Cohen Baruch Levy

Deshame entrar, y me azere lugar.

Let me enter, and I'll make a place for myself.

—Ladino proverb

Kantika

Constantinople, 1907

I

This, the beautiful time, the time of wingspans, leaps and open doors, of the heedless, headlong flow from here to there. This, the time before thought, the world arriving not as lists or harkening back or future tense, but as breath-filled music—*kantar*, sing.

Rebecca sings to the rhythm of the oars as the boat delivers her to school, and in school with the nuns—*tournez vos yeux vers Jésus*—and climbing ropes at Maccabi gymnastics, hand over hand and wrap your feet, girls, but what draws her up is less the instructor barking commands or the strength of her limbs than the unspooling thread of her own voice. In wordless tunes, nonsense sounds and ballads, in Ladino, French and bits of Turkish, Hebrew, Greek, she sings, as on the street the lemon man sings lemons, the Bulgarian sings pudding, the vegetable man sings eggplant, squash and artichokes—"fresh, cheap, ladies, how I wait for you with my aubergine!" She sings at school in chorus and for daily hymns, and at night her mother sings the children to sleep: "*Durme durme, kerido ijiko* . . ."—sleep sleep, darling boy, though two of them are girls. If the dull-eyed nightingale rarely makes a chirp, still her father stops by its cage most mornings to try to coax it into song, and he sings at synagogue—"you've given me a throat that has not gone dry for calling out to you"—and one strange morning after services, he leads Rebecca to the ark (she has just turned eight, still more baby than girl in his eyes), and she sings to the men below and the women above, her voice as unwavering as the cushioned freedoms and unspeakable good fortune of her childhood (still, her grandmother sews a *bonjuk* bead to the underside of every collar to ward off the evil eye).

Their house has three stories and is made of stone, which does not burn. Down the slope is Balat, where the poor Jews live, but her family lives at the top of the hill in Fener, their neighbors Greek diplomats, Armenian doctors, Jewish bankers and traders like her father, and it is with the daughters of these families and a few equally prosperous Muslim girls that Rebecca and her sister Corinne go to Catholic school. From their bedroom window, they can see the brick tower of the Greek School for Boys, and below it, the minarets of mosques, and beyond that, the Golden Horn with its blinking lighthouse and Hasköy and Galata on the other side.

Downstairs, a stream of people come and go, the door more invitation than barrier, men arriving in the evening to join Rebecca's father in prayer, and it is only after the guests kiss the mezuzah and file out into the dark that he locks the door and shuts the iron gate. On Sunday afternoons, her mother's friends and relatives arrive to play cards, gossip and assemble baskets for the poor, and so-and-so might be a second cousin or a cousin's cousin, or it's Rebecca's best friend, Rahelika, running up the stairs, or the dressmaker come for a fitting, or Oktay the music master instructing her father on the ney flute. During the week, her father is at the textile factory or out wandering the city, but on Fridays he returns to them, the house spotless, the children, too. Her mother covers her face, says the prayer and lights the candles, and as the wicks sputter and take hold, the sun goes down and the gleaming house falls quiet.

Saturday wakes to sound and light. Later in life, Rebecca will encounter Jews for whom the Sabbath is a solemn, davening affair—no apricots in syrup or pomegranates with their bloody pearls, just gefilte fish trembling in slime. Here, too, the meals are prepared ahead of time, and Gateel, the Armenian maid, arrives to start the fire, serve and wash the dishes, but the children are encouraged to dance and make merry on Shabbat, and in the afternoon, the family visits with relatives or takes a riverboat to the park, where the babies nap in a hammock tied to a tree, sometimes several babies to one tree, suspended like pendulous, damp fruit. For supper there's cold fish with lemon and egg, and *lokum* for dessert, and toasted melon seeds to snack on, and the ball comes out for catch, the tambourine for song. Later, at home, they will light the braided candle, then snuff it with wine and laugh out loud to show the evil spirits that though Shabbat is over, joy remains and has no place for them. Hahaha, hahaha!

Kyen no rizika, no rozika. Whoever doesn't laugh, doesn't bloom.

~

If Rebecca's father is not, even then, a loud or overtly cheerful man, still he laughs often, a reedy, high, almost wheezing sound, and while he is not tall in stature, he seems tall because of how other men tip their hats to him or clap him on the shoulder, whether at *kal*—synagogue—or in the marketplace or coffeehouse, and he is on friendly terms with important people: the pharmacist and dentist at the sultan's palace, the owner of the tobacco factory, who gives Rebecca candy cigarettes. He counts among his associates philosophers, scholars, bankers, even the chief rabbi, who comes to the house to discuss ideas or offer advice. Her father's friends call him Alberto, but his real name, Abraham, means "father of many," and her mother's name, Sultana, means "queen," and their family name, Cohen, means "high priest," which isn't something to brag about but something to know, just as Rebecca knows that her own name comes from her mother's mother and means "to bind or to tie," and that the name of their street, Çorbaci Çeşmesi, means "soup-maker's fountain," and one day, Rebecca and Corinne come home from school to find two bowls of steaming soup perched on the edge of the fountain and their mother telling them to thank the fountain and standing guard against the cats.

Every few years, they go to Studio Parnasse on Grande Rue de Péra, where an Armenian man with enormous hands covers himself with a dark cloth and takes their photograph. One year, their nanny, Victoria, who is also their second cousin, is with them and stands behind the children for the portrait. They're in a faux garden with a painted backdrop of a Doric column, silk flowers at their feet. It's supposed to be a choice—garden, palace, salon or imperial caïque—but their father always picks the garden, just as he always positions himself behind the photographer, hands up, a conductor mandating a pause.

Does he have something to prove? *Es de buena famiya.* Or something to preserve? He found his second marriage late in life and takes pleasure in his children's youthful beauty, even as he feels time panting down his neck. Or something to hide? He is rarely in the photographs himself. The children's feet ache from all the standing, but even as early as four or five years old, Rebecca notices how being photographed makes her feel more real, more seen. Alberto will frame the picture of the children with their cousin Victoria for his wife Sultana's birthday, though she is not in it, home resting in bed, which means pregnant again and at risk of another miscarriage or stillbirth. So take your pills shipped from France. So hang a sprig of *ruda*—rue, the queen of herbs—over your bedroom door and collect dew in a teacup on the windowsill (he puts no stock in this nonsense, but his wife does). Pray.

BEHIND THEIR HOUSE is a small, sloped garden with Alberto's roses and Sultana's herbs, and in spring, crocuses, tulips and grape hyacinths, and on the street side in winter, the cold stone fountain, and always, down the hill, Rebecca's father's first wife, Djentil Nahon. When a fire comes—in Balat, usually, or across the water—the watchman cries out, *Yangin var! Yangin var!*, and everyone climbs the brick steps to the highest point on the hill to watch the smoke below, flames rising, not their house, not quite their neighborhood, but don't feel too blessed, don't say you're lucky—this will curdle your luck. Just wait until the smoke clears and offer to help by giving money, food and clothes. The fire brigades spray some water, but mostly they dismantle the houses, bashing in doors, walls and windows so that the fire gobbling up one dwelling can't leap to the next, and soon there are no houses where the fire tore through, just ashy air that stings the eyes and mattresses lumbering through the streets, headless beasts on the bent backs of men.

Is this when Rebecca feels her first flicker of unease, standing snug between her mother and little brother, Isidoro, an adult's hand resting heavy on her hair? Is this when the skin of her eyelids first registers the possibility of sudden loss—how, for the people below, a house is a matchbox, its residents slender, red-tipped matches; strike them and they flare? The smoke smells musky sweet, the scene a shadow play lit from inside, and then the structure is on tiptoes, red ribs flaring, a fire scouring her wrists, chest, groin.

AT PURIM, THEY GIVE *biscochos* to the neighbors, and on Tu B'Shevat they pass out candied almonds to wish the trees a happy birthday. At Shavuot, they rent a boat and go for a picnic at the Sweet Waters of Europe, and at Orthodox Easter, the Papadopouloses next door bring them colored eggs. And if Rebecca is told not to cross in front of the church that week or go near the Easter parade with its rabbi effigy, so she is told not to do a great many things. Stay away from gypsies. Don't pick your father's flowers. Don't compliment a pretty baby, and if you forget, undo the words with more words, unsaying them, a common practice in Ladino, where evil spirits are called *buena djente*—good people—and a blind man is a *vistozo*, one who can see.

In school, you must always speak French, and if you're caught using another language, even during recess, you must put a coin in the pot for the needy. Christ is everywhere at Lycée Notre Dame de Sion—in the hallway alcove, in the classrooms, in the art studio, where they see images of Baby Jesus through the ages, naked or swaddled, dimpled or skinny, white to the point of glowing. Sometimes a porcelain baby doll in a white dress is set out on the table for them to draw. Most girls can't get beyond a few crude shapes, but Rebecca falls happily inside the task, following the curve of arm, the broad forehead, managing the splayed fingers by focusing on the shapes between.

Twice a week, while the Christian students receive catechism, the Jewish girls attend a separate religious history class (because there are so few Muslims at the school, they get to leave early). It is led by Monsieur Eskenazi, who teaches them about Jews being chased and Jews being run out of town and Jews being brave, while an old nun dozes in the corner so they're not left alone with a man. Who is Hashem? Monsieur intones. A hand shoots up—prissy Roza Valpreda's: He whose name cannot be said. Rebecca has never seen an image of El Dyo, and when her father speaks of Him, it is in mind-bendingly abstract ways, as the One Who Can Be Understood for What He Is Not, or the One Who Has No Human Form, or the One Who Is Said Through the Unsaid. He lectures his children like this, growing increasingly driven, until Rebecca's mother stops him, and so they lightly argue: But I need to teach them, Sultana!—But you talk too much, darling—Well, you talk too little—Not true, I talk plenty, just not of things impossible for a child to understand.

Be *sage* in the classroom, hands clasped, face to front, and curtsy when you see Notre Mère Marie-Godeleine, who takes a special interest in the Jewish girls because the school was founded by a Jewish-German convert whose dark oil portrait hangs in the front hall. Learn to sew and embroider—first with thick red wool, then with cotton, and finally with silk for your trousseau—and dress *à la Franca,* in outfits modeled on the latest fashions from Pareee. Be generous to the poor. Rebecca and Corinne go with their mother to bring packages to a Jewish orphanage in a neighborhood where the cratered streets have no name and women squat in doorways, cooking on outdoor grills. The girls are not allowed to leave the carriage, but they may wave from their perch to the orphan boys who hop up to get the bundles from the back. Their parents call this *benadamlik*—to be a good person—and at school the nuns write it in perfect cursive on the chalkboard as *le devoir avant tout.*

Whatever its name, Rebecca's childhood is steeped in it, and this both speaks to and goes against her nature, which is to open her hands, touch, offer, create—but also to grab, stow, hoard. And while she is too young to know that her father is a distracted, half-hearted businessman fast burning through the family fortune, and that the tides are turning against the Greeks and especially the Armenians but also the Jews, and that her people are only long-term guests here in an economy of tolerance, she is nonetheless the one, out of all her friends, most likely to spot the glint of a coin lodged between the cobblestones, hungry for the silvery taste of fished-out luck.

II

HALFWAY DOWN THE HILL live two important people—Rahelika and Djentil Nahon. Rebecca has always had a best friend and it has always been Rahelika, who goes to school with her and to gymnastics and to the summer house in Büyükdere, because their mothers are close friends, and Lika's father is a poorly paid teacher at an Alliance Israélite school, and they have no summer house. The two girls look alike, both dark-haired and petite. Strangers sometimes mistake them for twins, though Rebecca's eyes are lighter, and they tote around twin dolls, birthday gifts from Rebecca's father—Chérie and Bella, with blond ringlets and beatific smiles. Rebecca stands out at school at drawing, painting and singing, while Lika, on a scholarship to Sion, is gifted in math and science and would like to be a nurse, which the nuns say is possible if you pray and study hard enough. "Beccalika," Mère Mélanie (so young, pretty and mirth-filled that she seems more like an older sister than a nun) calls the girls, or "Likabecca," and by the time Rebecca is nine, her own home overrun with babies, she is allowed to walk alone to Lika's house, clutching Chérie, down the hill past the glassblower with his burned face, past the furrier, fishmonger, sesame oil maker, until she arrives at Lika's door.

There, she is fussed over, cooked for, doted on by Lika's mother and allowed to sink with Lika into hours of imaginary play, or they'll leaf through the illustrated French magazines Lika's father uses with his students—*Journal des Voyages* and *Je Sais Tout*—finding one day, among the shirtless whalers and feathered Indian chiefs, an illustrated folio on the Oriental Jew, and there, a lady with a black strap winding from beneath her chin to the top of her head and another strap circling her dress, hoisting up her enormous bosom. Her expression is dazed, her eyes beady; she might be a trussed bird. TYPICAL TURKISH JEWESS reads the caption. Between laughing fits, the girls stuff themselves with tea towels, bind each other in sashes and pretend to pose for photographs. Sometimes on Sunday nights, Rebecca sleeps at Lika's, bringing her school uniform with its white lace collar and black frock, and in winter, the black peacoat and wide-brimmed hat, and in spring, the straw hat made in France.

Djentil Nahon, Rebecca's father's first wife, lives upstairs from Lika, and Lika calls her *tiya*, for "aunt," though they're not related, so Rebecca does too. Several times a week, Tiya Djentil calls out the window or bangs on her floor, which is Lika's ceiling, and the girls know this means she has a task for them. When they come out to the street, she lowers money in a basket on a rope and sends them off to peddlers or shops, errands that Lika's mother says they must fulfill cheerfully because to be childless is a sorrow and Tiya worries about leaving her ancient mother on her own. Sometimes the girls make quick work of it and deliver the items into the basket. Other times Tiya Djentil says come up for a visit, *mi suvrinas*, I've made you a cake. So dutifully at first and then with increasing desire, they climb the steep stairs to the dark apartment, and as her old mother snores on the couch, Tiya Djentil offers them almond cakes and linden tea or black coffee with sugar, which they gulp down fast so she can read their fortunes in the muddy grounds. After the food is served and Tiya Djentil says *kome kon gana*—eat with desire—she settles her tiny, oddly girlish body into a massive wooden chair and tells them stories of the kind that Rebecca's father loathes and her mother tolerates and Rebecca hungers for.

"So one day last week, I banged and called—I'd made you cake—but you didn't come. First I thought, all right, so they're not coming, they're at school or helping their mothers, but soon it was late afternoon and I'd stopped calling but started to worry. Something terrible has happened! A kidnapping, accident or fire, even a rape—you shouldn't know what it is—but then I realized there were evil spirits, *shedim*, right here in my house, inhabiting my wooden spoon, because when I clipped my good mother's nails, I forgot to burn the parings. So I said, Mama, wake up, quick! There's trouble in our spoon! Notice I didn't say *shedim* aloud to her—if you name them in their presence, they'll come forward. My poor mother woke up and started whimpering—ahhh, ahhh, ahhh!—like somebody was poking her with a hot knife. They were there that day, the *shedim*! The spoon came after me, and my mother, too! But not you girls. I must have kept you away without realizing it. I knew in my bones before the spoon told me. I'm blessed with that kind of knowing. Maybe you have it, too."

Rebecca glances at Lika, whose lips are white with powdered sugar, and Lika, trying not to laugh, snorts instead, sugar puffing from her mouth. Something also rises in Rebecca, but it's not laughter. Might she also have that special kind of knowing? Does she want it? The objects on the table—the plate of cookies, tarnished *bombonyera* full of stale candies, jars of beads and cloves—take on a sudden weight, as if each has not a face, exactly, but a soul, a personality and will. Her dreams regularly contain things that are more than things—a wardrobe that walks but has no feet, a boat that laughs but has no mouth, people who are not quite people, though they appear to be. For as long as she can remember, she's seen faces everywhere, not just in the clouds, which is common, but in knots of wood and bowed iron window grilles and the flowers in her father's garden with their gaping mouths and silky heads. A few years ago at Pesach, she glimpsed the Prophet Elijah, just the cuff of his sleeve and his hand on the stem of a wineglass, but to see him at all is something that happens only to dogs and to people with a special gift.

"So then what happened?" she asks Tiya Djentil.

"The spoon in my hand got so hot that my skin, right here, started shedding, peeling off—" She holds up a finger with a shiny, raw tip.

"Oh, Tiya! You burned it!" says Lika. "You need to wrap it. Do you have any bandages? I can get some from my mother."

Djentil waves her off. "No need. I took care of it."

"How?" asks Rebecca.

Tiya shrugs. "Just sugar and paper."

"On your burned finger? You'll get an infection!" Lika sounds almost angry.

"Of course not! I put the sugar and paper under my pillow. Then the next day, you drink it with the dew. Like so, they leave. '*Vos do dulsuria, ke me desh sultura.*'" I give you sweetness that you may release me. "This is a reliable cure, but promise me you won't write it down. All true wisdom goes from mouth to ear. Until you tell, keep it shut away"—she raps twice on her forehead—"here."

In this manner, she goes on. Some of what she says is familiar to the girls, who have plenty of relatives who still believe in spirits and the evil eye, though at school the nuns will snip off their amulets if they spot them (but what of the wine as blood and the wafer as flesh; is this not equally far-fetched?). The girls' fathers are opposed to the old ways, but their mothers still reflexively neutralize a compliment with *sin ojo* or *ojo malo ke no tengan!*—without the eye; may the evil eye not get you. One day Djentil tells them that because sleep is one sixtieth part death, you can meet dead souls in dreams. The next, Rebecca's father tells them he just read that cosmic rays have been discovered by a scientist who climbed the Eiffel Tower. Why not? Either, both. One thing seems as plausible as the next.

More and more, Rebecca looks forward to her visits with Tiya Djentil. Everywhere she lives, works and studies contains a steady march toward order, from her home, which is a well-oiled machine despite its brood of children; to her school with its graph paper and polished floors; to her gymnastics club, where they parade military style, flexing their slight arms, because to be a Jew is to be strong is to be proud. At Tiya Djentil's, she finds another world. Despite its cramped size, the apartment reminds her of the forbidden quarters of the city she longs to explore: the Spice Bazaar, where she's only been once, on a school trip where they had to hold on to a length of communal rope, or the gypsy shows in the streets where a bear on a chain bangs a drum and slow-dances with his Romani master. Once, watching the bear from afar, she started panting with delight and would, if not restrained by her mother, have run straight into the arms of the dignified, sad, shuffling creature and buried her nose in the musk-oil blanket of its fur. Even then (she couldn't have been more than four), she knew it as a tale to tell and magnify, repeating it for months, though in her mind, it always took place yesterday: Yesterday I danced with the big bear! Tell the truth, Rebecca, her mother scolded from early on. Embroider your embroidery, that's all.

When her parents tell stories, the tales hold clear morals and almost never contain the word *I.* Not so with Djentil Nahon: Did I tell you about losing my *presyoza* mother in a fire? Did I tell you about the wild dog who snatched my baby in the night?

Afterward, when the girls emerge into the daylight, they take stock, and sometimes it's Rebecca who comforts Lika, who gets upset by Djentil's wanderings in a way that Rebecca rarely does, or sometimes it's Lika who dismantles the stories to find the chinks in them: She said it happened in July but it was snowing in the story; her mother isn't dead, she's on the couch! Now and then they sneak into their own mothers' gardens to pick herbs to put in potions or hang in the doorway, and if terrible things happen in their games (fire, illness, fanged creatures, maimed children, dead siblings), there's always a brew or spell to turn things around, and if they run out of stories or crave sweets, they can always run another errand for Tiya Djentil.

The fact that Rebecca's father used to be married to Djentil Nahon is simply how it is. It will take Rebecca a long time to think it noteworthy that her father even had a wife before her mother. That he is much older than her mother is also just how it is, and while she understands abstractly that her parents had lives before her, this doesn't much interest her, and they rarely speak of it. When finally, after spending the better part of an afternoon with Djentil Nahon, she asks her mother why her father's first marriage ended, she is told that Djentil Nahon could not have children.

A dog snatched her baby, Rebecca almost says, but something stops her. "Why didn't they find an orphan?"

"It's not that simple and not your business. Just be kind to her."

"I *am* kind. Yesterday we got her bread."

Her mother puts down her sewing and peers at her. "Lika's mother told me Sinyora Nahon has you up for tea. She says she's harmless. It's good of you to help her."

"I don't mind."

"Does she know who you are, that Papa is your father?"

In their neighborhood, doesn't everyone know everyone? "I think so. I don't know."

"Best not to mention it." Her mother is stitching again, something small and delicate, the needle dipping, rising, dipping in her right hand as her left rotates the hoop. "It might unsettle her to think of it."

"Why? Was Papa unkind to her?"

Her mother hesitates. "Not unkind, she just . . . she has troubles. Your papa helps her still. She has no little girl of her own." She sighs. "I've been—*ojo malo*—so lucky, even if my work never ends." She ties off a knot and cuts the tail with her teeth.

"How does he help her?"

"Enough, Rebecca."

"Does he give her money?"

"Do you ask this many questions in school? I pity your nuns."

Her mother has filled the corner of her mouth with pins now, the pearled ends sticking out as she releases the hoop and fastens the patch she's been working on to a bigger swathe, all of it white and gauzy, smelling clean. Rebecca sees that it will be a dress for her little sister, Elsa, with a smocked, embroidered center, and in the middle, a duck holding an umbrella in the rain, and beside the duck, a rabbit in galoshes. The rain is done in slanted gray running stitch, the boots in pink cross-stitch. The eyes—pink for the rabbit, black for the duck—are snug French knots. It is the most beautiful thing, and not for her.

"Hold this for me, please," says her mother through a mouth still stabbed with pins, but as Rebecca fights the urge to push the fabric away, Elsa starts crying from the nursery, which wakes Marko, who starts crying, too, and then the nanny is there—a new, stout one from Bulgaria—Elsa on her hip, Marko at her side, and her mother returns the pins to their plump rose cushion and rises with a backward glance—have you done your homework yet?—before descending on the little ones with open arms.

TIYA DJENTIL DOES NOT ASK THEM if they've done their homework. She does not even usually call them by name. Just, have some more tea, have another cookie, *listen*, so that in her presence the girls become four open ears, four eyes, two hungry mouths. Rebecca's father has been shutting the doors to his library of late, meeting to discuss important matters with business associates and men from the synagogue. Her parents have been speaking English over the children's heads. Rebecca is having a growth spurt and craves sugar more than ever. Her calves ache. She is rebuked by the nuns for jiggling her leg in class and singing louder than the other girls, by her mother for barreling down the stairs, by Corinne for rocking in bed at night, for she has discovered the rhythmic pleasure of her palm against her pelvic bone and relies on it now to fall asleep.

Tiya Djentil tells them about a creature with a boy's face and the body of a dolphin, about a spirit that is invisible but leaves chicken prints behind in the dirt, and a *zingana* Romani girl who is jilted by her lover so gives him a potion to make him break out in sores, and out of each sore a mushroom sprouts, and the girl makes a mushroom soup that he eats and falls back in love with her. "This one is true" is how Djentil begins each story. When her mother groans, Djentil rises to shift her position on the bed, spoon broth into her mouth or rub almond oil on her balding scalp, crooning as if her mother were a baby—*mi alma Mamasita, mi presyoza korazon.*

What is most peculiar to Rebecca about Tiya Djentil is not the nature of her stories, but how she can be at once so lost inside her fantastical worlds and so capable and caring at the same time. Her house, though stale and dusty, is stocked with delicious homemade food. Her mother, gnarled and curled, more dead than alive, is always clean, and at regular intervals Djentil kneels before the old woman, who is nearly twice her size, and slowly works her muscles, beginning with the fingers, moving to toes, feet, calves, singing softly before returning to her stories, so that it almost doesn't matter if the girls are there to listen, though if they get up to leave, she'll whip her head around and bid them stay.

Over time, Lika grows increasingly disturbed by the visits, though the sweets still tempt her. She should take her mother to a doctor, she says of Tiya Djentil. She should get her a chair on wheels and open the windows for fresh air. In school they have been learning about Florence Nightingale, who recently died, and Lika has started drawing pie charts and become a crusader for open windows, proper ventilation and clean hands.

"We should ignore her when she bangs on the floor. Maybe she'd open the window to call down if she sees us outside," Lika says one day. "It would air the place out."

"Stop, Lika. She's *lonely*," says Rebecca, as if she were the kinder, more generous soul, when in truth she wants the stories, shape-shifting and unruly, for herself.

"So one day—this is true, this is not a *konseja*—there was a rich lady living up the hill. Her husband took her on sightseeing trips to cities all over the world. One year, they went to Barcelona, Spain, and at the hotel, they spoke to the gentleman at the reception desk: 'Sinyor, we've come to see your fine city. Can you tell us what museums, what churches and castles to visit?' The manager says, 'Of course—go to this church, that exhibit, and afterward, if you have the courage, I'll show you something else.' The husband says, 'What do you mean by that, sinyor?' 'I mean if you have courage, the *guts*, I'll show you something right here at my hotel!' The husband still doesn't understand. 'Of course, we came to see your country, we want to see everything.' 'If you insist,' the manager tells him. 'I'll show you, but it's not my fault.'

"*Bueno*, so the couple visits all the sites and finally, on their last day, the manager takes them to the basement of his hotel. Now when you have a rug, what do you do with it in summer? You take it to the courtyard, pour hot water on it. Scrub. You clean it, roll it up, then store it in the basement for the winter. So this couple goes with the manager down to the hotel basement, and what they see is this: a big rug, rolled up. And the manager tells them it's made from our skin, the skin of our ancestors. Human skin. Jewish skin. 'I'm sorry to have to tell you this,' he says, 'but it's the truth.' On the walls, they see pictures, long tableaux, in all colors—again, made from our skin.

"I heard this story from the lady herself," says Tiya Djentil. "Sinyora Estella Caldora, of blessed memory. After that, she told everyone, 'So, my friends, go travel, see the wide world, *enjoy*, but promise me you'll never go back to Spain, because it suffers from a curse.' I'd never heard this before. I knew the Jews had their arms and legs broken in Spain, those who didn't leave or convert. They were burned or stoned, all kinds of things, but I'd never heard about the skin. Skin should disappear after you die. It's supposed to just, you know, return to the earth. Evaporate, disappear. This stayed. Can you imagine?"

She sighs, a long, rattling sound, and for a moment seems very far away, like someone else. "I don't know how they managed," says Tiya Djentil. "I just don't know."

III

For three years, Alberto had shared a home with Djentil Nahon, who for a time became Djentil Cohen when she married him. He was twenty-two when they married, and she eighteen, their union arranged by their parents when they were small. Somehow, as Djentil grew up, her family managed to keep largely hidden her strange ways, learned from their servants and from the older generations, or from the storm brewing in her brain. Or maybe Alberto was reeled in by his parents' desires or by the fact that Djentil was unusually pretty, tiny and big-eyed with long black curls, almond eyes and quick movements like a songbird, and Alberto was not a tall man and was a bit of a romantic (he loved flowers; he wrote the occasional line of verse). As was the custom, she moved in with him and his parents, and it was all right for a while. Their fathers were business associates, both in textiles, both prospering. The marriage strengthened the collaboration, and Djentil liked to sing and chatter and kept his mother company.

Though their marriage bed was a lively place, no child came, not the first year, not the second, and it was around this time that Djentil started leaving a glass outside on the balcony so she could drink the morning dew and mutter incantations, and soon she started drinking raki at all hours and wandering the streets at night, and one day at Alberto's cousin's son's Brit Milah, she burst out in the middle of the ceremony, asking for the foreskin so she could grind it into a potion to unblock her luck and get her with child, and the other women were both pitying and frightened, and some of the men turned it into a joke—hungry, lady? Have a bite!—and Alberto's humiliation was complete.

He found a doctor who specialized in ladies' troubles, and another who treated ailments of the mind. He even let Djentil's grandmother, who came from the interior near Ankara, do some *milizina de la kaza*, household cures, because there was power in thought and he was desperate, not for a child—that soon proved secondary—but to be able to take his wife on his arm to services and dinners hosted by his business associates and to charity and Purim balls, to come home and find her steady, clear-eyed, friendly, with his slippers and a glass of wine.

Djentil's grandmother split boiled eggs with a hair and had Djentil eat them. She made her rub her belly against the belly of a pregnant woman. Alberto's own mother watched helplessly and prayed. The doctors prescribed bed rest, poultices, pilules, fresh air, company, seclusion. Alberto began to gamble, just a little at first, at cards in the coffeehouse. Low stakes. A way to let off steam. Not only did Djentil not get pregnant, but she got sicker and sicker. She heard voices. She hacked off her hair and made it into jewelry, braiding in beads and beetle wings. Weeks when she spoke too much were followed by weeks when she did not speak at all. She sprinkled religion into her tales in ways that both frightened and disgusted him, claiming that Elijah the Prophet had entered her, leaving her with child. One day Alberto brought up his troubles to a man who had known the Nahons growing up, and the man said, Djentil, gone *loka*? I'm not surprised, she's always been a little— and he whistled and twirled his finger by his ear. For the first time, Alberto felt a fury that caused a dull ache in the roots of his teeth. Nobody warned me, he said.

There was a booming cotton business at the time in Manchester. Alberto's father, who had already more than doubled the size of the family's rare textiles enterprise, saw an opportunity for his son that involved the possibility of both profit and escape. Why not have a look, Alberto, why not see? They had a family friend over there, another Turkino, who was expanding. Alberto could learn the ropes, run exports, learn English, take a break from the troubles at home. So whose idea was it? He allowed himself to blame, or give credit to, his father. He left for only a month or two at first, then for longer stretches, sleeping in a twin bed across from his wife's when he returned but never touching her because if you didn't have a child after a certain amount of time—a long time, ten years—you could legally divorce your wife. In England, he found women in brothels and even took a gentile lover for a while. He managed to push aside memories of Djentil begging to come abroad with him and casting spells when he returned, how she'd straddle him in the middle of the night, bare-chested and never not beautiful, as small as a girl but with surprising curves and nipples the color of cinnamon and a probing tongue, then say there was something wrong with him—he must go for boys, he must be hexed—when he (such strength it took) refused. Take me with you, I promise to be good, she begged, but she'd have gone under in a place like Manchester, and Alberto's own rage frightened him, for he was not in his heart a good man, not really, he didn't think so. He had disturbing visions of slapping her silly until her *loka* thoughts bled out her ears and nose, and he was counting down the months and years.

Djentil moved back in with her parents. One time, he arrived home and went to drop off money only to be told she wasn't there, having been brought to a sanatorium. Every month he sent money from England, and for a while a gift on her birthday, a fine woolen shawl or velvet hat. He received a few letters from Djentil, which he was sure her mother wrote. Then the letters stopped. After two years, when he returned home for summer holidays, he didn't call on her, and eventually her father stopped doing business with his father. Alberto's brother, Maurice, had married well and produced two grandchildren, so his parents were kind enough to look the other way.

Alberto stayed in Manchester for ten years and six months (to be safe), with only the occasional brief visit home. It felt like a due and proper penance. England did not, as they said over there, *suit him*. It was gray and cold with tasteless food, and the language was difficult and held no charm. The gentile woman's husband returned from India. Alberto developed a connoisseur's interest in rare fabrics and learned to say *fustian*, *brocade* and *velveteen*, and stand at his spot in the Cotton Yard in a fez (should he add a snake in a basket, or a hookah pipe?) and broker deals, but the business world bored him, and numbers had never been his strength. It was during this time that he, never more than a passable student at the Talmud Torah and Alliance schools of his youth, began to read and study at night in his rooming house, first to improve his English and then, when a friend from Salonica lent him books in Ladino, Hebrew and French, to read the great Jewish thinkers. He found in the words of Saadia Gaon, Judah Halevi and especially Maimonides a way to think deeply and logically about things that mattered but also to find a path back to El Dyo, who had left him or whom he'd left, despite the fact that even before becoming a student of religion, he'd attended services at the Sephardic synagogue on Cheetham Hill Road because the pink marble columns and Moorish arch were the closest things, among all that gray, to home.

After the divorce, which took a good bit of money but was otherwise uncomplicated, he returned, to his relief, to Constantinople, a place he'd missed every day of his long absence. He came across Sultana barefoot and hanging laundry, of all things, when he was out walking on the island of Büyükada, where he had joined his parents on summer holiday. He'd been living the life of a bachelor for some years by then. He worked by day and frequented the cabarets, coffeehouses and bars by night, playing backgammon, poker and chess, gambling, discussing, disputing, listening to and playing music. Singing with the other men. After the bars, he read, and after he read, he prayed, and sometimes he prayed more than he drank, and other times he drank more than he prayed. Either way, the two things never felt at odds. On Friday nights and Saturday mornings, he went to the Ahrida synagogue, and most mornings he prayed at the small neighborhood *kal*, where he could also catch up with friends and discuss business over coffee served by a barefoot servant boy with a faint mustache. Every month, he sent money by way of a courier to Djentil Nahon, and if business was good, he sent a little more, and if bad, a little less. No one seemed particularly interested in arranging a match for him, not after he'd divorced his wife, and he was leery of marriage anyway and living, not unhappily, with his parents.

Sultana might, with her fresh face and bare arms piled high with laundry, have been a hired maid, but something stopped him—her goodness, maybe, or her sturdiness (unlike Djentil Nahon, she had some flesh on her bones), and the sea breeze ruffling her skirt and hair. He spoke to her and she answered that yes, it was a beautiful day, and he detected a slight lilt to her voice inside her Spanyol, a twang almost, a different kind of up-and-down. It turned out that she was no maid but a girl from a prosperous family who had spent much of her childhood in Ireland. Her father, Behor Camayor, was a successful tobacco merchant (upon his death, the Irish Embassy would bring in six white horses dressed in gold to pull the carriage that held his casket), and the family had gone back and forth among Ireland, Turkey and Malta until finally her father retired and came home. Might she like to go for ice cream later? She looked so young, he was afraid she would say no, but she said yes.

They spoke a fluid mix of French and Ladino together, but English was their secret language. "I'm a wee bit tired," she'd say to him at the dinner table at his parents' house, and he'd know it was time for a walk to the park, where they could neck in the shadows of the trees. She was quick and lively, hardworking, reasonable and full of affection, sane, and she didn't seem to judge him for having divorced another woman, though she felt terribly sorry for Djentil. She liked that he was bookish (though she was not particularly) and that he sang and played music. They married for love in the Ahrida synagogue, and because he had been living with his parents and was not a young man and she brought a good dowry, they could afford a house on the top of the hill in Fener. Soon, she gave birth to Corinne, then Rebecca, then Isidoro. Alberto came into more money from a bachelor uncle's death, and they bought the summer house in Büyükdere, which was not on the Princes' Islands, where most of their circle spent the summer, but it had a sprawling garden and was in an elite neighborhood near the summer embassies and not far from the city (he could, when duty called, commute an hour to work by boat), and you didn't run into your cousin or your cousin's cousin every time you stepped outside.

After that, Sultana lost two babies, to a miscarriage and a stillbirth, so that when her next child was born, a healthy boy, Alberto let her bend to old custom and send the infant off to live with relatives for a few days, and he came back dressed like a prince and with a new, second-chance name, Marko, which meant "sold." Elsa came next. Alberto didn't deserve it, but for some reason, El Dyo saw fit to bless him, so he tried to run a good business, balance the books and provide for his family. And he did, mostly, for a long time, though as the children multiplied and his responsibilities grew, so did his need for outside distractions. Not women—he wouldn't betray Sultana, though there was no harm in looking—but frequenting his old haunts, the bars, baths, coffeehouses, and perhaps most of all, mucking in his garden.

"Let us wander through the garden air and savor the smell of thistles and roses," wrote his beloved poet Judah Halevi. It was a deep, oddly forbidden pleasure to leave work in the middle of the day and hide in the garden for an hour or so when no one was home, Sultana at her mother's or doing charity work, the children with her or the nanny or at school, and he might rake or deadhead, prune or transplant, plant a new breed of tulip he'd ordered from Holland, wearing gloves so his hands wouldn't give him away, though sometimes he shed the gloves, wanting to touch the earth, and sometimes his trousers got smeared with dirt. Later, Sultana might see and roll her eyes—you're worse than the children!—but it was hardly a vice as vices went. Still, it might have been sex, it filled him up so, but gardening also brought him closer to God, erasing his worries and replacing them with blind roots descending, pale shoots rising, the onionskin sheath of a bud whose time was its own; it would open when it opened, shed its shroud.

So maybe he neglected to woo some potential new clients.

Maybe the business stopped growing and began contracting. Times were increasingly tough—not just for him, but for everyone. When the stress at work became too much, he'd go play poker, chess or backgammon for high stakes, winning just often enough to convince himself that gambling was a rational response to the situation (losing more, the cash disappearing as if his pockets had sprung holes, though Sultana kept his clothes in good repair now that they didn't have money to pay a seamstress for new suits). Times are hard. Times are not what they were. Was it his fault if happenstance was transforming him into (some piece of him even liked the notion of it) a fin de siècle, end-of-empire kind of man? His father had died by then and was not there to disapprove. Sultana had asked him not to gamble, but women couldn't frequent the clubs and the men covered for one another, and there was always—for a long time there was—enough money, so how was she to know?

If shame followed him around, coming out of the shadows on occasion to nip at his heels, so, equally, did pride. He discussed his troubles with no one. He dressed nattily, no matter the occasion, and walked with his shoulders squared. He kept moving, winding through his city, across neighborhoods where people knew him and tipped their caps, and ones where he was pleasantly anonymous. Sometimes he'd stop at a coffeehouse, or he'd amuse himself on a street corner with a simple game of chance that involved reaching into a cloth sack and pulling out a button, different colors yielding different prizes—ball, pipe, rag doll painted with the sultan's face. He'd come home with gifts for the children: Pick a hand, any hand! How they clamored, reaching, grabbing, so he'd stay for a little, then unpry their sticky, acquisitive hands—"Let go now, rascals, your papa has an important meeting"—and leave to wander once again.

IV

In Rebecca's tenth year, Djentil Nahon's mother dies. They learn about it from Nurie, Lika's mother, who, with Lika, has taken the ferry from the city to the summer house in Büyükdere to stay the week. The girls are in the garden, charged, along with Corinne, with watching over Rebecca's younger siblings, when they hear the two mothers on the veranda discussing the old lady's passing. The community has apparently set up a fund for the tombstone, but Djentil can't be trusted with arrangements, and doesn't her family have money from somewhere, they used to anyway, and wasn't there a sister in France and a brother in America, but nobody visits, the Nahons used to own the whole house, then sold off one floor, then another. Sad. How can her family abandon her like that? Who's left?

During the school year, the girls' visits to Tiya Djentil had dropped off but not stopped entirely. Rebecca is relieved that they weren't in the apartment when the old lady drew her last breath.

"Sorry to say so, but she already seemed dead—she was *five minutes to twelve*!" Lika whispers, using a phrase of their mothers', and together they laugh, but then Rebecca tries to unsay Lika's "dead" before it brings bad luck. "You mean *alive*," she says, bugging her eyes out at her friend, who looks briefly baffled, before saying, "Oh, right. She seemed alive. Very alive! Oh yes she did."

Eventually they lose interest and are obliged, anyway, to chase down Elsa, who has pulled herself up onto the garden wall while the boys play at swords under the linden tree and Corinne ignores everyone, head in a book, as the lizards freeze on the stones to watch them all. Then, from deep in the bushes, their father appears, dripping with sweat, almost glowing in his gardening hat and gloves. He yells harshly at the boys to stop their fighting and climbs the steps to the veranda, flinging his arms apart, as if to separate Sultana from Nurie, though they're just standing there talking, two mild mothers in floral dresses on a summer day.

Everything stops; even the little ones know to listen. Then their father is screaming loud enough for the neighbors to hear. Enough, don't bring me more shame, listen to me, there will be no fund from the community! How dare they—how dare you speak of this and bring me shame? Rebecca's mother says shhh, of course, you're right, darling, and calm down, and please, Alberto, the children, and at that he wheels around and stares, as if noticing his children and Lika for the first time.

"*Lo syento*," he apologizes, then repeats it to his wife, and a third time to Lika's mother, Nurie, sounding almost tearful. "I'm sorry, I'm sorry, I lost my head, please pardon me."

But he doesn't stop after that, just switches to English, the words, if slightly calmer, sharp and nasal, with *t*'s that spit. Tiya Nurie gathers the children—"Come, we're going to see the boats, and if you're good, I'll buy you ice cream"—pairing littles with bigs as she herds them out the gate, though they're all thinking not of ice cream but of two repeated words: Djentil Nahon, Djentil Nahon.

THAT FALL, AFTER THEY RETURN in the city, Tiya Djentil calls and calls for Rebecca and Lika, not once or twice a week, but day and night now, banging on her floor (Lika's ceiling), yelling out the window, and while at first she refers to them as her *suvrinas*, nieces, as has been her custom, soon she starts calling them her daughters: "Come, *m'ijikas*, I've got an errand for you to run! Come right now, I've made you treats!"

Their mothers agree that Djentil Nahon has truly lost her wits, and while they keep an eye on the poor woman and make sure she doesn't starve, they instruct their daughters to stay away. She can go out for herself, says Nurie, now that she doesn't have to care for her mother. It's good for her to leave the house. The charity ladies,

Sultana and Nurie among them, add her to their rotation. Rebecca and Lika don't protest; in fact, they are relieved. They are growing up, too old to spend their time visiting a crazy spinster, and the nuns have told them that too much sugar gives them spots, but more than that, Djentil scares them now, wanting them too badly, believing too much in the unseen, calling Mama, Mama into the night. Lika, for all her scientific objectivity, says she can't stop seeing the old lady still lying on the bed, flesh rotting, which disgusts her, and did Djentil Nahon tell anyone right away, and did she sew the shroud herself, and what if her mother's ghost returns? We should stay away from someone like that, Lika says with surprising coldness. We never should have called her *tiya.*

For her part, Rebecca feels sadness, coupled with a failing of belief, because how can you live in a world so peopled and storied that spoons have spirits and girls have wings, but then your own mother dies and you simply cannot find her, not in a spoon, not in a rug, not anywhere, and the girls who used to visit are not your daughters, not even your nieces, and don't come see you anymore, and the only man who ever married you is married now to someone else. For a while, Djentil Nahon still calls and bangs, bangs and calls. Then one day she stops. So it's over, just like that. Occasionally, Rebecca and Lika see her on the street, graying curls loose down her back, muttering into her basket or stopping to yank weeds from cracks, but she looks right through them, as if she no longer knows who they are.

REBECCA TURNS TWELVE. She registers the changes first as an internal thinning, a brittleness of thought and mood in inverse proportion to the spread and curve of her body. Her father comes home one evening and announces that she must give up gymnastics because he disagrees with Maccabi's focus on Palestine, which he views not only as a betrayal of their country but also as a false messianism not so different from the Sabbateans—he's taught her about them, was she listening, does she remember who they are? Yes, but it's not about that, Papa, Rebecca says. I'm getting so good, I'm one of the best. We have a performance coming up to raise money for the Turkish Fleet! I won't have you parading in front of people, he says. And believe me, the Turkish Fleet is just a front.

She appeals to him the next day but to no avail, and she cannot look to her mother for support because she's sick in bed from having had surgery after another difficult delivery. So now there's Josef, but Rebecca has had enough of babies, and her maternal grandmother is staying with them, making her fetch clothes and change diapers, and the baby spits up everywhere and cries a lot. Lika, whose mother has been blessed with a late-in-life baby boy after years of only having Lika, takes a job in a sewing notions shop because her scholarship at Sion has been reduced. Rebecca goes to school, comes home, does her chores and baby-minding, stays up late bent over homework. Sometimes on Sunday afternoons, she and Lika meet to dress up their baby brothers in comical outfits and take them in their prams along the shore, but the girls are too old for dolls, and unlike dolls, their brothers are a lot of trouble and can't be left alone if you get bored with them, so the pleasure quickly wears thin.

Still, there are advantages to growing older. Corinne begins to talk to Rebecca again, offering her advice or requesting that her sister braid her hair and coil it into an intricate bun. One day Sultana allows Rebecca to have a dress made—her wardrobe, except for her annual High Holidays outfit, is mostly hand-me-downs from Corinne. Rebecca works with the dressmaker, Amada Almaleh, on designing a sailor suit (she has always loved the jaunty, voyage-ready look) in dark blue raw silk with a red tie, princess waist and pearled buttons. She is told she has a keen eye for design and is invited to spend several afternoons each week at the dressmaker's shop, helping with the sewing lessons the dressmaker gives to little girls and learning tailoring techniques.

At *kal* and social gatherings, boys notice her, and one day, she goes on a picnic with Lika's extended family and meets, among other cousins, a boy named Sabetay Levy but called Samuel, who takes them in a paddleboat around a little pond, where they circle among swans and ducks. Samuel tells them about swans—how there are none in Africa or Antarctica, how they mate for life—and tracks Rebecca's movements with his eyes. Afterward, she asks Lika about him—where does he live, where does he go to school?—and Lika says Ortaköy, he had to drop out of school to work, his father ran off, they're terribly poor, a story that clashes with the fact-filled, nicely dressed boy and the sun on their hair and Rebecca's sense that, though the boat circled sleepily, they were all three headed toward bright futures. A pity, she tells her friend. He might have been someone. Lika bristles—everyone is someone before God—and Rebecca says, of course, that's not what I meant, even as she removes Lika's cousin from her mind.

ON NOVEMBER 14, 1914, she arrives at school to find a large sign on the front door: VACANCE DE GUERRE. For a moment, seeing the rushed, handwritten lettering, a childlike scrawl, she thinks it is a prank. But no: A real guard stands there, knees locked, shoulders squared. The adults' faces are ashen; Corinne grabs Rebecca and Lika tightly by their hands. Rebecca twists toward the sign, doubting her French. How can a war be a vacation? And which war anyway (the Balkan Wars, for which they wound bandages and knit scarves, are over, at least she thinks so)? She feels a flutter of perverse excitement—no school today!—even as she registers a chalky presentiment of loss.

The girls are not allowed inside their school—not to collect their needlework, notebooks and drawings, not to stand one last time in the marble courtyard where Baby Jesus cups Mother Mary's chin. Not even to say goodbye. They won't know all the pieces until later: how without any warning, the school was shut down, the nuns sent back to France or interned because they might (*might* they?) be spies, the boarding students dismissed onto the streets. More gendarmes gather outside, and with their red fezzes, gold tassels and blue uniforms, it looks like a parade is forming, but Monsieur Radkov, the usually gentle Albanian porter who escorts the girls to school each day, grabs Rebecca and Lika by their arms, squeezing too hard, tells Corinne to stay close and rushes them away.

So it is that Rebecca's childhood—the beautiful time, she will always think so—ends in a matter of hours. Her favorite teacher, Mère Mélanie, leaves for France without a goodbye, and you are not allowed to send letters to or from an enemy country. Lycée Notre Dame de Sion becomes an engineering school for the military, then a hospital. Within the month, Rebecca and Corinne are enrolled in the German School with its bare-bones classrooms, guttural sounds and stern teachers, no singing except for a few hymns, no art or statues, and when a girl needs disciplining, the teacher grabs her by the ear and twists. With Lika's father out of a job (every Alliance Israélite school in the city has been shut down because the instruction is in French), her family can't afford the German School, and there are too many girls looking for scholarships, floods of them uselessly jabbering in French. Rebecca asks her father if they can help with Lika's fees, but he says no, they're low on funds themselves. "But she's a better student," rejoins Rebecca. "And she likes school more." "*Chacun pour soi*," says her father coldly, but then he turns back to her and says, in a gentler voice, "Unfortunately, life isn't always fair, Rebecca. I'd have liked to be a scholar and teacher myself, for example, but instead I run a factory to provide for my family." Lika must quit school and work full days at the sewing shop, but not for long, because soon her family moves to Ortaköy to stay with relatives so they can pool resources and save up to leave for America, and Lika finds a new job in a bakery.

The two girls see each other every other week at first, then once a month. The following year, the military takes over the textile factory for uniforms, and Rebecca is obliged to tell the dressmaker, to whom she is still apprenticed, that she can only stay on if she is paid. This leads to more work in less time—Sinyora drives her harder when she's on the clock—packed hours after school basting hems and teaching sewing to ham-fisted, wiggly little girls.

On a Sunday in May, Lika returns to say goodbye before she leaves with her family for America.

"You're really going?" says Rebecca. Though it is not news to her, she had refused to consider it as a real possibility. She reaches to touch her friend's face, still so much like her own in her mind, though in person Lika looks older, pale and tense. "Don't leave me," Rebecca says. "What about our being next-door neighbors and raising our children together?"

"*Don't.*" Lika steps away from her touch. "I can't. We leave the day after tomorrow. My mother will come by later today to say goodbye. Please just wish me well."

"I'm sorry," Rebecca stumbles. "Of course I do, it's just . . . it's hard for me to imagine you're actually going. We were on the same path for so long—"

"No." Lika's voice is flat. "You always had more."

As Lika's gaze flickers over the tall stone house behind them, Rebecca remembers a game they used to play at school, a relay race where you handed off the seven deadly sins, and at the end, you claimed the sin you'd struggled with the most and meditated on it. Lika, she recalls, claimed envy and Rebecca vanity, but even then, she'd been aware that Lika's envy was justifiable in a way that her own vanity was not. She has always loved the pretty surface of things, her own face included, and been disturbed by ugliness to the point that her art teacher would chide her for ignoring the elements that brought authenticity to a *nature morte*—the chip on the pitcher's spout, the pear's brown bruise. For a week or so after that game, she had not looked in the mirror, a practice so disorienting that she soon gave it up. She wasn't Catholic, she told herself, and did not need to be tormented by the seven deadly sins.

"I'm sorry," she tells Lika, then, unable to stop herself, adds, "Everything's changing, for us, too. We've lost a lot."

Lika shrugs. "*Plus ça change.*"

"We still don't have the factory back. My father has to work for them now."

Lika looks surprised, almost pleased. "So come to New York. My cousins are already there. We can be neighbors in"—she says it in English—"*Spanish Har-lem.*"

"I'll ask my father," Rebecca says, but they both know that the idea of her leaving home is unimaginable and that her father has friends in high places and will surely find a way to work things out. Her family, especially her father, is from here the way the paving stones are from here, drawn from the very earth. When, rarely, he speaks of the decade he spent in England, he paints a gloomy picture of being homesick in a damp, dull place.

Lika takes off her silver locket and fastens it around Rebecca's neck. "I have to get back. Our initials are inside." She leans in close, her breath the dizzying green smell of childhood. "For you, Beccalika, but it's only a loan. You can return it when we see each other again."

Rebecca reaches up to remove her embossed gold hoop earrings, a gift from her parents that she removes only on holidays, when she replaces them with her Magen David earrings. "*Grasyas*, Likabecca. I'll never take it off. You take these."

"I can't, they're gold—it's too expensive."

"Good. If you ever need to, you can sell them."

"Over my dead body."

"*La boka mala*, Lika! Don't talk like that!"

Lika closes her hand around the earrings, and Rebecca kisses her friend, first on one cheek, then the other. "*Kaminos de leche i miel*"—paths of milk and honey.

Lika leaves without returning the kiss, running down the hill, weaving around people on the sidewalk, pivoting just once to wave. As Rebecca waves back, she remembers being in the Büyükdere kitchen with a splinter embedded deep in her heel. With Rebecca's nona instructing, Lika—they were maybe nine or ten—sterilized a needle with a match, steadied Rebecca's foot between her knees and went in with a deep, surgical plunge, a gouging swift and confident, with the splinter long and bloodied as the prize. The faster you go, the less it hurts. That might have been the same summer they plotted out a worldwide voyage using Lika's father's French magazines (neither of them had ever been farther than Izmir). India and China, Morocco, Polynesia, England. Ireland, where leprechauns squatted behind rocks. Paris and Rome, a few days in each, but never America; the magazines did not feature it, and it was so far away, and they didn't know anyone who'd been.

The faster you go, the less it hurts, but it had hurt quite a lot to get the splinter out, and afterward blood had sprung from the hole, followed by pus and something clear and cleansing, like tears. Now Rebecca steadies herself against the stone wall of her house, her insides scraped dry, as her friend descends the steep hill, and first Lika's body disappears and then her head and she is gone.

ONE DAY, SOME FIVE MONTHS after Lika leaves, Rebecca is walking home from work when she sees Djentil Nahon sitting at her bay window. She goes a bit farther before she stops at a cart and impulsively buys a bouquet of daisies, getting a deal because it's late in the day, then circles back and stops beneath the window, calling up but formal now: "Sinyora Nahon? Sinyora Nahon? *Buenas tardes!*"

The window opens; Djentil Nahon looks out. It is a warm fall day, but she's wrapped in a blanket, her gray hair loose around her shoulders. She looks even smaller than before, though the view is obstructed by the grapevines that threaten to swallow the house. The basket on a rope dangles at street level. Carefully, Rebecca lays the flowers in it, calls out, "I brought you some daisies!" and steps back to watch the bouquet rise. Djentil Nahon removes the flowers and abruptly drops the basket, which swings so wildly that Rebecca must duck and cover her head, but then the basket finds its place and settles, swaying mildly on its string.

Djentil stands at the window for a long moment, her downward gaze as intense as if it carried heat. She does not thank Rebecca or invite her up or tell her she needs onions. She does not say she forgives her for not visiting or forgives Alberto for divorcing her or El Dyo for not giving her a child or her mother for dying or Lika and her parents for moving away and leaving her with strangers in the downstairs apartment, which already looks run-down, its window boxes full of dead plants, dried mud splattered on the iron grille.

Rebecca bought the flowers out of a sudden, generous impulse—something pretty for someone alone. That the flowers remind her of her father, that he's connected to Djentil, that he seems sadder lately and more frightened, that Lika is gone (though she sends regular letters and appears to like America, where she has returned to school), that the past feels heavy, the present thin—all these are undercurrents too submerged for her to name, though she feels their tug. She tips her head back, meets Tiya Djentil's eyes and wills the old lady to dispense a blessing in return: "May you live and grow like the fish in the sea," or "May the angels come to your aid."

Djentil must read her mind, or perhaps you get what you get with a *loka* and it's more of the same, audible but losing substance, like the music on the aging wax cylinders on the phonograph

Alberto still keeps locked in a glass case, though he will need to sell it soon.

"*El Dyo te aga sigun lo ke azes por mi!*" Djentil calls from her window. May God do for you as you do for me.

"*Grasyas, Tiya!*" returns Rebecca, smiling.

But as she climbs the hill, she must wonder: Is it a blessing or a curse?

Istanbul, 1924

ALBERTO IS LATE. If he'd gone directly to the offices of the Jewish Refugee Relief Committee, he'd be there by now, but it's hard to walk in a straight line when you're drunk on raki and your heart is breaking, and if he goes to the appointment, he must say yes or no and then deliver the news to Sultana and the children. If he says yes, it will happen: They will *regresar*, return—though they've never been—to Spain. And there, in the former land of *Convivencia*, he will become a janitor.

Alberto is old. Soon he will turn seventy, and his youngest son, Josef, only ten. Old, drunk, tired, confused, sentimental, disappointed, though he knows he should be grateful for the opportunity. He walks fast in the wrong direction, down the hill, through the Balat Gate, into the tumbledown, cramped neighborhood they mockingly call Balat-sur-Mer, past the quai with its fruit and vegetable crates where refugees sleep beneath beached rowboats, and the next quai, with its firewood boats, past the Skala de los kayikes, which carries passengers and corpses to Hasköy because this side's Jewish cemetery is full. Feet marking out a beat, he tries to empty his mind and focus on the scene, for which he is already nostalgic, despite its grittiness. How fast he moves, like a much younger man. The agitation overrides the tiredness and gives him wings.

Six months have passed since he first approached the committee at his wife's insistence, writing not as he had in the past as a benefactor or supporter, but as a potential recipient: Having fallen on troubling times and hoping to find a better situation for my family, I seek employment opportunities for myself and my sons in France, the Americas or England. He did not say aloud that he had to get Isidoro out of town so he wouldn't be turned into an army slave (the walls have ears), but it was understood. A month or so later, the director, Jacobo Carvalho, called him in and said if you're open to Palestine, our colleagues at the World Zionist Organization might be able to help, but Alberto declined (he will go to Palestine only if invited directly by God).

"What about Cuba, where my eldest daughter and her husband are?" Alberto had asked. "They'll get into America from there."

"Good luck to them," Jacobo had said. "Try Cuba if you like, but plan to stay there, unless—" He rubbed his thumb and index finger together. "A lot. To grease the wheels."

"What about Egypt, or England?"

"Not unless you possess substantial funds." Jacobo had sighed. "We'll keep an eye out for you, but as you know, many countries have closed or tightened their borders, and we have thousands of refugees we're trying to place. Best, probably, to think about your own connections abroad."

Alberto had said of course he would, though in truth he has few connections left—he has gambled his fortune, burned a few bridges—and the deeper truth is that he does not want to go.

Then, nine days ago now—already late October, a slight chill in the air, Sukkot just over—he ran into an acquaintance at La Librairie Cohen Sœurs (no relation) on Rue Péra, where he'd brought a suitcase full of books to sell: business manuals in French, romance novels in Ladino, children's stories, school texts, a few old volumes of his father's; he has yet to pillage his own collection. The acquaintance spotted Alberto at the counter making small talk with Mazalto Cohen and said in French that Alberto's name had come up at the Refugee Committee and they thought they might have something for him. Alberto left Mazalto sorting books and led his acquaintance into one of the small, dark rooms at the rear of the shop. It could have been an illegal, lucrative deal they were brokering—that's how trembly and secretive he felt. "*Dites-moi.*" His whisper sounded raspy, hardly quiet. "So what is this opportunity you speak of? Where?"

"Espanya."

"*Espanya?*"

He had repeated the word, perhaps more than once, standing between high cases filled with antique leather-bound volumes with titles like *The Lives of the Ottoman Kings and Emperors.* He would not have been more surprised if he'd heard Timbuktu. Because what was Spain? It was where his people were from and where they were not from. It was where they'd been massacred, accused of blood libel, rounded up in town squares to be assigned saints' names or the names of trees. It was where—over four hundred years ago, for God's sake—they'd left. But Spain was also the origin of his *lingua de leche*, spoken from the cradle on (though he preferred French), and the birthplace of his hero Maimonides, and a place of great poetry, and closer to Europe, or even *in* Europe, depending on how you thought about it.

"Tell me more," he'd said.

The man informed him that Primo de Rivera, the prime minister of Spain, had issued a decree, to take effect in late December and good for up to six years, that offered Spanish nationality to its *Protegidos Españoles* and their descendants, including the Sephardads, and that there was a small synagogue in Barcelona—a modern city on the rise—in need of someone to help run it.

"Are you telling me there's a Jewish population there?" Alberto had asked skeptically. "Are you sure they're not New Christians, Conversos?"

"They're regular Jews," the man had told him. "Like you and me, from Turkey, the Levant, and a few from Russia and Germany and other places."

"How many?" Alberto had asked.

"A few hundred, maybe. Maybe more."

"And is it all right for them there? They're not forced to convert or . . . or hide who they are?"

The man had laughed, a tinkling sound. "No, apparently they like us now. They're calling Spain our homeland."

Alberto had also snorted out a laugh, even as he'd felt his chest contract. This city, the ground beneath his feet, here where he was born and his parents are buried—is his homeland. Not *next year in Jerusalem* (though he recites it in prayer and would be pleased to visit the holy sites before he dies) and certainly not Spain, a country that, when it doesn't call up bloodshed and *auto-da-fé*, invokes for him a kind of sloppy, outdated, feminine nostalgia for Spanish omelets and *romanseros*, old tales told in Spanyol—a language (if you can even call it that) that he speaks every day but considers jargon in its spoken form, kitchen-speak. "Why? Why now?"

"I don't know the intricacies, Monsieur Cohen. Someone mentioned that they're interested in expanding trade in Morocco and the Balkans, where our community has strong ties. Remember, they've lost a lot of empire. Or maybe they're regretting past actions. They lost a great richness when they kicked us out."

Surrounded by the august, outdated volumes on the shelves, Alberto had pushed aside the cynical, disbelieving thoughts that came too easily to him and allowed his mind to move to books and music, a scholar's life, the end of business dealings. A new beginning for his sons and daughters.

"So I'd be the hazan?" He is known to have a fine singing voice and often leads his congregation in both song and prayer.

"As I mentioned, I don't know the details," said his acquaintance with something like impatience. "Make an appointment at the office. They can tell you more."

TWO DAYS LATER, Alberto had gone to the office in Péra.

"No, not quite the hazan," said the young man behind the desk. "More like the gabbai or shammash. A kind of caretaker, from what I understand."

Alberto had winced. The shammashim he knew were simple, uneducated men who belted out "*tefila, tefila!*" through the streets to rouse people for morning prayers and patrolled with the watchman to make sure the shops were closed on Friday nights. The one at the Ahrida synagogue doubled as a volunteer firefighter and hawked brined fish on the street corner for extra cash.

"So why not a hazan?" He failed to sound casual.

"They're running on a budget and have a lot of needs."

"Such as?"

"Such as . . . I don't know, daily things, I suppose—opening and closing the *oratorio*, sweeping the stairs."

The young man had repeated the word *sweeping*, mimicking the gesture from his chair, and Alberto, surprising himself with a comic urge, had grabbed a folded black umbrella from a nearby stand and used it as a prop to perform an exaggerated sweeping routine across the carpet. Then, somewhat breathlessly, he had quoted from Proverbs—"Go to the ant, thou sluggard; consider her ways and be wise"—and the two of them shared a quick, relieving laugh.

"Who's the haham?" he asked next. "And the hazan?"

"It's a very small community, though they expect it to grow. I don't believe they have a regular rabbi or cantor. You'd live right there, adjacent to the sanctuary. It's in an apartment building, out of public view. A peaceful place. I think you'd be the only permanent staff member. There's a board, of course. They invite rabbis if they're passing through from France or other places."

"I see. So I'd be the . . ." *Boss*, he wanted to say. *El patron.* The guy in charge. "Shammash," he finished weakly instead.

The young man nodded and glanced at his watch. "This is a better opportunity than we can offer most people. You'd live right there with your family at no cost, in a nice new neighborhood. It's because you're well regarded, Monsieur Cohen, and have given so generously to the community."

This is true; he has given and given. He loves the feeling of it (more than he likes a day's work). "Thank you." He returned the umbrella to its stand. "Of course I need to think about it. I'll let you know."

"When?"

"Before too long,"

"No more than a week, Monsieur. Others will jump at this opportunity if you don't take it."

"A week should suffice."

And they'd made a date for today, for nearly an hour ago.

On and on he walks in the wrong direction, having missed his appointment at its allotted time, a windup toy veered off on its own inscrutable course. So what's wrong, *mon vieux* (what's not)? He has burned through his share of the family fortune or lost track of it, and he has no income because the state took over his (already failing) factory to make uniforms during the war, and the document required to get it back has disappeared. In his memory, it was no more than a half slip of frail paper. In his memory, he stowed it in the small safe in his library at home. That he hadn't fully understood the importance of the document is true—of course it was his factory; everybody knew so; his name was on the letterhead, the bank account! That the paper is missing is equally true. Could the government have somehow gotten to it? Could Alberto have lost it or misremembered where he put it? In the privacy of his study with the door locked from inside, he has emptied the safe more than once, gutted his desk, shaken the books where he sometimes tucks documents, all to no avail. The crooks won't honor the deed, he told Sultana, who shook her head in disbelief, then wept, then prayed that these men would see the error of their ways. How low he has sunk, to besmear others to save his name, to lie to his own good wife.

If, in another era, such a property dispute might have been remedied through a friend of a friend or fat donation, or through lawyers and the courts, now all systems have come undone, at least for a man of his background. The system wants to keep his factory from him; of this he has no doubt. He can't afford a lawyer, can't meet the children's school fees, can't pay the taxes or monthly upkeep to his first wife, Djentil Nahon, and while this last item should be the least of his worries (there is nothing legally binding;

he paid her ketubah decades ago), he feels perhaps most wretched about it and can no longer walk past her house but needs to take detours on side streets.

He's always liked them anyway, ducking off the main thoroughfare, the things he glimpses: veiled women with linked arms walking three abreast; potted plants on front stoops; cats threading along walls, and even if he's pressed for time, he'll stop to deadhead a spent flower or right a pot. At least Corinne is married off, though her husband, Israel, was forced to take the blame for his superior's smuggling activities in the army, so they fled to Marseille, then moved to Cuba, where they sell ready-to-wear ranch apparel in the countryside and wait for entrance to America. It is hardly the life he imagined for his oldest daughter, though at least he managed to supply her with a proper dowry. Rebecca, working for the dressmaker and with no marriage prospects, and Elsa, at the low-tuition Alliance Israélite School, are another story, and his sons—Josef also at the Alliance, Marko and Isidoro working for a pittance at dead-end jobs—are no better off, a source of roiling shame to him that he could not set them up for success.

He has nearly reached Eyüp and stops to rest, leaning on a pile of crates, his breath ragged. A swarm of cats appears, a mother and her litter, and he allows the kittens to climb on him, scrambling up, teetering, balancing on his arm, only to tumble onto the crate and, with a crouch and pounce, begin again. The story goes that because a cat once saved the Prophet Muhammad from a poisonous snake, the Muslims leave food and water out for cats (dogs, in contrast, are rounded up and carted off to islands to eat one another or starve). One of the kittens makes it as far as Alberto's shoulder. When he turns his head, it bats his beard and he startles, sending it tumbling to the street below, where it skids, then scampers off. In Barcelona, are there street cats? Do pigs hang bloody and fat-pearled in shopwindows? Do the ghosts of his beloved scholars and poets walk the streets?

Now that he's come to a stop, he can hear his own pulse. Job with all his troubles was being tested by God, but it's hard to believe that this current mess, born of the endless blunderings and plunderings of man (he includes himself) involves God's will. His brother will no longer do business with him because of his gambling habit and has blocked his access to the Swiss bank account that receives the small income from the family rental properties in Beyoğlu. They have long rented out to several brothels, which is why Alberto removed his name from the leases in the first place. He serves on boards, after all, and has a reputation to uphold. He gives (gave) abundantly to charity, and Sultana counts the prostitutes, abject girls from Romania and Odessa, among her many causes.

Rested now, he keeps going in the wrong direction, past the shuttered Imperial Fez factory, up the hill to the market street by the Grand Eyüp Sultan Mosque, which is thronged with shoppers, beggars, pilgrims and peddlers. There he buys a bag of roasted chestnuts and intends to devour them, though he stops after the first one scalds his tongue. A *pichiziko* street child appears in a quilted red shirt with a baby tied to his back, proffering grimy, empty hands. Impulsively Alberto offers up the chestnuts, and the boy snatches the bag and melts into the crowd.

Were there always this many beggars? Children raising children? While he was blindly going about his days, something has happened to his city (country, empire), first overrun with occupying armies, now full of refugees, while the Jews, and also the refugees, are leaving as fast as they can. Mustafa Kemal Atatürk's middle name means "perfection," and it is true that the new president has a lofty vision, but let it also be noted (if never said aloud) that this new republic could choke to death on its own rules. It used to be that a handshake and drink could seal a deal; now there is paperwork designed to leave an educated man feeling like a fool. No one is allowed to wear a fez (a hundred years ago, it was the turban outlawed for the fez) or have a religious symbol inside a Jewish school, where a state-appointed teacher must now teach five weekly Turkish lessons, which would be all right except that the rest of the time, the instruction must all be in Hebrew, ruled (absurdly) by the government to be the community's mother tongue. Even the name of his city has been changed and the place stripped of its ancient role as capital. Any day now, Isidoro could be conscripted into a military that will deny him kosher food and send him to the hinterlands to haul stones, and Marko is not far behind. Jewish boys are chopping off their pinkies and scalding their feet so they don't have to serve.

Alberto is all for progress and has long been a champion of modernization, but a man should wear the hat he wants to wear. Only Turkish Muslims can work at a foreign bank now or in public service. It doesn't even really matter that he's lost his business; he has almost no one to do business with. The Greeks have fled or been exchanged, the Armenians slaughtered in Anatolia or—as was the case for several of his friends and business associates—rounded up right here in the city and sent away while Alberto did nothing on their behalf except pray lamely to his own dozy God that justice be served. As for the Jews, the poor have left in droves for the Americas or Europe, while the Zionists have gone to Palestine to hack at rocky soil. A prominent Jewish trader recently committed suicide because of financial troubles. Even the chief rabbi has moved away, first to France and now to Egypt, despite having been granted the title of effendi and serving in the delegation at Lausanne.

Alberto has stayed. Why? Why not? He is rich (he used to be). An Ottoman Jew. A forward-thinking Jewish Turk. A Turk. This country has been good to him and to his father before him and his father's father before that. He is old.

But *why*?

He loves it here. Each spring and summer, he improves his garden in Büyükdere according to its need, adding chestnut bark mulch, crushed seashells and eggshells, coffee grounds, even rusty nails to bring out the blue in the hydrangeas, which Sultana teases him about, calling it witchcraft, though it's science. He loves the streets that wind through this city the poets like to call the navel of the earth, loves his pink-walled *kal* with its ark shaped like a ship's bow that might be Noah's ark or might be the boat that brought his people from Spain. He loves to stop on the corner and watch the ceramics fixer write numbers on the insides of the shards of a broken vase, drill tiny holes, brush the edges with egg white and secure them with wire, an act that gives him hope that anything shattered might, with enough skill and patience, be repaired. He loves the workshop of his music teacher, Oktay, on a narrow street deep in a Muslim quarter, the shop like a birdcage, hung with drying lengths of cane that Oktay fashions into neys, woodwind flutes whose sound—it was Rumi who said it—is not wind but fire.

Now the dervish lodges will be closed down for being antimodern. There will be no public whirling, no ney playing. If this is how the forward-thinking think, Alberto is tempted to don a white gown and join the Sufis, though they would not have him. Turn turn turn. Turn back. Even his own faith, the steady marrow of his days, feels thin to him, depleted.

Is this what old age is, to believe in less and less?

As he continues, entering the wide plaza, he spots the *pichiziko* in the red shirt and is pleased to see that the boy is with his friends and no longer charged with an infant's care. The group is playing catch because children are children and joy is free. It is only as Alberto draws closer that he registers that they're throwing not a ball but a baby, or no, it's a baby doll, unclothed, neck bent at an ugly angle, missing an arm—the boy's charge from the market street. On and on the urchins throw the splayed, naked creature, leaping and jeering, nearly knocking over the pilgrims in their path as they dive like filthy crows for carrion. Alberto's rising anger erases the fact that he didn't give the boy any money, just leftover chestnuts from a snack that had already burned his tongue. He wants to grab the child by the neck, call him out before the other boys for the fake and hypocrite he is, but he cannot; he is among strangers and these are not his people. How quickly, if provoked, the crowd could take him down.

The boys disappear into the throng, but Alberto stands there, rocking slightly and clutching his own elbows, feeling as unmoored as he ever has, despite being in the heart of the city he calls home. What you need right now, he instructs himself sternly, is to think of El Dyo, the One Who Has No Parts—no arms or legs, no back or front, no end or beginning. There is no *kal* in the neighborhood so he makes his way toward the mosque, where he takes off his shoes and hat, waits his turn to wash his feet, hands and face at the ablution fountain and enters the sanctuary.

How quiet it is, a world away from the packed square. The raki has largely worn off and left him with a throbbing headache. He tries to lose himself to the filtered light, the cool, white stone, the cats weaving between prayer rugs, the bent men facing Mecca, paused here in the middle of their day. While he has never set foot in a church, his faith permits him to enter a mosque, which has no false idols and just one god. Still, he feels slightly ill at ease, training his gaze not on the men but on the blue-and-white tiles, which he loves for their twining plant life and endless symmetry. Even when a wall ends, you can sense the design, like a taproot in a garden, persisting on.

If Alberto cannot quite pray here—it is not his place—he can at least think. Where is he going? Where has he been? Who (next) will he disappoint? In the vast, vaulted space of the mosque, the begging boy with the fake baby on his back feels tiny, his own anger at the child's ruse misplaced. The truth, like the veined marble floor beneath his feet, is both hard and slippery. If he wants to find a liar and hypocrite, he need only look at himself and the hundreds of small ways he skews the truth.

The praying men are rising now, almost in unison, retrieving their shoes from the rack, moving toward the obligations of the day. His own bare feet look newly young beneath him, pale and long-toed, like he could use them to scale trees. Alberto follows the men. Outside, the light is too bright. A woman is feeding the pigeons, and he sees that a stork has joined them, all sharp angles, one black leg raised, its wings spread so you can't tell if it has just landed or is about to fly.

He will go now to the refugee office in Péra, by tram, ferry, hired carriage, his own two feet, whatever it takes.

There, if they will meet with him despite his lateness, he will tell the truth.

I need your help. I accept your offer. I will scrub your fucking floors.

El Dyo willing, he will go.

He is shown into the same cramped, paper-strewn office that he visited the week before and given a glass of apple tea. The young fellow who helped him last time isn't there, but a balding middle-aged man who introduces himself as Monsieur Sasson greets him politely in French without mentioning his tardiness, consults a bulging folder on his desk and gets down to business.

"Will you be accepting our offer, Monsieur Cohen?"

Suddenly it isn't difficult. There is no choice, or only one. "*Si*," he says, then "*oui*."

Mr. Sasson nods. "I'm glad to hear it. I'll let our co-religionists in Barcelona know. You'll need to cover your own moving and setup expenses, if that's all right."

Alberto is aware of his tongue feeling fuzzy, scalded by the chestnuts. "Of course."

He is no charity case. He owns a house still, furniture. He has been selling off books, porcelain and silver, if at a dismal price, and can sell more, because what are possessions, what is a body, except a temporary cage to house a soul? He feels lighter now, but uncomfortably so. Everything—the man's desk, his face, the window with its leaded panes—looks flattened and unreal, a country on a map. There is a word in Ladino, *kayades*, silence, which is employed as shorthand for how you should behave outside your own small community: keep your head down, maintain good relations, avoid complaint. His head keeps nodding, puppetlike. He'd like to cuff himself on the back of his bobbly chicken neck.

"Very good, then," says Mr. Sasson. "We'll get back to you with further details. Plan to arrive by early January. I'm glad it's worked out. Our people have a proud history in Spain. Someday I'd like to go there myself."

"Why don't you?"

Mr. Sasson looks startled. "If they sent me, I'd go. We have small communities now in both Barcelona and Madrid. I wish you and your family well, Monsieur Cohen. *Shalom.*"

"*Shalom.*" Alberto gets up to leave but then blurts out the question that's been rising up in him. "Do you, unh, happen to know if there's a garden there, at the oratory, even a small one? I—it's just that, well, my wife loves to garden."

"Does she?" Mr. Sasson lets out a sharp laugh that fizzles into a sigh, and Alberto feels heat rush to his face. He has suffered no pogrom. His children have not gone hungry. He is neither stateless nor even quite technically a refugee. He is broke, a little broken. The desk is piled high with documents, with more stacked on the floor. Deliver my soul, O Lord, from lying lips. The truth is that his wife's thriving herbs would wither without his care and are more his than hers while in the ground. I'll make a donation, he thinks reflexively, before he remembers that he is deep in debt and has nothing left to give.

"Never mind," he says stiffly. "The garden doesn't matter. Thank you for your help, Monsieur."

"*Je vous en prie.*" Mr. Sasson closes the folder, clears his throat.

It is time to go, but Alberto does not move, glued to the floor by an inky sense of something missing. He isn't sure how long he stands there before Mr. Sasson rises and comes around to the other side of his desk as if to shake his hand, but then embraces him and says, "*Kon bien amaneskas*"—may you have good dawnings.

"*El Dyo ke te guarde,*" Alberto responds before he turns to go, feeling somehow smaller than he did when he arrived, a very old man in a pale gray suit, which, though tailored from Egyptian linen and custom-sewn to fit his frame, is too big on him now and has seen better days.

HE INVITES SULTANA to follow him to the stone bench in the garden, where they can be alone. It is early evening by the time they sit down in the shade of the sour plum tree. She has already brought him his slippers and a clean dressing gown, as she does each evening, and he has changed inside and washed his face. At the end of the garden, the sukkah he built with his three sons stands wind-torn and tattered, though birds still light on it and forage beneath for crumbs and seeds from the biscuits and fruits that hung from its laurel branches. The frailty of the sukkah is supposed to signify that life is transient and all men are equal in the eyes of God, a sentiment that Alberto used, from his high perch, to think was beautiful but that now fills him with panic. Sultana offers him the drink he has each night, red wine with apple slices floating in it. Tonight she has also poured one for herself. His voice unsteady, he tells her that he's said yes, they're going to Spain.

"You did it!" She leans to plant a kiss on his lips. "The boys won't be conscripted! *Mashallah!*"

How differently they see things. It is why his marriage never stops being a revelation to him, even after all these years. He has to try so hard, in a mental effort so strenuous it feels athletic, to see the good in life, while for his wife the world is naturally a place of blooming, and it's the sorrows that surprise her, despite their regular appearance, not the joys.

He nods. "As we suspected, there aren't a lot of options. We don't have to stay. It can be a stop along the way to somewhere else. We'll come back here if we can"—his voice breaks—"figure out how. Things will change again. They always do."

She looks at him with a level gaze. Is that pity in her eyes? "We'll see," she says, "but in the meantime, we'll make a home there. The children need us to, if they're to settle in. Anyway, I might prefer Spain to other places, certainly to America. It's warmer and sunnier—and closer, and we all speak the language."

"Or a version of it." He smiles thinly at her. "Though in Barcelona, I think they mostly speak Catalan. A kind of dialect."

"So we'll have our own dialect, too. Oh, so much to do! We'll have to figure out how much we can bring with us." She sips her wine. "Spain. Who would have thought, but it makes sense. It's where we're from."

"Maybe," he says almost perversely.

"What do you mean, *maybe*? Of course it is."

"We don't know that precisely. We assume it."

"Of course we know. *I* know."

It is what they've been told by their grandparents, who were told by their grandparents, but it's also true that their region has long been full of Jews from other places, both East and West, and many generations have passed and mixed. There's an old *konseja* that the Jews who fled Spain during the Inquisition kept the keys to their houses around their necks and passed them down through the generations. If Alberto views it as a grotesque and illogical tale (why save the keys to a house in a country that slaughtered, expelled you or forced you to convert?) and surely not true, Sultana finds it beautiful.

"Remember when we went to that party at the Spanish embassy?" she asks. The summer residence of the embassy is down the street from the house in Büyükdere. He used to stop there occasionally on his evening walks to chat with the bored sentries stationed under the linden tree outside its pale blue walls. With his kind of Spanish and their kind of Spanish, they got by. One warm June night, a sentry confessed to him under his breath that he was a Marrano, which meant he was a New Christian, which meant he was a Jew (also a swine, since that's what the word *marrano* meant). Then the man made the sign of the cross and went back into position, jaw set, eyes scanning the shoreline, as Alberto, dumbfounded, walked away.

A month or so after that encounter, he and Sultana were invited to a party there. It was not uncommon for them to find themselves at gatherings at the summer embassies, where, in a relaxed holiday ambience, you could enjoy yourself, make business connections, grease some wheels. They had dressed up, left the children with the nanny. Arm in arm, they walked down the boulevard, through the soft night air. How regal his wife had looked. Her hair had already turned an early white, as was common in her family, and that night she had reminded him—with her copper eyes and glowing white hair, a white fur stole around her neck—of the elegant Arctic fox on his cigar box label. They danced and drank and strolled along the terraced gardens and on the landing stage by the Bosphorus as a string quartet played and dark water lapped below.

Toward the end of the evening, a Spanish man of some importance—a doctor, maybe, Alberto doesn't recall his name—had pulled him aside, professed an interest in the Spanish Jews, and asked questions in Castilian interspersed, when Alberto failed to understand, with broken French: What do you eat, what songs do you sing, what is your business, what countries do you export to, do you do business in North Africa?

Alberto, more than a little drunk, had answered as best he could, if with a rising sense of unease. Why all these questions? he'd finally asked. You are elegant and cultured, said the man. A true aristocrat. But *why*? Alberto had asked, abruptly sober and with a pressing need to urinate. I'm on a bit of a quest, the man had said. The Sephardic race is a richness for my country and for our relations abroad; I hope to make you citizens. Are you Jewish yourself? Alberto had asked. Or a Converso? The man had looked startled. No, no, I'm Spanish, and you—the man took his hand, gripping it too hard—are an *Español sin patria*.

"They had a flamenco player," Sultana reminds him now. "And dancers in red lace. Do you remember? One let me try her castanets. I hadn't done it since I was a girl."

Sitting together on the bench, he and Sultana turn to details of the move—what to bring, what to try to sell or give away, and can they wait until school vacation for the younger children and when should they break it to them (soon, Sultana says, as in tonight, once they're all home) and to Sultana's mother, who is well situated at her brother's house in Taksim, but the thought of leaving her brings the first tears to his wife's eyes.

Not surprisingly, it is Rebecca who comes into the garden to find them there. She, of all the children, seems able to catch her father's thoughts as they enter the atmosphere, and she is not one to let things slide. She has returned from work at the dressmaker's and is wearing a sort of gypsy getup—a flowered vest and skirt, a shirt with billowy sleeves, a white wrap around her head—that she must have fashioned for herself. It would make a good Purim costume but is a ridiculous outfit for daily use. The dressmaker, though skilled at what she does, is from a different milieu, and hers is not the air he wishes for his daughter to breathe, another reason why they need to go. Still, Rebecca is beautiful and full of life, and it's hard for him not to be cheered by the sight of her. She plants herself in front of them, kisses her father on the hand and her mother on the cheek.

"*Ke haber?*" she asks.

Sultana raises a glass. "We're just enjoying our wine."

Rebecca reaches to take a sip, then returns the glass to her mother. "Besides that."

"We're enjoying the breeze from the water."

"Fine, Mama. But what are you discussing out here for such a long time? And in low voices? What happened? I know something did. Is everything all right?"

"Of course," Sultana says. "We're just going over some plans."

Alberto glances at his wife.

"What plans?" Rebecca asks.

"Wait until everyone sits down to supper," Sultana says. "Josef went to do an errand for me, and the other boys are out and about. And Elsa—" She glances over her shoulder. "Have you seen her? Is she still looking after the children down the street?"

"I know what it is, so you might as well say it."

"Now you're a mind reader?" says Alberto. "Is that why you're wearing this"—he waves toward it—"getup? Tell us, then, Mademoiselle Fortune-Teller. What is it?"

"We're moving," says Rebecca. "You sold the summer house, and you've been selling off our things. I saw how you tried to rearrange the books to hide the gaps. I told Isidoro it was happening, but he didn't believe me. We're going"—Alberto can't tell if she sounds excited or dismayed—"to America. We can live near Lika in New York. Did I tell you she's taking classes at night to become a nurse? It will take a long time, but I feel sure she can do it."

"Not America," he says.

She looks disappointed. "To Cuba, then, with Corinne?"

He shakes his head.

"France?"

Again he shakes his head

"Where, Papa? Just tell me. Why must you torture me?"

"You?" he scoffs. "I'm the one who's tortured, by these times."

Sultana makes a tsking sound. He looks toward his roses, which need to be pruned. Might he dig them up, roots and all, bundle them in burlap, and carry them to Spain? His father is buried across the water in Hasköy in the special section reserved for the Cohens, also known as Kohanim, with its scent of wild oregano. Each year on his father's *meldado*, the anniversary of his death, Alberto visits to say a prayer and leave a pebble on his grave. He sometimes wishes he could plant some flowers there—the English cemeteries were full of them—but it is the practice of his people to put stone on stone, and each time it moves him, the tiny rock set on the large one as if in protest, however small, against the maggots and the worms. How will he add his pebble from afar? "I don't know what's happening to my country," he says glumly.

"It's falling apart," says Rebecca cheerfully. "You say so every day. It does seem like I won't find a decent husband here, not without a dowry. But why not America, Papa? Lika likes it there."

"Read the newspaper, Rebecca. America has closed its doors to us."

"So Corinne will have to stay in Cuba? That was supposed to be temporary. She wants to leave. Where are we going, Papa? Is it Palestine?"

Wearily, he shakes his head.

"Is it—"

"Stop," Sultana interjects. "Please. Both of you. Alberto, why play this game with her? We decided we'd tell them all at once, and we will."

"*Where,* Papa?" Kneeling down on the grass, Rebecca takes her father's hand, still girlish in her motions, but though the spark in her eyes hasn't dimmed over the past few years, it has changed in quality; she often seems restive to him, even wild. She tries on costumes, parades and prances, puts on little plays with Elsa and Josef, though she is too old for such amusements. When she walks down the street, heads turn, and he worries she could end up with a Christian or Muslim. She did not like the German School and the fees were high, and while she might have gone on to a bookkeeping or stenography course, she apprenticed herself instead full-time to the dressmaker and is being paid a small sum that she should save for her dowry but spends instead on baubles like the glittery bracelets on her wrist and the cheap heart locket around her neck.

Sultana stands. "I need to start dinner. Come help me, Rebecca."

"Morocco? England?"

When no one responds, Rebecca too stands and moves away from them. In the dusk, her face looks suddenly hard to her father, drained of its prettiness, her clenched fists small gray balls. "I've run out of guesses. It's my life, too, you know. It's not a game. I can stay here and keep working for the dressmaker or start my own business. I'm plenty old enough. I'll just"—her voice turns breezy—"stay."

"You're my daughter," he says. "Where I go, you go."

"I'm not a child, Papa. I belong to no one but myself."

Before Alberto can remind Rebecca that in legal terms, a daughter belongs to her father until she marries, Sultana turns to him. "She's right, Alberto—she has a right to know. Why make her wait? Just tell her. Go ahead."

He does not want to be the one to utter the words. It is not his choice, this leaving, though it's at least partially the result of his own actions or inactions. Might a more capable boss have saved the factory? Why is it that his brother, Maurice, is, if not thriving, not drowning and has no plans to leave (though he has no sons to be conscripted)? His daughter and wife stare at him. From deep in his pocket, he hears the ticking of his Swiss watch, another thing he needs to sell. Once he releases the words, they will be so.

"It's Spain. We're going to Spain."

"Spain?" Rebecca laughs, an incongruous sound. "But why? Spain hates the Jews! They kicked us out!"

"That was over four hundred years ago."

"Still. I've heard terrible stories."

"Of course. From ancient history."

"No, Papa. More recently. I heard they made rugs from our skin, from the skin"—she lowers her voice—"of Jews."

Her mother, still listening, grabs her hand. "Who told you that?"

She hesitates. "An old lady I knew. She heard it from someone else."

"Of course!" Alberto downs the rest of his wine. "That's why it's an old wives' tale. You want true stories? Look what happened to the Armenians, right here. Solid citizens, good people, my business partners—" He chops at his throat with the side of his hand. "Atrocities. Injustices. May God take notice over time. Look at the Greeks. They've been emptied out of half the country. Those aren't stories, those are terrible, true facts. Things aren't what they used to be. You think we'll fare any better? It takes nothing at all for them to turn on us."

Where did it come from, this bashing of his beloved country? Though he speaks the truth, he could go on in the next breath to argue the opposite: We're not quite the same as those other populations, having never made a move for independence. We cower, stay quiet, *kayades.* Or we are children of Abraham, all one. And then the other side again, or maybe a third side: We have to leave because we've always had to leave, even if he doesn't remember, not in his heart; he is no Wandering Jew. He looks down the sloped garden at his sukkah's skeletal roof, which he wants to plait with reeds again, to hang with figs and dates, grapes and olive branches so he can study there and later lie on the straw mat with his young wife in his arms as the birds flock for a feast. "I can't even go to Ankara for business without permission now," he says. "We're running out of possibilities. There's nothing for us here."

"Well, we have a new opportunity," says Sultana. "*De la spina nase la roza.*" From the thorn is born the rose.

Suddenly Alberto is coughing, a racking, deep hack that appears out of nowhere, bending his torso, taking his breath—a shred of apple skin caught in his throat or God doing him a favor, keeping him from speech. Sultana starts thumping his back, and Rebecca, too, and though he tries to bat them away, he is heaving, making small, choked noises, and then finally is quiet again, his breath returned.

He sits depleted in the half light. "I swallowed wrong," he says hoarsely.

"Oh, Papa." Rebecca bends to stroke his beard, and Alberto senses, looking up at her, a terrible reversal. She, the child, and a girl no less, is worried for him, the father. It is a brutal passing, and he wants none of it.

"So. Spain," Rebecca says, almost brightly. "What will we do there? Which city will we go to? Do you have a job?"

And because there is no rule saying a shammash can't sing, and because he's a *kohen* from the priestly caste and thus honored with the first aliyah and the giver of the threefold blessing, and because dusk has arrived to blur the edges of his city, the faces of his wife and daughter, the story of his life, he says (*Deliver my soul, O Lord, from lying lips*), "I've been offered a position in Barcelona, as the hazan in a synagogue."

Barcelona, 1925

I

HER FATHER SWEEPS THE STAIRS. He sprinkles water on the side-walk and takes pumice and fine-grained scouring powder to the marble tile in the entryway, sinking down to his knees in his good gray suit to buff the milky stone. None of them understand it. For God's sake, Alberto, you have robust sons, you have sturdy daughters who can do such work, and though they'd rather not, they'd prefer it to seeing this each day: their father's bald dome or the dented top of his fedora, his old man hands laboring with a mix of martyrdom and fury, or maybe penitence or its performance—it's hard to tell.

When they first arrived at Carrer de Provença 250, Esquina Balmes, a few months earlier and saw him go on the attack against the dust and grime, their mother nudged them toward the brushes, rags and buckets, urging quietly—just go, don't ask, just help. She has raised her children to make their own beds, tidy their toys and maintain order in their satchels, assigning more substantial tasks—inside for the girls, outside for the boys—after the family could no longer afford paid help. Here, they quickly learn that if they try to assist with anything related to the synagogue, their father will turn on them, unleashing a torrent: Get away, leave me alone, go make something of yourself, or, to Rebecca (perhaps his cruelest comment), go find yourself a husband, you're not getting any younger! Do you want to be a hunchbacked spinster? For you to scrub floors on your knees, I left it all behind?

It is late March now, the air still fresh, the city's flowers in fragrant bloom. As Rebecca steps outside and edges past her father, she slips on the damp stairs, and though she catches her balance, she loses her grip on her basket and watches it sail to the ground and spill.

"Aye, my samples!" she cries as she picks her way down. "I hope they're not ruined."

Scrib-scrub. The sound, bristles against stone, is maddening. Why won't he answer, or at least look up? What samples, my daughter? I, too, hope they're not ruined. Where are you off to? Brave girl, going to seek your fortune, *mazal bueno*. She has put on a new pair of stockings and a navy dress with inset lace cutouts and a fitted waist that she only finished stitching the night before. The more her circumstances are reduced, the more care she takes with her clothes, carrying an instinctual sense of them as both mask and portal, but she may as well be invisible to her father. So have fun, Papa. *Adyo.* Silently, she brushes off the fallen items—a lace collar, a man's dress shirt, a baby's smocked gown, a velvet pillow cover she embroidered with gold swans—and leaves without another word.

Does her father lift his gaze and watch her walk away? She wouldn't know; she doesn't turn to see. As she rounds the corner, she picks up her pace, waving to the lady at the flower cart, smiling at a barefoot baby in a pram. A milkman unloads his silver jugs. The sky is blue, the sun is out. A workman eyes her appreciatively, tips his cap and says good morning in Catalan, and she smiles and returns the greeting. Earlier in the week, she and Elsa bobbed each other's hair in the latest style; now she feels lighter, free. Back home, even unveiled women had an invisible cloak around them, neither to be looked at nor to look. Here, an open city, open faces. If it scares her a little, it excites her more. Her dress, a play on a coat frock, came out even better than she'd hoped, a mix of a French pattern and her own improvisations, and she feels at once professional and stylish, a modern lady on the avenue. She has studied a map and memorized the turns between here and La Dreta, the adjoining neighborhood where the textile operations are.

Only the image of her father fierce-scrubbing the stairs dogs her as she walks on. How she mourns him, hates him (loves him). Staying together was supposed to be everything. What did a house matter—two houses, silver and china sets, books, divans, ivory carvings, paintings, bronze beds, silk carpets? What did a place matter, even, if you kept the people together, but what she is only now coming to understand is that the move itself can change the people in a corrosive, internal rearrangement, not a collapse, exactly—they are, she hopes, too tough for that—but a hardening, a shifting that fast becomes a kind of chronic misalignment if you aren't careful or can't help it or are too old or stubborn to take on a new shape, which she is not.

"Truth is the seal of the holy one, blessed is He," her father had taught them, so to arrive here and discover that he has lied to her—he's just a shammash, a glorified janitor; he's no hazan—was Rebecca's first real shock. Her second was to see him age so rapidly, for while he has always been older than her friends' fathers, Spain has turned him into an old man, the light drained from his eyes. And he's not the only one to have changed. Her brothers hold themselves differently on the streets of Barcelona, eyes appraising, muscles squared as if ready for a fight. Even inside the apartment, they are more guarded, shifty, causing their father to ask if the small sums of money they bring in were earned by legal means. Josef, at nearly eleven, hasn't enrolled in school here yet because he doesn't speak Catalan and the schools are all Catholic, which shouldn't be a problem—Rebecca and Corinne went to Catholic school—but apparently this is a different kind of Catholic, punishing, even Jew-hating according to their father (but is he too suspicious?), especially at the charity schools, the only kind they can afford, and where you need a certificate of baptism to be enrolled. Even Elsa looks sharper, a bit wolflike, out for herself, though their father's evolution is the most distinct.

Only their mother seems to have weathered the transition with anything like grace. Middle age suits her, or is it that she has already lived in many different places and knows how to accommodate? It was Sultana, often accompanied by Rebecca, who first found the local bakery, greengrocer and fish market, exchanged pleasantries with the neighbors, figured out how the currency worked, arranged for the community to install a telephone so they could better serve the people and made tea for Theodore Grunebaum, the Ashkenazi German president of the tiny Jewish community, who stops in regularly with lists of tasks or budgets, sitting at a small table in the oratory with Alberto, where they bump along between languages, resorting to drawings when words fail.

Only Sultana and Rebecca. What can she say? She likes it here. The doorways, the fountains, the metal folding chairs outside cafés, the street signs in Catalan, so many *x*'s, kisses tucked inside words. Even the name of the city—*BAR-sey-LONE-ah*—pleases her with its musical cadence. Finally, she can send postcards to Corinne in Cuba and Lika in America of palm trees and palaces, roller coasters and double-decker trams, mostly sights she has yet to encounter, though on clear days she can spot Mount Tibidabo with its lookout tower and aerial railway ride.

Their new home abuts the *oratorio* (half-hidden, cramped and lacking a rabbi, the place is not quite full-fledged enough to earn the moniker of *kal* or synagogue) on the ground floor of an elegant apartment tower in a modern neighborhood called L'Eixample, which Sinyor Grunebaum informed them means "wider part" in Catalan. The streets are indeed wide with angled corners, and the neighborhood has an air if not of ease exactly, then of sturdiness, spaciousness and frequent spots of beauty—doorways of stained glass, wrought iron filaments, the surprise of an Antoni Gaudí structure rising like a fairy-tale creature or inside-out body, as if to proclaim that a building (a body) can be anything: Come in! In comparison, their old neighborhood sits steep and hooded in Rebecca's memory, nooked, crannied and self-serious. Here, their apartment is modest and bare, lacking the rugs, furniture and books of home, but the kitchen opens to a sunken courtyard garden with a giant palm tree at its center and flower beds for her father, who, hoping against hope (so why can't you be a little happy now, Papa, a little gay?), brought along a valise so overstuffed with bulbs, seeds and bundled roots that he had to gird it with a leather belt.

~

"*Hola. Bon dia. Sóc una modista a la recerca d'una feina.*"

The first lady, in a windowless shop with Modista painted crookedly on the door, snorts with laughter when Rebecca blurts out an introduction cobbled from a Catalan pamphlet for new immigrants: "I am a dressmaker looking for a job." "*En Español, señora,*" the lady says, once her mirth is under control. Rebecca tries again: "*Soy una modista en busca de trabajo?*" Is that correct? Her family often refers to their home language as Spanyol or Spanyol Muestro, though she knows it's not modern Castilian but an archaic Jewish version, a little backward, according to her father, and mixed with other things, which is why her education was in French.

Don't mention that you're Jewish, her father had instructed on their first night in Spain, so they just say they're Turks. And don't bring up the synagogue to anyone outside the community. Why not? Marko had asked. I thought they wanted us back and knew we were here. We are permitted by the government to hold our services in private homes, their father had said stiffly, as if reciting a law. So why hide? asked Rebecca.

What do you want? he'd asked. To dance in the streets? To scream and shout? Be my guest, see what happens! They don't, he'd added glumly, shaking his head, know what we are.

Now she takes her samples from the basket, and the lady summons another worker from the depths of the workshop and spreads the items on a cutting table, where the two women finger them, turn them inside out, tug on their tight seams, nodding and jabbering in Catalan. Rebecca resists the urge to ask them to be gentler and wash their hands. Finally, the second lady tells her in Castilian that she has no work for her, nothing at the moment. Is something wrong with my samples, Rebecca wants to ask, but her brain is stuck, stuttering between too many languages. (Catalan feels halfway comprehensible, so full of French; she understands just enough to get a headache.) She collects her wares and is almost out the door when the first lady points to another workshop, so she tries there, too, but has no luck.

It is only at the third place, a few blocks away, in a neighborhood fast becoming dirtier and less appealing, that she finds someone—a middle-aged, sallow woman in a sack of a dress—who tells her what the problem is after, clumsily, Rebecca asks.

The lady hesitates, then says in Castilian, "*Usted es demasiado elegante.*" You dress like a rich lady. "You even walk like one. You hold yourself like one. I can hire a girl from the countryside. We're not fancy here. Our pay is low."

"Oh, I don't mind!" Rebecca tells her. "I have to start somewhere. I'm a hard worker. I can be paid by the piece, whatever you usually do."

The woman lets out a little puff of air. "You should see the beautiful gowns I have for myself at home, senyoreta. Our clients must be better dressed than we are—it's what they're used to and prefer."

"Of course, I'll wear different clothes. I just . . . I wanted to show you." Rebecca displays her arm with its cut-lace sleeve and velvet-covered buttons. "I only wore it to illustrate what I can do. But I'll wear something else, and I can sew anything, simple things—neckties or hems, collars, *perdes* . . ." The word for curtains, she thinks. "Whatever you need."

"*Perdes*?" The dressmaker squints. "*¿Qué?*"

"*Las perdes*," Rebecca says, realizing as she repeats the word that it must not mean curtains in either Castilian or Catalan. Her tongue in her mouth feels thick, the lady studying her with an intensity that makes her look away. "For the—you know—windows? To hang at the *ventana*," she tries. "The *fenêtre*? *Les rideaux?*" She sighs, caught between a sense of her own stupidity and the woman's. "You know, hanging cloth to block the light?"

The lady frowns. "In Catalan, *perde* is to lose, senyoreta. You might mean *una cortina*, yes?"

"*Una kourtina. Claro, si, si.*"

The *modista* takes hold of Rebecca's arm, running her finger down the fabric, inspecting the lacework and cuff. When she reaches Rebecca's hand, she flips it over so that the palm is facing up. Standing in the half-light with black flies buzzing and a sewing machine humming in the background, Rebecca remembers Tiya Djentil's warning that Spain was cursed and has a dart of involuntary fear that this lady is about to read her future and find it loveless or childless or cut tragically short. *Perdre.* In French, it also means to lose. But the dressmaker says nothing, just inspects the palm and fingers with her own warm, dry fingertips. Does she notice that the tip of Rebecca's left index finger has a greenish tint from the tarnish of the brass thimble? Does she register the pinpricks and small calluses, proof of a hard worker experienced at her job?

The lady returns her hand to her, almost reluctantly. "Somebody has trained you well. You do beautiful work. Did you tell me your name, senyoreta?"

"Rebecca."

"And your family name?"

"Cohen. Camayor *y* Cohen."

"Cohen?" The dressmaker takes a step back, bumping into the corner of a cutting table. "*Jueu,*" she says, and then, more softly, in Castilian, "*Judía.* As I thought."

From the depths of the room, a sewing machine stops, and another woman—older, with coiled white braids—appears and studies Rebecca, whose surprise is almost equaled by her irritation at her own foolishness. The name Cohen has always been a source of pride to her, the priestly caste, but to say it here was clearly a mistake. If, back home, there were places where it was unwise to announce your Jewishness, especially over the past few years, mostly her faith was just a fact about her, the way the city's synagogues with their ornate, announcing entryways were a fact. But here, the door to the so-called temple is unmarked, the mezuzah tucked inside. If you want to kiss it, you have to wait until you're through the door.

Her body feels abruptly heavy, a beetle pinned to a board, and she remembers the photograph of the swarthy, trussed-up Turkish Jewess from Lika's childhood magazine. But what has that to do with her? In fact, these two *modistas* could better pass for Jewesses from foreign climes.

"Where are you from?" asks the second lady sharply in Castilian.

"*Turquía.*" She reaches for the bump of the *bonjuk* bead that she keeps, against all reason and the formal tenets of her faith, pinned to the camisole beneath her clothes. "*Y Francia.*" No matter that she has never set foot in France; she went to a French school and speaks the language. What is "from," anyway? She has never been to the Land of Israel, but she is from there; she has been told so all her life. She had never been to Spain until now, but she is from here, has been told so all her life, even as it has been endlessly, tediously drilled into her that her people have no home, condemned to wandering. Where she is actually from, Constantinople, does not even exist anymore, turned into Istanbul. "I studied dressmaking in Paris," she adds. "*La haute couture.* Before that, I went to school at Lycée Notre Dame de Sion. The nuns taught us needlepoint starting at a very young . . ."

But the ladies are not listening, instead muttering to each other, and then the first dressmaker is taking Rebecca firmly by the arm and steering her toward, then out, the door. Outside, the day is bright. A band of men in workers' smocks and heavy shoes surges by, carrying placards and chanting, united in some angry end, some common goal. As Rebecca starts out in the other, quieter direction, the middle-aged dressmaker appears with the wicker basket of samples, whose existence had entirely slipped her mind.

"Here, senyoreta."

Rebecca takes the basket but will not say thank you or meet the woman's eyes.

"Next time"—the dressmaker leans in, her voice low—"you say this: 'I am Marie Blanco Camayor, from Paris, France.'"

"*Blanko?*"

"It's what we call the *orfes*."

Rebecca shakes her head.

"The *huérfanos*, the foundlings left at the door of the church." And the lady makes the sign of the cross.

Rebecca has witnessed the motion hundreds of times but never made it herself, despite itching to—not in school at Sion, not even when playing at teacher-nun with Lika, though they made crucifixes out of twigs and tea towel habits for their heads. Now her hand inscribes the air from forehead to chest, left to right. How easy it is, the gesture graceful, prayerful. Will her Dyo forgive her? Will the Christian one, called "Dios" in plural by the Spaniards because he's multiple, three-pronged, if he exists and takes notice of a girl like her? The sign of the cross comes almost too naturally to her, the practiced gesture of the Conversos who stayed in Spain, some of them living as Christians in the outside world but lighting their Shabbat candles in the cellar, out of sight. The Torah may consider the chameleon an impure animal, but God put chameleons on the earth for a reason, and Rebecca, who used to make a game with Lika of spotting the lizards in the garden in Büyükdere, has always been impressed by their ability to go from leafy green to stony gray to twiggy brown.

"*Soy Marie Blanko Camayor.*" She keeps her gaze steady. "*De París, Francia.*"

"*Encantat.*" The lady nods but does not extend her hand.

"Do you have a job for me?"

"I am sorry, senyoreta. I do not."

"But I do beautiful work. You said so yourself."

"I'm sorry." The dressmaker peers down the street and ushers her away. "I told you, there is nothing for you here."

~

The next day is Shabbat, so Rebecca stays home, though Isidoro and Marko, who have found jobs selling textiles in the Encantes outdoor market of San Antonio with a small group of Sephardim from the Balkans and Turkey, must go to work. Outside, the rain pours down. "Such a waste," her mother says, peering out the window. "The boys may as well be here."

The service is simple, with no rabbi and barely enough men to form a minyan. Still, the group gathers in the oratory, Rebecca, her mother and Elsa seated behind the lattice with a woman from Morocco and another from Izmir and their young daughters, and the men and boys—her father and Josef, Sinyor Grunebaum, a few others—on the four pews encircling the dais. The men say the prayers. Her father sings, and in the moment he seems close to his old self, and because there is no hazan to serve as cantor, he may as well be one, and he is complimented on his voice. After the service, the guests leave, and her father prays alone for a time while the rest of them snack on toasted melon seeds in the kitchen. Later, the skies clear, and her brothers return from work, and they all walk as a family to a little park, where they wipe down a few benches and share a simple picnic of bread, fruit, hard-boiled eggs, cold fish with lemon, cold frittata and cheese, just like they'd had at home. On the way back, her father, at his wife's unsubtle prompting, buys everyone sorbet from a street vendor. Briefly, Rebecca might be a child again, his pocket full of easy money, the sorbet identical in taste and texture to her memory of it, though sold by a Spanish woman at a stand, not a man with a yoke around his neck, and served in a cone, not a glass.

When evening falls, Josef comes in from the garden to say he has spotted three stars in the sky, and with the silver spice box and Kiddush cup they brought from home, they gather at the kitchen table for Havdalah, a ceremony Rebecca has always loved for how it marks the seam between sacred day and ordinary week.

Because they have no braided candle, her mother holds two candles together, and her father perches on a stool and says the prayer: Blessed art thou, O Lord, who separates between sacred and secular, *hamav'dil bein kodesh l'chol.* Then it's wine and laughter, fire and spice, the old familiar words, though uttered softly here and with the windows closed.

The laughing portion of the ritual is Rebecca's favorite part, but tonight it feels forced, her throat dry, her family a stooped, convulsing little circle: Hahaha! Still, she coughs it out and inhales the scent of lemon peel, spearmint and cinnamon bark, trying to move her thoughts beyond the previous day, which receded briefly with the picnic and sorbet but has otherwise been circling in her mind.

Why did the *modista* help and then unhelp her, offering a new name (though she didn't have the politesse to share her own) but not a job? *Blanko* as in white, as in blank. A foundling (but I'm not lost!). *You do beautiful work.*

"She's probably Jewish," her father had said when she visited him in his closet of an office after dinner that day and recounted what had happened. "Or part. They don't like to think about it, but many of them have Jewish blood."

"Who? The dressmakers?"

"The Spanish. Especially the Catalans—they're called the Jews of Spain. There were many Conversos. Also people like us who fled, from right around here."

"So we're from Catalunya?"

"We are Ottomans," he'd said sharply. "Ottoman Jews." But then his gaze softened, and he met her eyes. "You are who you are, Rebecca, a child of El Dyo. That's all that matters. If they ask who you are, say, 'I am who I am.'" He raised his hands, palms up. "That's it. End of story. Just tell them that."

~

Ken sos tu? I am Rebecca (Rivka, Rebekah) from my mother's mother and the wife of Isaac in the Bible. The name means "to tie firmly" or "to snare," which is why—or so her mother used to tell her when she struggled at sewing—she could, with practice, become skilled with a needle and thread. I am Camayor, from my mother's father, Behor Camayor of blessed memory, and also Cohen, high priests descended from the sons of Aaron, a name she feels she must live up to, though she'll hide it as needed and may God forgive her. I am from the pomegranate tree my father planted at my birth, from my nuns in white habits, my staircase with the worn ninth tread, the candlelight reflected in my fingernails. I am a gypsy girl, because to have no home place had once seemed romantic and she could do the dance, just as she could climb ropes at gymnastics, rising and lowering at will. Or was it actually that home, back then, was everywhere? On Sundays she had house-hopped, each door an opening, aunts and cousins, friends and friends of friends, visiting until she swelled with cake and apple tea.

This, the beautiful time. If there was blood (and there was blood) being shed in her city, she'd neither seen it nor smelled it. She hadn't been frightened, hardly ever. Her name was her name, the future abundant: when I grow up, when I get married and live near my best friend, when I travel the world and come home to my house at the top of the hill and my house at the edge of the sea. She had liked to watch the gypsies dance, to drop coins in their hat as her own hips swayed and her foot began to tap. Sometimes the dancers would reach out, inviting her to join the circle, but her mother always pulled her back; they'd been known to steal or bewitch children and were unclean. The *zinganas* set up camp in different spots throughout the city and melted away when you weren't quite looking, and though Rebecca had studied the faces of the girls her age, she rarely saw the same ones twice. At the time, their constant motion had seemed to her a kind of freedom—now you see me, now you don't—and it only recently occurred to her that maybe they moved because they couldn't stop (a door shut, another door shut), and that if they'd been paid to dance and sing, they were also paid, in some kind of twisted economy, to go away. Barcelona has them, too—they're called *gitanos* here—but she does not pause for them. She has no coins to spare and must keep her distance, dressed for the West, knocking on doors (a door shuts, another door shuts).

Where are you from? Between lightness and dark, between Israel and the Nations, between the seventh day of rest and six days of labor. With her eyes closed, she can enter the sound to become part of the vastness—a mote, a stitch, pure breath. Between night and day, water and air, fire and water. I am from *blanko*, nothingness, the self-erased, wiped clean.

ON MONDAY, SHE PUTS ON the drab brown dress she usually saves for housework, picks up her basket and sets out again, walking in the opposite direction now. Marie Blanko Camayor finds work in the second place she enters. She is paid in cash by the piece, the outfit a step above a small sweatshop, filled with girls at machines stitching silk neckties for peddlers to sell in cafés and restaurants, along with curtains, pillows and simple alterations. The tags on the ties—she stitches those on, too—are lies, reading *Fabriqué en France*. Customers, themselves no picture of elegance, get fitted for alterations behind a calico curtain walled in by piles of fabric bolts. The other workers are mostly peasant girls from the countryside, and though Rebecca is picking up some Catalan, many speak in dialects she can't follow.

On her third day there, her boss, an older, beefy man with a red mustache and wedding ring, pats her on the haunch and tells her loudly that she's pretty enough to eat.

"I'd make you sick," she says, and everyone laughs, maybe because it was a brash rejoinder, or maybe because she'd said something she hadn't intended ("I'd make you *bad*?").

At the end of the first week, she earns her first pesetas. She gives half to her mother (her father would throw the money in her face despite needing it) and saves half for herself, though whether for her dowry or a train ticket home or to Paris, she cannot say.

The work is dull, the air stifling, but the money pleases her and she likes the walk to and from her job, the busy streets, the shop windows filled with pastries, books, ladies' hats—even lace brassieres pinned flat to a display board like rare white butterflies, something you wouldn't see at home. She likes passing near the university with its arched doorways, hearing the church bells ring, the sound reminding her of the muezzin's call to prayer. Men look at her here as they did not at home. Some drop compliments, and if the man is young and appears to be someone of her (previous) class and station, she might meet his eyes and smile or even be drawn into conversation, and for the first time in her life, she allows herself to consider what it would be like to take up with a gentile, not that she would do it, but what about all people being God's children, and so many of the Spaniards look Jewish to her, whatever that means, just as she seems to look Spanish to them. Under it all, a gnawing worry, close to shame, and anger, too, for this is not what was supposed to happen to someone like her, and she is getting older every day.

There's a Catalan fellow, Andreu, employed as a mason at a building site across from the shop, who takes an interest in her, timing his breaks with hers and stopping to chat. One day he brings her a bakery box containing four little marzipan pears, green with a salmon blush and brown freckles, the almond paste as smooth, plump and insistent on her tongue as her own clotted desire. He asks her on a date, a walk in the park or a lemonade at an open-air café. *Moltes gràcies, senyor*, but I'm busy after work today, also tomorrow and the next day, my father is ill (not entirely a lie), my mother needs me (true), even as her hand defies her words by offering him a bite, and he lowers his lips and takes a nibble of her fingertip before snatching the candy with his mouth.

The next day, Friday, plums in a paper sack. The following Monday, a custard-filled pastry, which she refuses—she must put a stop to this and worries, anyway, that she's getting fat—turning away from him, though there's nothing down the street to rival the warm pressure of his gaze and ropy muscles of his arms. By then, she has spent Shabbat in prayer and can convince herself that she's rebuffing his attentions because he isn't Jewish, though the distance has also allowed her to reflect on his teeth, in poor condition, and the stone dust on his shoes, and his speech, which she can tell is not refined. Still, the gloss of his cowlick, the blue-black of a magpie's wing feathers. His teeth on her fingertip, bone to nail. The promise in the flick of tongue. Tuesday on her lunch break, she glimpses him across the street, but he doesn't approach her, nor does he come the rest of the week, though she sees him bent at work. The following Monday, she arrives to find a sealed stone path leading nowhere, like a bad joke about her life, the building still under construction and lacking a door. And so the masonry job is done, and he moves on.

As she walks through the city, she keeps close track of the clothes on the more fashionable female passersby, making a mental catalog of collars and buttons, pleats and folds, slits, belts, waistlines, and jotting down notes and sketches at night if she's not too tired. After a few weeks, El Patron moves from her rump to her breast, but she has seen him in action with the other girls and is ready, pricking him with a straight pin on the underbelly of his arm, which causes him to yelp and the other workers to titter behind cupped hands. He could fire her on the spot, but he does not; she is too fast and too good and might even intimidate him a little, for he seems, after that, a bit afraid of her.

There is one sweet, lonely girl, Consuelo, from a region called

Asturias, who becomes a sort of friend, though Rebecca never finds anything like the kind of intimacy she had with Lika, which seems a relic of the past. Sometimes she and Consuelo go down the street to a postage stamp park and eat lunch together. I'm saving to get married, Consuelo says. Me too, says Marie Blanko Camayor. She is older than Consuelo and the other workers (who might be sixteen, seventeen), but no one seems to notice, or if they do, they don't say. Instead, the girls ask her questions about Paris, and she does her best to answer, though really she's describing the Bosphorus, not the Seine: how the water glitters, how the pleasure boats take you here and there (she could make herself homesick, the way she talks). Beautiful, the girls sigh. But why did you come here? A sick aunt, some Spanish relatives, my father got a job. Sometimes she sings as she works, and the other girls say she could be a professional, and then a new girl comes who can sing even better, in improvised harmonies, so they do it together, teaching each other rounds, and even the girls who can't keep a tune join in. In this way, they amuse themselves and pass the time. There are six, seven, sometimes eight girls in that shop, depending on the week, all of them from somewhere else.

Her brother Marko has a friend at the market who has a sister, Klara Goldman, a Jewish girl from Austria, so Rebecca gets her a job, too, and gives her an alias—Ana Perez—to use, and while Klara doesn't know more than twenty words of Spanish or Catalan, she is a fast worker, if extremely shy. Sometimes Klara comes with her family to the temple for services, but the Ashkenazim mostly stick to themselves and have their own meetings after the service in a different room. Many weeks, they don't come at all. At work, Rebecca knows it would be the right thing to do to station herself beside Klara, but she has an easier time communicating with Consuelo, and Klara is so jumpy and distinctly foreign that it's hard not to feel she'll drag you down. The boss discourages talking but welcomes singing. He calls the girls his daughters, even as his eyes burn holes through their clothes. When work lets out, the girls scatter through the city, which grows hotter and heavier by the day.

Rebecca wakes, falls asleep and dreams to the sight of cheap silk ties. On the long summer evenings and weekends, whenever she can find the time—even on Shabbat—she works on her own dressmaking projects, fitting the items to Elsa, her mother or herself. After four months, she has held on to enough of her earnings to buy a small stock of quality fabrics and sewing notions wholesale from her brothers' wares and pay for a tune-up of her beloved black-and-gold Singer sewing machine, brought from home. Her brothers have told her about independent, highly skilled dressmakers who frequent the market. These are the true professionals who serve the upper class, working out of their own homes or in small workshops they set up, entering the ladies' homes for fittings. All you need is a calling card, a few connections. Skill. Some French can't hurt. Paris is a plus. All you need is your own smart elegance, which should be an asset, not a deficit (the worst thing about her job at the workshop is dressing down).

On June 26, Marie Blanko Camayor gives notice at her job. She feels a guilty pang at leaving a few of the girls but promises to hire them once she gets her business off the ground. On July 2, she sculpts her eyebrows, soaks her hands in milk, dresses in a simple but sophisticated linen shift, and joins Isidoro and Marko at the San Antoni Market, where she hangs a few pieces on a line suspended between two stalls and brings Josef along as her assistant. She displays a pale violet evening gown rimmed with white silk flowers that she repurposed from an old hat, an afternoon dress with a dropped waist and sheer overlay, and a child's seersucker frock, her mother's handiwork.

She does not hover or overtly eye the passersby but rather settles herself on a stool with a piece of embroidery of her own design, sunflowers rising by an open gate. The act of stitching anchors her, even as she is almost preternaturally aware of the wider scene: the well-dressed older lady whose pace slows at the sight of her wares, the shoeshine man eyeing her from across the way, her own hands, rhythmic and capable around the hoop of fabric but somehow not entirely attached to her. She wears Lika's heart necklace, though she will lose it within the month, the clasp come undone or the necklace snagged by one of the urchins who roam the marketplace and might think it valuable, though it's not, or only to her. Her business cards, set out on a corner of her brothers' stand in a blue-and-white china box from the flea market, are creamy white printed with cursive, her spelling of Blanko changed to Blanco by the haughty man at the printers, though in Ladino—will she never not give herself away?—Blanko is correct:

Rebecca Blanco Camayor

Couturière de Paris ~ Modista ~ Haute-Couture

II

Sultana takes the valise filled with roots, bulbs and seeds and dumps its contents into a corner of the weed-choked garden before leaving it on the patio, its lid open to the falling rain. The suitcase's innards are caked with dirt, bits of stem and dried seeds, but the rain, come to break the endless heat, will clean it or else soak through the fabric, detaching the lining and shrinking the leather until the cover separates from the frame, a heap of rags and bones. *Ke se vaiga a la profundina de la mar*—let it go to the bottom of the sea—*ni andi gayo kanta, ni pero yama*—where no cock crows and no dog barks.

What should happen next? The husband should look for her and find her there, bend close to say, Oh, what are you doing, my love, my life (my wife)? What has made you weep so, face tipped toward the sky, though your eyes are shut, shoulders heaving in the rain? If I'd known it mattered so much to you that I empty the suitcase and make use of God's green earth, I'd have done it in April, when you pulled the cursed thing out from under the bed, or surely in June, when you moved it into the kitchen and set it on a mat of newspaper, or most definitely by August. But you can't sow seeds in August, not in such heat, and she had largely given up on him by then, her own mood contracted, but did he even notice, did he *see*?

Now it's September, Spain's second planting season, Rosh Hashanah a mere two weeks away. Last night, the bloated sky finally split open, which should be a relief. This morning, she received news from Corinne in Cuba, which should be an occasion for joy. Instead, a dry, unforgiving anger, so unlike her that she feels possessed, as if *shedim* have climbed inside her limbs. For several weeks, she has been collecting dew in jars and leaving blue beads inside Alberto's pillowcase to ward off evil spirits, more out of desperation and inherited lore than firm belief. (So, too, is it a small rebellion, for he hates such things.) For weeks before that, she sought God's counsel—where is my husband, El Dyo? What must I do to get him back? But nothing came to her, no echo or dream, no word, not even a hunch, so that now, in addition to missing all the people and places she left behind and her mother most of all, she is homesick for the one thing that is supposed to be portable and ever-present: her God.

At the end of July, she'd made Alberto go to a doctor recommended by the man at the American Jewish Joint Distribution Committee office. He was deemed lacking in iron but otherwise healthy for his age. She cooked chicken liver and lamb kabobs, despite the absence of a kosher butcher—a man needs meat—but her husband refused it, turned rule-bound in a way he'd never been before. Her sons gulped it down instead. She made spinach pie, salads. Alberto picked and nibbled, stayed pale.

Then today, her body moving as if of its own accord, grabbing the valise by its worn leather handle, taking it outside as Corinne's letter swung inside her apron pocket, emptying the contents into the weed-choked garden bed among pottery shards and a trowel's rusty tip. Now she sits soaked and trembling on the stone bench, sapped from having put on the performance of a lifetime, but for whom? As she flung and dumped, Alberto had passed by the window inside the apartment but failed to notice her hauling, scattering, storming—she might have been a *loka* like the poor lady he married and abandoned. (What kind of man does a thing like that?)

If he had bothered to notice, bothered to ask what was happening in her soul, she might have reached inside and found the words. How it is one thing to leave behind her mother, house and home; to have no friends to stop by for a chat, no maid to help care for seven too-large bodies in a too-small space; to have to count each peseta but have, at least, her husband (who had always also been her friend and lover) by her side, and quite another thing to be doing it alone. She has made the best of the situation, grateful for the chance to start anew for the children and keep her sons out of the military, for the food on their plates, the roof over their heads, though she is still hoping for a way for Josef to attend school.

God willing, the children will find spouses and better prospects, all in good time. She is proud of them for learning the city, for finding work and retaining their sense of humor. Every joke they crack, every tune they hum or story they share is a small gift, and if the cramped apartment is too full of them at night—the boys with their sweat and stinky shoes, the girls with their perfumes and brassieres drying on curtain rods—the press of bodies is better than the empty feeling that arrives each morning when they go to work (she cleans the hairbrushes, puts beans to soak, airs linen, places three lemons in a bowl, one cut open for its scent—she will use the juice later with the beans. Notice the beauty, Sultana, blue against yellow, the sectioned symmetry), leaving her alone with him.

Because where is her husband? Too far, too close, too far. In their former life, he used to wander the city, stay out late. He gambled, drank and smoked hookah too freely and had a tendency to avoid his obligations, including mounting bills. His head turned at a pretty woman—she'd seen it more than once—and he regularly left work to garden or play backgammon or cards and made slippery excuses out of shame or cowardice. He could be sneaky, quick to criticize, pedantic and oversensitive to slights.

Sultana saw all this and more yet loved him still, because he was so full of life and art and elegance, because he was so full of love for *her*—a romantic at heart but also loyal as a dog. *From the moment I first saw you*, he'd say, and he loved her when her babies came out blue and she turned brittle with grief, and when her hair turned white too early. Most of the time, before the money ran out, she didn't really even mind his wanderings. They left her space; he would come home. On Shabbat he'd set her up with pillows and a hassock so she could rest her feet, and he regularly complimented her—how she had a head for numbers, how fine her cooking was, how many people she helped with her good works. Sultanita, Queen Shoshana, Malka, Reina, light of my life, my second chance. After her father died, Alberto brought her a flower each day for months, in a tiny vase shaped like a boat because her father had been a sea captain in addition to a cigar trader. In bed he loved her and throughout the days (months, years), often stopping to kiss her as he passed by, so that her friends spoke with envy of their marriage (it must be your name, her friend Viktoria said. He knows how to treat you like a queen), despite some of their husbands having risen higher in society and achieved more in their chosen professions.

And it was not just Sultana that Alberto loved. He loved their children and the world and the One Who Made the World, and understood, as she did, that such love was not just a gift but also a duty because El Dyo was bodiless, in each leaf and drop of water, each heartbeat, each bite of food, and it was a lifelong calling to notice Him and let Him in. When, years ago, she accepted Alberto's marriage proposal, her mother had warned her that with their age difference, she might wake up one day still young but married to an old man. Sultana had not quite believed it. Alberto, though twenty-two years her senior, had seemed plenty young, scrambling up a hillside to introduce himself to her. He was full of impulses to taste and learn: cafés and books, ideas and music, flowers and their habits. Her body, which he played as if it were an instrument. Sex had embarrassed her, her own pleasure, too, but he'd kept at it until he made her sing. He'd not been cheerful, exactly—there was always a dark philosophical undertow; maybe he saw too much—but always, he had kept a finger on the pulse of life.

Has he turned suddenly old here, the move dragging him not just across space but also time? That's not it, or not entirely. He is still plenty strong and, despite his iron deficiency, hardly seems anemic—see how he bends and scrubs. His mind is sharp; he reads the Spanish newspapers and keeps the community's accounts in better order than he did those of the textile factory. No, this is something else: a giving up, a faithlessness, for all his endless tending of the synagogue. A turning inward that leads to selfishness, even distrust. His breath has gone vaguely sour; his eyes, when they're not lit with outrage, are flat. He has not touched her for months, and the few times she approached him (patting his arm, once, stroking his cheek with an outstretched finger), he jumped as if he had been stung.

When Jews—sailors, refugees, traders, merchants—find their way to the unmarked temple, Sultana prepares coffee, tea and *biscochos*, and when the men finish with their prayers, she brings the tray and talks to them in gestures and whatever common language they can summon. Where are you going, where have you been? Do you have children? How was the voyage? What is the news of the world? What can I do for you? Please, sit. Eat. She'll give them the name of Villa Erna, the pension on Carrer del Modolell run by a Jewish family, and Café Cómico, where the Sephardim can learn about jobs, and for the Ashkenazim, the corner café on Còrsega, where they might find Yiddish speakers. Tell them you've been to us, she says warmly. Say you're a friend of a friend. If the visitors are stateless or, like her older sons, fleeing military service and considered deserters, she'll pass on the address of the Ezra Aid office, which can help them apply for a Permit of Stay or small business loan and let them use its address on their business cards. She'll tell them about the market where her sons have stalls, and the razor blade factory started by a man from Smyrna, and the zipper import outfit run by a German Jew who settled here some time ago. In Turkey, I was a surgeon, one man said bitterly a few months ago. Wonderful, replied Sultana. You know how to cut and zip! To orient the strangers, she'll unfold a map of the city with Carrer de Provença 250 marked with a red dot and the words, in her own hand: *Estas Aki.*

Sometimes the travelers, almost all male, seem surprised that she, the wife, is the one to engage with them, but what choice does she have? "Love the sojourner for you were once sojourners in the land of Egypt." In truth, she is still a sojourner herself, more or less brand-new here and hardly at home, but no need to share her private troubles with her guests. This is a beautiful city, she tells them. Great Jewish sages used to walk these streets. If a visitor is single and seems like a prospect for Rebecca or Elsa, she might invite him to dinner. Her daughters flirt and prattle, though later they'll take her to task (he's a fisherman, Mama, he smells of fish!). Alberto hovers in the background or leaves the table with his meal half-eaten to prowl in the untended garden in the dark.

Yesterday he told her he'd hired a mason to install glass shards in cement on the top of the brick wall along the street.

"*Ke?*" She'd set down her paring knife on the kitchen table. "You didn't, Alberto. Why would you do that?"

Her husband did not lift his eyes from the ledger of the community's accounts. He shrugged. "Things have happened."

"Such as?"

He wrote something down. "Different things. Graffiti. A pig's head thrown into the garden."

She shook her head. "I was there when Sinyor Grunebaum told us those stories. That was years ago. Things are better now. We've no reason to think it will happen again."

"Of course it will, sooner or later. It's just a question of time."

"Alberto, don't say that!" She reached for the *bonjuk* bead pinned inside her collar and murmured *leshos de mi*—far from me—though the expression has always struck her as selfish, implying that the misfortune should land on other people somewhere else. "Please."

"Say it or not, it makes no difference. It's the truth."

"The truth," she said, "is that if you spit at the sky, you hit yourself in the face."

"Sultana," said her husband wearily, as if to a dullard child. "Who is spitting? I've seen more than you. Read more. Traveled more."

You're a cranky old man, she had an urge to say. I go out on the streets and smile at strangers while you stay locked inside these walls. I still look out at the world, and up to God.

But a wife did not address her husband in this way, and anyway, she didn't have it in her to be cruel. Her husband was still a good man, trying to protect his family, but she wouldn't allow him to infect her with fear. The neighbors seemed like nice people. They'd brought over cakes; she'd complimented their baking because it was tasty but also because a *boka dulse avre puertas de fierro*—a sweet mouth opens doors of iron. You had to look for people's good side, not greet them with a wall of broken glass. Back home, they'd been on friendly terms with all kinds. Alberto had played music with the Muslims, done business with the Christians. Her sons and daughters went to school with *bien élevés* children of many stripes, and her own charity efforts, while primarily focused on Jewish orphans, were variously directed at people of different creeds.

"No glass on the wall, Alberto," she had begged. "Please. It will cause more problems than it solves."

But the mason had already arrived and was using a paddle knife to smear cement on the top of the brick wall on the Carrer de Balmes side, then inserting shards, sculptural, glistening; they might have been festive if they weren't so ghastly. Sultana returned to her carrots, chopping and chopping, pushing the minced bits into a colorful pile with the edge of her knife. The onions were next; then at least she could cry. What had they come to? In another life, she had loved glass. Alberto, who had a knack for finding treasures as he wandered the city, used to give her gifts of it: a hobnail pale blue perfume set, glass flowers from Bohemia, gold-rimmed fluted Pesach cups, all of it sold off before the move.

"I'm doing it for you," her husband went on, even as his hand, awkwardly bent—he'd been born left-handed but had been made to switch to right—kept writing in his book. "To keep you and the children safe."

She banged down the knife. "For me?"

He looked at her sternly. "Yes. That's what I said."

"Well, I don't want it."

"You *need* it. That's what I'm telling you."

"That"—she looked at her feet—"is a matter of opinion."

"No," he said. "I know more than you. I read the papers. I've read books about Spain. I've talked to many people. I see what's happening in the world. What do you know?"

"Goodness. Friendly neighbors. No one trying to undermine us. What I see with my own two eyes."

"Surfaces lie. You've told me that yourself. Look underneath."

Now, having not yet gone near an onion, she was crying. "So why are we even here, Alberto, if it's such a terrible place? Why did you bring us here? Tell me that."

"Why?" He spoke very softly. "I failed."

"*Ke?*"

"I failed! Should I say it louder?" He got up and went to the open window, poking his head out and putting his hands to his mouth to amplify his voice. "I failed!"

"Stop it, Alberto. Have some dignity. I beg of you."

The mason turned to look, and Sultana, reddening, waved and watched the puzzled man wave back.

"*J'ai échoué,*" Alberto repeated, switching into French, and then (how many ways could he hammer it in?) to English. "*I failed.*"

"Why not take out an ad in the newspaper about it?" she said sharply in their mother tongue. "Shout it from the rooftops! Invite the neighborhood!"

She went to close the windows, far from tears now. An old man? Hardly. It turned out she was married to a child. "Our country failed us, that's what happened," she told him. "Why do you think so many Jews left before we did? Thousands have left, more every year. You think we're alone in this? You're not so important, that you should put it all on yourself."

"So I'm a nobody."

She rolled her eyes.

"You said so yourself," he told her. "You married a nobody. I'm sorry for you."

"*Basta*, Alberto! Where is your head?"

"I don't know."

He looked around, and for a moment she thought his mood had turned and he was about to make a joke—is that my head on a platter, is it up on a shelf? But his eyes held no mirth.

"You married a nobody," he repeated.

"Don't insult me. Or yourself. You know better, Alberto. No one is a nobody before God."

"I can't find Him, Sultana. I can't—"

A tenderness came over her, but she would not bow to it. "Try," she said.

"I have."

"Try harder."

He looked up, his face twisted and ugly. "I'm an old man. I'm all done trying."

"For that," she told her husband, "you should be ashamed."

THAT NIGHT (which was just last night, though it feels like days ago), she did not sleep but sat in the garden where the rain had not yet come, the heat oppressive, and no cats visited because they would bloody their paws on the top of the wall, and no one came for her or noticed that she was not inside. She sat and sat, a garden statue, her thoughts gone blank, and woke wet from the rain, her neck in a cramp (so she must have slept a little), and went inside to make breakfast for her family, not out of love or generosity, but because it was her job.

Then this morning, through the slot in the door, a blessing from afar: Corinne and Israel expecting a baby, El Dyo willing, in Cuba. Alberto had only been a few feet away as she'd opened the letter, but she'd read it silently and slid it into her apron pocket, where it had stayed, a hoarded secret, while she got the valise, took it outside and dumped it out. Then back to the bench, where she'd sat in a daze, is sitting still, as the rain slows and stops (the garden gleams).

"WHERE IS JOSEF, that little bastard!"

Abruptly she is up from the bench and on her feet, ready to protect her son.

"He took my suitcase!" screams Alberto. "He dumped my plants! How dare he do such a thing! Where is that idiot boy? I'll throttle him! I'll wring his neck!"

With surprising strength, he lifts and hurls the suitcase across the courtyard. Sultana watches it teeter and settle on the flagstone with a thump.

"Calm yourself," she says. "And keep your voice down, the neighbors will hear." She steadies herself on the trunk of the palm tree, dizzy from having stood up too fast. What time is it? Are all the children home? Is Josef? She looks through the windows into the apartment but sees no sign of him.

"Where is he? I'll find him at the market!" Alberto says. "Where is it? What's the street called?"

"Leave Josef be. It wasn't him."

"Who, then? Marko? Isidoro? One of the girls? Who would do a thing like that? My"—he looks briefly desperate, helpless, then furious again, still in his dressing gown, the sash untied, his pajamas, fine Egyptian cotton, frayed now, hanging loosely on his frame—"plants from home."

"It wasn't the children, Alberto. It was me."

It is El Dyo who leads them; they agree on this later. It is El Dyo who shows Alberto his wife, rain-washed, drained of tears. Unafraid.

"You?" he flings back, and she nods, and he shocks her by coming at her ready to strike (on rare occasions, he will take the switch to the boys, but he has never raised a hand at her or their daughters), but stops suddenly and drops his arm down, and whatever is to happen will now happen. She is that calm, that far away.

She moves forward in silence, not toward her husband but toward the far corner of the garden where she dumped the bulbs, roots and seeds. The garden has always been Alberto's world, but how hard can it be to untangle the roots, lay the bulbs out in a row on the nearby patio stones, turn toward the garden bed, fill her fists with weeds and tug?

The soil, damp on the surface but dry below, yields easily as she pulls two-fisted, dropping the weeds in a pile by her side. And then he is there beside her, they are on their knees, removing dead growth, making room for the new, and he is correcting her but mildly, as if nothing unusual had just transpired between them—leave that one, it's not a weed, take these out, here, that's it—and he's shuffling off to the shed against the courtyard's back wall and coming back with a rusty pitchfork, shovel, spade. Some of the bulbs are desiccated and unfit for planting. These he sets to one side. Others are solid to the touch or sprout pale green shoots the color of endives. These he plants. Though the suitcase had seemed full when Sultana emptied it, in truth it's no more than an overnight bag and held just enough bulbs for a few square feet of jonquils, tulips or hyacinths, along with several envelopes (now soaked) embossed with the name of the textile factory, full of seeds. Alberto lays down newspaper on the low stone wall and spreads seeds out to dry on yesterday's news, while Sultana deposits the weeds in a spot he points out between the shed and wall.

It is El Dyo who keeps her from saying that a valise, even a ruined one, is good for one thing only, to be filled with clothes (not just her own but also the baby clothes she has been stitching for her future grandchildren), and El Dyo who prevents her from calling out that she's had enough, she'll find her way to Corinne in Cuba or to her mother back home, take Josef with her because he's too young to be left with a father who is ready to throttle him without proof of wrongdoing and promises to tutor him but never does. *Adyo*.

When finally they stop their work, they are filthy, feral, like someone's (not hers) untended children of the earth, she in yesterday's clothes, he still in his pajamas and dressing gown. It is time, then, to return inside, boil water and bathe in the tin tub. Sultana goes first, drawing the curtain she strung up in the kitchen to give the illusion of privacy. She alternates between the kettle and the stoneware pitcher, and if at first the water is too cold, too hot, too cold, eventually she gets it right, and the copper rinsing bowl is the same one she used to bring to the hamam during the hours reserved for the Jewish women, its curved, hammered shape taking her back to the enormous *göbek taşı* stone where the bath ladies loofahed her skin, her cares dissolving painfully until she was reduced to what? A woman among women, a body's breath, a nub. On her *noche de novia*, her mother, aunts and friends surrounded her there, chanting *kolay i liviano*, easy and light, and wishing her a fruitful marriage, as she later would chant for her own firstborn daughter. And now Corinne has (still Sultana guards the news) a baby in her womb.

She comes out from behind the curtain wrapped in a towel and does not meet her husband's eyes. The kettle she put on for Alberto's hot water spits steam through its spout, but he ignores it and steps behind the curtain to bathe in her leftovers, so she takes the kettle off. Terribly sleepy suddenly, she goes into their tiny bedroom, hangs her towel on its hook—in truth just a nail on the door—slips on her nightdress and climbs into bed, where she pulls the covers up and sleeps, or maybe not, because soon Alberto is there, too, real or in a dream, clean enough, still damp, smelling of wet leaves. Without exchanging a word, they arrange themselves to spoon together as they did for so many nights, so many years (but not once in the past few months), except it's not night but daytime now, everything changed and far away and turned around save for maybe this, a small return: her back to his front, their breath settling into the same smooth rhythm, set by her.

How much time goes by? Has she slept again? Alberto must have latched the inside shutters on the window and shut the bedroom door. It must be past dinnertime but no one has made dinner; there is no smell of food. From her sleep, Sultana feels a mouth on her skin, hands on her hips, and he is back, her husband, kissing her shoulder, sliding his head down, her nightdress up. He has (is she dreaming?) his mouth on her droopy *tetas*—first one, then the other—flicking, suckling, tasting, drinking her, and she shivers from the crown of her head to the root of her spine, candle wax first resisting, then melting in the flame.

A few minutes later, with her husband inside her, she gives up the news, her mouth at his ear—we got a letter today, Corinne and Israel are having a baby, she was five months along when she wrote it, she didn't want to tell us until they knew it would stick—and her words have an unintended effect for he goes promptly limp, pulls out, rolls off and turns away. For a moment she is frightened: Is he angry that she waited to tell him? Unhappy with the news? Replaced, the generations barreling on? Then she realizes that Alberto is crying, silent tears running diagonally down his tipped face, and she reaches over his shoulder to wipe his cheeks with her open palm. He turns, then, says *lo syento*, I'm so sorry, Sultana, I'll do better, I'll try harder. All about himself again, as if he hadn't even heard the news, so she repeats it: Corinne and Israel are expecting a baby in Cuba, did you even hear me? And he says of course I heard, thanks to El Dyo, a baby, why do you think I'm crying? I'll be a grandfather, I'm an idiot! A baby, God willing. *Mashallah!* Aye, Sultana, I'm an old, sentimental fool.

Then they are laughing and crying together in the dark, trying and failing to be quiet, giddy with good fortune, although she's also aware (she started eleven children in her womb and raised only six) of how uncertain the passage is, and Corinne is far away in an unknown country, and a pregnant daughter should have her mother by her side. Still, a baby. Their first grandchild. God willing, it will be a boy in good health. She hears Josef in the kitchen: Where's dinner, where's Mama, I'm starving, and Elsa joining in—I'm starving, too—so that you'd think (she pulls on her clothes, arranges her face) that she hadn't taught her brood how to boil green beans and fry an egg.

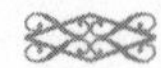

Barcelona, 1926

I

SHE MARRIES HIM BECAUSE HE ASKS HER TO. Barcelona is in short supply of Jewish bachelors, and Rebecca is almost twenty-four, overripe and ready, on her way (*grasyas*, Papa, for reminding me) to hunchbacked spinsterhood. Her older sister, Corinne, is already a mother and has moved from Cuba to New York, where—Rebecca tries to tamp down her jealousy—she spends time with Lika, who has married her cousin from Ortaköy, Sabetay Levy, and is expecting a baby. If the child is a girl, Lika writes, we will give her Rivka, after you, as her middle name.

Rebecca knows Mishon (who goes by Luis) Baruch by sight from his visits to the temple, Luis one of only half a dozen single men filing through the unmarked door on Shabbat and holidays to find the tallits, embroidered by Rebecca, on the rack. Why him over the others? He is neither too old—just six years her senior—nor too young. He is Sephardic, from Adrianople in Eastern Turkey, where his parents still live. He has (Sultana asks around) a job. More to the point, *la ija del Judio no keda sin kazar*, the daughter of a Jew does not remain unmarried. On both sides, the families are angling, Luis's sister Palomba more than a little anxious to get her brother settled with a wife. One day after services, Sultana invites Luis, along with Palomba, her husband, and their small son, Manuel, to stay for tea, where Palomba and her husband entertain the group with funny tales. The next week, the same thing. Luis doesn't say much, Rebecca observes to her mother afterward. A man of few words, says Sultana, is better than one who never shuts up. The following Wednesday, an invitation signed by Luis tumbles through the mail slot: "We hope your family will join us after services on Saturday for a picnic in the park." How elegant of him, says Elsa, for the letter arrived rolled into a scroll, secured by a blue bow. That was his sister's doing, Rebecca says.

She takes a liking to Palomba, who is warm and plays the guitar and has a keen eye for social mores but doesn't put on airs. The family has humble origins, but Palomba married well, and her husband already owns his own small auto repair business. They're saving to send Manuel to the expensive Lycée Français, where Sultana tried but failed to get a scholarship for Josef. For the first time since she arrived in Spain, Rebecca has a friend to visit with. As for Luis, how is he? A good boy, Palomba says, and it's true that he is pleasant enough. Polite—he holds open doors, carries picnic hampers. Quiet. Dreamy, maybe? In the park, he plays catch with Josef and Manuel, the most animated Rebecca has seen him. Later he disappears for a time and returns with a pinwheel, which he presents to Rebecca with a bow.

"Charming," she writes to Lika. "Handsome," though in truth, she finds him so-so in the looks department, short and broad with a high forehead, thinning hair and pink, plumpish lips that would be a gift on a woman but appear slightly feverish and mannered on a man (years later, at a vaudeville show, she will see a clacking ventriloquist's dummy that looks exactly like Luis). Still, his eyes are an attractive shade of blue—unusual among the Sephardim—and his hands well-shaped, though each time she tries to picture him coming close to her, her mind summons Andreu, the glossy-haired Catalan who brought her marzipan.

Luis is not rich, not remotely, but somehow he manages to woo her in style, and she finds herself out and about in the city on a man's arm. "We went on a harbor cruise," she writes to Lika. "He took me to a Charlie Chaplin movie, *The Gold Rush*. Have you seen it? Charlie boils and eats his own shoe!" Luis works at his brother-in-law's automotive repair business, and soon Marko (who is quarreling with Isidoro and fed up with hawking wares) gets some shifts there, and they hire Josef for a few hours a week to run errands. On occasion, Rebecca and Marko have dinner with the family in the flat above the shop, or Luis will stay at Carrer de Provença for a meal after services.

That boy doesn't have much to say for himself, even Alberto remarks after one such dinner. How could he? says Sultana. No one ever stops blabbing in this family. Speak for yourself, Alberto says, and it's true that he talks far less than he used to, though his mood seems to have lifted a little and he has planted a fall crop of vegetables and begun to read again. *La mijor palavra es la ke no se avla*—the best word is the word unspoken, offers Sultana predictably. You might take your own advice more, mutters Rebecca and watches hurt flash across her mother's eyes and rushes to offer her a hug. She is too old to live cheek to jowl like this, receiving adages at her mother's knee.

So Luis isn't perfect. Rebecca has her own pocketful of adages for trying times: "Look on the bright side!", "Seek the good!" The nuns used to have a teaching game: Here is a picture of a sad, sad house (lame horse, empty larder). Reducing suffering through charitable works is one important obligation, but another—pay attention, girls—is to find the good in what you have. The girls would strain to think of it. Maybe the lame horse likes to stay in the house? Perhaps food tastes better if you're starving? Or this (they'd all chime in): Down the road is a homeless family and they find the house and live in it, and though the lame horse can't walk or pull a wagon, he can fertilize the garden with his poop (at this last, Lika's observation, gales of laughter; even Mère Mélanie joined in). At recess, the girls, most of whom lacked for nothing, would reframe the story back to misery. The lame horse starves in the sad house. *Tant pis, c'est la vie!*—a chant to jump rope to, though when the nuns came close, they had to stop.

If Luis speaks too slowly—Rebecca's thoughts wander off between his words—his hands hold talents that his tongue does not. He can repair an automobile and swap parts out to turn two broken clocks into one that works. He can build a chicken coop out of scrap wood for the corner of the garden (her father has started raising chickens so he can slaughter them according to their practice, since they still don't have a shohet) and build a house from playing cards. He is from a family of butter peddlers, laborers, though in Barcelona he has held many different jobs—driving a cab, selling carpets or newspapers, shining shoes, working in a factory. Back home, he'd have sold them butter and gone on his way. His name, Baruch, means "blessed."

The wedding is a small affair in early January, held on a Friday for good luck. Luis's parents, still in Adrianople, are not present. For Rebecca, there is no going to the mikveh (no mikveh) with her mother, sisters and girlfriends, no festive party at the summer house (no summer house). No dowry, though she brought her trousseau from home: the pillowcases, bedspread and bed jacket, the piano runner (no piano) made of velvet silk and embroidered in gold with pomegranates and figs. She brought the cutwork baby bib she stitched when she was twelve, and another bib that was her own, made by her mother, and doilies and crocheted booties for both adult and infant, all of it packed in her trunk between sheets of brown paper and sprigs of lavender and rue.

She does not display the items around the room for viewing and for the elders to note down and include in the marriage contract. It's an outdated custom, says her mother, but in truth the community here is a small, bedraggled group and transient, so many people just passing through on their way to somewhere else, which is also why there is no formal *entrevista* gathering as the match is being made. How can you gather to assess when you have no grandmothers, aunts or longtime neighbors guiding you along the current formed by their collective judgment, base prejudices, gut feelings? (How does he stand? How does he eat? What does the shape of his head indicate about his potential? Is his gaze shifty? Is his shirt simple but well-made, or stylish but cheap? Is he nice to his sister when he thinks no one is watching? Does he eye the other ladies? When he sits, does he rearrange his parts in a way that indicates too much or too little in the bank? Does he slurp, burp, fart?) Swat them away, those meddlesome ladies. It would be a farce anyway to pretend to decide between this one and that when Rebecca's choice, if you can call it that, is singular. Man Bachelor Jew = Luis.

Still, the families do their best to make the occasion festive. The day before the wedding, Alberto enlists Isidoro to borrow a car and drive him and Rebecca to the Cementiri de les Corts on the outskirts of the city where, among the ornate, towering Catholic tombs, they find an out-of-the-way corner where they can clip branches from evergreen plants—artemisia, hare's-ear, cedar—and if anyone asks, they will pretend they've come to decorate a relative's grave, and may El Dyo forgive them. Rebecca is pleased to come along. She is in business for herself now but has taken off the week and needs to stay occupied to calm her nerves, and now that she has a way out, she is suddenly filled with an outsize sentimental attachment to her family. She learns from her father how to clip in a way that helps the plants—always at a juncture, with an angled cut. On the way back, they stop at a flower market, where Alberto selects lilies for the table and white roses for Rebecca's bridal bouquet, then at a wine shop down the road. In a matter of hours, he spends a month's worth of the family's household budget. I only have one Rebecca, he tells her as she basks in his attention. I can contribute, Papa, she says (in an economy where everyone complains about how hard it is to get ahead, her business is doing well). He shakes his head. Is he crying? This is my small gift to you, he says, but in the direction of the flowers. God willing, Rebecca, you will only marry once.

She sews her own gown, and her mother sits by the window where the light is good and stitches hundreds of seed pearls to the bodice, and Elsa and Palomba make marmalades and candied citron for the tray of sweets. Isidoro, Marko and Josef build a long table from two doors and set it up in the meeting room adjoining the oratory, where the Ashkenazim usually meet after shared services. A traveling French rabbi performs the religious ceremony in the oratory, which Alberto has festooned with fragrant greens. The civil ceremony is scheduled for the following Monday, to be followed by a visit to the photography studio. Rebecca's wedding dress, an ivory silk sheath of her own design, is pretty in an understated way. For the civil ceremony, she makes a simple below-the-knee dress with two layers, adding mink trim near the hem at the last minute because she has a remnant on hand and the dress had looked too plain.

LATER, AFTER THE wedding photograph is developed and printed in portrait size and as a postcard to send to friends and family, Rebecca is troubled by the fact that the image shows her staring off into the distance, frozen as a wax doll, her eyes rolled slightly back into her head. She dislikes how her arm appears more like a leg, oddly swollen and ringed by a bracelet that looks too small, though it fit just a few days prior to the wedding when her mother, who received it from her own mother, gave it as a gift. The mink border of her dress looks like a dying animal has attached itself to her. "*A keepsake of our unending love and friendship*," she writes on the postcards. "*Rebecca y Luis*."

Even the studio set looks odd in retrospect. Something is wrong with the table, its legs neither bird nor beast and caught in a perpetual cramp, its top not a seat, though a man is seated on it, gazing (raptly? dumbly?) at his new bride as she looks away.

Something is wrong with the man.

NO ONE TELLS HER that Luis fought for the Turkish Army on the German front in the Great War and is sickly from the aftereffects of mustard gas, or that he has ongoing digestive maladies (she'd allowed herself to think it was just a stomach bug followed by wedding butterflies) and struggles to read and write. A few days after the wedding, a cold front sweeps across Europe and a giant storm arrives in Barcelona, breaking moorings in the harbor, damaging whole fleets. As wind gusts and rain sheets down outside the flat above the auto parts store that they share with Palomba and her husband, Luis labors over a headline in the paper, tracing the print with an index finger. "How will I go see my parents now?" he asks plaintively (she'd known of no such plan). His tongue darts out to lick his finger, smudged with ink. "I guess," he says, "I've got to wait."

No one warns her that he'll get gut cramps and need to leave the room each time she suggests they look into renting a small flat of their own, or that when, fishing for a compliment, she asks him why he married her, he'll say, with childlike simplicity, "My sister told me to." No one hints that after the storm passes, he'll make her groan with blind pleasure, spill his seed, then leave to go to Adrianople, Tétouan, the Canary Islands, who knows where else, a restless soul, a butt in a bad seat, as her grandmother used to say, returning just long enough to spill a small pile of foreign coins onto the table and bed her again.

The first time he disappears, she is shocked, even hurt, and confused—where does he get the funds for the fare?; the second time, less so (he appears to earn money mostly to be able to flee again); then not at all. He's not the only husband she knows who travels far for work, and for a while, bolstered by Palomba's defense of her brother, she convinces herself that Luis's trips are at least partly in service of setting up a life for them, for at various points he has business schemes: exporting carpets, importing tiles or (such a market for them!) brass bells. Even when she no longer believes this, it remains a necessary public fiction. My husband is in Morocco looking into trading. My husband is exploring opportunities in Turkey (why he should be able to come and go from there when her brothers can't is a detail she overlooks, only to realize later that the Turkish Army wouldn't want Luis, having already chewed him up and spit him out).

That she misses Luis is something that puzzles her. Any illusions she'd had about him being a good match are gone, but still she yearns for him—or maybe it's not him at all. She yearns for touch—the plush, heady pull of it, the shedding of clothes, salt and heat of skin and clink of teeth, to feel at once powerful for awakening such lust and dizzyingly incidental, a stray leaf in a stream. It might almost make her think she loves him, or else she's just a rutting animal.

She does her best to banish such feelings, but they persist until she gets pregnant on one of Luis's brief visits back to Spain. Then, as if a spell were cast, her desire evaporates, replaced by nausea and a heightened sense of smell and taste. Pregnancy is a trial, especially in the first few months. She vomits and vomits, and most smells, even ones she used to love—lavender, roasting chicken, chocolate—fill her with disgust. But being pregnant also restores her in some measure to herself, redrawing her boundaries. She wants to be touched by no one and nothing, not even seams or the zipper on her dress, though she is also aware of being newly plural and begins to sing a *kantika* to the baby inside her once she can feel it move, picturing it, always, as a little girl.

In July, a letter arrives from Corinne with the tragic news that Lika's baby, a boy, did not survive the birth. "Write to her, please, Rebecca," Corinne says in her letter. "She's very blue, and I worry for her spirits. A letter from you would do her good." Rebecca writes one letter and then, when she doesn't hear back, another, but Lika does not answer. She knows she should try again, but Lika's stillborn child feels like a bad omen for her own pregnancy, and she convinces herself that Lika has replaced her with Corinne and does not want to hear from her, at least not now, when her own pregnancy is (*ojo malo*) in full bloom.

In October, Rebecca gives birth to a healthy son, with her mother and a Spanish midwife attending the blindingly quick home birth. Reluctantly following the custom, she names the boy David after Luis's father in Adrianople, which may or may not be where her husband is the day his son is born. When the baby is three months old, she decides to move back in with her parents. "Your brother is forever away and not supporting us," she tells Palomba. "I need to find more work. My mother is glad to watch my son." She keeps her head high but her voice wobbles, and Palomba, who is the only good thing about that family, hugs her hard and says, "I understand, *mi ermana*, just make sure you visit often. And please give my brother another chance. I promise you—he's a good man, an innocent soul. He'll be back. He means no harm."

Then to her new (old) life at Carrer de Provença 250. Her parents welcome them, and her mother is glad to have the baby there, but Rebecca can feel their disappointment. Isidoro and Marko have moved out to live with some other young men from the market. Elsa takes over their tiny room, with Josef camping out on a pallet on the kitchen floor, and Rebecca returns to her old room with her son, a watchful, solemn baby who prefers his avuela to his mother except at night, when Rebecca sleeps with him and he burrows into her, nursing and patting her arms, letting out small grunts, a solid brown-eyed bear cub in the dark. These are among her happiest moments, to nuzzle the top of her son's head and the nape of his chunky neck, to feel his touch and nourish him with her milk.

The rest—earning enough to provide for him and contribute to the household, rushing home after work at the atelier where she has rented a corner for her sewing machine to greet a baby who bats her away, covering up for her absent husband—is a grind, and though she has never been an angry person, something shifts during the first year of her son's life. Her voice grows stronger, her stride longer. She is hungry all the time from nursing David and hasn't shed the weight she put on when she carried him, but while she might appear softer to the world, a curvy, well-dressed young mother, baby on her hip, inside she is wraith thin, focused, hard.

She pulls away from Palomba, who can't go two minutes without providing justifications for Luis's bad behavior. She pulls away from her father, who disapproves of a young lady working all the time, and whom she silently blames for the mess her family is in. She even distances herself from her beloved mother, jealous of David and Sultana for how they exchange smiles and coos and are each other's daily companions in the kitchen, garden, park. If, on an evening or weekend, Rebecca is holding David and he fusses, she is quick to hand him off to her mother. Just jiggle him a little, give him something to play with, her mother will suggest. Or sing—he loves your songs! So Rebecca sings, and David wails, reaching for his avuela, tracking her every motion with his eyes. Just take him, Mama, please, I have a dress to finish. And I'm not in the middle of making dinner? her mother will retort, but in the end she always takes the baby. My little shadow, she murmurs close to David's ear when she thinks no one is listening. My precious boy.

Of course she has her own loneliness; they all do.

II
1927

Now and again, Luis returns. Rebecca never knows when it will happen—he rarely sends letters—but she'll come home from work ready to wolf down some food, nurse her son and soak her feet to find her husband drinking coffee in the kitchen or sitting cross-legged on the floor, playing clapping games with David. Watching from the doorway, you might think Luis Baruch a present and devoted father. He can make like a dog and woof, do a monkey walk, throw the boy in the air and catch him, and he sometimes comes bearing gifts—a shell necklace for Rebecca, a tin spinning top for the boy, spices for Sultana (though Rebecca suspects that Palomba is behind the offerings and that they're from the local marketplace). It is hard not to appreciate how the baby perks up at the sight of his father, despite being shy in general and not (with the exception of his uncle Josef, who is still a boy and plays with him) a fan of men.

Come to my sister's, Luis whispers to Rebecca before long. She's leaving us the apartment for a couple of hours, your mother can watch the baby. I'm not feeling well, maybe tomorrow, she'll say, and then tomorrow arrives—he sleeps at his sister's as if still a bachelor—and he asks again, but no, Luis, sorry, not today, I'm under the weather, David, too, I think we're getting a cold, I better stay with him. Until what can she do, he nibbles her neck, wears her down. It is her wifely duty to go to bed with him, but also she is lonely, and there is something about Luis—how openly he wants her, maybe. How blue his eyes are, and how guileless, the eyes of a child. How sweet he is, essentially, or is it plain daftness? She hears her father whisper that he is *vaziyo*, empty-headed, not all there. What is your *plan*, she asks Luis. You need to focus on one thing! He chews his lower lip. Rebecca imagines slapping him, first one cheek, then the other, until her own palms sting, but at the same time, she feels sorry for him. He seems as uncertain how he married her as she is how she married him, and it's not his fault that he was damaged by the war.

In the dark with the shutters closed, Luis's skin is salty, complex, fully human. All he has to do is rub against her at a certain angle and she'll climax, though she has no name for what is happening, just the feeling of something lengthening, traveling up her spinal column, of her forehead tightening, a pinpricked dazzling—it might be a headache or a fever's grip. And he is bucking, moaning, emptied out, and they lie there spent, not touching, terrible strangers as her anger and loneliness return and gather force, surprising even her and making her feel, long before her time, that she is old.

"No more, Luis," she tells him after one such encounter, turning her back on him and reaching for her clothes. "You'll get me pregnant with another baby to raise by myself."

"A baby!" Luis says happily.

She starts to get up to make ginger tea—it's supposed to help stop a pregnancy from taking hold—but he grabs her by the waist and pulls her down.

"I'm starting a lace business," he says. It is something she'd suggested the week before, after noticing a shortage of decent quality, reasonably priced lace at the market. "As soon as it gets going good, I'll send for you."

"Send for me where?"

He shrugs. "Where it is."

"*Where* is that, Luis? Where will it be?"

"Uh, Adrianople? Or Morocco? I'm figuring it out. Someplace good for lace."

"Why not here? Our son needs his grandmother, I need my mother. It's a port. I could sell your lace to my clients. We have a base here already, with my brothers' textiles and my business."

"All right," he says agreeably, nuzzling her arm.

"Where will you get it from?"

"What?"

"The lace, for your business—will you import it from somewhere or manufacture it?"

"Yes," he says.

She twists away, grabs his face in her hands and makes him look her in the eye. "Which?"

"Ow," he protests. "You're hurting me!" but she has released him from her grip and is gone, on her way to the kitchen to peel and cut ginger for her tea. As the water heats, she takes a pinch of shredded spice from the cutting board and swallows it raw and pungent, a root to stop a root. For days, her fingertips will smell of ginger and bring hot tears to her eyes. In another life, she would have loved a second child, but she is filled with terror at the thought and has begun to scrutinize David and compare him to the babies she sees on the street, afraid he has inherited deficits from his blockhead father, though her mother, experienced in such matters, says not to worry, he's developing on course.

It's a heartache, really, to peek inside Luis's little mind.

LUIS IS NOT THERE the day their second son, Alberto, is born sixteen months after David's birth, though he returns a few months later, staying just long enough for another picnic Palomba arranges in the park. A friend of Palomba's husband takes their photograph. Later, Rebecca will be struck by the lie of it, for in the picture she looks happy, settled, surrounded by a clan of friends and family: her brothers, a few friends from the congregation, Sultana, Elsa, Palomba with her guitar, even her father, Alberto Grande, as they have taken to calling him (they call the new baby Berto), who almost never ventures out anymore. A month prior, someone threw bloody bones—from what animal was unclear, though it was probably a pig—over the wall into the garden at Provença, so Alberto sent his sons to the animal market to buy two puppies to raise into guard dogs, though in the photograph, the pups look like pets intended for the children, loose-jointed and floppy, full of play.

Luis, kneeling next to David with a puppy, appears sturdier and older than before, a man of the world, though in fact he is in ill health and belching, gaseous and restless throughout the picnic lunch. Next to him, in Rebecca's arms, is baby Alberto, but while Luis still has a fondness for David, he gets irritated when Rebecca nurses Berto and shows more interest in the puppies than in his second son. That visit, Rebecca does not ask Luis for money, nor does she lobby him to stay. Go sleep at your sister's, she tells him sharply the evening after the picnic, when they're back at Provença. He has finished drinking coffee with her parents—her father started grilling him about his business plans but soon gave up—and come into Rebecca's room, where she's been lying beside David on the bed, trying not to listen through the door. Both boys are sound asleep, but as Luis approaches, Rebecca starts rocking Berto's cradle with an outstretched arm. Luis lies down next to her and tries to kiss her. She pecks him on the forehead, turns away.

"You'll wake the boys," she whispers. "They're barely sleeping."

He goes for under her skirt.

"Listen, Luis." Rebecca slides away and sits up, keeps her voice soft but grave. "I have something to tell you. Please concentrate, all right? I have . . . it's a kind of female ailment, I've just been to the doctor. Apparently it's from too much feeding of the babies. But the thing is, Luis, it can give you"—she leans closer—"warts on your *pipi*."

"Warts?" He clamps a hand over his crotch.

She nods gravely. "Yes, and then, well, they told me it can sometimes atrophy."

"*Ke?*"

Again she nods. She has his complete attention now and feels, in equal measure, a sense of triumph and of sorrow—that he is so easy to trick, that it has come to this. "Your thingee becomes useless," she adds. "No good, like dead wood. *Kaput.*"

"Aye! I've never heard of this!"

She sniffs. "It's not uncommon, but they just figured out the cause. It's a dreadful malady."

In truth, the nurse she saw after Berto's birth told her to stay away from Luis because he docked in many ports. Those were her words: A traveling man like your husband *docks in many ports.* If Rebecca had felt more than a flutter of jealousy at the idea of it, something might have been salvaged, but she felt nothing except surprise at the idea of Luis possibly having the wherewithal to take up with other women, along with a powerful desire to avoid contagion or another pregnancy.

~

LUIS GETS UP, goes to his sister's. The next day he leaves town without saying goodbye. For herself, Rebecca feels mostly embarrassment; she does not want to be the object of pity, the abandoned wife. But what about David, already smitten with his father, and Berto, too young to know him? This, she cannot forgive. In the months to follow, Palomba will bring small presents for the children or stop by, wanting to take David out for ice cream or leave some cash. My brother will come back, she says. Or he'll send for you, I made him promise. In the meantime, though, take a little something. It's not much, Rebecca, but it can help with the children. Please.

Thank you but no thank you. Give it to the temple if you want, but not to me.

An aunt is not a father. Rebecca's dressmaking business is growing. Her old determination has been strengthened to almost bullish proportions by the birth of her children and the pathetic behavior of their so-called father. So she is proud. Is it a sin? The nuns thought so, but her own people have the story of the rabbi who said to keep two truths, one in each pocket, and take them out as needed, or together:

It was for me the world was created.

I am but ashes and dust.

Thank you but no thank you. We are fine.

BORN TO SILKS AND LACES, Rebecca sews now for the Spanish upper class and a few well-heeled members of Barcelona's small Jewish community. Men's underwear, ladies' dresses, evening gowns, christening gowns. Elsa, who started out as a clerk at a paste jewelry store, finds a job at a higher-end boutique using her many languages.

At night Rebecca sleeps with her sons, one on each side and

both still night-nursing, but she does not mind, finds comfort, even a dim erotic tingle, in their four hands patting, coaxing down her milk, while outside the guard dogs sniff and bay. At the end of each week, she passes over half her earnings to Sultana and keeps half for herself, spending a little on life's small pleasures—a lipstick or stockings, a toy boat for David and rattle for Berto—and saving the rest to put toward setting up an atelier of her own. At work she collects empty spools of thread for the boys to stack and, when she can steal a few minutes, stitches simple hand puppets—lion, mouse, sailor—from fabric scraps. From worsted wool left over from a high-end suit, she makes her sons Shabbat trousers in English schoolboy style. At home in the garden, if David, learning to walk, staggers into a flower bed or beheads a bloom, he might get a weak thwack on the bottom from his grandfather, who is truly an old man now, with an old man's sudden flares and dozy dreams. And then Avuela coming fast, to rescue them both: *Ven, mi chiko, deshalo en paz!* Come, my child, leave him in peace!

The letter, which arrives on a Monday in December 1928, is brief and to the point—"I'm feeling better, come to Adrianople, bring the children"—and in Luis's own hand, the *b*'s and *d*'s reversed. Rebecca reads it, folds it up, returns the page to its envelope. Later, after the boys are asleep, she takes it out again. Every boy should have a father, and it is a daily humiliation to be raising two children on your own when you're not even a widow, and she feels, beneath the polished face she offers to the world, like damaged goods. At the same time, it seems utterly foolish to set off to an unknown, faraway city to find Luis, a man she doesn't love, much less respect. Could he have changed?

But also this: At the end of the letter, below his initials, he has drawn a man, just a simple stick figure but with one leg kicked up in a jaunty stance, and next to it, a little heart, and finally, it is the drawing—the extra effort of it, the figure's simple, rakish charm, the heart—that reels her in.

Not that she has much choice. He is her husband. "You married before God," her father says sadly when Rebecca shows him the letter, and her mother, standing behind him as he sits at the kitchen table, hands on his shoulders, does not disagree.

"What if I just threw away the letter?" Rebecca asks. "No one has to know."

Her mother shakes her head. "Maybe he's better. Maybe they cured him over there. Everyone deserves a second chance, and you deserve a husband. You can always come back or leave the babies here with us until you're sure he's for real."

"No! They're my children!" Rebecca gets up from the table, fighting back a childlike desire to pound her fists and stomp her feet. "I'm their *mother*. I'm not leaving them behind."

Her mother nods, looking almost victorious. "It will do them good to spend this time with you. May God be with you on your journey. Just in case, I'll sew the return fare into your clothes."

Adrianople, 1929

THE NEW YEAR ARRIVES. A few days later, Rebecca fills a suitcase, and her parents bring her and her two sons to the boat. Berto is plump and snuggly in her arms, but David is already walking, running, eyes on the nearest exit. For the voyage, she sews him a harness and leash. They go to France first, to Marseille, and from Marseille on another boat to Turkey. They arrive in Istanbul in the afternoon, having wired ahead. Her father's brother, Maurice, meets them at the port, takes them to his elegant house on a hill and invites them to spend the night and leave for Adrianople the next morning, but Rebecca declines: "Thank you, but my husband is expecting us." In truth, the idea of being home but not home is just too upsetting, and her ancient grandmother, who lives with Tiyo Maurice, has grown senile and does not recognize her, instead spitting in her direction, and it's only a matter of time before David breaks a piece of china or rams into a wall.

I am going to my husband. The relatives gather, all from her father's side (her maternal grandmother is in poor health and cannot come). Apple tea, *biscochos* and baklava are served. Rebecca, who eats like a sow when she is nursing, gobbles down two, four, six sweets before, in danger of popping the buttons on her already-tight dress, she sits on her own sticky hands. There is nothing she hates more than pity, and she feels it in their careful tone and skittish gazes. How are your parents? Fine. Your father's job? It suits him, he has time to read. I like your hair, says her cousin Zimbul (Rebecca has cut it short and blocky like a picture in one of her pattern magazines, a grim but temporary mistake); is that a Spanish style? I hate to leave, but we should go to the train station, says Rebecca finally. Stay, implores Maurice's wife, Grasya. Just for the night, to get rested, and for the children—they need a good night's sleep, and you look . . . drawn. We're *fine*, Tiya.

Rebecca's impatience shows in her voice. Sitting with a tulip glass of apple tea on a wide, low bench in the salon with high windows and antique kilim rugs and embossed leather books as Berto sleeps in her arms and David plays in a nearby room with Zimbul's son under a nanny's watchful eye, she feels acutely aware of this being a world no longer hers. Her father was never close to Maurice, who is at least a decade younger. There were . . . what? . . . dealings, grudges, maybe. Shared properties. Squabbles about money. Who knows? Probably her father squandered it. There was something—a scrap of memory returns to her, a conversation overheard—about a rooming house and prostitutes, a shameful business deal gone bad. What's done is done; it hardly matters anymore. What is harder to ignore is the fact that Maurice has stayed here and appears to be doing just fine, which calls into question Rebecca's father's story that they had to leave because there's nothing left for the Jews in Turkey. That they are refugees. Maurice has no sons, only daughters, and need not worry about mandatory military conscription, so maybe that's the difference, and he only goes to services for major holidays, so maybe that's it—he can blend in. But perhaps he just managed things better, thought ahead, drank and gambled less, worked harder, constructing and preserving a life for himself and his family. (Rebecca will do the same, she vows, despite being a woman and headed into the wilderness.)

She takes her boys into a small salon to change their clothes and diapers, nurses Berto, having resolved to wean David, who does not protest, and rejoins the family to eat a light supper and accept the picnic basket Grasya has prepared. Overcome with an acute desire to be recognized, she kisses her grandmother goodbye, and this time Nona treats her tenderly, cupping her face between her hands. *Kaminos de leche i miel*, says Grasya, and the others echo her: paths of milk and honey. Maurice tries to give Rebecca cash for the journey, in case something happens; Rebecca says thank you but no thank you, we are fine (is it the only word she knows?). It is getting dark by the time Maurice takes them to the station, where Rebecca buys her ticket and sends a telegram to Luis as Berto whimpers in her arms and David tugs on his leash while people stare.

We arrive tomorrow around 4 in the morning STOP Please meet us at the train STOP Your loving wife Rebecca STOP

THEY ARRIVE IN ADRIANOPLE to a dark and wintry world, the ground dusted with snow. For the last hour, the train was nearly empty, just the three of them and a well-dressed older Turkish couple in their car. The motion had been soothing; after a round of polite conversation across several languages, they'd all slept. When Rebecca disembarks with her sons, the Turkish couple gets off, too, the man helping with her valise and the woman assisting with David, who is still half-asleep and stumbles along drunkenly until the lady scoops him up. They enter the station to find the place empty, the ticket window shuttered.

Rebecca looks around, searching her mind for Turkish words, which have receded during her years in Spain. "My husband"—her voice echoes in the large space—"is late."

"We'll wait with you. We're not leaving you here alone."

The woman sets David on the bench and sits down beside him; her husband adds Rebecca's valise to their own pile, which makes her suddenly, unaccountably sad. Inside it, a photograph of her parents and, distributed among the hems of several dresses, enough money for the return trip.

The station has a ceiling and three walls, with its fourth side open to the outside. In the cavernous, cold space, they wait for half an hour, an hour, an hour and a half. The man builds a fire in the stove in the corner, and Rebecca sits near it, rocking Berto. His wife takes off her coat to wrap David, who is shivering, and the man disappears and returns with hot tea, having found an open stand, and together, they finish off the bread, cheese, dried apricots and olives from Grasya's picnic basket.

"Thank you." Rebecca speaks to the couple in broken Turkish mixed with French, as they know a little bit. "Thank you very much, but you can leave now. It's getting light. My husband will be here soon."

"Maybe he didn't get your telegram, *chérie*," the Turkish lady says. "Or he had trouble with his carriage in the snow. You said he lives in the mountains? What is the town? We're from around here. Maybe we can tell you where it is."

Rebecca finds the piece of paper with the address of Luis's cousin's house in her purse and hands it to the lady, who gives it to her husband.

"Oh, that's high up in the countryside." The man returns the paper to her.

"Is the road twisty?" asks Rebecca, and the man says yes, very, and she fumbles for her *bonjuk* bead beneath her coat, shuts her eyes and speaks to El Dyo—may Luis not be lying in a ditch by the side of the road; may I open my eyes to see him coming toward me—but when she opens her eyes, it is David she sees, sprawled on the dirty floor like a pauper boy, paddling his arms and legs.

Anger rises in her, partly at Luis but more at herself for marrying an overgrown child, and at her parents: You married in the eyes of God; when your husband sends for you, you go. What about your first wife, Papa (she had not said), the one you abandoned, driving her to madness? Did *you* marry in the eyes of God?

The couple stays; the embers glow. Rebecca collects David from the floor and starts to sing—*ah lye leh, ku ba bey*—a nonsense song that arrives in her mouth from who knows where, and she rocks her children beneath her shawl and sings some more, *durme durme, kerido ijiko*, until her voice grows hoarse. Finally, both boys fall asleep at the same time—a small miracle, *grasyas Dyo*—so she puts them in the makeshift crib the man has improvised from benches and a wall. She returns to sit beside the Turkish woman, then, and a kind of peace descends. They are so small, all of them, and though the station has a roof, she can see the scene as if from above: five figures, three big, two small. They might be made of clay and wire, homemade dolls bent instinctively toward each other and the fire. And finally, her head on the Turkish woman's shoulder, she sleeps, too.

It is six, six-thirty, not yet light. The ticket window opens and a few people arrive to buy tickets or pick up passengers, but not Luis. There is a driver outside, a man with a carriage waiting for customers, but he says he can't wait much longer; he has to go somewhere else to look for the next job. You go with him, Rebecca tells the couple, but they say they live near the station; when it's time for them to go, they'll walk.

At half past seven, the driver says he has to leave if Rebecca can't make use of his services, so finally she gets into the carriage, Berto in her arms, David pressed to her side, all of them under fur. She pulls her hand out from beneath the dense pelt to wave goodbye to the Turkish couple, calling *grasyas grasyas*—it's not their language but it's what comes out of her—and as they disappear from view, she has the queasy sense of leaving something good and valuable to go toward something not. Slowly, the sun comes up. They drive past people on the road, in carriages, on foot, carrying water, herding goats. As she sees turbaned men and veiled women like visitors from her childhood, she begins to feel happy, peaceful again (am I freezing to death? she wonders calmly), and David peeks his head out from the fur and looks around, wide-eyed, newly awake and squirming, while Berto sleeps.

They pass a marketplace waking with morning life. They pass a tall yellow synagogue with twin towers and Magen Davids in stained glass, and she feels a flood of desire to live in a place where she doesn't need to hide her faith, though she hadn't known she'd minded it so much. As the sun grows stronger, she makes out minarets in the distance and hears the call to prayer coming from several directions at once, and a sound escapes her own lips, a song or moan. She sits up taller, points things out to David, who is alert and curious, and who is, after all, a little Turkish boy, or Turkish Hebrew, as it says on his passport, despite—for reasons Rebecca doesn't fully understand but that infuriate her father—his having been born (yet never made a citizen. We were *promised*) in Spain.

Then they are going out through the city gates and up a steep road, snow everywhere, and the bumpy passage of the carriage on the rocky path is soothing, nothing to do except jostle, slide, sway and hold the children tight. David's eyelids start to flutter and he soon falls back asleep beneath the fur blanket. Chin resting on the top of his hard little head, Rebecca shuts her eyes. A Turkish song returns to her: *köpek uçmak istemiş, birgün kargaya gitmiş.* The dog wants to fly so he goes to see the crow. The washerwoman used to sing it, back when they had a washerwoman. And another one: *dandini dandini dandasta*. Finally, her babies damp and heavy against her, she also sleeps.

She wakes to the driver cursing and stabbing his pickax at a trough of frozen water so the horse can drink, and then they set out again, climbing still higher and on narrower roads, and the driver stops several times to ask directions until finally they arrive at Luis's cousin Oro's house.

Oro, who comes outside with a blanket over her shoulders, shrieks when she sees them. "You didn't let us know you were coming! You're his wife? You're Rebecca? We didn't know you were coming! We didn't know!"

"But I did! I sent a telegram. He gave me your address."

"We never got a telegram. The weather has been awful, the roads were blocked for weeks, but anyway, we can only get letters up here. It's too remote. Come in! Your children are cold. You're all cold, poor things!" And then to the carriage driver, in Turkish, "You, too, mister. I'll feed you before you turn around, and you can get hay and water for the horse. Everybody, let me shut the door, the heat is escaping. Please come in."

The house is like a barn, not even a real floor, just dirt, with farm animals living on the lower level and Oro's two sons, school-aged boys (in time they will grow up to be esteemed rabbis in Israel), doing homework under blankets by the fire. Even in the cold, the stench of hay and manure are strong. Rebecca has never seen a house like this and must suppress the urge to flee, but Oro, who has a pretty, round face and whose name means "gold," is pulling up a chair and offering fragrant lentil soup and bread, and so all of them eat together by the fire, and then Rebecca pays the carriage man, who wishes her luck and tips his cap before going out to feed his horse and drive away.

"Where is my husband, Oro?" Rebecca asks that night before bed, and again in the morning as she helps Oro fold laundry stiff with cold and drinks tea and nurses Berto and even offers David her breast because he seems so glum, but Luis is not there, and one day, two days, three days pass, though time is a dream here, endless and watery, and she has trouble keeping track. "Where is Luis, where is Mishon? Why doesn't he come? My sons want to see their father. He told us to come! Is something wrong, Oro? Why did my husband write for us to come?"

"He's working," Oro keeps saying. "Somewhere a little far away."

"Is he a liar, Oro?" Rebecca asks on the fourth morning as she rocks Berto in a rough pine cradle with her foot. "Truth be told, I never quite understood him. Can you help me? Was he always so . . ." Dim-witted, she might say. Vacant. Tricky, though that might give him too much credit. Dumb. "What was he like when he was young?" she tries instead.

"He was"—Oro looks pained, like she might start to cry—"a nice boy. Sweet. I used to play with him. He didn't tease me like my other boy cousins. He had a gentle soul. He loved to run."

"Ha!" says Rebecca so bitterly that David, by her feet on the floor, looks up from the pot he's pounding with a wooden spoon. "Nothing has changed. Was he slow as a boy? A little feebleminded? Did he have trouble focusing in school?"

"Slow? I don't think so, but we don't have much schooling over here except for religious study, which I'm making sure my boys do. Mishon had to start working at the age of nine or ten. Later, I think he got some injuries in the war."

"Well, they must have left his jewels alone," Rebecca says crassly. "That man walks into a room and I get pregnant. I'd love another child, a daughter especially, but until he proves he can earn a living and stay by our side, that's it for me. Where is your own husband, Oro, if you don't mind me asking?"

"Working. There's not a lot of work up here. You have to go down. He stays with his cousin in the town."

"Why don't my in-laws want to come meet us, to see their grandsons, Oro? I thought—"

"They're coming, Rebecca, just wait a little. Please." Oro gets up and won't meet Rebecca's gaze. "Everyone is busy, that's all."

~

THEN ONE MORNING, Rebecca looks out the window and sees the rabbi coming up the steep road to the house. She sees women approaching, all in black, like crows climbing up the hill.

"Oro!" she says. "Why are all these people coming here? What's wrong?"

"Don't worry, Rebecca, they'll tell you."

A woman enters the house, sits down next to her, puts a hand on her arm and says, "My sweet girl, I'm so sorry, I'm so sorry what happened to you. It happened to me, the exact same thing. I was very young when I lost my husband. Aye, it happened to me, too!"

"What do you mean? What do you mean, that I lost my husband? The way you talk! Don't talk to me like this!"

"I'm so sorry, my sweet," says the woman, "but that's what happened."

Rebecca's breakfast rises up, and there's a floaty feeling, a watercolor bleeding so soft as to be almost pleasant, followed by a hailstorm battering her eyelids, and her vision swims. Later, the rabbi will tell her that she fainted and fell off the chair, and that she's lucky because the dirt floor saved her head.

AFTER A TIME, THEY bring something to revive her, salts to wake her up, and Oro confesses that Luis fell very ill after he returned home, and then he, well, he just . . . may his memory be a blessing, but he *died.* He's been buried already; he is gone, in the ground. "I'm so sorry," Oro stumbles. "I didn't know how to tell you, what to do, you came from so far, your boys are so small . . ."

Apparently, Luis's father had written to Palomba with the news, asking her not to send Rebecca to Turkey, and if she'd already left to tell her to turn back, but it was too late. She was on the high seas by then. It was too late for them to find her. She was gone.

When she gets over the initial shock, her first thought is how to return to Spain to her family, but the roads to Adrianople are impassable—an ice storm has come, it's winter still, time passing so slowly that days feel like weeks feel like months. Anyway, Luis's family has other plans. Now that Rebecca knows the dismal truth, his parents are at Oro's house all the time, country people with broad accents who stink of garlic, and though she shrinks from them, she can't help also feeling a little pity for his mother, Bohosa, who has lost her eldest son and moves like a sleepwalker, racked with grief. Stay for a few months, let us get to know our grandsons, his mother keeps saying, forever pulling the boys into her arms, and as if she has cast a spell, Berto starts smiling at her and then David develops a bad cough. You can't travel with him sick like that, begins the chorus. It's still winter and so cold! Stay a little (bearing broth and rue, poultices and potions, wooden farm animals carved for the boys by Luis's father, who turns out to have a hidden talent). Your sons are the spitting image of Luis, everyone keeps saying, especially of David, even as Rebecca tries to wipe Luis's face from her mind.

Later, it will all feel like a terrible dream: David getting better but passing the cough on to Rebecca, who hacks until her ribs ache; the rabbi reappearing on a Friday to circumcise Berto, which they hadn't had a way to do in Spain; four men, including Oro's husband, who is back now, dour and large, holding down a thrashing, screaming Berto (in Spain, for David, a mohel had been passing through, and Rebecca's father had held the baby, who'd remained wide-eyed and calm until after the cut); Rebecca lunging for Berto as Oro and Luis's mother keep her back. Between coughing fits, she screams bloody murder, having become some other, nightmarish version of herself, a vulgar woman with no manners, a rabid animal, as the rabbi drones on about how beautiful the baby is, so blond, so fat.

"*Ojo malo*," she calls out in front of everyone. "Keep your hands off my baby! He never screams like this! A curse on all of you! You're hurting him! Give him back to me!"

Then Berto is in her arms, his cheek smeared with his own blood from the crude cut on his tiny penis, and she is murmuring into her son's flushed, bewildered face and grabbing David by the hand and stumbling outside into the cold air, where she sits on the edge of a stone wall and unbuttons her dress, murmuring I'm so sorry, I'm so sorry, my darlings—I'll get us out of here, I'll take you home, I'll get us out, as she puts her wailing baby to her breast.

Eventually, Berto's wound heals, and in late February, he has his first birthday. Rebecca's cough goes away and the roads start to clear. Spring is coming. The tight-fisted buds bring hope. Oro's sons give David piggybacks across the rocky fields. Rebecca can finally mail a letter to her parents. Weeks pass, but eventually she receives a letter back from her mother saying come on the next train, the next boat. We miss you and our grandsons! Come home to us, don't delay. Rebecca says, listen, Oro, thank you for your hospitality, but I'm leaving with my sons, going to my mother and father—we're going back to Spain. Oro, a lonely woman with no mother or sisters, starts to weep and begs Rebecca to stay. What will I do all day long, says Oro, without your singing and your company, but Rebecca is unable to entirely forgive her for withholding the news that Luis was dead, and although she embraces her and promises to stay in touch, in her heart, she is unmoved.

People come from the temple, a different rabbi this time, younger, handsome, with a thatch of curly hair. Again, some women come with him: Rebecca, stay with us, stay here in this village, don't leave! Luis's parents want their grandsons close by but not to live with them, maybe because they're too poor or have something to hide. The whole time she is staying with Oro, Rebecca never even sees their house.

"If you stay here, sinyora," the rabbi says, "we'll take your sons and put them in a nice clean orphanage and give them the best education. Don't worry, we won't steal them away. They're *your* children, but to help to nourish them, you can get a job in a household with a family of means and see them on the weekends. And in the meantime, we'll look for a man to marry you."

"Rabbi," she says, "with all due respect, please stop. It's decided already. I'm going back to Spain with my children."

"Oh no, but you can't. A young lady alone on a journey that long with two babies, this is very dangerous. You'll perish along the way!"

"We made it here," she says, "and we will make it home."

Barcelona, 1929

A FILMMAKER KNOCKS ON THE DOOR. He has no appointment but luck is on his side because Rebecca—born too friendly, in Alberto's opinion; she'd chat up a paving stone and is a flirt—answers the door and invites the stranger in. It's a Sunday in November. Alberto is in the garden doing fall cleanup when he looks up to see his daughter leading a tall man through the apartment and into the garden. The man is filming, so that the first thing Alberto sees, before he glimpses a pasty complexion and sharp eyes behind thick, black-framed glasses, is a movie camera, aimed at him.

"Put that down!" he says reflexively in Ladino, and then, when the man does not, repeats it in Castilian and tacks on "*por favor*."

The man lowers the whirring machine, fiddles with a button and shuts it off. "My apologies, señor," he answers in Castilian.

"Of course." Awkwardly, he extends a hand, elbow still crooked around the camera. Alberto sets down his broom to shake.

"Ernesto Giménez Caballero, from Madrid." The man makes a small bow. He is dressed nattily, in a patterned suit and tie, a handkerchief peeking from his pocket. "I cannot express how pleased I am to find you. You're the rabbi, señor? And the father of this lovely lady?"

Alberto glances at Rebecca, who lingers behind the stranger, with Berto and David clinging to her skirt. Take them inside, he commands sternly with his eyes.

"*Bueno*," says the man after the door clicks shut. "Rabbi, I've met several of your colleagues in the Balkan communities—Rabbi Alcalai from Belgrade, Rabbi Levy from Sarajevo, and others in North Africa. Wonderful men. I've also had the good fortune to meet Sephardic politicians, bankers, philologists, along with people of more humble trades. It's been an inspiring journey. But"—he smiles broadly—"perhaps the most exciting part of my little exploration is to return home and find a rabbi right here, in Spain!"

Why does Alberto feel he's being mocked? And that Rebecca is listening through the closed door, holding her father to the truth? (He still feels a stab of shame each time he remembers how he lied to her about his job here.)

"I'm not actually the rabbi, señor. I'm the shammash," he admits, aiming again for Castilian in his speech, though despite his daily reading of the newspaper, he's not always sure what's what.

The man looks puzzled (so he is, as Alberto suspected, no Jew).

"I look after the place," Alberto explains. "We have a rabbi part-time when we can, but I live here . . . it's—"

Mine, he is tempted to say. My apartment, tucked half-underground, my oratory with its dais, tallits and worn siddurs, my meeting room and closet of an office, my garden. Has he not made a peculiar little kingdom here, taking cramped, circumscribed quarters rimmed by dead pigs, crucifixes and strangers and populating them with chickens, hounds, a fig tree, vegetables, healthy greenery and blooms, though most of the seeds and bulbs he brought from home have failed to thrive? Never one for numbers, he has made a valiant effort to keep the budget balanced, appealing to the Joint Distribution Center and a few local donors when—every other day, it seems—the community runs low on funds. He has locked and unlocked the doors with the keys on the brass ring, smoothed ruffled feathers between the Sephardim, who came here first, and the Ashkenazim, who arrive each month in ever greater numbers. He does not scrub the stairs anymore—his back was giving out and Sultana insisted that Josef take over—but he still prepares the oratory for worship, and he still makes a point of greeting every person who files in: *Shabbat shalom, shabbat shalom.* Sometimes he'll invite an older refugee to sit beneath the palm tree and have a glass of wine. He's more tired than he used to be; they're tired, too. They proceed in patchworks, bits of English mixed with bits of Hebrew and French, the conversation limited, in contrast to the rapid-fire repartee he enjoyed at home. Sometimes they play chess or backgammon (the Russians clobber him). More often they just sit. He is moved by their stories, though they cannot always tell them. Most of the men are only passing through, but Alberto lives here. It's been almost five years. Every day he hates the place, and each day he improves it, by far the hardest thing he's ever done.

"I manage the budget and help run the services," he explains.

"Oh, I'd love to film a Jewish service, with your permission!"

"No cameras in the sanctuary. It's the rule."

The hounds, locked in their kennel, hear his stern tone and start to bay. "Be *quiet*!" Alberto calls to his dogs.

"Of course, señor." The man's fingers flutter over his machine. "As you wish."

"So tell me, why have you come here with your camera?" Alberto asks. The dogs have stopped baying, but their ready alertness fills the air. He hears his wife singing lilting nursery melodies to David and Berto in the kitchen and wishes she'd stop, the songs too lovely and private for this stranger's ears. "We don't have many visitors from Madrid, or who aren't—"

"*Judíos.*" The man looks down at his hand as if it's marked with a cross or stigmata. "It's true, I'm not, but how did you know?"

Alberto lets out a thin laugh. "For one thing, you speak fluent Castilian. Most of us haven't been here long enough for that."

"Allow me to disagree, Señor—?"

"Cohen."

The man nods. "The truth, Señor Cohen, is that with your *Judeoespañol*, you speak a purer Castilian than I do. It's the Spanish of Cervantes, after all."

Alberto rolls his eyes. "It's a hodgepodge, a patois. *Je préfère le Français.*"

The man—who can't be more than thirty and has the tightly wound affect of a scholarship boy intent on making a mark—looks stricken. "That's because the French took control of your educational system for their own purposes. The children of the Judíos Sefardíes should be taught in their ancestral Spanish. That is one of our proposed goals."

"*Whose* goals? Who is 'we'?" Alberto asks, though he understands more than he lets on. He has seen this sort of thing before, the past yoked in service of the Ottomans or a new republic. Spain, having lost colonies in the Caribbean and Pacific, must be shoring up its presence in the Balkans and North Africa, both regions with Sephardic Jews. "Señor, can you tell me why you're here? I am"—he lies (his days are long, his tasks relatively few)—"a busy man."

"But of course." The man smiles. "I'd like to tell you about my film. Might we sit for a moment, if it's not too much to ask? It won't take long."

Alberto sighs. "Come to my office, but please, leave your camera in the meeting room."

~

THE FILMMAKER HAS RETURNED from a tour of Sarajevo, Bucharest, Istanbul, Tétouan, Salonica—so many exotic places! With support from the Spanish Ministry of State, he has taken on the dual task of offering Sephardic Jews a deeper knowledge of their Iberian heritage and making a little film to educate Spaniards about the national treasure of the half a million Spanish Jews abroad.

"Why?" Alberto asks.

"Of course, that's the central question, though many people fail to ask it. For the Judíos Sefardíes, Spain is still a *patria*."

Alberto shuffles some papers on his desk. "At the risk of offending you, señor, we've made our lives elsewhere. Spain is hardly my *patria*—and I've come back here, unlike most of us."

"'Back,' you say. Back! The pull of a homeland is nothing to scoff at." Giménez Caballero looks around in the dim light of Alberto's tiny office, really no more than a closet with a single-paned window, narrow desk, two kitchen chairs, books on a plank shelf and the ney flute in its case in the corner, next to a bucket and mop. On a second shelf—this one slightly tilted, poorly attached to the wall—a row of prayer books, Haggadahs and an illustrated Children's Bible, dog-eared from how many times he read the stories to his children. A locked metal trunk houses the ledger books and records of the community.

After a long pause, Giménez Caballero says, "You seem—I hope you don't mind my saying so—a highly educated, even sophisticated man." He taps his temple. "Smart. Were you a . . . did you also serve as the shimmish of a synagogue in Turkey?"

"Sh*am*mash. I did not."

"What was your line of work?"

"Textiles."

"Ah, I see. And you came here for . . . ?"

"Opportunities."

The man scans the cramped space. "Have you found them?"

Alberto snorts. "Beyond my wildest dreams."

"To leave everything behind must have been painful, Señor Cohen. I'm sorry."

Alberto hates nothing so much as pity, at the same time that he feels an involuntary softening toward the man across from him, who meets his gaze now and whose tone has turned direct, even tender. Once, Alberto was also a young man full of ideas and restless energy, and tending toward the pompous. Someday, if this jiggly little schoolboy lives long enough and suffers hard enough, he, too, will be a stooped, sour old man. "Let's get back to your film project," Alberto says.

The filmmaker nods. "I'd like to include your synagogue, just the exterior could be enough, though I'd be honored to show the inside, with the people, your family, if you're willing. Your grandsons are charming, and your daughter is a beauty. A brief shot, perhaps, to show the world that there are actual, modern Jews living in Spain. It's not just ancient history."

Alberto leans forward in his chair. "So does your government want to invite us back here, then? A mass migration? That could be interesting, especially given that you still haven't gotten around to revoking the Alhambra Decree that kicked my people out. It's only been, what, four hundred–some years?"

"It's long overdue, I agree with you. Be assured, that's part of my larger goal, but these things can take time."

Alberto shakes his head. "My family was promised Spanish citizenship, señor, but it's yet to happen. Even my two grandsons, born right here in Barcelona, are listed on their birth certificates as Turkish Hebrews, which will severely limit their opportunities."

"I can help with that. As I said, I admire your people."

"Would you say your film is propaganda?"

"I consider myself an avant-garde artist and editor. Look at the Bible—a work of poetry, but the lessons it holds!"

"Did you happen to notice, señor, that our synagogue has no signs or symbols on the exterior, nothing to reveal its function to the passerby? We are, how should I put it, uncertain about our standing here, in just about every way."

"People are ignorant. I'd like to help change that."

"Good luck to you."

The filmmaker sighs. "Forget about the film—it's not important. What is your biggest concern, Señor Cohen? About the community here and your family's place in it, or your future in Spain? What's your most pressing desire, your number one priority, if you had to say?"

To return to my stone house in Fener and my summer house in Büyükdere, Alberto wants to respond. To tend my old gardens, pick mulberries and figs. To see my mother and pay a visit to my father's grave. To give my children the lives they were born into, my wife the old age she deserves. To be home.

"I'm not sure," he says instead.

The filmmaker leans forward. He is asking more questions—how long have you been here, what do your sons do for work? (That Alberto's daughters also work outside the house feels too shameful to mention.) Then the man starts talking about Maimonides, Alberto's sweet spot. Have you been to Córdoba yet, Señor Cohen? Did you know that we're working on erecting a statue to honor the great man? I'd welcome a piece from you on a great Sephardic thinker, señor. A homage, a meditation for the small literary review I founded, *La Gaceta Literaria* (he pulls a volume from his satchel).

"You flatter me, but I'm no writer," says Alberto. "A reader, yes, when I have time, and a bit of a musician. Back home, I used to play"—he points to the ney in its case—"and sing a little. But a writer, no."

"Ah! Wonderful! Might I hear you play?"

How much time passes? Maybe an hour, maybe more. Alberto tells Giménez Caballero about Maftirim music, Hebrew verse set to Turkish melody, and plays a few notes on the ney, though the reed is dry and the sound lamentable; he hasn't played since Isidoro's wedding a year ago. They talk about poetry, philosophy. His own children don't read, not like he does, and among the many emotions he feels crowding the small room is a surprising wish that he could wipe this young man clean of lineage and nationalist fervor and take him on as a conversation partner, a kind of friend. The filmmaker tells him about Ángel Pulido, a Spanish doctor who advocates for the Sephardic cause, and a stray memory returns to Alberto of the Spaniard who questioned him at the party at the Spanish summer embassy in Büyükdere.

"I may have met him once, years ago," he says. "Did he tell you to come see me?"

"No. I was given this address by the president of Madrid's small Jewish community, but I'll tell Ángel we met. He'll be delighted."

Alberto hears noise from outside—his grandsons laughing, then one of them wailing, someone arriving, maybe Isidoro with Ida, his Bulgarian wife—but the office door is shut, as is the door to the meeting room beyond it, and he feels cocooned or perhaps trapped; it's hard to say.

"About my film—" Giménez Caballero leans forward in his chair.

Alberto leans back, still holding his ney. "Señor, we are guests in a strange land." How archaic he sounds, straight out of the Bible. "I must respect my family's and the community's privacy. I'm sorry I cannot be of service. Good luck to you."

Giménez Caballero stands and retrieves his satchel. "Thank you for your time, Señor Cohen. It's been a true pleasure." He opens the door, speaking over his shoulder. "You never did tell me—"

"*Ke?*"

"Your number one priority, what it would be."

"My number one priority . . ."

And then Alberto is soft-tumbling backward through time to a hushed place of poplar trees and pebbles on slabs, of rosemary for remembrance, letters etched in stone and blurred by lichen and the scrub and scour of rain and sun. His father is there, but he is not. The soil is there, but his wife, children and grandchildren are not. God is there, but he is not.

Baruch dayan emet. Blessed is the true judge.

"I suppose," he says, "there is the matter of our dead."

THEY CUT A DEAL. Ernesto Giménez Caballero will go to the office of the City Council's Delegate Assistant Municipal Director of Beneficence and Cemeteries, where both Theodore Grunebaum and Alberto have sent letters (five, between them) over the past two years but not received the courtesy of a reply. There, he will inquire about the allocation of land for a small, walled Jewish cemetery in Barcelona. Madrid has such a cemetery plot; Sevilla does, too. It's not a lot to ask of the city, given, well, everything. Alberto will provide Señor with the name of the man at the office—one Señor Ventalló—and tell him the most likely place for such a Hebrew precinct—namely on an empty parcel of land in the southwest portion of the Cementiri de les Corts, where he gathered branches for Rebecca and Luis's wedding and which has ample room.

Because really, if you want to welcome the Jews "back," you better put your money where your mouth is, the sad truth being that some disturbing things have happened—a funeral procession stopped by the police because the coffin bore a Magen David, people yelling insults to mourners in the streets, community members buried in civil plots with no markings of their faith, and in elevated niches instead of sunken graves. Not to mention hundreds of years of buildings constructed from the ransacked gravestones of Jews; parks, houses and Catholic cemeteries built on top of Hebrew burial sites (why do you think Montjuïc is called Montjuïc, for example?), and yes, our population may be small, but it is growing, and in the natural order, people pass on (he may be next himself).

"Graves aboveground," he explains, "are counter to our practice—'for you are dust and to dust you will return'—but also, señor, in our tradition, no person is higher or lower than another in death."

"A poetic sentiment." Giménez Caballero scribbles something in a notebook, then returns it to his jacket pocket. "I'll look into the question tomorrow or the next day, before I return to Madrid."

They are out in the meeting room now. Rebecca has appeared with the movie camera, which she must have spotted lying on the table. Smiling, she returns it to its owner, who bows in thanks.

"Are you going to film us, señor?" she asks boldly in Castilian. She has changed into a flowered dress and put on lipstick. A costume jewelry clip—Elsa sells them at the boutique where she works—glimmers in her hair. She bats her eyelashes and unfurls an invisible fan.

"*Rebecca*," Alberto admonishes, then turns to the guest. "My daughter fancies herself a movie star."

Giménez Caballero bows again. Is he blushing? Alberto feels suddenly extraneous, though this man should assume that his daughter, who has two children, is a married woman, unless he has looked closely enough to spot her ringless hand.

"As well she should. I could film a little now and a little later," the filmmaker says. "My government is not known for its expediency, as I'm sure you've figured out. I'm in Barcelona only occasionally, since I make my home in Madrid, so if it would work to get started today—"

"I'll find the boys—" Rebecca starts, but Alberto cuts her off.

"Nothing today. Bring me a letter of permission from the municipality, señor. Then we can discuss your film."

~

THE PERMISSIONS TAKE OVER TWO MONTHS to work out, so that by the time the filmmaker returns with the letter, it is mid-January, a low season for the garden, which is a disappointment to Alberto, but even worse is how Giménez Caballero does not want to film the family underneath the giant palm tree or by the rhododendron bush. Instead, he arranges them by the plain door leading from kitchen to patio, where there is nothing but a few potted (unflowering) birds of paradise. Is the filmmaker hoping for pathos? Is he looking down on them despite his ornate compliments, hoping to portray them as poor, downtrodden, simple folk in need of rescuing? Rebecca is there with her boys. Elsa is there, and Josef. The filming takes all of three minutes. They stand, they smile, Rebecca nudges David forward. She has washed and combed his hair, and Berto's, too, though it sticks out in a profuse blond halo—she refuses to cut it—and the boy presents as a wild, unkempt girl.

¡Mira! An actual, living Jewish Spanish family! In Spain, their *patria*! Sultana declines to be in the film, and though Giménez Caballero tries briefly to convince her, Alberto steps in. "My wife said no. Respect her wishes, please."

He is already rehearsing what he'll say to Sinyor Nahum, the part-time rabbi, and Sinyor Grunebaum: "I have managed to obtain a letter from the city. They're granting us the dignity of a Beit Olam, a permanent cemetery that is ours alone." He would prefer with every cell in his body to be buried in Hasköy, but he has inquired about the cost and technicalities of transporting remains (in the past, some bigwigs did it—Abraham Camondo arranged to have his body returned from France), and there's no going back, not at this point, and it's not just him and his fellow Turkinos who need a proper resting place; there are all the other Jews: Russians, Hungarians, Bulgarians, Moroccans, Poles. He must admit it is no small achievement to have procured for his ragtag community a cemetery of its own, a legacy that he, a mere shammash, a shuffling *viejiziko*, can leave.

The plot will be on the grounds of the Cementiri de les Corts but its own separate thing—a sunken space, almost like a sunken garden, not large but ample enough for perhaps one hundred graves if laid out cleverly. It is a start. They will need a water source, a small sink, a walled enclosure. Their own door in the wall, from the street. The city will provide some funds, along with the families of the deceased. The Joint Distribution Committee will chip in, too. Though the rules forbid a *kohen* from entering a cemetery or tending to the dead beyond his own family (as a boy, Alberto wasn't even allowed under the trees outside the cemetery fence, since they shaded the graves on the other side), there are exceptions if there's no one else to manage the burial, as will surely be the case for some of the people here.

O Lord, make me know my end and what is the measure of my days; let me know how fleeting I am. The soil is rich, as befits a place that's nourished by the dead. A few shrubs might be permitted, and a fruit tree if there's room, to draw the birds. On his last visit to Les Corts, he'd spotted a flock of parrots chattering from a nearby plane tree, escaped pets, perhaps, turned wild now, or maybe even native to these parts. He welcomes the thought of a splash of color in the form of these clever, garish birds peering down at him, or what remains of him. Superstition holds that it's better to call a cemetery *beit hahayim*, house of the living, than *beit kevorot*, house of the graves. So. House of the living. Here, a yellow wing, there a cobalt flight feather, the stony overbite of beak, and at night the birds will huddle together in the branches, old kings in velvet cloaks.

It could almost make you look forward to being dead.

~

HE MUST NOT HAVE NOTICED that as he was clearing his garden of stray sticks, the camera was switched on and following him. It is not until some months later, in a high-ceilinged room at Barcelona's Ministry of Culture, that he attends the screening and sees the finished silent film. *Los judíos de patria española* is a deeply strange affair, from its opening shot of Giménez Caballero in woolen pantaloons on a rooftop with a camera, to the fat, bearded rabbi on a brass bed in the Balkans, to a man slitting the throat of a hen and another moving along a row of seated women, examining their teeth. People walk through the tumbled streets of the old *Juderías* of Toledo, Córdoba and Sevilla—the last a place where actual Jewish almond paste makers now live!

Then there's Alberto (a tottering little fellow in a cardigan; he looks so old, so small) on the front steps of the building with Josef and shuffling around the garden, broken pots in the periphery, a plant in an urn, a decaying shutter. Half the time, his head is chopped off by a camera he ignores. He used to consider himself handsome and took care with his physical appearance, and though he has been vaguely aware of having let himself go, the film is a rude reminder—and now a record for all the world to see.

Then Rebecca and Elsa fill the screen, and Josef, and the little boys. Everyone is moving but jerkily; they might be puppets in a plotless play. And then the film (that's *it*?) leaves behind the assemblage—a flesh-and-blood Jewish family in Barcelona!—to comment on the "authentic Sephardic features" of a young writer in Madrid and proceed to this politician, that diplomat. You'd think the whole of Spain was devoted to this little cause. Here is Señor Ángel Pulido, who might indeed—though years have passed and the film is grainy so it's hard to tell—be the man they met at the embassy in Büyükdere. "Our motto must be, once again," proclaims the final subtitle, "Spaniard, return to where you once lived!"

The film ends fourteen minutes after it began, leaving Alberto with a headache and dry mouth. Rebecca and Elsa had wanted to come to the screening, but the invitation had been for only two people and Sultana loves a party. *I'm taking your mother.* A date for the two of them. The children and grandchildren had applauded when the elders left the house dressed for a rare night on the town, but now Alberto wishes he'd sent a daughter in his stead. After a smattering of polite applause, the audience files out into the antechamber, and Alberto is paraded around the room by Giménez Caballero. Sultana, in a pale blue silk dress made by Rebecca, chats easily with the wives, and it's almost like the old days, servers with wine and canapés, the twinkling of a chandelier, the upper crust, except that he feels distressingly out of place, like a curiosity at the Constantinople Museum of Natural History, which boasts such anomalies as a two-headed baby and a goat with seven legs.

"We are honored to have in our midst this evening a few local Jews, subjects from our little film," proclaims Giménez Caballero, who will become a Fascist and get sent off to a low-profile diplomatic post in Paraguay, but not before attempting unsuccessfully to Catholicize the Führer and strengthen Spain by marrying off Pilar Primo de Rivera to Hitler.

Meet Señor Alberto Cohen, our esteemed local rabbi, says Giménez Caballero now, with no apparent irony. Alberto glimpses his wife, out of earshot on the far side of the room, her posture dignified, her white hair glowing, and even the love he feels for her is painful. A large gentleman with a mustache extends a hand: Rabbi Cohen, so very pleased to meet you.

Encantado, señor.

Alberto could set the record straight, or he could not.

Barcelona, 1934

15 January 1934
The Bronx, New York

Kerida Rebecca,

I write only to you, to let you think on this first, with an idea that Israel and I hope you will consider. Even after four years, the sorrow of Rahelika's passing is a dark cloud over us here, as I know it must still be for you as well. Even harder is to watch her little motherless girl, Fanny Luna. The child, as you may remember, was born early with some resulting health troubles but has a strong spirit and loving temperament. Her father, Samuel (Sam) Levy, is her greatest champion. I've never seen a father so devoted to a child. Sam is a good man, honest and hardworking. They live in Astoria, a section of New York not too far from the Bronx, where we are. Sam has a candy and newspaper shop that's doing better than most things around here—I guess people always need the news, and sweets to sugarcoat it! Sam's mother (also named Fanny) looks after Luna, which is what they call the little girl, who must be six or seven years old. The child is impeccably dressed, with ribbons in her hair, and doted on.

But to come to my point: Sam needs a wife and you need a husband, and your sons need a father and Luna a mother. Being married to a United States citizen, which Sam already is, would be a sure way to get you to America. Our efforts to bring the whole family over at once are going nowhere. We go every few months to the Turkish Consulate, and we tried the Spanish one, but we get turned away. They're not letting in Turks, and, as you know, even your sons are listed as Hebrew/Turkish on their papers. How to bring you over is increasingly on our minds when we read about what is happening in Europe. Israel follows it closely and says that even if Spain is safe for the moment, there is general unrest and factions among the people, to say nothing of what is happening in Germany, especially for the Jews. I don't know what you've seen, Rebecca, but he showed me an article about a Spanish poster, widely distributed over there, that called Jews a sinister force, along with Bolsheviks and Freemasons. In short, it seems like the tide is turning and could really turn.

Here is our thinking: If you approve of Sam Levy upon meeting him, you marry him, gaining a husband and a father for your sons and giving Luna a mother in you, which I feel sure would have been Lika's strongest wish. You would marry in Cuba so you could gain entrance to America as Sam's wife, but that's simple to do, and the perfect place for a honeymoon. Sam even has a cousin in Havana who can perform the ceremony, and I can tell you which sights to see. Once you're settled in America, we'll have a stronger argument to bring the rest of the family.

If you'll consider this idea, send me a recent photograph of you and the boys. I enclose one of Sam so you have something to picture. I think you'll agree that he is a good-looking man and looks wise, despite his youth. In real life, he does not look so swarthy as in the picture, and he speaks good English and seems quite American. He knows of our little plot and is open to considering it because of your bond with Lika, his friendship with Israel and me, and his undying love for his little daughter. He says that, being Lika's cousin, he even met you a few times at home—do you remember it? You must have made a good impression—you were always the prettiest girl in the room. If you won't consider this plan, I will of course respect your decision, though I'll worry that you're not getting a bird's-eye view. Israel is gifted at that, as you can see from when he got us out of Turkey, a move I cannot regret, though I regret our family scattered to the winds.

Shalom, *tu hermana* Corinne

AS SHE PREPARES TO LEAVE the apartment on a chilly morning by Barcelona standards in late January, Rebecca finds the letter face-down on the floor beneath the mail slot. Setting out for work—she has her own atelier now and employs five girls—she fishes a crochet needle from her purse and uses it to slit open the envelope, then stops on the sidewalk to scan the letter and squint at the photograph while the morning crowd flows past. Rahelika's husband? That she should *marry* him? If her sister had sent a picture of Clark Gable as a potential spouse, she could not have been more astonished. On the page, the word *marido* looks foreign, in need of translation, despite being written in Corinne's hand. In her flustered state, Rebecca loses her grip on the crochet needle and watches it fly, a silver arrow, into the street, where it is run over by a bicycle, surely a portent of bad luck.

The news of Lika's death in childbirth four years prior had also reached her in a letter from Corinne, the irreality of the event compounded by the actual distance so that her grief had felt trapped and muffled, which both intensified it and made it somehow easy to ignore. By that point, it had been many years since she had seen Lika. At first, they had regularly exchanged letters, but after she learned from Corinne that Lika lost her first baby, a boy, most of Rebecca's letters went unanswered until the correspondence slowly, painfully, petered out. When, in the years before her friend's death, she heard news of Lika, it was usually from Corinne, who seemed to have replaced her as Lika's best friend. Then Lika died, terribly, while giving birth to a baby girl who perished, too, leaving the one surviving middle child—also a girl, Samuel Levy's little daughter, Luna—motherless.

She finishes reading and returns the letter and photograph to the envelope, slipping them into her coat pocket, where they burn a hole. *If you'll consider this idea.* On she walks, looking like . . . what? A woman. A Spaniard. A woman walking to work or (for she makes a point of dressing like a lady who doesn't have to work) on her way to meet a friend at the museum. Her employees arrive at nine, and she has the only key and should not linger, but as she waits to cross the street a few blocks from the atelier, she fishes out the envelope again. The man in the photograph is no movie star, his chin a little weak and jawline soft, but he is handsome enough, with a thoughtful air about him, and well dressed. Poor fellow, she thinks, to have lost his wife—her friend, his cousin—and two infants and been left to care for a motherless girl. His expression is inscrutable, but everything in the image—hair, shoulders, ears, even the nap of his suit—seems tilted slightly backward, as if tethered to the past by invisible strings.

At work, she hangs her coat on its hook by her station, the one with the nicest machine, and transfers the envelope to her apron pocket. In and out it goes as the day wears on, in a rhythm not unlike the start and stop of the sewing machines. She supervises her workers, takes orders, butters up a fat old *señora* with a creamy young throat who wants an evening gown in green brocade (don't lie to them, exactly, she tells the girls. Just find something good to say). At lunch, she reads the letter again, and once more after the girls go home.

As she starts to lock up, she begins to absorb the bigger picture. (But what do Corinne and Israel know from so far away?) They want her to come to America, but without the rest of the family. *It seems like the tide is turning and could really turn.* It is true, there have been some incidents in the city—a bombing in December in which some people were hurt, strikes and unrest in the streets. Her landlord at the atelier recently installed grilles on the ground-floor windows and doors to protect against nighttime marauders, and the shopgirls regularly gossip about relatives feuding over politics and sometimes even argue among themselves, but Rebecca has never roamed the streets after dark and hadn't thought the wider canvas would have much bearing on her family, as long as they kept to themselves. Now, though, as she lowers and locks the grille, a sliver of fear enters her, and she scans the street for trouble, finding none (a cat threads along the sidewalk, a lady holds a toddler by the hand). Has she been stupid, keeping her head down, not reading the newspaper? Might her reaction to her father's pessimism—it galls her, casting a shadow over everything—have caused her to put blinders on?

By the time she gets home, dusk falling, she has nearly memorized her sister's words, and it feels like days, weeks, have passed since the morning, so that it does not occur to her to delay sharing the letter's contents with her parents. She delivers the news in the kitchen—you won't believe the letter I got from Corinne!—before she even greets her sons, who are visible through the window, playing in the garden in the dying light.

"I'm glad she finally wrote to you," Sultana blurts, then clamps her hand over her mouth.

"What, Mama? You knew about this?" Rebecca asks, newly incredulous. "Why did she pretend to ask me first? She said 'only for me.' She *lied*!"

"Lied is a strong word," Sultana says. "Maybe she hoped to give you time to think it over before discussing it with us."

"But she'd already written you behind my back! Why would she do that? Why didn't you say something? I'm not a chess piece you can move around at will."

"Nobody thinks that." Her father speaks into his wineglass.

"But you knew? You wanted her to ask me this? Is that what you want? To send me away?" She tries to sound angry, but the hurt breaks through. "To get rid of me?"

Her father looks up at her with his watery eyes. "Don't ever say that. We want to be together, all of us. But we also want our children to have a future, and for our grandchildren to grow up safe and not feel ashamed."

Rebecca circles the kitchen table, pounding the tiles, though her feet throb from her day at work. Outside, her sons are giving each other wheelbarrow rides along the garden path. They are flushed and laughing in the dusk, wearing matching blue peacoats she designed and had one of her workers stitch, and red caps knitted by her mother.

"Look at them." She points at the window. "Look. These are happy children. Loved. So maybe their life isn't perfect, but whose is?"

"It could be worse," her father agrees. "But that's part of what concerns us—where we're heading."

"What do you mean? What's happening? Do you know something, Papa? Will there be a war?"

He shrugs. "I don't know the ins and outs here. I try to stay abreast, but it's not my country. But I know this is no life for your children. They don't know who they are, they have to hide. They're not in school. David is seven years old and still can't read a word. Do you want your sons to grow up to be illiterate dummies with dead-end jobs, like their—"

"Alberto," Sultana cuts in. "*Doucement.* She's doing her best for them, she works so hard—"

"I'll find them a school," Rebecca says.

She'd tried that fall to send David to a neighborhood charity school, but the director gave her trouble because he had no baptism certificate and then, when the school agreed to make an exception, traumatized her son with strict rules and a statue of Jesus as a bloody dead man, naked but for the scrap of cloth around his waist. For punishment, the children had to kneel in front of the statue and beg forgiveness, a fate that befell David when he bolted for home a few weeks into the school year. After that, Rebecca decided he'd be taught by her father at home, but the boy was fidgety and sensitive to slights, and Alberto often lost his temper, and her mother had too much on her hands to take on the role.

"There must be a better school for them," she says. "It's all right if it's Catholic as long as it's friendly. You know how much I loved Sion. I can pay some fees now if it's not too much, or get them scholarships. I'll start looking tomorrow. I'll ask my clients."

"It's not just about school," her father says. "This isn't a nice place for us, and it's not a stable country. For people like us, America has fewer ghosts."

"So why did you bring us here?" Rebecca asks hotly. "I suggested New York—I'd have gone in a second and been with Rahelika and Corinne. I never wanted to come, but I won't be forced out or . . . or leave without you. I'm calling in my sons for supper, then I'll give them their bath. *Don't* try to help, Mama. I want time with my children."

As she pushes back her chair, her mother whispers something in her father's ear, and he raises his hand like a schoolboy waiting to be called on.

"*Ke?*" Rebecca asks.

"I just—" He clears his throat. "*I* wrote to Israel and Corinne. I'm the one who started this, just to look into it, to ask about possibilities. They can't get us all in, not now, but I thought maybe you and the children, if you could marry an American, and then we'd be in a better position to see about the rest. It was Corinne who came up with the idea of this Samuel Levy. We'd like for you to be married, Rebecca, to not have to work so hard. To have a friend, a companion for your days. You know I also had a difficult first marriage, but then God brought me your mother, the great blessing of my life."

Rebecca goes to the cupboard and takes down three bowls, three glasses, three spoons for herself and her sons, as if her family has suddenly shrunk. Then she returns a bowl to the shelf—the thought of eating makes her stomach roil—and turns toward the window, where her boys streak by, a flash of blue and red. A friend, a companion for her days. It is hard to imagine such a thing from where she stands, even as she is touched by her father wanting it for her—the wish of it, the noticing. She is not a complainer—she is much too proud—but she carries around a softly clinking daily loneliness, like toting a pocketful of little stones.

"How would I do it?" she says and, unable to prevent herself, flings herself into her mother's waiting arms. "It's so far to travel with the children, and what if he's not a good person or drops dead before I get there? I won't go through that again, I swear I'd kill myse—"

"*Ojo malo*, stop it, and may El Dyo protect you." Her mother pats her back. "It would be step by step. You'd leave the boys with us, just for a few weeks, and go see what he's like. If he doesn't suit you for any reason at all—anything—you'll turn around. *Adyo*, that's it."

"Leave them? Why would I do that?"

"To see what he's like. To make sure it makes sense."

"But I could change my mind?"

"Yes," her mother says firmly. "You could. You'd make that clear to him. But I have a good feeling about him, for whatever it's worth. And you'd be with your sister, she'd help you get settled."

"Then you'd come with the boys? They can't travel alone."

Over her mother's response, or before it takes shape, the door pushes open and her sons storm in, hungry and prattling, muddy and squabbling, and there is chicken stew being served, and bread and olive oil being passed around, and wine for the adults and apple juice for the boys, and Marko stops by for a bite and brings honey cakes for dessert.

After dinner, Rebecca and Sultana boil water and bathe the boys together in the galvanized tin tub, steam rising, towels warming by the stove, and when Berto and David are clean, dry and tucked in bed, Sultana refreshes the bath with more hot water and a sprig of lavender. Alberto retreats to his office, then, and Rebecca bathes as her mother, kneeling by the tub, sings to her—*durme durme ermoza ijika,* sleep sleep beautiful little daughter, *sin ansia i dolor*, without worry and pain—shampoos her hair and soaps her back, for what feels like the first or last time.

Havana, 1934

Cuba is a dream. Outside of time, outside of place, even, unless you count the room at the end of the hall on the second story of Hotel de Flor in Centro Habana, with its pale blue walls, turquoise drapes and corner sink, the faucet plinking out a rusty tune. The bed, built for two, is dark wood tented with mosquito netting, the satin coverlet light green. Rebecca falls inside the space as if inside the narrow berth on the SS Cristóbal Colón where, for the past few weeks, she'd dozed, slept, floated in a watery hibernation while her roommates, two horse-faced Spanish sisters, went up on deck or to the dining room or slept behind curtains strung on wire that were, along with a child-size pillow and flimsy blanket, the amenities of second class.

Usually exacting and quick to improvise her own improvements, Rebecca had not been bothered by the ship's accommodations. Usually social, she'd barely spoken to her new companions. Usually hungry, she'd seen her appetite evaporate, though neither was she seasick; she was satiated, in suspension, full. Her thirty-second birthday came and went on the ship, and she didn't even realize it until the next day. For the first time in years, she'd had no work to go to, no children to wipe, coax, soothe or discipline, no father to placate or mother to amuse with stories of the day. Under her pillow, she stowed her French Bible and a photograph of herself flanked by her sons in the white US sailor suits she'd made them—the picture a copy of the one she'd sent to Corinne to give to Samuel Levy: Look, a pretty lady! Look, her adorable sons, already patriotic Americans! She kept a *bulsika*—amulet pouch—from her mother around her neck (her father had sent her off with a small packet of rue seeds), said the Shema twice daily and asked God to watch over her children, but she didn't take the photograph out much nor linger on her prayers. She was tired; that was why. The ocean rocked her, *durme durme* (she was a baby; that was why. You couldn't be a mother and baby at the same time). Sometimes as she lay alone in the cabin on the edge of sleep, her hands roamed her body to find it thinner than before and vaguely desirous, and so untethered from its normal obligations that it may as well have belonged to someone else.

From ship to land she'd gone, from dream to dream, to find herself here, in Havana, lying half naked in her childhood best friend's husband's arms. What came in between—the meeting and greeting, the drive from port to hotel, the glimpses of the city (pink walls; black, brown, white skin; blue cars) was a child's picture book, a set of cut-out shapes. In the taxi, Samuel Levy, who had arrived by boat from New York a day early, was quiet to the point of rudeness, leaving Rebecca to make conversation enough for two. Have you been to Cuba before? *Si.* When was that? Some time ago. Did you like it? A nod at the straw Panama hat resting on his knees.

Did Lika ever come to Cuba, she was tempted to ask, her friend their main shared reference point, but the subject seemed off-limits, and she'd felt a sudden sense of shame, as if Lika were watching them, saying (though Corinne seemed convinced that she would welcome their union, given the circumstances) keep your hands off my husband, stay away!

"I like the pink buildings," Rebecca offered brightly to Samuel as they drove. Again, a nod. Could this man—who was half a head taller than she and well proportioned but ramrod stiff with a receding hairline (in the photograph Corinne had sent to Spain, tucked now in her suitcase, he'd had considerably more hair)—not speak? Had she once again been sold a batch of damaged goods? There's a good chance I'll turn around and come right back, she'd told her parents before she set off like an explorer for the New World. Split between her purse and a pouch suspended from a cord inside her dress was enough cash from the sale of her fabric stock and all but one sewing machine for a return ticket to Spain if the match proved unsuitable. Samuel Levy had offered to pay for her ticket from Spain to Cuba, but Rebecca declined; she will not be beholden. She'd laid out her terms from the start, in her first letter to him: I'm not saying yes, I'm not saying no. Be forewarned that (1) I come as a package deal with both my sons, and (2) I need to meet you to decide.

The taxicab had pulled up to Hotel de Flor and they'd left the hot outside air for the cooler, shaded foyer of the hotel, where Samuel got a key and a wiry brown-skinned porter in a crisp white uniform took her bag—her trunk and sewing machine were still in transit—and led them through a courtyard to the back of the hotel, up one steep flight, then another, down a narrow hall to the far end, before the porter traded the bag for a coin and departed with a bow. Samuel Levy, who told her to call him Sam (he pronounced it in what must be the American way, flat and nasal, *Sæm*) would be staying with a cousin who lived in Havana until after—*if*, he corrected himself, before she had to—he and Rebecca got married. He'd ushered her inside the room, set her bag down and lit a cigarette.

"I'll, unh, leave you to settle in," he'd muttered. "I'll return in an hour," and she'd said *bueno*, though it was far from all right to be left by an unknown man in an unknown room in an unknown city on some island at the end of the world.

But then he did not leave. She moved toward the window, but not before a few rogue tears escaped her eye, a humiliation. She was not a crier; she was a *mère de famille*, a businesswoman, a private school girl from a prominent family. I'm going to New York to get married, she'd announced to the girls in her atelier in February, and though jobs were scarcer by the day and none of them could afford to buy her out, they had clapped and cheered for her, exclaiming over Sam Levy's picture *¡Un Americano! ¡Muy guapo!* She saw no need to mention that the man in the photograph was actually from Turkey and a Jew (with the exception of the one Ashkenazi girl she'd hired through the synagogue and who hid her own faith, her workers still didn't know she was Jewish herself), or that she was sailing first to Cuba, which didn't have the cachet of New York.

Now, two choices: going forward with this bumbling man whose accent in Spanyol—so far as she could detect from his minimal speech—betrayed his lower class, or returning to Barcelona having failed in her quest, a small, jerky figure in a film run backward—down the stairs, into the taxi, onto the ship, back, back, back to Carrer de Provença. *I'm* (though it was not and never would be) *home.*

Sam Levy stepped in front of her and, for the first time in their brief acquaintance, looked her in the eye. His own were so dark brown as to appear almost black. Something shifted then, a mutual locking in, however brief. His gaze held layers: appraisal, reserve, a deep and keen intelligence. Grief—or was she reading too much in? And something else. A heat, the unmistakable, heady musk of male desire.

"I remember you." Sam Levy's voice was husky. "From home." He let out an embarrassed laugh. "You were beautiful then and you're beautiful now."

"*Sin ojo*," Rebecca said, only half joking. She flipped over her collar to show him the *bonjuk* bead, and, after stubbing out his cigarette in an ashtray on a side table, he reached to touch it.

"*Mashallah*. Do you believe in it?" he asked.

She shrugged, and his finger on the bead shrugged with her. "No. Yes and no. I don't know."

His finger stayed, another joined it and then his whole hand was on her collar.

"Why take a chance?" her voice prattled on, though her pulse had quickened and her heart had left the conversation. Smooth me, iron me. Could he hear the hoofbeats clip-clopping in her head? "Do *you* believe in it?" she asked.

"No. Not really."

His voice was dim, but his hand spoke freely now, abandoning collar for neck, finding her face, the curve of chin, her cheek still damp with tears, her brow, and she shut her eyes and turned her head to taste his open palm with its salt and soap and padded heel, its lines a fortune-teller might read to predict a life long or short, a marriage happy or not. *You will go on a voyage, meet a man.* He felt brand new and, at the same time, deeply familiar, and why not? Lika, her almost-twin, had been held by these selfsame arms. Before long they were kissing, then caressing and shuffling, still at it, to the bed. You started it, he would tell her later. No, you started it—you touched my bead. You ate my hand. I kissed it. *Licked.* I was starving, she'd retort, laughing and ducking away just far enough to make him reach for her. I'd been stuck on a ship for weeks. Did it ever occur to you to offer me a meal?

Now his hands on her hips pull her down. Now his tongue travels her ear from lobe to inner whorl, and it might be a fire licking clean her flesh, so sharp is the flare that shoots down her spine, making her arch for more. It is daytime still. They are unmarried still; she is unbathed, unfed, her legs wobbly from her days at sea. The room is blue and green, but the place they go is smoky pink and dark: his armpit with its thatch of talc-dusted, lightly sweaty, slightly sour hair, the plush of inner cheek, the ancient (or is it newborn?) heat when they press together under the mosquito netting, belly to belly, tooth to tooth. Where Luis's torso had been almost hairless, Sam is softly furred on his chest, back and arms, a quality Rebecca finds surprisingly appealing, a thicket where she can lose her way. She does not let him enter her, nor does he try—they keep their undergarments on—but as for the rest, they shed, taste, meet with as much ease as they'd previously been separated by awkwardness, and there is nothing unexpected about Sam Levy's wide chest, narrow hips and stocky legs, the span of his big hands around her ribs and hefting each breast out of its satin cup, their legs entangled, the dense weight of his head, even the smell of him—coffee and soap, tobacco and a complex intermingled scent she will later come to associate with the shop: papery, dry, bearing impossible news in a language she will never quite master, and sweet—bubble gum wrappers, sugar and rock salt, the metal of an ice cream churn so cold it aches.

It is dawn when they untwine their bodies. Rebecca puts on slippers and the tea-dyed silk robe she stitched for her first trousseau and walks to the shared bathroom down the hall, where she relieves herself and sits for a long moment on the toilet seat, staring down at knees that jut out newly unfamiliar, faceless dolls or amputated limbs. The toilet is in the same room as the bathtub and flushes with a lever, not a chain. A plain wooden crucifix hangs by the mirror, the most familiar thing in sight (but who is that love-mussed woman? Who is that squinting, wrung-out, chapped-lipped girl? She has lost weight on the journey and hardly recognizes herself). Though she washed herself as best she could on the ship, she was hardly clean upon arrival and should have bathed (married) before she touched a man.

Now, after washing her hands, saying a prayer and begging forgiveness from Lika and El Dyo, she strips and squats naked in the tub, where a brass caddy supplies a bar of soap but no washcloth or loofah, and the water heats to warm but not to hot. Still, she plugs the drain and sets to work on herself, wishing for the kind of Shabbat cleaning she used to receive as a girl, when she'd lie on the marble *göbek taşı* stone at the hamam as her mother or the bath lady took a sponge to her, husking her from head to toe until she emerged smarting, rosy and brand new.

Breakfast is under the outdoor arcade at the small hotel restaurant on the ground floor: *café con leche*, *tostada*, a quivering slab of pink jelly, sliced tropical fruits. Also bacon, although Rebecca gets rid of hers immediately, using an extra fork to deposit it on her coffee saucer. Sam Levy eats his.

"You eat pork!" she exclaims.

He looks startled, then chagrined. "Not at home but at some of the places I've worked—hotels, the club where I was a hat check boy. There wasn't always a lot of choice, I'm not so strict, I could be stricter . . ."

"But you're"—she lowers her voice; Spain has taught her not to say the word aloud—"all Jewish?"

He laughs. "Of course."

Her bacon curls on the saucer, glistening and pocketed with fat, and she slides the plate toward him. "Have mine, too. You may as well, now that you've started. Get rid of it."

Her voice comes out harsher than she intended, and he looks startled. "I shouldn't have," he says. "I don't need to eat it, it's not a—"

"Do you believe in God?" Rebecca interrupts.

He looks surprised, then nods.

"But not," she presses, "in *la Ley*?"

"In certain matters, I believe," he says, and something in his tone—slightly formal and pedantic, beyond reproach—reminds her of her father. "You could say I'm more devoted to the spirit than the letter of the law where religious practice is concerned. I enjoy reading about Jewish history, there were many wise men, but I don't have much free time."

"Esther was no dummy either, and Judith. Not to mention Rebecca."

"Of course, but I was speaking more of the philosophers, like Maimonides and Hillel."

"Could they water a camel? Convince a king?"

He is gazing at her steadily, with something like amusement. When he doesn't answer, she forges on. "Do you go to *kal*?"

"When I can. For the big holidays. I usually have to work on Saturdays. In New York, they only close the newspaper shops on Sunday afternoons, for the Christian sabbath."

"Did Lika go? And your little girl?"

"We went when we could. Lika liked going. There's a temple just a few blocks away."

"We *live* at the temple in Barcelona," says Rebecca. "I embroidered the ark curtain and tefillin bags. You should know, Sam Levy, that it matters very much to me to raise my children inside the faith, and I'll never let a pig, dead or alive, inside my home."

He nods. “That’s not a problem.”

“Which?”

“Neither. I’d like it for my daughter, too.”

After that, they have nothing much to say. Small talk seems trivial after the night they’ve had, but the rest is too vast. Rebecca has a host of questions but no good way to get them out: Ah, what a pretty morning and are you of sound mind and body and is your job as steady as my sister claims and are you an honest man and just how sick is your little girl and what do you expect from a wife and will you love me and leave me and when you look at me, do you see Lika or Likabeccabeccalika or myself, and can you *dance*? They’ve gotten ahead of themselves with their nighttime escapades, that’s one problem, but also Sam Levy confuses her, for while various markers—the cut and fabric of his ready-to-wear suit, slight differences in his speech—reveal a less refined background, he seems educated and has an air of authority she finds almost intimidating. He is only two years her senior but seems older than that, or is it that this journey has launched her forward in distance but back in time, to before she was a mother, business owner, wife? She has eaten her whole breakfast except for the bacon and is still hungry. If she were alone, she’d be tempted to eat the bacon, too, for in truth, she has tasted pork herself on occasion because when a rich Spanish lady offers Marie Blanco Camayor an antipasto plate at a home fitting, it’s bad for business to decline.

“What is your little daughter like?” Rebecca asks.

Sam brightens. “Luna? She’s the light of my life. I adore her. We all do.”

“My sister told me she has some health troubles?”

He nods.

“Such as—if you don’t mind my asking?”

“She has . . . it’s mostly muscle weakness, from a complicated birth. We found a specialist doctor for her, and my mother helps.”

"My mother helps me, too. She's like another mother to my sons. So far I've been blessed"—Rebecca reaches for her bead—"with healthy children."

"And what are your sons like?"

"Oh, they're good little boys. They make me laugh. Berto, the younger one, is a clown. They need to get out more, but I have to work to support them, and my parents, especially my father, aren't young. Sometimes my brother Josef takes them to see the boats. David especially loves ships."

"Do they go to school?"

"Not yet. We tried for David, but it didn't work out." She doesn't disclose that her older son has trouble paying attention, a fragile disposition and a temper, reminding her too much of Luis. "The school was Catholic, of course, like everything there, but it was nothing like my nice Catholic school at home. He lasted less than a month. He was terrified."

"In America," Sam says, "they have public schools open to everyone, no matter your income or your religion."

"That's what Corinne said. Her daughters go to one."

They lapse into silence then. Rebecca, hit by a wave of exhaustion, is tempted to rest her head on the table. Sam has turned away to watch a group of old men as they stop at the intersection and talk in an animated cluster.

"Who are they?" she asks sleepily, sinking deeper into her seat.

"*Ke?*"

"Those men you're watching."

"Oh. I don't know, I have no idea."

He turns back to her and lights another cigarette (he goes through them at a startling pace). In the daylight, Sam Levy has soulful, heavy-lidded eyes and an olive skin tone, reminding her of the Turks at the Grand Bazaar, where her father used to take her as a treat. Sometimes a young boy would step out of the shadows to tie string around a box or offer apple tea, and her father might give the boy a coin, but Rebecca was not allowed to speak to him because Muslim or Christian girls were all right (she went to school with them and counted them among her friends), but Muslim or Christian boys were not—you might fall for one if you weren't careful; be polite but nothing more. So, too, with Jewish boys from families that were overly religious and insular, or not religious enough, or obsessed with Palestine, or didn't know French, or went to charity schools, or didn't go to school at all. You had one life to lead; there was never any question. She can picture Sam Levy, not as he was when she met him with Lika at the paddleboats, but as a little boy with scuffed knees and a head of close-cropped hair, running through the steep lanes at home, scrambling up the brick stairs, playing street games (or was he too serious, the eldest in the family, trundling forward, shoulders squared?), not in her neighborhood but across the Golden Horn in Ortaköy, where her mother brought food to the poor.

She yawns again.

"You're tired," Sam says tenderly. "Do you want to go upstairs to rest?"

Something clicks inside Rebecca then, the bobbin settling into its slot in the sewing machine. Already, he is looking out for her. Could she love this man? Make a life with him? He is not what, in the old days, she would have set her sights on, but these are not the old days. What are our future husbands doing now? she and Lika used to wonder when they were ten or eleven, and Rebecca would picture a house like her house, a boy like her brothers but better-looking. It had never occurred to them that the future might land them with the selfsame man. The plan was to live next door to each other, and marrying the same man would mean that one of them—a thought so strange and grim as to be unthinkable—would have to die.

"If I take a nap, I'll be up all night," she tells Sam, "but I'd love another coffee. I have a few more questions, if you don't mind. I can answer for you, too, about myself. Are you—forgive me for asking, but I—it's just with my first husband, I didn't know. Would you say you're in good health?"

Sam gestures for the waiter. "Very. I haven't even had a cold in years."

"The same for me. Do you consider yourself honest?"

He nods. "In everything, from my business dealings to my home. I don't abide liars. Of all the virtues, this one probably matters most to me. And you?"

"Yes." Rebecca is wide awake now. "Most of the time," she adds. "A little white lie here and there if I'm to be"—she giggles—"totally honest. Truth be told, I should tell you that"—she lowers her voice, not that anyone cares—"I've tasted pork, in Spain, when it was offered to me by an important customer. But no pork in my home. No *aught dahgs*."

He looks confused.

"*La salchika*," she says. "*Aught dahgs*, no? I saw it in a magazine. The English word for sausage made from pigs?"

She lets out a pig snort and snuffle—she has practice from the barnyard song she sings with her sons—and Sam says "*Hot dogs!*" and laughs from deep in his belly, the sound fuller and less restrained than you might expect from the man at the table, though it jibes with what she learned of him in bed. She joins in, and hearing them, the couple at the nearby table starts laughing, too, though the old man a few tables away casts them a dour look before returning to his newspaper.

Finally Sam stops and wipes his eyes. "Oh, it does a man good to laugh like that."

He reaches for her hand as it lies palm down on the table and flips it, and they are palm to palm, then interlaced. She exhales deeply, dizzy with a potent mix of exhaustion and lust—to stop talking, to find his mouth with hers. Let's go upstairs, she'd like to suggest, but first things first, just get it over with. Does he not understand that he needs to pop the question, address what they're here for, the unspoken, ever-present agenda of the trip? She wills it with her mind, a real proposal—*Rebecca, will you marry me?*—and she'll say yes, and the other diners will clap, and she'll blush, a young virgin bride, a tourist eloping for a honeymoon in a tropical playground, and have a story for the ages: *He proposed in Cuba, over breakfast at a restaurant at the Hotel de Flor.*

She sighs too hard, an edgy, irritated sound.

Sam releases her hand and sits back in his seat. "I'll walk you upstairs and leave you to rest. Or we could take in the sights if you're not too tired."

Under the arcade, the air is fresh, still morning cool. Birds land on the potted plants and trade calls back and forth. A skinny calico street cat like the ones from home weaves across the patio and flicks its tail against Rebecca's bare leg, sending a shiver up her calf. Is it good luck or bad? Across the distance, her mother speaks: *Si no hay demandador, no hay respondedor.*

"If you want to do it," Rebecca blurts, "I mean, if you think I'm okay, just get it over with."

"Are you saying—" Sam Levy looks panicked.

"I'm a lady. I'm not saying a thing."

He doesn't smile. He looks down at his lap, then grabs hold of her hand. Are those tears in his eyes? Are those tears in her own? "Would you like—" he says hoarsely.

"Say my name, say *Rebecca*, or it's very bad luck."

She grips his hand. She is plummeting now, toward an uncertain future from a past shot through with holes.

Sam Levy speaks to the crust of his toast. (*He got down on one knee, with a rose in his hand. Everybody clapped, then they brought out champagne!*) "Rebecca, will you marry me?"

CUBA IS A DREAM. Husband and wife now, they eat and fuck, drink and dance (he doesn't know how, but he's a quick learner, and Rebecca likes to teach and can do both parts), smoke cigarettes. Though Rebecca had tried smoking a few times in Spain with the girls at her workshop, it never stuck, but now she finds that she loves to put a cigarette in her mouth and lean toward Sam for a light, just as she loves to blow smoke rings together and watch the twin streams rise, blend, disappear. They take the trolley to Habana Vieja to walk arm in arm along the Malecón seawall, where a Chinese man sells them coconut ice cream served in the shell and topped with tiny paper umbrellas.

Rebecca saves the two umbrellas for her sons and stops at a stall to buy Sam's daughter and Corinne's two girls topsy-turvy rag dolls, each with one body but two heads, one brown, the other white, and you flip the skirt around to reveal the hidden head. "Lou-Lou Mary-Lou, Lou-Lou Mary-Lou!" sings the vendor, fast-flipping the sample doll's skirt. Midtransaction, as Rebecca is fishing for the money pouch suspended beneath her dress, Sam steps in to pay, but Rebecca thinks the price is inflated and tries to bargain down. Sam demurs and pays the asking price, telling Rebecca afterward that the vendor needs the money because people like her are second-class citizens and Cuba—with its mansions, plantations, grand hotels—was built on the backs of slaves and sugarcane. But she's running a business, says Rebecca. She expects us to bargain, that's how it goes. Sam looks stern, almost angry. For a moment, she might be a little afraid of him, even as she thinks, though she can't find the words to say so, that to not bargain is to treat the lady, old enough to be her mother, like a child. Maybe so, Sam says finally, but we're American (speak for yourself!), and I think her price was fair.

Later, on a side street on the edge of a poor neighborhood that they wander into by mistake, they pass a vodú offering—charcoaled *x*'s and *y*'s on the stucco wall of a house, jars of amber liquid, a piece of dried cactus nailed to a door. Rebecca lingers, feeling a powerful urge to ask the old woman watching them from behind a shutter if she can bless them in their marriage, wish them luck. The woman, dressed all in white with a deeply lined, dignified brown face, steps outside and begins, quietly, to speak, but Sam puts his hand on Rebecca's shoulder and hurries her along. It's backward, he says heatedly once they're out of earshot. Ignorant superstition, and she's likely to grab your purse! I thought, Rebecca says, tightening her grip on it, that you wanted to support them. For reasons she can't quite name, she feels drawn to the woman with the vodú offering, while the saleswoman, who looked shrewd and out for herself, set her on edge, reminding her of her own days hawking market wares, when she'd set the asking price at twice the item's worth in case a sucker bit.

"I can't support stupidity posing as religion," Sam says.

Rebecca fingers the *bonjuk* bead that she repins each day to the collar of whatever dress she has picked out. "Life is full of mystery," she says.

They are only just glimpsing the thousands of ways there are to disagree.

On they walk, past vendors, schoolchildren, street photographers, sailors, necking couples. In the Plaza de Armas, vagrants doze on the grass near the used-book stands as ladies pass by in silk afternoon dresses and tremendous ostrich feather hats. Rebecca catalogs the fashions even though she does not need to; as a married woman with a steadily employed husband in America, her job (she thinks, she hopes) will be managing children and a home. Some people—they must be American tourists or businessmen—in the plaza are speaking English, which she can recognize but not understand except for a few words: *thank you, hello, goodbye*. At El Capitolio, she and Sam climb the white stairs and pose for a picture, which they purchase and arrange to retrieve the next day. The photographer is a Turkish Sepharad like them (with this fellow, Sam has no problem bargaining for a better price), from Silivri. Sam grows talkative around the man and introduces Rebecca proudly as his wife.

The sea, when they return to the Malecón at dusk and stare out, is dark green, though Rebecca had hoped for turquoise, like on the postcard Corinne sent when she was here. On the other side of the ocean, David and Berto are eating, playing or squabbling at this very moment. Her mother is in the kitchen, her father in the garden or the temple, which has grown crowded with German refugees needing everything from soup to prayers. Or Josef could have taken the boys to the park, and her mother is wheeling her hamper back from the market, and her father is shut in his tiny office, where he claims to work but mostly naps and stews. Or everyone is asleep in bed. It is a different time in Spain; she has lost track. How many times a day does her family speak or think of her? Do her sons cry out for her? (Berto wept lavishly at the dock as the boat pulled away, while David turned his back.) Are they eating enough, behaving for their grandparents, missing their mother? She should have missed them more on the boat, and may El Dyo forgive her.

Flooded by loneliness (or is it guilt?), she turns and kisses Sam Levy right there on the walkway, and he enfolds her. Look at those two lovebirds. Where are they from? Hard to say; she might be Puerto Rican, or even Irish (the fair complexion, hazel eyes). He might be an Arab or from India or who knows where. They could be Spanish, French, American or *Polacos*—what the Cubans call the Jews, even the Sephardim. It turns out that there are a lot of Jews in Havana, and though Cuba, like Spain, is a Catholic country, Jews practice openly here and no one seems to mind. Some shops—a butcher, a bakery, a leather goods boutique—have signs in Hebrew and mezuzahs on the doorframes. There is even a little synagogue above the hardware store on Calle Inquisidor (oops!), its colorful painted sign bearing a Magen David and the name: Templo Union Hebrea Chevet Achim.

The next day is Shabbat and they go to services, where Rebecca, wearing her Magen David earrings in public for the first time since she left Turkey, is one of a handful of women behind the screen. Many of the congregants speak Yiddish to one another; she can understand a little from her time at the German School, but not enough to converse. Sam's cousin Miguel is there and invites them back to his home—to see your cousins and celebrate your marriage—but while Rebecca would like to go, Sam seems uncomfortable with the notion: We don't want to put you out, we have somewhere to be. Back at the hotel, he tells Rebecca that in New York they'll have a party with his family, with music and dancing, the works. "After we get married again there," he explains. "For legal reasons, we need to do it twice." They are in bed again, though for the first time, Rebecca must suppress an urge to push him away; she is sore from all the sex, chafed and raw.

"Good," she says. "My sister can celebrate with us in New York. But why not go for a meal with your relatives here? Don't you like them? Is there something between you?"

"I like them fine, but"—he licks a path between her breasts—"I like you more."

In the middle of the night, Rebecca wakes to stomach cramps and stumbles to the toilet to expel a burning torrent of diarrhea. She has been freely consuming street food, along with plates of fruit, mint mojitos and ice cream, and must have overdone it or gotten food poisoning—or she might, God help her, already be pregnant since they haven't used protection, though the symptoms wouldn't likely show this soon. She is doubled over, shivering on the toilet, when her monthly blood arrives in a big clot, adding insult to injury, though it's also a relief and helps explain the cramps.

Back in the bedroom, she tiptoes past Sam lightly snoring to find a shawl and retrieve her supply of little cloths (her mother helped her pack and thought of everything), returning to the bathroom to scrub out her underpants and clean herself in the tub. Then once more to the toilet. The cramps are like labor; each time she catches her breath and thinks she has nothing left, her body roils and crests, expels. *Aye, Mama*, she mutters, and now her nose is running, too, though her mouth is parched. Is God punishing her for rushing into marriage, propelled by lust? She almost never gets sick and doesn't know how it's supposed to feel. Back in bed, she is freezing, then much too hot. She slides to the far side of the mattress near the open window and casts the blanket off. Still Sam sleeps on, oblivious, his snores creating a painful racket in her ears.

When eventually he wakes to find her unwell, he jumps up, horrified, and gets to work, preparing a cool washcloth to wipe her brow. He leaves the room to return with two aspirin from the hotel desk and a weak cup of tea *because you need liquid when you're feverish, it's the most important thing*. He plumps her pillow and hums a lullaby. Even in her sorry state, Rebecca is astounded. Is it because his daughter lacks a mother? And are such attentions an asset or unbecoming in a man (she likes hers big and strong)? The rest of the day is a blur, sleeping and waking, more trips to the toilet, a headache that turns from mild to blinding, a vise around her skull. At some point, she half opens her eyes to find Sam setting a plate of crackers and bottle of water on the bedside table. I need to go to the port, he whispers, to see about our tickets to New York. And I'll pick up our photograph and get you more aspirin, and some broth. Will you be all right on your own for an hour or a little more? She nods and burrows into the pillows. All she wants to do is sleep.

SHE WAKES TO HER FEVER having broken and Sam still out. She consults her wristwatch to find that more than four hours have passed. It's late afternoon already. Where could he be? Did something happen? And then suspicion (she feels it too readily after Luis, and it has aged her). Could Sam Levy be that kind of man, the kind that doesn't return? She swings her legs over the side of the bed, slides her feet into her slippers and stands to take a few tentative steps, growing steadier with each one.

Then she is back, as if her sickness never happened. Her headache is gone, and she is starving. Is that her excuse? Later, she will wonder. But also this: Her new husband is gone; she is alone. I was hungry and needed Cuban pesos to get a meal at the restaurant downstairs, she'll explain to Sam (though they both know she has her own stash of Spanish money that the restaurant would take). I was looking for aspirin. I was cold and wanted to borrow a sweater. I was . . . what? Nosy (she will not say). Suspicious. Looking for trouble. Missing you. Scarred and scared.

She brings his suitcase to the bed, flips open the lid and empties out the contents, beginning slowly, then giving into it and gutting the valise to see what she can find. The bed is now a surface meant for viewing evidence. The fever dream is over, the skin on her hands dry, her fingers fast. The Cuba dream is over: honeymoon and sex, belly to belly, the slip of coconut ice cream down your throat. She is gripped instead by a forward-looking, backward-seeking nervousness. She might be a magpie scanning, or a boss with a critical, inspecting eye (her father, over lessons to David and Berto before he gave up trying to instruct them; herself, over a shopgirl's careless work). But also this: As a child she was not above snatching a piece of fruit from a vendor's cart, because she was good at it, because she could. *I have my flaws.*

Is it not a wife's duty to refold her husband's clothes, examining them for missing buttons and frayed hems? To run her hands along the inside walls of his valise, which is lined in silky gold fabric with a faint leopard skin pattern that looks so familiar that she thinks the suitcase must have belonged to Rahelika, which means that it is also (for once upon a time, they had shared everything) hers.

Sam Levy's clothes are worn but not too worn, mostly factory made, not up to her standards but clean and well cared for. One of the shirts, an unimpressive garment with poor stitch density and an unsplit back yoke (easier to make but bad for fit), has a label, surely a sham, that reads *Fabriqué en France*. She finds a little notebook where he's been marking down every expenditure of the trip, down to the tips he gives the porters at the hotel. Also in the notebook are a few names and addresses: Hayyim Marzouk in Havana, Ayna Levy (a relation?) in Cienfuegos. She finds the topsy-turvy dolls, and a handkerchief embroidered with a jaunty man in a blue hat and *Habana Cuba* that she hadn't known he'd bought, and cigarette paper and a tin of tobacco. His socks are nested inside each other, the row of snug black bundles filling her with a momentary tenderness, as if she'd stumbled upon a nest of baby birds.

The small side inside pocket of the suitcase holds a shoehorn, a pair of shoelaces, a razor and a letter. With the utmost care, she lays each item on the bed. The letter is in an unsealed envelope, just as the suitcase was half-open. She looks around, feeling an old desire to make the sign of the cross, a motion she used to itch to make at her Catholic school because it was balletic and aimed at a God who would forgive you for your every sin, and because it was off-limits to the Jewish girls.

But it is not her sign (it is not her letter). She reaches in.

~

Sam Levy returns at six o'clock, bearing hot broth for Rebecca, the photograph of them on the steps of El Capitolio and two second-class tickets to set sail on March 30, three days from now, from Havana to New York.

"I'm sorry I took so long." He holds out the tickets. "The line went all the way around the corner. You look better. Are you? You're all dressed and out of bed."

"I am fine. I will need to obtain a different ticket."

Rebecca stands stiffly by the window, dressed to travel. She has packed her things. She has repacked Sam Levy's suitcase (though retained the letter) and returned it to the luggage stand, where it sits slightly open, as it was before. She has her money pouch around her neck. "Please take me to the office or give me the address so I can get a taxi," she says. "I'll pay for it myself."

"A different one? What do you mean? What happened?" He comes toward her, but she steps away.

"Havana to Barcelona, one way. Also I'll need an *anulación*. Is that what it's called? A reversal of our so-called marriage." She tries to speak lightly, almost merrily, over his shoulder, as if to the windowpane. "*Adyo*. It's been nice knowing you, Sam Levy, and I wish you, and especially your little girl, the best, but I'm going back to Spain."

He gasps. "Spain?"

Then out with it; she must explain. But first, make him wait; she has never been so hungry. She gulps down the broth right out of its carton, burning her mouth so that the words that follow are coated with cotton wool, though they still come out fast. How he lied to her, told her he was healthy when really he is sick, told her he was honest when really he's a liar, which comes as no surprise because all men are alike—even her own father, whom she loves and misses, hates—but I'm no idiot, I'm not a child, I'm the mother of two children, I run my own business, I've been tricked before, but I was young and stupid then, and I won't be tricked again.

Sam Levy stands frozen by the window as she paces the room. Never again, she says, and from under the pillow produces the letter, addressed to Sam from one Pedro de Medina at Cuba's Secretary of Justice, having the peculiar feeling of being an actress in a stage play. Soon it will be over—a brief interval in a long life: took boat, met man, took boat. *Because the couple is of urgent need to move abroad to obtain the cure for the disease suffered by Mr. Levy,* she reads aloud (still he stands by the window, mouth open wide enough to catch a fly; he is suddenly homely, even ugly, losing his hair, with a hawklike nose, his eyebrows fat black caterpillars), *they request that they be granted exemption from the publication of the Edicts required by Article 89 of the Civil Code so that their marriage can be authorized.*

"You're a sick man," she says when she has finished reading. "In more ways than one. You didn't tell me you have a disease. I am sorry about your condition, but I didn't come all this way to be tricked into marrying a sick or, God help you, dying man."

"No, no, Rebecca, it's not correct! Please, let me explain. It's not true, it's—"

"Not true?"

"It's a lie, a white lie, to—"

"Ha!" She feels almost victorious now. "I thought the truth was *the most important thing* to you. The Cuban government says you gave evidence—or that *we* did, thank you for including me!—proving that right after your marriage, you have to go abroad to obtain the cure for your malady. Is it not true? I thought you were an honest man."

"I *am* an honest man. I try to be. But I misspoke, I should have . . . how can I put it? I should have said that honesty is the most important thing after my daughter, Luna. My little girl is everything to me."

"So you'll trap a new mother for her so that if you drop dead, she's not alone? For this I left my sons, who are also 'everything to me,' to come to you?"

"No." His face is red now. He paces the room. "I'm healthy, I swear to God, very healthy. I just . . . I can't leave her for more than a few days, Rebecca. I've got to get back. She—"

He stops to find a cigarette, which he lights. For a long moment, he is silent. The chatter of strangers rises up from the street below. "It's not easy for me to speak of this," he says finally. "The truth is, I'm ashamed. It goes against my nature to try to bend the rules."

"What rules?"

"It's just, how to explain, they make you stay for months when you get married here. They have to publish it in the paper, here and in Spain, maybe other places, too, Turkey, wherever you're from—that such and such a man has married such and such a woman, so that if there's someone else—another wife or a hidden marriage, somebody can come forward and say wait, this is not a lawful union, I object! That all takes time so they make you wait, unless you can prove you have a reason you can't stay here. I'm afraid such waiting is impossible for me. I'm supporting my mother and daughter and helping other members of my family, too. I'm the oldest son, Rebecca. It all falls on me. Each day I'm here, I don't get paid. And my child has no mother. I . . ." His voice cracks. "I sit by her bed each night when I get home from the store and sing to her, even if she's already sleeping. I teach her things, to read and add. I read her stories. And my mother has no husband, I'm all she has. Everyone"—for a moment he sounds resentful—"depends on me."

"What happened to your father?" Rebecca asks.

He shakes his head. Time has slowed in the blue-green room, a fish slow-circling.

"I . . . we don't know where he is, but if he's still alive—" Sam looks out the window, ignoring the lit cigarette in his hand, and she watches a bit of ash fall to the carpet—"I guess he might be here."

"What?" She looks around. "In Cuba? Really? In Havana?"

"Maybe," he says wearily. "Last I heard. He came here years ago from Turkey. He had a cousin doing import-export. At first he returned to us sometimes, but eventually he stayed. I have seven younger siblings. We had nothing to live on, we had to move in with relatives. My mother sent me to find him, that's why I came here a long time ago, but when I arrived—" He turns to her. His eyes are damp, though he holds his head high. "I prefer not to speak of it."

"You've been looking for him, haven't you?" Rebecca says. "Even now. On the street."

Sam seems stricken.

"I'm sorry," she says more gently. "I—it's just, I had no idea. I didn't know."

He nods. "I'm not like him, Rebecca. I'm cut from different cloth. He wasn't an honest man, he was a bad person, may I be forgiven for saying so."

"Did you find him when you came here the first time?" She feels a rising sense of guilt that she has snooped and opened up this wound. She is hardly from a perfect family herself. Didn't her own father (not to mention Luis) also abandon a marriage for another country, leaving behind not a too-large family but a childless *loka* sitting alone in her window and scanning the street for little girls?

"He'd remarried," says Sam glumly, "though technically he was still married to my mother. He took up with a Cubana, a gentile. He changed his name. He—there were more children, my half-siblings, I guess you'd call them. Many."

"You saw him?"

"Long enough to ask him for money for my mother, which he didn't have. His poor children were hungry. I got them some food. I went home to Turkey after that. Later, I went to Mexico with my brother, then to New York, and we worked and saved until we could get the rest of the family over. I'm a forgiving man, Rebecca, but I will never forgive him for what he did to us. I had to drop out of school to work, even before I knew he wasn't coming back. I loved to study more than anything. I was eleven years old, but I already had a family to support."

"Do you think he's still here?" Rebecca asks.

She is sure now that Sam's slight distractedness, his eyes tracking the path of a certain subset of older men, is him looking, staring, everywhere they go. They had visited the racetrack. It was empty of horses—it's the wrong season—but full of pariah dogs, with a handful of men fixing fences and painting jumps, and others playing dominos in the empty stands. Rebecca had been ready to move on, but Sam had lingered, watched. They had gone to the pier, walked by men selling fruit, men betting on bingo numbers set up on sandwich boards. Always, as Rebecca noted fashion and flowers, food and boats, people from every walk of life, Sam had been watching the men go by. He was searching for his father, all this time.

He shrugs and stubs out the spent cigarette in the cut glass ashtray. "My uncle, Miguel's father, might see him sometimes, but he knows better than to bring him up with me. Maybe they have business dealings now and then. He might live in the countryside, or here. I don't ask."

He takes a deep breath, in and out, then steps toward her, and she lets him lead her to the bed, where they perch on the edge a few feet apart, facing the closed door. Sam reaches for her hand. "Your fever has broken."

She nods.

"That's good. Listen, Rebecca. You have to believe me—I'm not sick. I'm as healthy as can be. It's . . ." He sighs. "It's my daughter who has some health problems, but I already told you that."

"How sick is she?" Rebecca asks, more sharply than she means to.

"She . . . the truth of it is," Sam says miserably, "she can't walk, not yet, and she has some trouble speaking comprehensibly, though we can understand her. She's smart. I've taught her to read, and she's learning English. She loves to learn. She was born too early, and they thought—we all did for a while—that she was a lost cause. The doctor said to let her die or put her away someplace. It's a miracle she survived. I live for her, my mother lives for her." He pauses. "She's so excited to have a new mother. Lika would have wanted you for Luna's mother. Out of anybody in the world, she would have wanted you."

He is silent, then, staring at his lap.

"Do you have a picture of your daughter?" Rebecca asks.

He shakes his head. "No. Not here."

"Does she look like Lika?"

"I think so. Yes."

"So like me?"

He looks confused.

"People thought we were twins when we were little," Rebecca explains. "Beccalika, Likabecca."

"Ah. Lika gained quite a lot of weight by the end—she had something with her glands, she wasn't well—but maybe I can see it, from before. Luna has beautiful eyes, dark brown, like her mother's. Yours have more green and gray."

"In the letter from the Secretary of Justice, I'm referred to as Rivka Cohen. Why is that?" Rebecca asks, Rivka being her Hebrew name and Cohen her family name, though her passport reads Rebecca Baruch.

"That's what Corinne gave me. I thought it was the official one. What name would you like?" Sam scoots closer, cups her face, kisses her forehead. "How about what it says on our marriage license, Rebecca Levy?"

She speaks close to his ear. "You must never lie to me or keep things from me. *La verdad va enriva como la azete.*" Truth, like oil, rises to the surface. "Is this understood? Do you promise?"

"I do. I promise before God."

He is nuzzling her neck, and she yearns for him again, though she is light-headed with hunger, her stomach gurgling loudly enough to hear. She detaches his hands, stands and brushes off her dress.

"Rebecca Levy is starving," she announces. "She could eat an ox."

Astoria, 1934

I

HIS DAUGHTER IS AN ANIMAL. It's a terrible thought that crosses Rebecca's mind upon meeting Luna, who has been primped and preened for her and Sam's arrival from Cuba—a pert bow in her hair, lace-trimmed ankle socks, a pink dress, the sash askew—but is so twisted and wild-eyed that they might have forced clothing on a raging, captive creature (Rebecca, having just set foot on

American soil, already feels similarly trapped). The guttural noises rising from the child's throat sound at first like random moans, but it soon becomes evident that they're aimed at Sam, who unstraps his daughter from her chair, scoops her up and drapes her arms around his neck, her legs splayed out, her bent hand hammering his back.

It is then, as Sam starts to rock and kiss Luna, that Rebecca assigns sense to the sounds coming from the girl's mouth—*pawwwpawpawaaaaapaaaapapaaa*—and Sam pivots so that Luna faces Rebecca—"This is your new mother, Lunita!"—and the sounds morph into a bleating *maaaaaaaaaaa*, the meaning clear, aimed straight at her. Pushing past a revulsion that makes her despise herself and the child at the same time, Rebecca steps forward to deposit a kiss on Luna's cheek, which is slick with drool and tears. A terrific scream issues forth, as if the girl has been shocked.

Rebecca pulls away. "Oh, I'm sorry! I'm so sorry, Sam—did I hurt her?"

"No, no." He pivots his daughter's head to face his own. "Everything all right, Lunita?"

Luna makes a gravelly noise, and Sam laughs. "She's just excited to meet you, and that her papa's home."

An older woman (she must be Sam's mother; the room is full of women observing the scene) comes over with a cloth to wipe the child's face, but Luna twists violently away. "*Maaaaamaaaa!*" she cries again, then falls abruptly quiet.

Rebecca retreats farther, colliding with a kitchen cabinet, and finds herself pinned in place by the intensity of Luna's gaze, the irises a liquid brown, the pupils large, the stare full of hunger and, it seems, a kind of complex challenge: *Don't mess with me, deliver me, come near me, stay away.* Here, as Sam had said, are Lika's eyes—the same color, like staring into a well, the same thick, dark lashes, the same heat and sharp intelligence (Sam has said the girl can already read)—but Lika trapped inside a cage of brokenness, all wrong, just as the word *mama* is all wrong, coming at Rebecca from the wrong child's mouth. In Cuba, she had managed the separation from her sons with alarming ease—they were safe with her parents, and she was on a kind of honeymoon—but as soon as she stepped onto American soil, their absence became physically painful, her empty hands twitching at her sides.

"Soon you'll meet my two little boys," she tells Luna too loudly. "They're right around your age!" then, registering the gold hoop earrings in the child's ears, adds, "Oh! You have my earrings on—I gave those to your mother!" which comes out sounding harsh—why bring up the dead mother?—and also possessive in a way she didn't (mean to) mean. All eyes on her, she looks at Sam, who looks away, and she realizes he has been dreading these introductions, too. "I'm glad to see them on you," she adds to Luna. "And now you'll have a new mother, and two new brothers—"

"*Annaairmanonoaakaaana*," Luna says incomprehensibly.

Sam shakes his head and whispers something in his daughter's ear. Rebecca turns to the door, wishing Corinne would hurry up and appear, or even better, Lika, although if she were alive, none of this would be happening. Lika, who had the best deep laugh, might have found some comedy in the scene: Rebecca's flailing, the improbability of it and, at the same time, the skewed symmetry: *You married my husband, you're my daughter's mother!* As children, the two girls had regularly completed each other's sentences in their imaginary games, passing roles back and forth in easy, swinging improvisations. Whatever happened to Chérie and Bella, their twin porcelain dolls? Those dolls, who with their blue eyes and blond sausage curls looked nothing like their mothers, were chased by hounds and suffered curses, plagues, fires and broken bones, but Likabecca always set things right before dreaming up another obstacle.

"We made *tishpishti* for you," announces a woman who Rebecca will soon learn is Rachel, Sam's sister.

"Wonderful!" says Sam. "And we have gifts for everyone from Cuba." He lowers Luna down to her chair, straps her in and looks out the window. "Israel must still be parking—they had to circle the block. Corinne is down there with the luggage. I'll go help."

"I'll come!" Rebecca says. Fresh air, a glimpse of sky and space.

"No need, *mi kerida*," Sam tells her. "It's heavy. I can make a few trips. Stay here and settle in."

Sam's mother's eyebrows rise at her son's use of the endearment, and before she can stop herself, Rebecca flashes her a look. She might tell Sam that she is built like a workhorse—in Spain, she transported bolts of fabric, carried her children, hauled pews around the temple—but the truth is that she feels dizzy and tired, if also longing for fresh air and to be beside her sister, even as she already suspects Corinne of avoiding these introductions to bypass witnessing the shock. Instead, she says nothing. Sam carries more authority here than he did in Cuba and is also distinctly less hers. This is his family, his daughter, his life she's stepped into, but she is already longing for the moment when they can shut the bedroom door and fall into each other's arms. His mother—a skinny woman in a faded apron and tight gray bun—comes forward with a glass of water as Sam starts down the stairs.

"Welcome to America." She leans to peck Rebecca's cheek.

Rebecca laughs thinly, accepts the water and returns the kiss. "*Munchas grasyas.*"

"I'm Fanny, his mother. This is his sister Rachel and his sister Sarah."

Rebecca nods to each of them. "*Enkantada.*"

"*Elmueeevonooviaeeermmoowzza*," drawls Luna from her chair.

Sam's sister Rachel looks up from cutting the cake. "She says you're beautiful: *the new bride is beautiful.*"

"Oh no, I'm really not at my best, but thank you, Luna! You're beautiful, too. I . . . I like your dress."

Then the child is saying something incomprehensible again and trying to lurch forward, though she is bound to the chair. Her grandmother is at her side, propping her head with pillows, shushing her, wiping her chin and telling her to be quiet—*kayades, Luna!*—and something else in what must be English: *CAWMDOWN.*

"She's overexcited," Fanny says.

"I understand. I am, too." Rebecca suppresses a gag as a fetid odor fills the room. "I'm"—her vision swims—"a little dizzy." She steadies herself on the back of a chair, spilling some water as she sets the glass down on the table.

"You need to lie down." Rachel swoops in with a rag. "You're white as a ghost."

"I'm fine," protests Rebecca. "Just tired from the trip."

"You can go in there, but I need to change her first." Fanny juts her chin toward an open door, through which Rebecca sees a low bed with a white nubbed coverlet. "I do it in there."

"She's *faint*, Mama," says the other sister, Sarah.

"I'm fine," Rebecca repeats, and it's true; the room has come back into focus: the red-checked oilcloth, the bare walls, the dance—or is it a battle?—of women pushing, pulling. Already she is part of it, and she must stake her claim. Luna is silent now, watching with something like fascination.

Sam and Israel arrive with Rebecca's trunk, and Corinne comes up the stairs with her two young daughters, carrying the sewing machine in its lacquered wooden case. At the port, where Rebecca's line moved quickly because she had the prize of an American husband, she had rushed into her waiting sister's hug, but now she can't look at her, afraid of what might spill from her own eyes. Why hadn't Corinne told her about the extent of Luna's difficulties? "The child," Corinne had written in her letter to Rebecca in Spain, "was born early with some resulting health troubles but has a strong spirit and loving temperament"—if not an outright lie, at least less than the truth, so that Rebecca again has a queasy sense of reliving what happened with Luis, when she was kept in the dark about his war injuries and poor health.

Corinne joins Rachel at the kitchen counter, where they busy themselves with arranging plates and cutlery for the cake. Fanny unstraps Luna and carries her to the bedroom, and in her grandmother's slight arms, the girl looks bigger than she did in her father's, her head large and bobbling, her legs dangling down, stick thin except for her kneecaps, which bulge out. From this angle Rebecca can see the white cloth of a diaper. Have they tried to teach the child to use the toilet? Have they taught her much of anything? Rebecca sits down to drink the water, though her hand trembles as she holds the glass, as if her limbs, like Luna's, might start to fling and jerk. Fanny returns with Luna, having changed the child into an ordinary brown dress, and sets her on the floor, where, skirt hiked up and diaper flashing white, she heaves and hauls herself like a dogged inchworm in the direction of her father.

From his valise, Sam retrieves cigars, perfume and handkerchiefs, and, for each of the three girls, one of the topsy-turvy rag dolls, which had seemed charming in Havana despite their inflated price but now seem in poor taste for having no legs and two heads.

THIS, THE BEGINNING. Before it gets better, it will get much worse. A bureaucratic logjam, if not something more sinister, has stalled David's and Berto's departures from Spain, and it seems increasingly unlikely that other family members will be cleared to accompany them. Unless something shifts, the boys will need to travel on their own—but they are much too young, how can this happen?—and leave their grandparents behind. Corinne lives far away on the Grand Concourse in the Bronx, on a tree-lined street in a roomy apartment with high windows. When Rebecca confronts her about her letter—how it underplayed Luna's challenges and implied that Sam was a shop owner when in truth he's just a manager, paid by the hour—she bursts into uncharacteristic tears, then tries to shift the blame to their father and Israel: *They scared me, Rebecca. They said we had to get you out.* Sam's mother is predisposed to dislike Rebecca from the start because she comes from a higher social class but has nothing to show for it except (Fanny seems convinced) a snobby attitude, and comes—or will, after her sons arrive—with two more mouths to feed.

Rebecca plants the rue seeds from her father in a pretty blue-and-white pot since there is no garden here, and Fanny, who already has rue growing in a different pot, doesn't try to hide her irritation—we're short on space, why do you need your own? Fanny grumbles about Rebecca spending Sam's earnings (in fact they're her own, saved from Spain, and from the alterations she quickly takes on) on cut flowers and fabric for new curtains, and, after Rebecca learns about the great American invention called a *rummage sale*, on a secondhand oak stand for her sewing machine that she pays two boys to carry, along with two small paintings—lemons in a blue bowl, a stand of birch trees that reminds her of the poplars in the Anatolian countryside, one planted for each new child's birth—to cheer up the apartment's drab beige walls.

How much did you pay, Fanny will ask, though price tags still dot the frames. And later, to Sam, though she must know Rebecca can hear through the flimsy walls: She's quite the shopper! Doesn't she know you're trying to save for your own store? As if it's a crime to spend fifty cents on something beautiful. But you could fault a person for much less: the watery, flat taste of Fanny's lentil soup, for instance, oversalted and underspiced, and her dense *tishpishti* cake, with its aftertaste of cheap rose soap. The small noises she makes in the cramped apartment above the store, aggrieved sighs, mutterings and gloomy, slippered shuffles, the world too much for her except when it comes to Luna; there she is all endless energy and sharp opinions, a guard bee circling the hive. The girl can move about with her own strained brand of nimbleness, relying on her buttocks and trunk more than her underdeveloped, wayward limbs, but no matter how often they sweep the floor, she gets dusty creeping around, which makes her wheeze, or she'll bump into a table leg and emit loud grunts and groans, so Fanny doesn't let her out of the chair for more than a few minutes at a time.

As for Luna's toileting, the bathroom, shared with the neighbors, is located five steps down off a small landing at the top of a long, steep flight of stairs. This poses a challenge but not, to Rebecca's mind, an insurmountable one. Did you ever think of teaching her to go in a pot for a start? she asks, but Fanny brushes her off. Spare in most ways, Fanny keeps an elaborate store of talcs and lotions and a stack of snowy white diapers and is forever crooning over the child, brushing her hair, wiping her face, feeding her with a baby spoon, the scene oddly familiar to Rebecca, though she can't think why until one day it occurs to her: Fanny is like Djentil Nahon with her old mother, except that the mother was ancient and dying, and Luna, at almost seven, is a growing girl.

For an hour each afternoon, Sam gives Luna lessons, teaching her to sound out the words he writes on butcher paper and doing math with peppermints: Count to thirty and you can have one! Take away half, what's left? Get it right, Lunita, and you can have one. In his teacherly bent, he reminds Rebecca of her father, though he is gentler and considerably more patient, and while Alberto's instruction tended toward religion and philosophy, Sam introduces Luna to the natural world—the stars and tides, how clouds make rain, the layers of the earth. Luna's speech is garbled, and at first Rebecca thinks Sam might be indulging in an elaborate charade where he supplies both question and answer, but she soon begins to decipher the child's words and sees that Luna has a brain that is a throbbing railway station on the one hand, all chaos and missed connections, and a verdant, fertile valley on the other, with nothing like a clear path in between. At the end of the lesson, Sam often picks up an illustrated *Grimms' Fairy Tales*, reading in

English to teach it to Luna and improve his own but translating portions for Rebecca, who puts down her sewing or pauses in her housework to listen to the story like a little girl.

Luna has a knack for math and loves the fairy tales, but she is spoiled and quick to get frustrated, kicking, screaming and strategically soiling her diaper if she gets an answer wrong or doesn't know it, or if her father withholds candy or pushes her too hard. Fanny doesn't like the lessons. That's enough, Sam—she's tired and it's time for her bath, she'll cut in after half an hour, having come up from the store. Or please, Sam, no more school for today, she won't eat dinner after all that sugar. But Sam, who gives in to his mother about most things, resists—just a little longer, Mother, go back down, please, I'll get you when we're done—and there is something almost sacred about his big, balding head leaning over his daughter's small, dark one, his large hand guiding her tiny, overflexed wrist and stiff fingers along the block words on the butcher paper—*CAT DOG OPEN SHUT SKY SUN.* Watching them, Rebecca falls into a different, deeper kind of love with him and registers the stirrings of something like affection for Luna, even as she feels herself grow smaller, for father and child are an inviolable pair, a sealed world unto themselves.

"LUNA IS SMART. Why doesn't she go to school?" she asks Sam one night in bed. "There must be one someplace in New York for her."

America seems to have schools for everything and everyone. In their neighborhood alone, there is a school for driving and a school for hairdressing, as well as a large, forbidding brick elementary school where Rachel took her to inquire about enrolling David and Berto once they arrive. At the church around the corner, there is even a free program for learning English. Rebecca saw a flyer for it in Spanish on the church door and plans to sign up for the next cycle.

Sam runs a hand over her nightgown, along her hip. "There's nothing close enough."

"We could take her on the bus, or drive her. I could help. I want to learn to drive."

He shakes his head. "Driving is dangerous here. Anyway, I went last year to see a school for handicapped children. It was a miserable place, full of feebleminded children, like a jail."

"Are you sure they were all feebleminded? Forgive me for saying so, Sam, but people might think Luna—"

"No, they weren't like her. You could tell. Even if some of them started out okay in the head, a place like that will do you in. I'm telling you, it was like a prison, Rebecca, with bars on the window. The children had to sleep there." He shudders. "I'd never seen anything like it. I was so ashamed."

"Ashamed? Why? It's not your fault."

"As a society, as an American."

"Oh." She tries to hide her surprise. An American? He's a foreigner, isn't he? A Jew, as she is. A Sepharad and Turk. They speak Spanyol at home, though Sam keeps an English dictionary on the kitchen table and reads the newspaper with it by his side.

"Then what about a regular school?" she asks. "She's plenty smart enough."

"Of course she is, but you have to be able to use a toilet and to walk, for fire drills."

"What's that?"

"Where they pretend there's a fire and teach the children the best way out."

"Really? What a good idea!"

In the shared city of their childhood, fires regularly tore through neighborhoods. Afterward, the survivors rebuilt their tinderbox wooden houses on the ashes of the old ones, clutched their amulets and prayed that next time the winds would take the fire someplace else. Even Rebecca's father accepted misfortune with a maddening passivity—she still doesn't understand why he couldn't get his textile factory back—but Rebecca is not one to take trouble lying down, and America has a can-do attitude that appeals to her. She rolls onto her side and strokes the evening stubble on her husband's face.

"Listen, Sam, I think I could toilet train Luna and work on strengthening her muscles. I've been watching her. She has plenty of willpower, and I have some ideas. In time, maybe I could even teach her how to walk. Then she could go to a regular school, like a normal child."

Sam sits up and speaks in a sharp whisper. "Don't get her hopes up—promise me. She has severe inborn limits and always will. They . . . I don't like to speak of it, especially in front of Luna, but when she was born, they had to use high forceps on her head. Lika nearly died, and Luna came out blue. It's a miracle they both survived."

Rebecca touches Sam's back, but he stiffens and she withdraws her hand. "I wish I could have helped," she says. "I didn't know. I just—Lika hardly wrote to me. She wrote once during her first pregnancy, the one before Luna, to say that if the baby was a girl, it would have Rivka as her middle name, after me. It was Corinne who told me what happened to that poor baby, may his memory be a blessing. Did Luna end up having Rivka in her name?"

Sam looks pained. "No, she's Fanny Luna, but Lika didn't forget you. She just, how to explain—she was damaged by losing the first baby, and then Luna was born and had such difficulties. It all . . . I guess it just broke Lika's heart. She wasn't well. Anyway, it's over and done, may she rest in peace, but to give Luna false hope would be unkind."

"It doesn't have to be false."

"You just got here," Sam says sternly. "You can't see the whole picture. I'm her father."

"You married me. I'm her mother now." Rebecca speaks to the ceiling, its surface striped by the moonlight coming through the cracks between the curtains. "If you wanted a dishrag for a wife, you picked the wrong lady. I won't sit back and watch a life go down the drain. I wasn't raised like that. She can control when she makes *caca*—she times it to get what she wants. She has enough willpower for ten children, but she's spoiled and she doesn't understand what's possible. I can work with her, Sam, if you're on my side and show her she can trust me. I can get somewhere with her—I feel it in my bones. You know how much *dignity* it would give her to use the toilet like other girls?"

"She's not like other girls. The stairs are steep. We share the bathroom."

"So she starts out with a pot, like I told your mother."

"You did? What did she say?"

"She ignored me, of course, like I don't even exist. Does she really want to be changing diapers her whole life? That's not my plan."

"So that's what this is about!" Sam says, almost triumphantly. "My mother adores Luna and takes good care of her. Leave Luna to her, then. She doesn't mind."

"Did you hear what I said? You married *me*. *I'm* here now." Rebecca's voice comes out aggrieved. "What does the doctor say about her prospects?"

The previous week, she'd gone with Luna, Sam and his mother to an appointment at Columbia Presbyterian Hospital, the waiting room filled with handicapped children, many in even worse shape than Luna, though a few could walk with the aid of braces and crutches. Next to the doctor's office was a room where a little boy with blond curls like Berto's and bowed legs walked with the help of leg braces and a contraption on wheels while a nurse observed from the sidelines, hands laced behind her back. Rebecca had stood on tiptoes and watched through the window in the door until the nurse spotted her and, scowling, swatted her away as if guarding the secrets of her trade, or perhaps the child's privacy.

Later, the doctor, Dr. Carlson—a surprisingly young man, himself in a wheelchair with cerebral palsy—had examined Luna with the help of a nurse as she thrashed, screamed and soiled her diaper. What does she like? the doctor asked Sam over her cries, and Sam translated to Rebecca. *Like?* Yes, what does she enjoy? Sam had looked stymied, rattled by the whole encounter, so Rebecca supplied answers, which Sam translated. She likes candy, fairy tales, baubles. Her papa. A red coiled lollipop materialized, and the doctor started in on a story (in America, they all begin with *Once upon a time*). Luna's screams slowed, then stopped, and the doctor examined her some more and told them they'd need to get an (expensive) X-ray of her brain. When it was over, his assistant gave Luna another lollipop to take home and handed Sam the bill. Then the doctor said a few more things in English, patted Luna on the head with his own clenched hand and sent them home.

"Her *prospects*?" says Sam. "She's severely limited. She always will be. You don't need a doctor to see that."

"Why does she have leg braces?"

"To try to keep the bones from curving."

"But then why doesn't she wear them?"

"They're heavy and uncomfortable, especially when she's having a growth spurt. We tried, and we might try again, but the doctor says her comfort is more important for now. Her legs will never be normal, Rebecca, but she was blessed with a sharp mind. I try to keep her engaged. It's not easy for me—I told you, I had hardly any schooling, it's my biggest regret—but I do my best."

Rebecca nods. "I know. You're a wonderful teacher for her, but she also has a body."

"Yes. So do I." He turns to face the wall. "Mine needs sleep. Enough of this, please. I appreciate your concern, but your hopes are too high. She'll never walk. She doesn't have the bones for it. Good night."

But Rebecca cannot stop. "My grandmother designated me a healer, Sam. She taught me some of her *kuras de kaza*. I think maybe I can help Luna, at least a little, but your mother doesn't let me near her. It's been over a month. The way she treats me, you'd think I'd never raised a child."

"Keep your voice down please," Sam murmurs. "She could hear you."

The closet-like room where Fanny and Luna sleep is on the other side of the apartment, separated from the bedroom by the kitchen, though it's true that the walls are thin. "Luna doesn't even call me Mama anymore," Rebecca says more quietly. "Not since the first few days."

Sam turns around and takes her hand under the covers. "What does she call you?"

"Nothing. Ever. She'll"—she shrugs—"maybe grunt in my direction. That's all. I understand, these things take time, but she wants something from me. Her eyes are always on me, following me around. Nothing is lost on that child."

"I know," Sam says proudly. "She's really something."

Outside, a dog barks, a sharp, lonely sound, and then again. For a long time, no one speaks.

"When she was born," Sam whispers finally, kneading Rebecca's hand so hard it hurts, "they told us to leave her there to die or . . . or put her away in a place for *throwaway children*—that's what they call them, children you toss away like . . . trash. We were ready to do it. Lika was sick from losing too much blood, and Luna had come too early. They had to feed her with a dropper, like a bird. Everybody said to let her go—Lika couldn't hold her, couldn't even look at her—she was covered with hair and the size of a doll—but when I went to say . . . to say *goodbye*, Luna just"—he sniffs—"she stared at me, Rebecca. She stared and stared. She could only open one eye, but I'm telling you, she saw into my very soul. We'd already lost one child—maybe our blood was too close from being cousins, and Lika wasn't built for giving birth. They'd said not to have more, but Lika wanted it so, and it . . . well, it happened, and then they said they'd cut the baby out, do a surgery, but Luna arrived first on her own, before they could. She looked at me, and that was that." He releases Rebecca's hand. When he speaks again, it is with a rare anger. "My father abandoned me. I'd never do that to a child. I'm far from perfect, but I do my best."

"Of course you do." Rebecca, crying freely now, strokes his cheeks to find them dry. "You're a good man, Sam. Why do you think I married you? But love can blind, and so can fear. Look at me. I'm a good example. I should have found a school in Spain for my children, but David had a terrible time with the nuns, and I got . . . I just got scared. I should have brought them with me to Cuba, but I thought what if it doesn't work out with this stranger, this *Samuel Levy*? What if the ship goes down along the way? I'd already taken them all the way to Adrianople only to find their father dead and gone. So now again? Like jumping off a cliff into a fire."

"You did the right thing leaving them with your parents while you came ahead." Sam kisses her wet face. "Sometimes being cautious is the right path."

"It wasn't, though." She sits up in bed. "Now they're stuck in Spain. What kind of country keeps a child from its mother? They say *be patient, Mrs. Levy*. I sit around, waiting and waiting—I've never felt so helpless—but maybe I can help Luna, I can try. Your mother won't take her outside because she's afraid of the stairs, and that people will stare. So, all right, let's find a first-floor apartment and teach Luna some manners. Let the sun put color on her cheeks. So maybe people stare a little until they get to know her. So what? Be my guest! They stare at me. Who is this strange, foreign lady come into the neighborhood? Did I tell you I tried to buy a chicken the other day but asked for a *keet-chen*? When we figured it out, I burst into laughter, and so they laughed, too. Stare all you want." She bugs her eyes out. "I'll stare right back."

Sam shakes his head. "They stare at you because you're beautiful. They stare at her because she's not."

"She's beautiful, too."

"Really?" he asks hopefully. "Do you think so?"

She nods. "She has Lika's eyes, and thick hair and the prettiest skin, but she needs to learn how to drool less, and to say please and thank you and hold her head up. To be proud. Give me an hour a day to work with her, Sam. Tell your mother to let us be. She can go to your sisters' or sit in the park, do something nice for herself."

"I can ask," he says doubtfully.

"Don't ask. *Tell.*"

"She won't like it."

"The last time I checked, you were the man of the house." She sends her hand beneath the covers along the furred skin of his belly and down his undershorts.

"Is that how it works?" He laughs. "I'm the man of the house if I obey my wife?"

"Of course. You didn't know?"

Then—so much for exhausted—he is kissing her collarbone and neck, her jawline, temple, the pathways of her ear, and pushing up her nightgown, and before long they are both naked and he has entered her. A wife is supposed to feel burdened by her husband's urges, but Rebecca mostly finds their lovemaking a pleasure, the only place in America where she feels at home. Tonight, though, her thoughts stay on a separate track, because what if she can't help Luna, and where will her sons sleep when they finally arrive from Spain, and *when* will they arrive, and what about the rest of the family? And how will her boys adjust to Luna and to learning a new language, and to a new grandmother with no room in her heart for them, who never sings?

Rebecca has never thought of herself as a nervous person, but she has a recurring dream that David and Berto have caught Luna's illness (though she knows it's a birth defect and not contagious), and another in which her parents speak at a rapid clip in a language she can't understand. When Sam is asleep and snoring, she reaches for her nightgown, needing the protection of a second skin, and lies fitfully awake. It is later in Spain, or earlier, depending on how you think of it, the wolfhounds stirring, the sun coming up over the shards on the garden wall. Has the cock crowed yet? Are her babies still asleep, reaching for their mother but finding only each other, or maybe Avuela, in the night? Did they have a bath before bed, emerging pink and scrubbed?

Did they get her last letter with the drawing she made: two smiling boys in a boat, in sailor suits like the ones she sewed? *Be good boys. I'll see you soon. Send me a picture. Kisses from your mother who adores you.* Have they—she both wants and mourns it—grown? In a frame on her bedside table is a photograph of her flanked by David and Berto in those same sailor suits and, on the reverse side, her first attempt at writing in English, undertaken a few weeks after she arrived. *There in Spain my dollings.* Sam had pointed out the misspellings when he saw them, and though Rebecca shrugged off the correction, it had stung.

Later, in the bathroom, she will clean herself with a soapy cloth, and although she doesn't know it at the time, this is the night that Jacob—to be called Jack once he starts school—takes hold, her only redheaded son, a beautiful (*sin ojo*) infant and the first of her children, if you don't count Luna (Rebecca will and she won't) to be Made in America, but high-strung and fussy from the start, for being born to a *nerviosa* mother on nervous soil.

II

Newmother is at the doctor for the baby in her belly and Papa is at work and Luna is hungry but they're out of bread. How about an egg? asks Nona, but Luna says no. How about yogurt, offers Nona, or *kashkaval*, but Luna wants a sweet roll, the kind with white icing stripes and a plump dot of apricot jelly at its center. Also she wants to go outside—it's sunny out the window and she hears children playing on the street—but she never can unless Papa is home to carry her down because Nona is scared of falling with her on the stairs.

Luna bats her lashes, her eyes one of the few body parts she can control at will. "Please, Nonita? Pleasepleaseplease, can we go out?"

There's an Italian bakery down the street, and Papa is at the store. He'll smile when he sees her; he'll give her licorice. Her red wagon waits in the supply room behind the store. "Every child needs fresh air," Luna adds, quoting Newmother, and Nona snorts but then takes her hat from its peg and bends by Luna's chair to work socks onto her feet and buckle her patent leather shoes. Then a bow in Luna's hair, a wet cloth circling her face, the stove turned off. Nona's purse, Nona's house slippers exchanged for her brown lace-up shoes, Luna's bow adjusted. Nona's stockings pulled up from the outside, her hands making expert laddered pinching motions on her skirt. "What I do for you," Nona says finally, which is what Newmother says, too (Papa never does; she is his sun moon stars), and, bending from the knees and staggering backward a few steps, Nona lifts her with a groan.

They are barely on the landing when Nona trips and falls down the long, narrow staircase with Luna in her arms, a lurching, forward tumble, Luna's jaw slamming shut, the dusty, splintered scent of fear. Luna closes her eyes to a spangled blur, clinging to Nona, who clings to her, as they fall head over heels, then bump along sideways at a twisted angle, the next stair down, the next and next until they land in a tangle at the bottom.

For a long moment, Luna can't breathe. Everything goes quiet, white and still. Then her breath returns, and she coughs violently, as if expelling salt water from her lungs.

"*Lunita*," Nona gasps, sitting up partway, then flopping back with a thud. "El Dyo have mercy, are you all right, are you *alive*?" and Luna says, "I'm alive, Nonita. Are *you*?" which might even be funny because of course Nona is—she just spoke, didn't she?—except Nona doesn't answer; she is whimpering now, an awful sound, and Luna can see her own bent arm and Nona's brown shoe sticking out beneath her leg and the wall with its smudge of fingerprints, but Nona isn't where she should be; she's twisted here and there, the angles wrong, and Luna cannot find her face.

Noooonaaaaaa? No-NAH?

Nothing.

FANNY, Luna tries.

A low, vibrating groan.

Nona? TALK, Nona, please! Nona, are you hurt*?* Can you *talk*?

But her grandmother has gone still and silent. Is she dead? Luna tries to pray (Newmother has been teaching her the Shema), but the words won't come. "Papa?" she calls into the air. "Papa! *Ayuda!*" but her father, though only next door in the store, may as well be miles away, and even if she could move, she is afraid to because any motion could hurt Nona if she isn't already dead, and if she is dead, then the worst thing will have happened, and Luna is lying with a corpse.

Nona groans again. So she's alive! A fly buzzes close, then circles away. Somebody? Anybody? Help? What to do? As Luna lies there, it occurs to her that she and Nona might die together at the bottom of the stairs, which might not be so bad; she could be laid out like Snow White and mourned by an owl, raven and dove, and her prince would come and she'd wake up a princess or something even better—a bird that can fly like the pigeons that land on the windowsill, where Newmother has started a flower box because "my Papa taught me how to garden when I was a girl like you and sent me to America with seeds," and so that Luna has "something to see and something to tend." Each morning, Newmother hoists her up ("*Guay de mi*, Rebecca—don't let her fall!"), and they water the seedlings and leave crumbs for the birds, who gather *like rats* but have feathers like rainbows and fold their knobby pink feet to take off into the sky (they lift, and Luna's heart lifts with them).

She tries to separate her limbs from Nona's, but her left arm springs out and whacks Nona in the chest, which makes her yelp. *Imsorrynonaimsosorrynona.* Luna is crying now, her limbs still jabbing and poking, a random firestorm. A familiar antipathy rises in her for her body, which is dead set against her even as it's her closest companion and full of hungers—for compliments, sunlight, sugar, touch. She tries again to pray—*shemayisraeladonaieloheinu*—and this time her limbs start to settle, the sounds rerouting her in a kind of sidelong trick.

Baruchshemk'vod. Her leg slides out from under Nona's.

Vahavtaiadonaielohecha. She tries to lift—she lifts—her arm.

FREE AT LAST, Luna scooches to the door and bangs on it with the crown of her head, the prayer still looping through her mind. It will be several years before she learns what the Shema actually means—"When you are home and when you are away and when you lie down and when you rise up"—the recitation by then a daily habit. Now she says the words anyway as she bangs her skull on the door, yelling and headbutting, until finally the door swings open and a lady in a hat peers in—"Holy Mother of God, child!

What happened to you?"—and, abandoning a plaid shopping caddy on the sidewalk, rushes to the store, where Papa is.

Briefly, Luna is a hero—you saved the day, you saved your nona, you got help!—and her elbow heals, but Nona's hip is broken, and she will never again walk without a cane. Nona blames Newmother for the fall, for *planting ideas in the child's mind*, but Luna knows it was her own fault for being greedy, wanting a sweet roll and wearing Nona down, and Newmother, who has eyes in the back of her head, also knows it but doesn't say so, the silence almost worse than being blamed.

When Nona gets out of the hospital, she goes to stay with Tiya Sarah, who lives a few blocks away in a ground-floor apartment. Newmother makes Nona a silky coral bed jacket and a pot of chicken soup with lemon and egg, then turns to Luna with something like victory in her eyes and gets to work.

NEWMOTHER TORTURES HER. For the past month, she has been taking her through a set of exercises for an hour a day, but with Nona gone, the hour becomes two, then three, divided into one grueling session in the morning and another in the afternoon. Luna must lie on the rug and lift, drop, lift her limbs, first one at a time (she can do it, though it's hard), then two arms together (harder), then arm with opposite leg (*ahCAN'T!* She kicks, screams, arches her back, flaps her hands, pees in a warm release) to the count of ten. Newmother makes her heft cans of soup and grab at fistfuls of slippery uncooked rice and drink a glass of water with no straw or lid and *don't get upset if a little spills* (it does, she does).

Newmother knots a dish towel around Luna's neck and gives her a cup of creamy chocolate milk—her favorite drink—and when it spills, forces Luna to clean up the mess herself with a rag cut from her favorite outgrown nightie, white flannel dotted with blue sprigs. When the lesson is over, she offers Luna chocolate milk again, this time with a lid and straw from the store, but Luna sucks up a mouthful and spits it out, spattering (whoops!) all over Newmother's white and yellow gingham dress. Newmother unbuttons the dress down the front with her quicksilver hands and steps out to reveal a satin slip and lace-trimmed pink brassiere, a far cry from the practical, severe underclothes that Nona wears. Her stomach sticks out; there's a baby in there just starting to show. She turns away for a moment, hand on her middle, and draws in her breath, and when she turns back to Luna, she has a big, fake smile on her face as if it were all a joke, but it is no joke; Luna *wanted* to ruin that dress, even more than she wanted to be the person inside it, a beautiful lady with beautiful clothes, a cold heart and Papa's love, a wicked stepmother in a fairy tale.

"We can wash out the stain," Newmother says cheerfully, like she's proposing an outing to the park. "Soap and vinegar, a magic potion. Set yourself up at the sink while I change, and I'll show you how."

Years later, when Luna is working as a ward clerk at the New York City Department of Hospitals, she will receive a birthday gift from an office friend of a wooden paddle toy with two geese who peck each other when you pull the string, and in the endless staccato bow and stab of the little carved birds, she will remember herself and Newmother in those early days in Astoria, when they were each marking territory and fighting, though in different ways, for their lives. Lie down lift up one two three, I can't, you can, I won't, you will, you're *hurting* me, I'll tell on you to Papa! Go right ahead, tell away, Luna—you think this is fun for me, the way you carry on? Your papa knows I'm doing it for you.

Sometimes she pretends to cry, theatrical, loud wails, and then she really does cry, choking on her own spit until Newmother thumps her back and begs her to stop and kisses her face all over—cheeks, forehead, chin, it's all right, Lunita, shhh, shhh—and once in a rare while, she makes Newmother cry, too, and for a fleeting moment, she feels her sadness, how she is without her real children, far from her mother, far from home, and they rest, depleted, in each other's arms.

The reprieves never last long.

"Nice girls eat with a spoon, Luna—you're not an animal in a barn."

"Nona says it's all right how I do it, that I can eat like this."

"Well, I say no, and I'm your mother."

"My mother is *dead*!"

Then a scream with no words. Luna puts her all into it, crying holy hell.

"A little louder," Newmother says dryly when Luna stops to catch her breath. "Please. Go ahead and yell it to the sky so the neighbors know to call an ambulance."

ONLY ON SUNDAYS, when the store closes at 11:00 a.m., does Luna get a break from the routine, because Sundays are for outings: to visit Nona or go to the park, or to the Bronx to see Newmother's sister, or to the Concord Hotel in the Catskills, where Papa's brother Leo is a waiter and gives them *COOO-pons* (Newmother makes the word sound like a pigeon's burble) for family discounts on a meal. In the big dining room with red velvet chairs and a grand piano, Newmother gets up in front of everyone and sings, and the other diners cheer and clap and Papa glows, but no one talks to Luna; the mothers drop their gazes and hold their children close. In her mind, Luna shrinks Newmother and stuffs her headfirst into the open maw of the piano, then slams the lid.

"*Se mi korason ventana tenia de poder adientro mirar—*" Newmother sings with full-throated abandon. If my heart had a window and I could look inside—"*kampos i vinyas se despertavan de veder tanta dolor—*" fields and vineyards would awaken from so much pain.

The music is lovely, if searingly sad, but Luna cannot let it in, too racked with jealousy toward the woman who is its easy instrument.

ONE SUNDAY AFTERNOON, they drive to the beach, and Papa carries Luna into the sea, where she turns soft and watery, squealing with delight in his furry arms. But Newmother is there, her face blocking the sky: "Try tipping your head back, Luna, you can float on your back! The salt water holds you—it's amazing, like I'm not even pregnant!"

Papa shifts Luna onto her back until her head touches the water, but she howls, terrified, so he gathers her up and wipes her eyes. "No need, Rebecca. Let it go, please—this is just for fun."

Newmother swims away, then, arm over arm, heading straight out to sea. She had lessons as a girl at her summer house and can "swim like a fish" (and will tell you so), while Papa, who never had lessons, swims clumsily, though he tries not to draw attention to this fact.

"Swim along the shore!" Papa calls, but Newmother doesn't hear or will not listen, so he calls out again, heading to the beach, where he can see her better, with Luna in his arms—"Turn around, Rebecca, I'm not joking!"—and finally she swims parallel to the shore: big dot, small dot, a kick, a burst of spray, and only when she is nearly out of sight (even Luna feels a spark of fear) does she begin to swim back.

"What were you *doing*?" Papa asks when she finally joins them on the sand, but she doesn't answer, lying dripping on her towel, panting a little, rubbing her stomach where the baby pushes out beneath her swimsuit.

"She was swimming to Spain," Luna offers from the adjacent towel.

"Spain?"

"To her sons."

"Of course, that's right. She knows." Newmother rolls over and leans to kiss Luna on the forehead. "You know, *m'ijika*."

Before she can stop to think, Luna flings an arm around Newmother's wet neck. And for a lopsided moment, it's the just two of them, with Papa watching—just a girl with her mama on the beach.

OVER AND OVER, Newmother demands and Luna resists, the windows now shut during the exercises because *people will think I'm torturing you, the way you carry on!* To Luna's limbs, Newmother applies heat (too hot) and ice (too cold). She tries to massage Luna's fingers, but they're glued together like the flies on the sticky amber flypaper spiraling above the kitchen sink, except those flies are dead and Luna's fingers are (were) alive and cozy, snuggling, or they're a fist out for blood: punch her in the lip, smack her in the jaw (she lands to one side of Newmother's ear and is—the very worst thing—ignored).

Newmother makes Luna stretch her arms using bands of cloth she ties to her wrists and holds at the other end. Pretend it's a boat and you're rowing! Row out to the island. See the giant palm tree? See the parrots? Row, Luna, row! She ties beanbags to her legs. This one's just a featherweight, now lift. A little higher, you can do it! Your body is a wild horse, but you're the rider! Let it know who's boss! Don't you want to be a big girl? FDR has paralysis, but does he let it stop him? You can be someone! You have what it takes. Look at Dr. Carlson. He started out like you, maybe worse off, and now he's a big doctor. Don't you want to go to school and make friends? You can do it! You just need to think before you act!

Ithinkithinkithink. In a deeply buried corner of herself, Luna wants nothing more than to go to school, make friends, be someone, but the truth is that thinking ruins everything. If she thinks left, her hand moves right, especially if anyone is watching. If she tries the opposite approach and thinks left for right, her hand—either one, surprise!—might smack her in the face, like Charlie Chaplin bonked in the head by his own rake. If she thinks school, friends, new baby, new brothers—a framed picture of Newmother's two sons hangs on the wall, where there are no photographs of her—she is swamped by a toxic brew of emotions that slams her head to one side, sends her limbs akimbo and makes drool dribble from her mouth.

For a few days after Newmother arrived, Luna called her Mama. Then she stopped. She doesn't fully know it yet, except in her bones, but she has always longed for a mother, even before she entirely lost her own (a large, blurry figure lies on a bed, turning away). Then one day Papa said he'd found one; he'd have to go away to get her, but only for a little bit. This new mother had been best friends with the old mother and wanted a daughter and was coming to them from across the sea.

He didn't tell Luna that the new mother would also be his wife and that she'd have to share her Papa with a stranger. He didn't say that this mother already had two children of her own and would look at Luna first with horror and then with a fierce determination to fix her so she could stand (all alone) on her own two feet. Does Newmother think Luna can't hear when she complains to Papa in the bedroom about how spoiled she is, or when the two of them moan and groan at night, disgusting, fascinating sounds? Papa calls Newmother *prensesa*—also his pet name for Luna—and kisses her on the lips in the kitchen and pats her hip and tells Luna to *please cooperate, she's trying to help you*, and *it's not easy to make a whole new life and have your children so far away.*

At first, Luna lies on the rug for her exercises, but then Newmother has Papa build her a special table, copying it from a sketch she makes of the one at the hospital, where Luna now has physiotherapy after her monthly doctor's appointment and where the nurse, a German lady married to Dr. Carlson, lets Newmother watch and assist so they can repeat the therapies at home. The table, which takes up a good part of the living room, has holes drilled in its sides where Newmother strings ropes, lengths of bandage and old stockings. Beside it sits a crate filled with beanbags, bubble wands, rubber balls—items that might, to an unsuspecting observer, look like toys but are actually torture devices.

The first time Luna sees herself reflected in a hand mirror, she is in her chair after a beanbag session. Newmother, who has been asking Luna for help with the English words in a pamphlet from the hospital (Ex-tend*? No se.* Swa-llow*? El pasharo*. Are you sure, Luna—a *bird*?), says she has a fun new activity to help with Luna's speech and produces the mirror. Luna has only ever seen her own image as a watery reflection in the windowpane, and her first encounter with the contorted face looking back at her is so devastating that she spits, hitting her target with a blustery spray and sending the mirror flying from Newmother's hand.

"*Guay de mi!*" cries Newmother. "Never do that again, it's very bad luck! Love yourself, Luna. Love your own self, a gift from God."

Luna spits at Newmother and flails an arm, hitting her in the side so that she steps away, hands on her belly, and says, "*Stop* it, Luna—you'll hurt the baby!" Legs planted wide, she stoops to pick up the mirror. "I'll clean it, and we'll try again." But then she pauses, breathing heavily and leaning on the wall. "Or should we just give up? Is that what you want? It's your life, Luna. You only get one. Do you really want to spend it stuck by the window like a potted plant?"

Luna does not say yes, she does not say no.

"I'm tired," says Newmother plainly. Then, as if to herself, "And so sick. I can't keep anything down. Maybe it means I'll finally get a girl." She takes the mirror to the sink and starts to scrub. "This exercise is to help you speak more clearly and not drool. Don't you want that? So you can go to school and play with other girls, go shopping, make a friend? This is why I'm trying to learn English. People look at me like I'm a numbskull with no brains, but inside I have a thousand thoughts, like little seeds. So what do I do? I try and try until my head is about to explode, so I can let my little thoughts into the sun, where they will grow."

A few minutes later, Newmother returns with the mirror and two spoons, each dabbed with a blob of candied orange *confitura*. She props the mirror on Papa's English dictionary on the window-sill, level with Luna's face. "You stick out your tongue and watch in the mirror. Out like a snake, the snake wants the jam. Like so . . ."

Her face looms over the chair, her pink tongue flickering. The tongue bumps the spoon, grabs the *confitura*, returns to her mouth. Newmother swallows; you can see the ripple moving down her neck.

"This *confitura* is delicious!" she says, like they're at a tea party. "Nurse Carlson showed me while you were in with the doctor. Isn't it sweet that they're married? They must have met at the hospital. So romantic."

With an outstretched arm and keeping her stomach out of range, she holds the second spoon, dotted with candied fruit, in front of the mirror. Luna leans toward the treat but finds the ugly face instead and spits at it again, then pees in her underwear, warm liquid pooling, an old friend. Leaving diapers behind has been the only easy thing. In a matter of days, she learned to sit on a low chair with the seat cut out and go into a pot and then to use the toilet in the bathroom off the landing, and she loves beyond reason her set of underpants, four with bows and three with coiled pink satin rosebuds, a gift from Corinne and Israel, who sell children's clothes.

Newmother throws up her hands when she sees the puddle on the floor. "That's it—we're done. We'll try again tomorrow. Thank you very much."

Luna starts to cry, first playing up the wails, then borne away in a flood of wordless grief. Lately, after her sessions if she does a good job, Newmother gives her a prize, small, shiny magpie things, some hard to grasp or use—a penny whistle or wax crayon—but others so alluring that her fingers find a way to manipulate them. A diamond-encrusted brooch, a glass rabbit, a Turkish *hamsa* amulet, the treasures stored in a Cuban cigar box that smells like Papa, of cinnamon, cigarettes and toast.

What she cannot say: She's been broken by the mirror, split in two, inside and out, old and new. While she has long known that other children played outside as she sat at the window, she still lived in her mind as a girl like the ones she sees on the street and in picture books: round cheeks, clear eyes, straight legs, hair topped with a bow. What she cannot say: If she has hurt the baby inside Newmother, she will never forgive herself, but she'll also be happy because a broken baby will be hers, a perfect match, and sad as well, because who can love a broken thing?

What she cannot say: Why "finally get a girl"? What about me? What she cannot say: I want my prize.

She is rocking now, side to side, and doesn't notice when Newmother comes up behind her. Slowly, she becomes aware of slight pressure on her shoulders and hair, and then Newmother has moved to the front of the chair and is lifting her chin, supporting her neck with one hand and washing her face in slow circles with a warm cloth with the other. Newmother unstraps her and scoops her up, moving awkwardly because of her big belly, but still says nothing, carrying her to the bedroom and sliding off her wet underwear, cleaning her and sprinkling talc and sliding on a fresh pair and lying beside Luna on the bed. Humming a little, then singing: *Camini por altas torres, navegui por las fortunas*—I walked among high towers, I sailed through storms.

Tired beyond measure, Luna closes her eyes. As she drifts toward sleep, Newmother massages one of her fists, wrists, her arm up to her shoulder, firmly but softly, each squeeze followed by a stroke, then fingertips pattering like rain. When she reaches Luna's neck, she changes position and begins on the other side, singing all the while. As Luna shivers and yawns, both her hands open up beyond thought or intention, so relaxed that you could pass a pencil through the spaces between her fingers, you could pass a spool of thread between her fingers and her thumb.

The room—it's where Luna used to sleep with Nona before Newmother arrived—has new blue curtains and is tippy, tilting, its corners rounded in the afternoon light. Newmother finishes with the second arm and says, quite formally, I should not have pushed you so hard, Luna, it was my mistake and I am sorry. Luna thinks but does not say *what if I hurt the baby*, and then says it aloud, and Newmother says don't worry—you didn't hit me where the baby is, but it's true that you can never hit me. If you want me to help you, you have to promise not to hit.

Luna does, she promises, forgetting in the moment that she doesn't want Newmother to help her. Did you really never see yourself in the mirror before? asks Newmother, and Luna says no, she never did, and Newmother says well I hope you noticed that you have beautiful eyes, just like your first mother's. Stroking Luna's forehead, she says my mother used to tell me that everyone has an inside self and an outside self, but it's the inside self that matters in the eyes of God. She yawns, and Luna yawns, too. We wear each other out, Newmother says. How about we take a little nap?

Luna has questions: What was my mother like? (Newmother is the only one to speak of her, though every year a birthday present—necklace, bracelet or earrings—arrives from her dead mother's parents, whom she has never met, at least not in her memory, and who have a jewelry business in Mexico City.) And why, if it's the inside self that matters, do you look in the mirror so much (oval with a violet painted frame, it hangs on the wall near the table, too high for Luna), lifting your chin, frowning or smiling, plucking a hair from above your lip with silver tweezers, catching sight of what everyone knows is a pleasing face—even Nona said it once, *that one's too pretty for her own good*—and why does the snake want the spoon? But Newmother has fallen asleep, a hand on Luna's shoulder, and soon Luna's breath slows to match hers.

ONE DAY IN LATE JULY, Newmother ties one end of a long rope to the top of the banister and the other end around Luna's waist and stands behind her on the landing by the long staircase, the slack length of rope in her hand.

"I can't carry you down anymore with a baby inside me," she says. "And it's a beautiful day. Go down on your *kulo*, seated, one step at a time. Tip yourself back, toward me. I've got the rope, I won't let you fall. You can have school with Papa in the store—I'll work the counter—and then we'll go to the park and visit Nona. You can bring her butterscotch. We'll have a day out. Ready set? I'll count to three. *Uno dos tres*, now go!"

Luna stares down the steep, scuffed wooden staircase. There are twenty steps—she has counted them before—and says *Icannascare-ahitifellifellafell*, her speech already hurtling down the stairs, a blur, but Newmother says, "No, *Nona* fell. You were fine, remember? You"—she switches to English—"*saved the day*"—then back to Ladino. "Papa is waiting. I told him you'd be coming. Let's go. I can't stay on my feet too long, and I'm thirsty for fresh air. *Uno dos tres*."

Luna scootches herself in the wrong direction on the landing, past Newmother's black pumps and swollen ankles, until she is pressed against the bathroom door. Gotta go potty, she says, and Newmother says you just went, and Luna says *caca*. Newmother sighs: Fine, go, but then it's down the stairs with you. The rope is untied, she's set up on the toilet, Newmother turns away to give her privacy and because Luna can't relax her muscles with anyone watching, but still nothing comes out. She is empty—she's been caught.

On the landing again, Newmother stands behind her, retying the rope. "Papa has a Popsicle for you if you can do it, but you've got to get there first. Picture it in your head. That's how I used to do gymnastics. I'd see myself climb to the top of the rope, and then from seeing it, I'd go. Think: I can go down the stairs, I can go down the stairs, *uno dos*—"

Luna flaps her hands, drums her heels and shrieks. With Papa or Newmother spotting her, she has already learned to bump along on her *kulo* down the four stairs from the apartment to the landing, but this is different, steeper, longer, and it's where her life flashed past her eyes and Nona broke her hip, then moved away. She wants a grape Popsicle, the purple frosty slide, and to see Papa and Nona and go to the park, but *uno dos tres* jams up her limbs and clacks her teeth.

"Sing," she says, without quite meaning to.

"*Ke?*" asks Newmother.

"Sing, don't count. And don't say 'try.'"

"No problem. You know I love to sing!"

The song is in a language Luna doesn't recognize—*qui peut faire de la voile sans vent, qui peut ramer sans rames?*—the sound a wave, a current carrying her to a place unmarked on any map. What is there? Nothing much, just sound beyond sense, a child as yet unborn (unhurt, unmarked), the bones still soft, slow-turning in the womb. She lurches forward, jerks back. Newmother stops singing to adjust the rope, Luna's voice a bark now.

Sing.

LATER, THEY WILL COME TO UNDERSTAND that there's a logic to this approach, Luna's body carried forward by a kind of trickery to a sweet spot between trying and not trying. Luna taught me, Newmother will tell Dr. Carlson in one of Luna's proudest moments. She showed me how to do it, and Dr. Carlson will say, if the mother can listen—and you clearly can, Mrs. Levy, you've made excellent progress together—the children usually do.

Et qui peut quitter son ami sans verser de larmes, Newmother sings, and Luna tips herself forward, and it's bumpety-bump, the rope tightening around her waist, her eyes squeezed shut, her mouth a spout of wet, scared sound. Thought returns—*stop me help me no!*—but it's too late to stop, she is thumpety-thump and her dress hiked up and a splinter piercing her thigh, her waist cinched by the rope, then clapping and the rope undone, Newmother hoisting her up by the armpits. You did it, Luna! Bravo, I knew you could! You did it, let's go tell Papa!

Luna opens her eyes to the blinding street, sun, people staring, she is howling with happiness, her papa is reaching for her, lifting her high in front of the store, her legs fast-peddling so that she nearly kicks him in the chest, and he says, in English, holy smokes, you did it, Luna! You went down the stairs, your mother has worked miracles!—and the people are clapping and Mama is laughing and clapping, too, her hands a blur, and from high in her papa's arms, Luna tries but fails to greet her good audience with a bow.

Astoria, 1937

I

David is deep inside a comic book—Popeye swinging a fat fist at a scarecrow, Pops gone off to get Luna at the bus from her School for Crippled Children—when Miss Hill arrives one afternoon in early November, the bell jingling wildly at her entrance. He looks up to feel the jolt of two worlds colliding: his fifth grade teacher, in the same dark blue dress she wore at school today, here, inside the store. Instinctively, he hides the comic on the shelf behind the counter. His tasks include sweeping, wiping down surfaces, restocking jars, oiling the wide plank floor, collecting coins from the newsstand honor box out front, but a customer is the signal to drop everything and stand tall. Good afternoon, may I help you, and the person points and David grabs, using tongs for the penny candy and bare hands for the rest, dropping items in a paper bag and marking the price and item in the ledger.

It has only been a few months that Pops has left him alone in the store for brief periods, and he is not yet allowed to go into the cash register—Pops holds the key—but there's a jar with change tucked on the shelf under the counter, and he can do basic arithmetic, numbers reaching him more easily than words. Pops makes him count out the change aloud in English *so you don't make mistakes and so they know you're on the up-and-up*. If they give him more than a fiver, he's to say, sorry I can't make change but my father will be right back, and if the customer seems at all shady (they shouldn't, says his mother a few too many times. It's a safe neighborhood, with the florist next door and the locksmith on the other side. Everyone respects your father), he is to walk backward (Rule #1: Never take your eyes off the customer) into the storeroom, bolt the door to the shop and exit out the back to find an adult (Pops, his mother, Aunt Rachel, Aunt Sarah, Nona, in that order, and, as a last resort, his cousin Robert, Aunt Rachel's studious, unfriendly teenaged son) and call the police. This has never happened, but he almost wants it to, the chances being good that he'd get points for having handled it well and be freed from working at the store.

"David!" says Miss Hill. "Hello! I thought I might find you here."

In the sickly sweet spiral that is time slowing down, he realizes that his teacher's visit to the shop is no coincidence. Miss Hill is staring at him, her pale blue eyes magnified by her spectacles. What has he done? What should he do? If he has learned anything in his three years in America, it is that there are endless rules, most of them unspoken, and if he can follow them, they might become him, and if they become him, he might escape the vibrating doubleness that dogs his every waking hour so that he is always two boys, Dah-VEED and DAVE-id, the former at home in his skin, at home in Spain, the latter thick-jawed, stuttery and bent with nostalgia like an old man, stuck in fifth grade when he belongs in sixth.

Can I help you, he tries to say but instead emits a fishlike bubble sound.

"What a sweet, tidy little store!" observes his teacher. "I was in the neighborhood, DAVE-id. I live over in Flushing, but I stayed late at school organizing props for the play. Rehearsals start in two days. What a rigmarole. I'm swamped!"

David nods, despite not fully understanding her. "Can . . . *may* I help you?" he tries again.

His teacher looks startled. "Oh, thanks for asking. I wasn't—I'm not a big candy person, well, truthfully, I'm keeping an eye on my waistline . . ." She giggles girlishly and glances down at her curvy figure. "But my little nephews certainly wouldn't turn down candy. Maybe I should—"

She leans over the showcase. With her head bent, David can see the straight part in her blond hair and a row of perfectly aligned bobby pins, and he has a new and not unpleasant sense of her as human, as female (she must undress, she must take baths). In the three months since she became his teacher, she has hardly registered with him, being neither very young nor very old, especially ugly or especially pretty (though suddenly—her upturned wrist, pink scalp and parted lips—she is), extra nice or mean, just an adult demanding things of him and being regularly disappointed like the rest.

Miss Hill straightens up. "What might you recommend?"

David shrugs. It's a stupid question—it depends on what you like—but he must answer it. Standing before her, he feels the turgid mix of emotions he gets in the classroom each time a teacher calls on him, how even if he knows the answer, he can't retrieve it because his head starts swimming; how he is bigger, slower and more foreign than the other boys, and, at the same time, older and more worldly (he sailed the seas, he has a job, his father died, he has a *story*, though he guards it greedily, like the candy he filches from the store, chewing the wrappers into spitballs until they're small enough to swallow). Though theirs is an immigrant neighborhood, most of the arrivals are not recent, and his classmates read as bona fide Americans to him, with the exception of a nearly mute boy from Mexico and a math whiz moon-faced girl from Russia. Once, at the urging of his mother, David tried to talk to the boy from Mexico in what he thought was Spanish but was in fact a mangled mix of Castilian, Ladino and Catalan, and the boy had the nerve to laugh at him.

"Snickers are pretty good," he offers now.

"Thank you." His teacher nods gravely. "Did you know that *snicker* means to laugh? In a not-so-nice way? We should add it to the Word Wall tomorrow! I'll take two Snickers bars, please. No, make it three, why not one for me, too—it's been quite a day. Or four, let's get one for you, David, or do you get your fill of candy helping out here?"

He shakes his head, and Miss Hill looks at him curiously, maybe even a little sadly, which pleases him. "All right, then, David. Make it four."

As he snaps open a paper bag and drops the bars in, she turns toward the shop window, where his mother recently suspended real fall leaves that she and Al ironed between wax paper and hung from fishing line. While David is stuck working for Pops in the store after school, Berto—called Al now—has become mother's little helper, threading needles, amusing the babies, making her laugh with his antics and cartoon drawings. They don't have room for a real window display; the store is a small space and overstuffed with wares. Pops is saving up to open a store of his own, which is why he doesn't pay David and why David is supposed to think of the job as an *apprenticeship*. Pops grills him on addition and subtraction and explains *this is why* and *this is how* and reads the news headlines aloud and insists on speaking English and looking up words to get the proper definitions from the dictionary he keeps under the counter. He occasionally offers David a candy bar or soda, but only when he, Pops, wants to, or as a reward for a job well done, never just because.

"I love the leaves in the window!" Miss Hill is saying. "How clever to hang them like that."

David folds over the top of the sack and marks the ledger. "Five, ten, fifteen . . . twenty cents, please."

Miss Hill hands him two dimes, which he drops into the change jar.

"You're a good boy, working here after school, aren't you? That's a big responsibility. Is it just you here, or are you usually with your father?"

"Yeah."

"*Yes* what, David?"

He scowls. Grown-ups don't like him; he gets under their skin. He doesn't much like them either, except for Avuela, whom he adores and misses every day.

"Usually with my father," he echoes back.

"Where is he now?" Miss Hill asks.

"Um . . . he has to find my sister at her bus."

"Huh. So you're all alone here?"

Something in her voice sets him on high alert. "Just for a minute, and my mother"—the lie slips out of him; after baby Suzanne was born last year, they moved across the street to a bigger apartment, but it's close enough—"is right upstairs."

He retrieves a rag and starts to wipe down the marble countertop, feeling his teacher's eyes on him. For all Pop's exacting standards, he has a bad habit of setting down lit cigarettes when he's handling cash, staining the marble counter with permanent burn marks that David, indifferent to most mess, has a persistent desire to erase.

"So he won't be gone long? That's good. I'd like to have a word with him." His teacher takes a bite of her bar, chews and swallows. "Yum. I haven't had one of these in ages. I'll just enjoy it and browse the magazines. Don't let me disturb you, David. I know you have work to do. I can wait."

Standing before Miss Hill, separated only by the counter, David absorbs the news that she is here for Pops. Abruptly, his teacher's blue dress with its double-breasted gold buttons looks like a cop's uniform, her efforts to chat and buy him candy designed to trick or distract. Over the buzzing neon Coca-Cola sign, he hears her chewing the Snickers bar. He might walk backward to the storeroom, close the bolt, slip out the rear door and run, but he is glued to the floor with the queasy knowledge that if anyone is a suspicious character, it's him.

His crimes are considerable. On the ship from Spain, he was halfway to hoisting Al over the railing for tossing his best toy soldier overboard, and it was only the bosun intervening that made him release his sniveling, unsorry brother to the deck. He has stolen candy from the store, but worse, he has swiped coins from the honor box outside and snuck over to Mr. Romano, the competitor down the street, to buy penny candy (*Your old man don't got enough for you, sonny?*). Last spring, Mr. Romano snitched on him, and Pops used one arm to pin him down in the storeroom and another to whack him on the *kulo*, then sent him home without a word. Later, at home, his mother thwacked his open palm with a wooden spoon, though not hard enough to really hurt. Then her tears started: I left everything to get you a father and an education, Sam took us in, a widow and two children, I told him you were good boys. Did I lie to him? Do you want him to send us back?

Yes, he'd said, and she'd looked briefly baffled, then said acidly so that's what you're trying to do, ruin everything so we get sent back to a war zone—now I understand. No, he'd said, because that wasn't it, or not in a planned way, though he does love ships, planes and soldiers and might not mind being sent into a war zone, especially if it meant he could see Avuela and not have to go to school. He was grounded for two weeks after that. For the first few days, his mother froze him out, cooing and singing with Jack and Suzanne, laughing with Al, complimenting Luna like she'd set a world record by slicing a stupid cucumber with a paring knife. For David, a squaring of her shoulders, her eyes skimming over him as she set down his dinner plate or passed him his lunch box. He'd have preferred another thwacking with a wooden spoon.

If his deeds are bad, the crimes of his thoughts are even worse. He has prayed to God that the war leaves Spain and lands here instead so they'll be forced to move. He's made devil's bargains to trade Pops for Avuela and pictured his teacher—not Miss Hill, but a different one from third grade—wet and naked, his face pressed up between her knockers, and spied on his sister Luna, who's not really his sister, through the half-open bathroom door as she undertakes the long, arduous ordeal of getting dressed. He has thumb-wrestled with an older neighborhood boy in an alley while chanting *1 2 3 4, I declare a thumb war! 5 6 7 8, I use this hand to masturbate!*, and even tried it a few times, though he's wedged in a bed with Al and Jack now that Suzanne is in Jack's crib (we're *overflowing*, complains his mother; the apartment across from the store has three small bedrooms but is still a squeeze).

Then the door is jingling and Pops has arrived with Luna, her hand in his, her legs in braces, her hair, like his teacher's, tamed by a neat row of bobby pins. She smiles broadly at him—*HaaaloDAYvid!* When they are alone, she can be merciless, pointing out how much better she reads and how he still speaks English with an accent, or she'll flaunt the candy necklaces Pops gives her when she gets off the school bus without help (so what, David returns. They're for *girls*), but she puts on a show for the adults.

Miss Hill turns with a smile, then sees his sister and does something funny with her face.

"*Pops*." David's voice comes out too high.

"David." Pops drops Luna's hand and goes around to the other side of the counter, where he rummages for a cigarette. He looks from Miss Hill to David, then back again. "Good afternoon," he says in English. "May I help you, ma'am?"

Miss Hill bends her knees in a sort of curtsey. "I'm David's fifth grade teacher, Miss Hill. Josephine Hill. It's a pleasure to meet you, Mr. Baruch."

Pops drops his lit cigarette directly on the marble counter and smiles. "The pleasure is for me, madame!"

He has a thing for school, for teachers, the way other people worship movie stars. From his station behind the candy counter, David watches the cigarette begin its staining work.

"*Eeetsmeeesterleeeveeee*," Luna corrects in the labored, throaty drawl that is how she talks. Short to begin with and shorter because she can't stand up straight, she folds at the waist and extends a curled hand to the lady. *"Ahmlunalevy pleeezedtameeyoooo!"*

Miss Hill reaches to tap Luna's knuckle with her outstretched index finger, then takes a step back, rubs her hand against her skirt and says, too loudly, "Oh, you precious child!"

Adults are scared of Luna or pity her, or both. They think she's backward because of how she talks, and they think she has polio because she's spastic, but neither is true (she is, if anything, too smart). At home, David mostly feels jealousy mixed with irritation toward his stepsister, who receives outsize attention from his mother and can do no wrong in Pop's eyes, but when they're in public, he can't help wanting to defend her to the wider world. Once, a few months earlier, he witnessed a boy taunting her with "lunatic" and "Looney Tunes" and doing gargly, spitty imitations of her speech, and though he knew that to take Luna's side would come at a cost and that he has no capital to spare, he went in with both fists swinging and got a shiner on her behalf, earning an afternoon of pampering from his mother and an ice cream sundae from Pops.

"*Levytellerdayveedlevynawmistabaruch!*" Luna instructs him now.

David points to Pops. "She says his name is Mr. Levy, not Mr. Baruch."

"I'm afraid"—Miss Hill furrows her brow—"I don't understand. I'm looking, I believe I was looking for a Mr. Baruch? For your father, David, no?"

"*Heeesrealfoddersdead!*" pipes Luna almost merrily.

Above them, the stuffed animals suspended by string from the ceiling sway in the heat from the radiator and roll their googly eyes, but the people, including Luna, stand stock-still. Then she lets out a sob and casts her eyes past the animals to the heavens. "*Anmimuddatoo!*"

"Pardon me?" Miss Hill, sweat beading on her forehead, looks to Pops, but as he starts to speak, the door jingles and Mr. Sheridan, a regular, walks in and orders a cream soda.

"Unh, she said . . . it's just—her mother died," David translates, leaving out the part about his real father dying, too.

Pops speaks carefully from behind the soda fountain. "Let me explain. My wife and I lost our first . . . we were widows, a *widow* and a widow*er*. I had Luna"—he points—"and Rebecca, my wife, had already two sons when she came to me, David and his brother Albert."

"Oh, I'm so very sorry, Mr. Levy, I had no idea." Miss Hill blushes to the roots of her blond hair. "I'm sorry for your losses, I shouldn't have assumed, I'm a fool, I . . ." She touches her neck, turned rashy red. "I don't know what to say."

"Nothing to say," Pops replies bluntly, and even David can tell it's not the best way to phrase it and feels briefly sorry for Pops, who repeats phrases after the radio announcer to try to shed his accent and has Mama trim his nose and ear hairs so he won't *look like a hairy immigrant* (the fact that he's balding seems not to factor in).

Pops passes a cream soda and carton of Camels to Mr. Sheridan—"How's your better half, Mr. Sheridan? Please give her my regards"—notes the amount and returns to Miss Hill.

"Don't apologize. My wife and I have the blessing of two more children together," he tells her. "I'm a lucky man. Maybe this is because his name"—he points to David—"means 'blessed.' *Baruch*. A good name for a good boy, at least he tries." He eyes Miss Hill, trying to gauge her reaction, and David stiffens. "School isn't so easy for him—he started late over here, he was born in Spain—but he understands that education is the most important thing."

"Your name means 'blessed,' David?" Miss Hill is smiling now. "You never told me that. We've been discussing the meaning of family names in class, how Smith came from Blacksmith and Lincoln and Washington are towns in England. But *blessed*! It's like D'Angelo in Italian, 'of the angel.' In what language, David?"

David looks to Pops. In Spain, he was under strict instructions not to tell anyone he was Jewish, and while it's more acceptable here and there are more Jews, it's still nobody's business and some people might get you for it, so be proud of who you are but no need to take it to the streets.

Pop hesitates, then looks into Miss Hill's eyes and says, "*Ee-broo*."

"Hebrew! An ancient language. Some of my finest students have been of the Jewish—"

"*Ahneed*—" interrupts Luna, bobbing up and down and jabbing an elbow toward her crotch. Does she really need to go or is she offering David an exit strategy, since Pops doesn't let her cross the street or climb the stairs to the apartment alone, and there is no bathroom at the store? Mr. Sheridan has sat down on his customary stool to read the paper. Miss Hill and Pops lean toward each other.

"Luna needs to go—" David interjects in a whisper. He can't bring himself to say "toilet" or even "bathroom" or "girls' room," none of which sit right in his mouth, even now that he knows the difference and won't stumble into the wrong room like he did in his first week at school in America, desperate to go, undoing his fly on his way through the door, only to look up and see two girls at the sink, their faces visible in the mirror, filled first with outrage, then with horror and finally helpless mirth as a puddle formed around his new snow boots on the floor. He doesn't know why he and Albert are still Baruchs when their mother is a Levy, but he's attached to his last name and has some sense that it's a safety measure, like the store's back exit or the blue glass beads his mother—who makes a joke of it but does it anyway—sews into their coat linings for good luck, or maybe it's just hard to change your name. Pops is going to officially adopt them, whatever that means, but it all takes time, forms and money and hasn't happened yet.

"*Tengo ke pishar, Papa,*" Luna says.

Pops nods. "Walk her home, please, David. Be very careful crossing the street. Mother should be there. Unless"—he turns to Miss Hill—"you need him here."

She starts to answer, but David already has Luna by the arm and is out of there, moving as fast as her lopsided gait will allow. He grips her until they reach the sidewalk and she pulls free of him, heading straight into the street so that a laundry van, white and massive, must screech to a sudden halt. David steps into the crosswalk and raises his hand like a traffic cop, and magically, the cars all stop at the four-way intersection between Twenty-Eighth Avenue and Steinway as Luna weaves and bobs her way across. And then, close behind her, running toward or away, his lungs gulping down the sharp November air, David crosses, too.

So it comes to be that he is neither chastised nor punished, shamed nor blamed, but is instead enlisted to be a soldier in the afterschool play. It wasn't his idea; he didn't want a part. Miss Hill had already tried to convince him to take a role, and while he'd offered the most-ready excuse—I've gotta work after school—the truth was that he had no interest, or less than no interest: The thought of speaking lines onstage made him want to puke. His mother loves that sort of thing, to click castanets in the kitchen and sway her hips, tell stories for an audience. Al also loves to put on a show, and so does Luna if she can be the queen or princess. Sometimes Al and Luna do performances together, using a sheet for a curtain and getting Jack to play a dog or Suzanne to be a kidnapped baby, but they don't bother to ask David anymore. He tells himself he's too old for such games, but the truth is that public speech confounds him, especially in English, and being looked at hurts his skin.

Which is maybe why Miss Hill makes him her special project, and why his mother fashions a soldier's uniform out of olive-green wool from a worn men's overcoat, and why Pops closes the store early on the day of the play, and everybody comes to see him, even Nona, tiny, wizened and clapping from her wheelchair, though she's losing her marbles and can't always remember his name. He does not forget his lines (he has two: "Hark, they are coming over the hill!" And "Be brave, fellow soldiers!"), and it might be all right, it might even be good, because backstage, he plays jacks with the other boys, they joke around, he talks to a pretty girl named Joannie and escapes, for a time, the store—except that at curtain call, when he steps out of the line to bow as instructed (folding from the waist with hands behind his back like an actual soldier), his mother stands up—she is the only one standing in the crowded room—in her red dress and red lipstick and calls, *Bravo, DahVEED, bravissimo, DahVEED!*, hefting some (girly) roses like a torch—and the whole audience turns away from him to stare at her.

David flees, tangling with the velvet curtain before breaking free to stand backstage, sweating and panting in the dark. And then Miss Hill is there, hand on his shoulder.

"She's just proud of you, David," she says, so close to his ear that he can feel the warm tickle of her breath. "As she should be. You did such a nice job. Allow her that—a mother's pride." She turns him around and nudges him toward the gap in the curtain. "Be a brave soldier. Go back for the final bow."

SHE HAD A SOFT SPOT for him, Miss Hill. He hardly noticed at the time; that's how stuck inside himself and his own misery he was. Maybe at first she saw him as a pity project, but over time, she also glimpsed how his anger could translate into determination, his watchfulness into perception. Her own people, she shared with him one day, came over not so long ago, one side from Australia, the other from Ireland. Maybe she knew what it was like. She was not even a beloved or particularly gifted teacher, the kind most students remembered, but she saw the goodness in David—that he was, or could be, good.

What amazes him is that Pops says yes, he can be in the play, and tells Mama, who says but what about the store, Sam, don't you need him there? Pops (David hears it all, lying in bed, ear pressed to the wall) says not really, not so much—it's more for him than me, to teach him math and responsibility, to give him a few skills. Mama says thank you, Sam, to think of him, to put him first, but how will you go to the jobbers or meet Luna at the bus, I can't do it myself, not often anyway, not with the little ones, and it's the highlight of Luna's day to find you there. And Pops says it's not a problem, I can close the store for a few minutes and when I'm there, Al can help—he's getting old enough to learn the ropes. Al, listening, too, groans into his pillow and kicks David in the shin.

A week after the play ends, David is back in the store with cash register privileges, and though he's still not paid, he is now permitted a daily soda or a candy bar as long as he writes it down. Something has changed. He stands a little taller. He still hates school but finds in himself small competencies. He's not bad with machines. He can hold his own at stickball and is shedding his accent. He makes a friend or two, boys on the margins like himself but not the sorriest cases. He stops filching candy from the store. His mother is running a full-fledged sewing business now. Ladies come to the house for fittings and stay for coffee, and sometimes she reads their (mostly happy with a few mishaps thrown in for authenticity) fortunes in the grounds, claiming she has gypsy blood, and she laughs more than she used to, and on Saturdays, she troops the children to the local synagogue, though the services are gloomy, the men keening and davening, the music like a dirge. So go to the Sephardim, Pops says when she complains, but those services are far away and Pops works on Saturdays so they have no ride.

The truth is that what she is looking for—David understands instinctively because he feels it, too—is nowhere to be found in America. For her, the synagogue in Turkey where she spent her childhood; for him, the wooden pew at Carrer de Provença where his uncle Josef helped him carve his name under the seat; for both of them, the ark shaped like a ship but one going nowhere, even as David (even as his mother) was forced to leave. Every Sunday, she counts out her week's earnings on the kitchen table, dividing the money into piles: one for the fund to bring her family from Spain, another to supplement the household allowance from Pops and a third, if there's anything left, for the Dream House, a term she picked up from her women's magazines.

It's New Year's 1938, and then Valentine's Day, the store full of hearts now, full of chocolates, white doilies slow-spinning in the window, and it's St. Patrick's Day, the window hung with lucky four-leaf clovers while in Barcelona, Italian bombers with Spanish markings drop forty-four tons of bombs over the course of three days and nights. David finally has reason to heed Pops's call to pick up the newspaper, which is full of news from Spain: bombs and explosions like in his cartoons—KABOOM, KAPOW, WHAMM!—but real now, though also unreal, his childhood idyll turned grainy as a photograph and full of broken bits. The *New York Times* reports that the air-raid alarm system in Barcelona has been rendered useless, Franco's airstrikes, led by Fascist Italy and Nazi Germany, so close together that you can't tell if a siren marks the beginning or end. Some antipersonnel bombs are marked *chocolatti* so that children will pick them up and get their hands blown off. His mother receives a bare-bones telegram from Josef that she shares with David and Al because *you're old enough now.*

> *Bombings Eixample STOP synagogue ransacked*
> *STOP all alive parents with Elsa STOP*

In March, on his mother's birthday, Corinne comes from the Bronx with flowers and Papa gets a cake, but Mama says she isn't hungry. A few weeks later, a letter arrives from Josef saying that Marko had his head bashed in by Franco's henchmen, suffered brain damage and is in the hospital, and David's mother makes a terrible, inhuman sound and goes across the street to the store, where there's a phone, to call Corinne. Whether Marko got beaten because he was a Jew or foreigner, Freemason or Bolshevik (swindler, smuggler, hero, do-gooder, rebel, *Rojo*, keeper of the peace), or because he was simply in the wrong place at the wrong time, they will never know. Some Jews in Spain are accused of being capitalists and others of being communists (the same thing, Pops explains, as Reds), but *our family is neither*, Mama keeps saying—we keep our heads down, they just want to get by, get out.

One day she tells David that when she was a little girl in Turkey, a lady warned her to stay away from Spain, and that it turns out she was right. Your mother knew her, too, she says, and for a moment David thinks she's going crazy or that there's some dark secret coming out, but then she shakes her head and says wait, what am I saying, not your mother—*Luna's* mother, Lika, Rahelika, I'm all mixed up, don't listen to me, it's driving me nuts what's happening over there! I'm—she pulls him in for a tight hug—losing track of what's what.

She mails letters and sends money to Spain but few letters come back and those that do are censored, whole sentences blackened or cut out. She visits offices across the city, and one afternoon she brings David to a place with long lines and tells him to cry and say *my grandparents are stuck over there, old and sick, their home and religion have been attacked*, but he can't cry on command so she berates him half the way home in several languages, until finally she stops to kiss him right there on the street and apologize. The next time, she brings Al, who produces a torrent of fat, fake tears, but it does no good. Avuela and Avuelo are too Turkish and not Spanish enough, or too Jewish or not Jewish enough, or too poor (we used to be *rich*, the same old story. No one cares!) or too old. Corinne's husband gets involved, something about greasing the wheels, and then Mama and Pops argue—Pops is opposed to bribery or cheating for any reason, in any form, but, says Mama, the whole system is unfair, they'll die there, people are starving, Jewish boys are going over to help but nobody realizes there are actual Jews living there, my family, other families—nobody is helping them! You can't be on your high horse at a time like this!

It's Pesach, which they celebrate at Tiya Corinne's on the Grand Concourse, but his mother and Corinne start arguing in the middle of the meal, switching to French so the children can't follow, and there are extra wineglasses set out, the customary one for Elijah, plus two for Avuela and Avuelo as if they'll walk through the open door. Of course no one comes, and an hour later, Elijah's glass is empty (who drank? Who *saw*?), but the other two are full.

And then, in June, another telegram arrives from Josef, bearing the news that Avuelo, malnourished and weakened by the food shortages and the ransacking of the synagogue, is dead, זכר צדיק וקדוש לברכה, and may his memory be a blessing.

II

This is how to cut the cloth at the *kortar mortaja*, the communal gathering to make the burial shroud—from a bolt of white cotton, the plain fabric the same no matter your station; death comes for all and knows no rank. This is how to baste and hem the garment, and if you've lived a righteous life and are lucky before God, you might have the privilege of taking needle and thread to your own shroud, gathering over tea and pastries to sew. As a girl, instructed by her mother, Rebecca contributed stitches to baby clothes for Elsa and Josef, as for the siblings who came out blue, their swaddling wraps turned overnight to shrouds. Whether the occasion is birth or death, the women always shared the tasks, the needle passed from hand to hand to stitch the passage *de la fasha asta la mortaja*, from the cradle to the grave.

To mourn on the wrong side of the ocean and with only Corinne to share the grief is a heartache. Rebecca is a mother, but she needs her mother. She is a grown woman, tripping over her tongue in English class, though she used to pick up languages easily (how much it cost? Do it cost? *Guay de mi*—does!), in between wiping noses, tying shoes, unjamming the bobbin, forcing Luna through her exercises, pleading her parents'—now just her mother's—case at the Spanish consulate, splitting chicken breasts in one blow with a steel cleaver. Is that bone-cracking rage on top of grief? Saying the Shema, though God knows God is far from her, she is far from herself, and the Psalms, when she recites them from her French Bible—*toute la nuit j'inonde mon lit de pleurs*—are still beautiful in a faraway way but release no tears. She is scraped dry.

For the first time in her life, barring pregnancy and her voyage to Cuba, she cannot eat. Her food rises up; her bowels turn liquid. She leaves Luna or the boys to keep an eye on Jack and Suzanne—always a risky proposition—and rushes to the toilet, where she rides out the cramps until someone starts wailing or she hears an object crash to the floor, and, guts still roiling, hurries back. She gained weight from Suzanne, but now she loses it and then some, her wedding ring from Sam (Depression-era mass-market but beloved to her with its latticework, silver in the middle and gold rims) swimming on her finger until one day she leaves it in a pouch inside her trunk.

Usually quick to find pleasure in her children—their compact bodies, small accomplishments, comical ways—she views them now as if through a pane of glass. Fine-tuned barometers, they sense her distance, and the little ones turn clingy, Luna grows more irritable, and David and Al back away from this distracted lady who burns the soup because she's writing letters to her mother, whose return letters—none come for weeks, then three or four arrive at once—are brief and repetitive, the handwriting shaky, phrases (what could there be to censor?) blocked out or cut out, leaving empty squares. *I count the days until I see you again.* ██████████ *I count the days.*

In bed in Sam's arms, she can't stop talking, and even after he goes to sleep, she often lies awake for hours.

"I shouldn't have abandoned my family in Spain," she tells him one night.

"You came here for your children," Sam says. "Your parents wanted it, and it was the right thing to do."

"But I've got to go back, to help my mother and brothers and . . . and visit my father at his grave. To leave a stone."

"It's not safe in Spain, or anywhere in Europe, especially for us. If that changes, I'll tell you. Believe me, darling, I'm keeping close track. I read at least two newspapers a day."

"I read them, too!" she says hotly, though in truth, the news of the world upsets her too much, and the newspaper she tends toward is the local one, with its advice columns, recipes and simple poems—both amusing and helpful for her English—and ads for restaurants and hats. "It must be safe enough in Spain for Americans," she argues. "Look at all those Jewish American boys going over there to help. Doris Rosenberg has two sons over there right now."

"They're risking their lives, and you're not a boy," says Sam with the first hint of impatience (it is after midnight; he must rise at dawn).

"Meaning what?"

"You're a mother with five children, and a wife." He touches her hair. "We love you and depend on you."

Rebecca pulls away and sits up in the dark. "I failed my family. Do you understand that? I could fail you, too."

"You saved my daughter." Sam pulls her back down, and she gives in to his embrace. "You've given her a life. What's happening over there is much bigger than us, bigger than anyone—it's history."

Abruptly, she can see it: Marko, his skull shaved and sutured, curled half-naked on a hospital bed. Her mother, rocking alone in the chair in the garden behind the temple, but no, that's not right: She has moved in with Elsa, to a third-floor apartment that Rebecca has never visited and cannot picture, though she knows the address—Carrer de la Diputació, 127—by heart, having written it on so many envelopes. She can see her father's grave, still just a plot of dirt in the modest Jewish cemetery that was his life's last hope and deed. And up above, in a nearby tree, a parrot, hook-beaked and inscrutable, looking down.

HE LOVED TO READ, she tells her family in the weeks following her father's death. He was a good man, which is true but also partial because her father was not uncomplicated. He would, she thinks, have approved of Sam despite his lack of education, but they never met and now they never will. He will not know the grandchildren born in America, though she sent a few pictures. David and Albert only knew their avuelo as a stern old man and seem more uncomfortable than sad to learn of his passing.

Only Corinne shares Rebecca's grief. Together they turn the mirrors to face the walls and sit a wan little *siete* in Corinne's apartment, though not for long because her sister is in the middle of packing up, she and Israel having just signed the purchase and sale for a house in a leafy neighborhood in Great Neck on Long Island, a town where Rebecca would also love to move but can't afford. Anyway, there is work to be done, children to tend, packages to send to Spain: a scarf for Marko crocheted by Rebecca, and from Corinne, monogrammed men's silk underwear, though these are mere gestures for Josef has written that Marko spews gibberish and doesn't recognize the trick-the-gods name he received because his birth followed a miscarriage and stillbirth.

Si los anios calleron, los dedos quedaron. If the rings fall off, at least the fingers remain. *Mas tura un tiesto roto ke uno sano.* A broken pot lasts longer than a whole one.

Get up, *mi alma* (says Rebecca's mother, who often speaks to her across the distance). Put on lipstick and brush your hair. Take the children to the park.

I can't, Mama.

Do it for me, and for his memory. Go on. Good girl. Get *up*.

Rebecca gets up. What choice does she have? Five mouths, ten hands, fifty sticky fingers reach for her. July turns to August, beastly hot. She makes pleated fans out of butcher paper and passes out apple juice ice cubes to her children and the neighbors', along with watermelon slices, the fruit trucked in from the countryside. She puts on lipstick and takes the children to the park. No public pools—they might catch polio—but a few times on Sunday afternoons, when Sam is off work, they drive to the Catskills and rent a rowboat for the day, and they all go in the lake to swim, even Luna, with a rubber tube around her waist and her father beside her. Rebecca doesn't get out when the rest of them do. She floats on her back, ears filling with water despite her petaled swim cap, sunlight spackling her eyelids, her children's happy voices like a far-off song.

Somewhere in there, despite the heat, her appetite returns, and then she is starving, cleaning her plate and getting up in the middle of the night for more. She craves sweets especially, plucking gumdrops from the jar at the store when Sam's back is turned, and once Luna catches her in the act and so they have a secret: *Don't tell!* The children return to school except for the littlest ones, and the sewing business picks up, and Rebecca starts to enjoy lovemaking again, a little, then a lot, returned to her body and the body of her husband, who is a beautiful, loamy animal in the darkness of their room with a vulnerable side that moves her—his small sounds, the way he clings to her—though by day they bicker plenty, especially about anything having to do with Luna, David or Al, where their root allegiances are clear.

On a snowy morning, some eight months after her father's death, she opens her trunk to retrieve her wedding ring, only to find it is now too small. So she is pregnant again—her last, late child; she will get her tubes tied in the hospital (thank you, Doctor, I am *done*). At first, she cries at the news—six children is too many, she feels like a sow, they don't have enough room—but she soon gives into it, aided by Sam's excitement and the fact that for the first time in her life, pregnancy makes her feel dreamy and pleasant instead of sick.

In July 1939, for $4,500 with a thirty-year mortgage, they buy a 1,200-square-foot house in Cambria Heights, a new housing development in southeast Queens that will sell property to Jews. On September 1, the day that Germany invades Poland and World War II begins, they move in. Though the house is modest, a quarter of the size of Rebecca's childhood home, it has enough room for them all, and for Sultana when, God willing, she comes from Spain. On nearby Linden Boulevard, Sam opens his own newspaper, stationery and candy store, with the hope of eventually expanding to include a luncheonette. Luna passes the fire drill test and is cleared to attend the local school. Sam tells the younger children to call him Daddy now instead of Papa, so then he is Papa to Luna, Pops to David and Al, and Daddy to Jack and Suzanne, three different fathers under one roof.

Cambria Heights is almost in the country. Farm fields stretch behind the grid of roads. Children play stickball in the street and the mailman knows your name, and while the trees on their block are new, frail saplings wound with bandages, they, like the children, have room to grow. Rebecca is seven months pregnant when they move in but possessed of an almost manic energy. Before she even hangs curtains, she waddles down to A-Z Hardware to buy a pitchfork and spade so she can plant the rue she grew in Astoria from her father's seeds, along with tulip bulbs to bloom in spring.

It is to this house, with its mouthful of an address—114-32 226th Street—that Franklyn Benjamin Levy is delivered home, plump and sturdy, the most American of all their children and the first not to be named after a relative, having inherited his name from two of Sam's heroes (Rebecca lets him choose this time): Benjamin Franklin and FDR.

Cambria Heights, 1942

I

Luna hates her school. She'd wanted to go there so badly, just as badly as she'd wanted to believe Mother when she said you can be like the other girls if you work hard enough—if you look in the mirror and swallow your spit, if you relax your jaw and do your stretches, if you dress with care, use your God-given mind, let people see how funny and smart (she does not say pretty) you are. If you *show them what you're like underneath*, which is something Luna rarely thought about in their old neighborhood, where first she was inside all the time and then she was outside more but always with a protector at her side, so that she became a sort of local mascot, *Sam Levy's little girl*, and the cops would tip their caps to her, the baker offer her a cookie, and the nicer people were, the more relaxed she grew, so that soon she could remember to say thank you, take the cookie without dropping it and guide it on the wobbly path to her mouth.

In Cambria Heights, she caught up fast and did well in her classes, but she slogged through seventh, eighth and most of ninth grade without making a single friend. The loneliness of the school day is a torment, but even worse is how alone and consumed with jealousy she is when she's at home. Her siblings, each at different stages, have moved further out into the world. Her father, too, has less time for her now, working longer hours at the new store and coming home to make repairs and improvements on the house. As for Mother (Luna opted for this over Mama, for its Americanness and—irreproachable because polite—slight edge of cold), she is forever nagging Luna: Do this, do that, do more, do better! Work harder! I know it's not easy, but we all have to do it. Look at your father and me—we worked day and night to buy this house and now we're here, but have we stopped? You can't stop, not in America, not if you want to get ahead.

This, like many of Mother's claims, is an exaggeration; they do work hard, but they also stop. Sunday afternoons are reserved for family outings to the beach or park or to visit relatives. Daily, Mother stops to sit on the front stoop and chat with the other mothers, or once in a while she'll pop into a neighbor's house for tea or a game of mahjong, Frank toddling behind. She stops to sing in Spanish across the street with old Mr. Espinoza from Cuba—they do duets; he calls her his *pajarita*, little bird. Each Friday night, she stops to light the Shabbat candles, covering her eyes, and after the prayer ends and the rest of them disperse, Mother stays on, eyes still shut, rocking slightly, mumbling, and they know not to bother her (she is praying or talking to her mother) and to keep an eye on the younger children. Out of nowhere, she'll park the car, swerving to the curb and lurching to a stop—she has learned to drive but only recently—if she sees a sign for a rummage sale or a garden she admires, or a snowman in winter, or baby ducks in spring. And everywhere she goes, she chats. She'll roll down the window or get out of the car, smile, nod, charm, compliment, inquire, present Frank like a chubby offering. Make friends.

Why is it that she—foreign, with broken English and peculiar ways—can make friends so easily when Luna cannot? The answer, Luna is convinced, is simple: Mother is beautiful; people want to look, not look away. While she can't help being beautiful (she was *born like that*), she also labors at it, tweezing stray facial hair until the skin smarts red, soaking and pumicing her feet, sewing a new outfit or refashioning an old one for Rosh Hashanah or the Fourth of July, even if it means staying up until dawn. She pauses before leaving the house to put on what Luna thinks of as her outside face, no makeup other than lipstick—she says it's bad for your skin—but proud, almost imperious, with a ready smile, whether real or fake. She seeks out her reflection in shop and car windows, mirrors, even water, like Narcissus in Luna's book of Greek myths—all surfaces that Luna willfully ignores.

There is care to it all, a strategy. Mother might slip a business card into the conversation—*Rebecca Levy ~ Alterations, Curtains, Dresses ~ You Dream It, I'll Make It!*—or drop mention of the store (say you're my friend—my husband will give to your son a lollipop!). She pays attention to what the other mothers wear on the street, in the garden, at services at the little storefront synagogue she helped start up because the nearest one was in St. Albans, and consults the women's magazines in the store without creasing the pages so they can still be sold. One day, she announces that it has become fashionable for ladies to wear trousers in the garden, and lickety-split, she has altered an old pair of David's pants for herself and a pair of Al's for Essie Zimmerman next door, and stitched blue-and-white striped kerchiefs for their heads. Mrs. Zimmerman looks like a stuffed sausage in her new getup, but Mother might be a sailor girl in a musical, and soon half the neighborhood women are in their Victory Gardens in trousers and kerchiefs sold to them at cost, with *a leedle beet added for my time*. So maybe it's work, all that self-fashioning, but it is also fun.

You can be like the other girls. It takes Luna twice as long to walk to the bus stop so the other girls don't walk with her, and if, rarely, a few join up—under pressure, surely, for they are always the daughters of her mother's friends—you can tell how much they itch to spring forward, how badly they want to stretch and run, and though Lisa Bergman is no beauty, with a piggy nose and no waist to speak of (Luna, like Mother, is a merciless observer), Margie Frangipani has swingy dark hair and long legs and is nice besides. As they walk, Lisa and Margie move unconsciously faster, giggling about this boy or that, Luna struggling to keep up, and sometimes they talk to her, asking stilted questions, but Luna's voice jams if she tries to answer and the girls can't look her in the eye. Before long, she invents something—a stone in my shoe, a book left at home—and sets them free, accompanied now only by her rage, aimed not at the girls (she'd be just like them if she could), but at Mother, for dangling the transformation before her, an endlessly receding prize.

At her old school, which Dr. Carlson found for her, she'd been (it was etched in stone above the door, *The School for Crippled Children*) among many of her kind. Some children couldn't walk, others were feebleminded, and the schoolwork was too easy so she was bored a lot, but the days were soft, only kind words and gentleness, and the school was small, an experiment of sorts, with therapeutic exercises performed to classical music, classrooms painted in pastel shades, even a much-photographed outing to the zoo (cut short because of all the wheelchairs and crutches, and a group of jeering schoolchildren). People came to observe them as if they were themselves zoo animals, scribbling notes, but no one cared if you took ten minutes, complete with sound effects, to retrieve a dropped pencil, the room full of such extended labors and blunt noises. Luna made some friends there—Roxie, a smart, spastic, caustically funny girl much like herself, a few polios—but when Roxie wrote to her after they'd both switched schools, she answered the first letter but ignored the next, keen to shed her past, and soon the letters stopped.

Her current school, Andrew Jackson High, is housed in an enormous new brick-and-limestone building serving Cambria Heights and adjacent towns. When the bell rings, students flood the hallways and stairwells with a great din, though Luna has permission to leave class a few minutes early to navigate the halls before the crush. To enter, she must use the banister and her stick to maneuver her way up the slippery stone stairs—a harrowing journey in rain or snow—but once she's inside, her classes are all on the first floor except for Exercises class, which takes place in the basement, accessed by a freight elevator used only by staff and Special Children (there are just a few). For an hour each day, when most of her grade gets to go to gym, music or art, Luna is collected by an aide and taken to the basement for a session with a sad-eyed lady who gives her dough to squeeze and marbles to put in her mouth and mutters *good job* no matter what Luna does or does not do.

Mother knows more, asks what do they teach you over there, and then she'll take it and make it ten times harder, while also making sure that Luna, like that other blighted stepchild, Cinderella, does more than her fair share of chores along the way. The result is that Luna can now slice vegetables, fold pillowcases, paint phyllo dough with melted butter (she hasn't yet mastered folding the delicate papery dough into triangles, though Mother makes her try). After a year of failed effort, she can knit a simple scarf with her wrists tied together so her arms don't fly apart and stitch needlepoints that look as good, or nearly as good, on the back as on the front, which is what girls do in Turkey for their dowries, except that Luna's needlepoints are enormous, the backs knotted off with fat, wormy yarn.

She makes a huge rose—Mother draws the pattern first with marking chalk—and a yellow Magen David rimmed in blue. Beautiful, Mother says when the star is finally complete. You can give it to your husband for your dowry. Nobody does that here, Luna says scornfully, but inside, she is flattered; inside, she is picturing Brian Ahearn, a tall, warm-eyed basketball player who once asked her for help with an algebra problem and greets her in the hall with nothing like mockery in his voice. Brian Ahearn isn't Jewish, which, Luna tells herself sardonically, might pose a little problem with her family, but that night, after she climbs into bed in the small, first-floor room she shares with Suzanne, she lets her fist find the pulse between her legs, and then she and Brian Ahearn are kissing, he is carrying her across a threshold. It is dark where they go, a velvet erasure, but Brian Ahearn can see into her very center, where a new rose opens, one smooth, unmangled petal at a time.

In Astoria, Luna used to clown around with Al and put on plays, and David helped her cross the street and defended her from teasing. David started out with her at Andrew Jackson High, but after two months of bringing home failing grades, he switched to the technical school. He and Al help at the store in the afternoon and play stickball or bike around the neighborhood in their free time, so she hardly sees them anymore. They are good with their hands—Al draws comic strips and David makes model ships and fixes radios—but have never done well in school. Why, Papa laments sometimes, did the girls get all the brains? Mother says that's not fair because David and Al had no school in Spain and came to English late, but Luna thinks Papa has a point because Jack, American-born, struggles to read at seven years old, whereas Suzanne reads full sentences at five, and Luna regularly makes the honor roll.

When she started high school, her father got her a used pale green typewriter and built her a small corner desk in the room she shares with Suzanne. She can type using her left hand to steady her right, and though it's a slow process, she loves to watch her thoughts imprint on paper, loves the typewriter itself—its dinging carriage, each letter with its own true-aim metal arm. She loves, especially, to add the final flourish, *BY LUNA LEVY*, all in caps. Papa may wish for studious sons, but he also tells her to work hard in school so she can get a job with a pension with the city, which she takes as grim evidence that he thinks nobody will want to marry her. In her heart of hearts, a sealed-off, airless place, she wants three things: (1) to be a mother to a pretty, normal little girl, (2) to be a wife to a handsome, doting, funny (normal) man and (3) to be a famous romance writer (here, normal matters less, since you can lop off your body for the photo on your book). That the daughter in her mind looks just like Suzanne and the man like a cross between Papa and Brian Ahearn is, she understands, a failure of imagination and evidence of her too-small life. She has started writing a few love stories, modeling them on the dime-store romances Mother will spring for at rummage sales if Luna completes the transaction herself, but she never gets beyond the first paragraph or two.

Just show them what you're like underneath. Come on in! Ten cents a ticket! Do you want a guided tour? Here, on the left, the brain that makes me stagger and slur my words like a drunk; down this way—watch your step!—tendons tight as a stretched rubber band, except that a rubber band, released, will fly (will wound), and I can only vibrate, twang. Here, a tablespoon of bitterness, an oily little cesspool. A vein of jealousy. An artery of arrogance. A bladder leaking shame. What's that on my shoulder? It's a chip!

Usually Papa has already left for the store by the time Luna goes into the kitchen before school, but occasionally she crosses paths with him in his undershirt and trousers, his face dabbed with toilet paper from shaving nicks, his ironed shirt hanging from the curtain rod. "Tell your old man something interesting you learned in school," he'll say as he pours his coffee, so she stockpiles tidbits to impress him—about refraction, or how sound travels, or the carpetbaggers after the Civil War. Sometimes she says, "No, *you* tell *me* something, Papa," and he tells her how the store is doing and who came in this week—a circuit court judge, the local mother with triplets, Father Kelly, the parish priest, who enjoys discussing world affairs.

Papa refuses to give graft to the health inspectors who visit the store, despite it being common practice among local business owners. Instead, he keeps the place sparkling clean, beyond reproach, though sometimes they fine him anyway because they feel like it, or because he's an immigrant or Jew. He works tirelessly, washing floors, stocking shelves, keeping the books, opening and closing the store in a never-ending cycle, though he should have been a scholar or a judge because that's how smart—how *just*—he is.

"How's my good girl?" he greets Luna one morning in the kitchen, and Luna, still on the edge of sleep and trying to shed a nightmare where she was under arrest for an unspecified crime, blurts, "I'm not actually good, Papa, not deep down."

"Of course you are, Luna. You're the best girl in the world, you and your sister." Papa pauses, then adds, in a quieter voice, "And your other sister, too, of blessed memory."

They sit in silence. Luna can hear the ticking of the cuckoo clock, and from upstairs, the thump of Frank's feet hitting the floor as he gets out of bed. Papa stands to go wash up at the kitchen sink, first his face and then—soaping, lathering, rinsing, thorough as always—his hands. What was the name of my other sister, Luna wants to ask, and did she come out dead or die soon afterward, and did you see her, hold her, and who died first, my mother or the baby, and did *I* see her, and was she damaged like me, a throwaway child?

But you do not ask Papa these sorts of questions. Unlike Mother, who is full of stories of her fairy-tale childhood and the slew of troubles that came after it, he rarely talks about his past. When he turns away from the sink, his face is zipped shut. He takes his shirt from the curtain rod and puts it on over his undershirt, fastening the buttons without looking down. Then he plants a kiss on Luna's forehead, grabs his hat from its hook and cigarettes from the counter and is gone, though she catches one last glimpse of him through the kitchen window. He is leaning forward, almost running through the bruised purple air, trailing smoke as dawn changes into day.

THEY ARE HAVING DINNER when Tiya Rachel first brings up the school in the Bronx. They've just finished eating, the table a riot of dishes, silverware and crumpled napkins, and Luna is sleepily full. Papa's relatives—usually just Nona and Rachel but sometimes also Sarah and her family—come to Cambria Heights once a month or so for dinner, always on Sundays when the store is closed, though Luna would rather go with Papa to the Bronx, where no one expects her to help clean up and she can gorge on candied oranges and baklava.

"Somebody pays for this school," Tiya Rachel goes on. "A rich couple who had a crippled child who died, and they made a school for crippled children but only unusually bright ones—you have to get in, they make you take a test, and if you get in, you don't pay a cent. It's a private school, but *free*! The lady who told me about it sent her son there. He went on to City College and now he's an accountant, doing very well for himself. He even got married to a girl he met at the school. Maybe you should take a look, Luna, just to see?"

Rachel is asking *her*? Luna feels suddenly adult, her very future in her hands, but before she can respond, Papa says curtly, "Thank you but no thank you, Rachel—we know about this school from Dr. Carlson, but Luna is thriving at her regular school. Did I tell you she's on the honor roll?" (Luna rolls her eyes. Only a thousand times.)

Tiya Rachel looks at Luna, who looks at her plate. On her last visit to the Bronx, in a rare moment of candor, she had confided to her aunt about how much she disliked the high school, not because of the work but because she has no friends. Tiya Rachel had listened, sitting beside her on the couch. When Luna was done, she had cried into the starch-scented calico of her aunt's knobby shoulder, but only for a few seconds—she is no crybaby, not with her teasing, tough-guy brothers, and she has her pride. Rachel, out of all Papa's siblings, is by far the nicest. Even Mother, no fan of his family, admires her and counts her as a friend. She was born with one leg shorter than the other and wears a clunky shoe with a rubber lift, and her husband, a drunk no-goodnik, abandoned her a few years ago for a younger woman so she's a *divorcée*, and sometimes her pain shows in her eyes, but she is also practical and smart and has one son in college and another in medical school, and she supports her family with a job in the garment district and takes care of Nona, too. Luna appreciates Rachel because she doesn't talk down to her, but now she feels a ripple of mistrust. Did she open up to her aunt only to feed a plan to dump her in another cripple school?

"They have professors from the Teachers College who come in

to lecture," Rachel is saying. "It might be unique in the world to have a school like this. She'd have a chance to meet other children like herself, bright ones but with physical challenges. To make friends. And did I mention that it's free?"

Papa clears his throat. "You mentioned," he says dryly. "Thank you, Rachel, but I'm a homeowner now, a small business owner. We don't need to accept charity. Anyway, the Bronx is much too far. There's no way I could drive her every day."

"Oh no, she'd live with us and see you every weekend. And it's not charity, it's a *scholarship*, for every child who goes there. That's just how it works. She'd stay with us."

Nona, who might have been sleeping from the look of her, jerks her head up and echoes, "With us!"

Papa shakes his head. "I'm not sending my daughter to live away from home and go to school on some rich stranger's dime. Luna's only fourteen. Her public school is excellent, with top teachers. That school is why we're here, right, Rebecca? It was the first thing we looked for in a neighborhood. The first and last."

Mother, who has been busying herself with herding crumbs into a small pile with the edge of her butter knife, looks up. "That's right. She'll make friends, it just takes time. We're like in the Bible"—she laughs lightly, though nothing is funny and the laugh is strained—"strangers in a strange land. *Pasensya*."

Then David pipes up, speaking English. "That school nearly did me in."

Luna turns toward him; they all do. David never says much—he keeps to himself and has had an eye on the door ever since he first showed up, a sullen little boy from Spain—so when he speaks, you listen.

"*Ke?*" asks Mother. "What is this, *deed me een*?"

He turns his hand into a gun and takes aim—POP POP—at his own forehead as if to blow his brains out. "It almost killed me," he says. "There's a reason it's called Andrew Jackass High. That place is a hellhole, for Luna, too. She walks to the bus alone and cries in her room. Haven't you heard her? How can you not? Every night, she cries. If it were me, I'd get the hell out. I mean"—he shrugs—"I did."

"Watch your mouth," Papa says. "*You* were failing your courses. A lazy numbskull when it comes to school, I'm sorry to say. Luna brings home straight A's."

David's face floods with color, and Luna feels a stab of sympathy for him and is tempted to tell him he's no numbskull and that Papa knows so, too (she once overheard him tell Mother that David was dumb like a fox and just didn't apply himself in school), and that last term she got a B in Math, which Papa also knows. But she says nothing. Mostly, they are—at least to the outside world—one big, happy-enough family, but when the lines get drawn, it's her and Papa against Mother, David and Albert, back to the beginning, back to blood.

"David"—Mother turns to Papa—"is mechanical. No need to insult him. Every person has some gift. Just look at this chandelier he built for me, like a sculpture, you could sell it for a lot of—"

"*Stop*, Ma." David claps, a sharp sound. "Please stop."

"It's a lovely piece of work. And you're so right, Rebecca, everyone has something," says Rachel. "But we were talking about Luna, how she cries in her room. We were discussing what's best for her."

"*Luna* is here," Luna cries out finally. "*I* am *here*!"

"Of course you are, *mi alma*," says Mother.

They all turn to look at Luna. Her arms have started flapping wildly, but no one notices, or if they do, they don't pay any mind because (sometimes it's all she wants in the world) they're used to her.

"Do you cry in your room?" asks Papa tenderly.

Only later will it occur to Luna that if the others have heard her crying, he must have, too, though he gets home late and rises early so maybe he missed it, or maybe he turns the noise into a different one, for Papa is not a crier or complainer and doesn't like to see it in a child.

"Sometimes she does," confirms Suzanne. "Me, too, if I'm sad or can't find Dolly."

"Buncha crybabies," says Al scornfully, and then, as if on cue, Frank is wailing, falling apart—it's past his bedtime—and Papa is pushing back his chair and telling Nona and Rachel that he must drive them home, it's getting late, he still has to balance the books when he gets back. Mother unstraps Frank from the high chair and hoists him to her hip, and the other children get up and start to clear. Luna is supposed to help, but as her family clatters into motion all around her, she lowers her head to the table, feeling the slick surface of the oilcloth against her cheek, and shuts her eyes.

"Get up, Lazy Loony!" Al chants as he pokes her in the shoulder.

She opens one eye. Above her, the chandelier, an imitation ship's wheel that David built for Mother in wood shop, casts its ring of watery golden light. Mother carries Frank up to bed, her footfalls sounding on the stairs.

Luna is exhausted but also strangely happy, at the center of the circle. Rachel and Nona want her. Mother called her *mi alma*. David noticed her. She will, she vows, make friends with him, beginning by telling him how Papa said he was dumb like a fox (so not at all).

II

REBECCA IS WEEDING the hopeful pansy and petunia patch she planted for her mother by the basement window when she sees them, David and Al kneeling on the basement floor, Luna sitting on the step stool, her blouse unbuttoned, her brassiere pushed down, and they are leaning, reaching (which boy? Both boys, hands like ham hocks; she wants to shut her eyes, unsee, but because she is a mother, she must look) for Luna's breasts.

Rap on the basement window (she cannot move). Yell (she cannot speak). What happens next? There is no next. Time slows and pleats, drops down on buckled knees, and so Rebecca gapes and stares but does not—maybe for five seconds, maybe ten—act, instead observing through the windowpane: two boy-men with their arms raised as if in supplication, the girl sitting strangely still, eyes shut, mouth an open O of . . . what? Protest and shock? Invitation? ("She planned it," each boy will later insist when questioned separately. And Luna: "They forced me, made me show"). Even in the horror of the moment, it is impossible not to register something of the tableau-like nature of the scene: three lush heads of hair, black, brown and blond; three young bodies, at once foreign and familiar—two Rebecca knit, one she repaired—poised between childhood and adulthood. And at the center of it all, the pale, lit spectacle of Luna's perfect new breasts.

A lunge, a hand (whose hand?) reaching out. Luna lets out a pained sound, barely audible through the glass, and Rebecca lurches into motion, rapping both fists on the windowpane and calling out in several languages. "*Guay de mi! No se tokes! Kanios con lodos!* Don't touch her! You get away from her right now!"

And then (because despite eight years in America, citizenship papers signed and sealed, a sturdy marriage with six children between them, she will never not feel a little afraid), she adds, hand pressed to her mouth, "Do you want him to send us back?"

A scurrying in the basement room she fixed up for her mother but has allowed, as time wore on and hope dimmed, to be taken over by the boys. Legs scrambling, ducked heads. She rocks onto her heels and stands up too fast, her vision swimming, and shuts her eyes to steady herself against the rough, sun-warmed bricks of the house. When she opens her eyes, the yard looks different, smaller maybe, and coated with a dust of shame. Did the neighbors hear her call out? The younger children are at the park with the high school girl from down the street. Sam is at the store. Not generally a keeper of secrets—she has a reputation among the other mothers for saying it how it is—she is already aware of having been forced into a complicated danger zone and having too many people—Luna, her sons, herself—to protect.

When she looks again, Luna is alone and fumbling at her clothes, and then she has pitched forward to the floor, where she lies bent over herself in a twisted shape, her throat exposed, one bare breast, too, the size of a new peach and pale, almost glowing in the light from above, save for its startlingly dark pink tip.

Luna starts crying, or not crying, exactly—moaning, from low in her throat, a keening, remarkably complex sound that harkens back to when she couldn't control her limbs or bladder or put words to any but her most basic needs but could produce this sound, at once animal and mechanical, like metal scraping bone. It's been years since Rebecca last heard it, and the effect is shattering, as if all Luna's hard work and all her own have come undone—the years of drudge and haul, push and pull, sit up, stand proud; the years, too, of gluing together a family from shards the way the ceramics fixer of her childhood repaired a broken vase.

"I'm coming, Luna!" she calls through the window, and then she is running: up the back steps, down the hall and steep basement stairs to Luna's side, where she kneels and takes Luna, moaning still and thrashing, alone down there—where are David and Al?—into her arms.

~

First Mother slaps David, a sharp, resounding smack on his right cheek; then she slaps Al. She is so acrobatic, it's as if she was born slapping her own children; slap slap go her hands as Luna watches, torn between horror and vindication, from the stool. It all happened so quickly, one of them (which?) lunging at Luna after she'd said *look, don't touch*, the hand squeezing hard, a burst of sparkling pain inside her chest, then a rap on the window, her brothers (they're not really her brothers) scramming, Mother rushing down. A scream—Luna's own—and she'd toppled off the step stool, registering a sick humiliation at having lost control. By then Mother was at her side, pulling up her brassiere, fast-buttoning her blouse. She'd helped Luna back onto the stool and started up in English—*I'm so SAW-ree, dolling, I'm so SAW-ree what they done to you!*—before switching into Ladino and issuing commands: "Stop screaming, Luna. Breathe in, breathe out, to the count of three. *Uno dos tres*, get ahold of your breath. You'll give yourself a heart attack. Enough now. Stop!"

But Luna could not or would not stop, too far gone by then, the sound splitting her open but also strangely centering, even purifying. It has been years since she has screamed like this, but she remembers it from her earliest days: How they'd ignore her and ignore her as she lay prone in her crib or sat strapped to her chair, and she'd want something—her papa's strong arms or a piece of candy or to see out the window or for the new lady to kiss her/love her/see her/fix her/disappear/drop dead, or her diaper was full though she was no baby, she was six, seven years old, a big girl, a *basket case*, a *sorry sight* ("She no deaf, madame!" Mother would fling back at the lady on the street. "You want people should talk of you like this?"), but when she screamed, her fury lifted her high atop a column of sound. She could see herself from above, then, down to the straight part of her hair and her knobby knees, could see their faces turning toward her, shocked pale platters. Then they'd come.

Slap slap go Mother's hands now on David's and Al's cheeks, another round for each of them, even though if there's one cardinal rule in this house, it is to never strike another person on the head; it can injure the brain, look what happened to Luna, her skull squeezed by forceps because *Rahelika's baby tunnel* (what other mother talks like this?) *was too small*, and Mother's brother in Spain is brain-damaged from being beaten in the head. Still, Mother found her own two sons hiding in the basement bathroom, fished them out, lined them up, then smacked them hard enough to make their heads whip around, the act shocking Luna into silence. Papa has been known to take a strap to the older boys if they lie or steal, and if you cross Mother in the kitchen, grazing while she cooks, she'll lunge at you, often half laughing, with a wooden spoon, but this is different, head-on, meant to hurt. Finally, Mother drops her hands to her sides. Al has started crying, thick, gulpy sobs, but David stands with his jaw set and fists clenched, staring at the floor.

"*Silans, Alberto!*" Mother stands on tiptoes in her green gardening galoshes, squinting up at the boys, who have shot past her in height. "Stop crying, be quiet. Which one of you grabbed her? Or did you both? What happened? Tell me, I'm all ears. Tell the truth."

The boys shift and shuffle, exchanging glances, but they will not turn each other in.

Mother groans. "Right now, and may God forgive me, I'm ashamed to call you my sons. Luna, who grabbed you on your poor *bosoms*?"

Luna wants to think it was David—she is closer to Al—but suspects the opposite, for Al is all impulse, and younger and stupider, though they're both plenty stupid, which is why Al will follow David to technical school, but also not stupid, with an ease in the outside world (they have friends, they ride bikes, they've kissed girls—this one is *stacked*, that one's a *looker*) that fills her with an acid jealousy.

"David," Luna says, and then, as his gaze bores into her, adds, "I think, I'm not sure," because in fact it happened so fast, she has no idea.

"It was Al," says David, and for the first time in Luna's memory, she thinks he might be about to cry. Then his voice grows hard, and he switches into English. "But Luna started it. She followed us down here, said she had something to show us, and then she just"—he shrugs—"took 'em out. Right, Al?" He looks at his brother, who nods. "But it was Al who grabbed her. It wasn't me." David shudders. "I wouldn't touch her with a ten-foot pole."

Al blubbers, sobs and spills more crocodile tears from his big blue eyes. "I'm sorry, I'm so sorry—Lunita, Mother, Mama, can you ever forgive me, I'm a wicked boy, I don't know what happened, can you find it in your hearts"—suddenly he has summoned great powers of oration—"to forgive me?"

Luna, far from tears now, says coldly, "Not on your life, I will never forgive you," though already she has started to and is even a little flattered that she evoked such hunger and that he couldn't help himself (but why the squeeze, the bruise?). The sad truth is that she is more upset with David for telling Mother that she started it, and especially for his comment about the ten-foot pole.

Beneath her clothes, her *bosoms* are burning. Just this morning, they were her own best thing, but now they have been ruined, laid to waste. She had not planned to show them to her (step)brothers, but as she was leaving the first-floor bathroom, they'd walked by whispering, heads bent close, and she'd had an unruly urge to—what? Command their attention. Stop them in their tracks. See herself reflected back, made real. Something has happened without her even trying: She has made a perfect thing, and it is part of her. After a lifetime of avoiding her own reflection, she looks in the mirror all the time now, locking the bathroom door from inside and running the water to make it seem like she's busy in there. It's what girls her age do, primp alone or together, with a key variation: Luna narrows her vision, like looking through a camera lens to frame only what she wants to see. Two pale eggs, two powdery, pink-topped bakery buns, and if she strokes them, they shiver, and if she lifts and squeezes them, she can make a passage—*cleavage*—for the silver minnows darting up and down her body like electric shocks. A half hour might pass, even longer, before someone raps on the door and boots her out.

"The children"—Mother looks at her watch and sounds suddenly panicked—"will be home soon. Sam will be home."

"Please don't tell Papa!" Luna's head starts to wobble.

"Don't, Ma!" says Al. "It won't happen again."

"Never," says David. "I'll make sure of it."

Mother looks at each of them in turn. They're all a little afraid of Papa, not because he's mean (he's not, though he can be strict with the boys), but because he has high standards and they live in fear of disappointing him. Mother steps out of the square. In her khaki gardening trousers and beige blouse, she might be a curvy army sergeant, but her lipstick and the purple pansy tucked behind her ear add another element. And something else. Luna, who has been reading Mother closely since the minute she showed up in the first apartment in Astoria on Papa's arm, can see it in her eyes: She's scared.

"Fine," Mother says, but she won't look at them. "No need for us to bother him with this. It would only upset him, and he might overreact. It will stay between us. I won't tell."

She bends down to still Luna's bobbing head with her hands, and abruptly she is a mother again, poised and sure. "You made something beautiful, Luna," she says. "Of course you're proud. But you have to understand—they're yours to save, a gift from God."

She turns toward the boys. "You keep your lousy hands off her, do you hear me? If it happens again—or anything like it, no matter how slight—I'm going straight to Sam, who'll beat you to within an inch of your life and send you away without a penny to your name. But first"—she flings out her arm as if brandishing a sword—"I'll cut your little *pipis* off."

A FEW WEEKS AFTER THE INCIDENT, Mother comes into the girls' bedroom after Suzanne is asleep, holding a sock with a darning egg stuffed in its toe. Luna has been reading by the light of her gooseneck lamp but slides the book—a dime-store novel about a rich American girl abroad and her Swiss romance—under the covers.

"I've been thinking," Mother says in a half whisper. "Thinking and praying. And I think—I really think, Luna, that it might be time for you to spread your wings." She perches on the edge of the bed, pulls a needle from the sock and begins to mend, squinting in the dim light. "You deserve to meet nice boys who appreciate you. To have a best friend, like I had with your mother, of blessed memory. To *belong*. I called that school in the Bronx, just to see. The lady was so nice, a good person—I could tell from her voice. She said you'd need to take an entrance exam, and I told her that's no problem, Luna is intelligent and a hard worker. You can see for yourself, I said to her. They help their students go to college or find jobs. She said they'd love to meet you. They have a few openings for the fall."

Luna pulls herself up to sit. "You want to get rid of me, because of what happened! You want to stick me in some awful cripple school! You're kicking me out, but it wasn't my fault, I wasn't the one who—"

"*Shhh*. You'll wake her." Mother points at Suzanne, who sleeps like a log. "Who said anything was your fault? You haven't told your fa—?"

"No! Did you?"

"Of course not. It's in the past. I'm focused on your future now. Will you give some thought to this school, Luna, just to learn a little more, to see?"

"I don't need a place like that. I can go to a regular school."

"Of course you can. You *are*. We know you can. But you're not happy, you cry in your room. You deserve better. It's no way to live."

Mother moves closer, sets the darning on the bedside table and strokes Luna's arm through the fabric of the bedspread. "Let me tell you a story. When I was young, I married the first man who came along, a real good-for-nothing, missing something up here." She taps her forehead. "With your father, it was different. I was a mother twice over by then, a widow. I'd been around the block. Of course I was scared, terrified, really, to give up everything I'd ever known, but my children needed more—*I* needed more—so I took a chance, and then—well, you know the rest." She shrugs. "I made a life. We made one. If you don't like this school, Luna, right away when you see it, or after a month or five months, you just walk away, come home. You don't even need to cross an ocean. You just call us up and say come get me, I am *done*. But not to look, not to see . . ."

Luna wants to ask: Are you doing this to protect David and Al, sending me away to keep them home? Are you afraid it will happen again, which it won't, though the other day Al did say *oooh la la* when she walked by, and he outlined a curvy lady with his hands. She should have spit at him or told, but she didn't—she was flattered, she's pathetic, she *loves* Al, for how easy he is with her, jokey and accepting. David is more like her, darker and brooding, damaged somehow, though with working limbs. He's only fifteen, but he's already talking about quitting school to work or lying about his age and joining the Navy, though Papa says he has to stay in school, and Mother says she's not sending her son off to war, not after all they've been through; even once he's seventeen, she won't sign the consent form. Do you love your real children more than me? Luna almost asks, but Mother reaches out to stroke her face with fingers so deft as to possess a kind of witchery, knowing just where to press the temples and massage the jaw, turning Luna's thoughts to mush.

After a time, Mother takes back her hand and sits rocking slightly as, outside, the neighborhood tomcat yowls. Luna can hear her breath, in and out, and Suzanne's, too, a shallow, light rhythm she has come to depend on, and sometimes when she can't sleep, she climbs into her little sister's bed just to feel the warm pads of her feet and her small belly rising and falling beneath her flannel nightgown.

Finally, Mother speaks. "All my life, I thought people were good. It's how I was raised, what my mother taught me, what I saw. But lately, I don't know. I thought my father was crazy, putting glass on the walls to keep people out, but look what happened to him and to his synagogue, look what's happening in Europe now. I don't know anymore." She turns toward Luna, her face half in shadows but still (always) too beautiful, the curve of cheek, her earring catching the light. "I was sure you'd make friends. I mean, why not? You're a nice girl, smart and well dressed, polite and funny. *Interesting.* But people are small, they can't see past their noses. It's been almost three years, and you're . . . I think you're stuck. That's what I see now. It's not your fault, but enough is enough. I'm sorry, *mi alma.* I"—her voice falters—"expected too much, not from you but from the world. I was wrong."

"I will never be normal," Luna tells her. "I will never be beautiful, or even pretty. *Don't* say I am."

Mother says nothing.

"So I'm not. You're saying I'm not!"

Mother laughs. "Shhh. You'll wake her. You said not to speak! I can't see you from outside, not anymore. All my children are beautiful to me."

She stands, reaches for her darning, turns off the light and plants a quick kiss on Luna's cheek. "Don't forget to say your prayers. Ask what should I—Fanny Luna Levy—do with my one life to live? Then go to sleep. God willing, El Dyo will pay a visit in your dreams."

III

LUNA'S NEW SCHOOL in the Bronx needs a photograph for the records and for use in a pamphlet to send out to donors, so Mother sews her a new tea-dyed muslin blouse and slim white skirt with a kick pleat, and one Sunday afternoon in July, they drive to a field on the outskirts of town, Papa, Mother and Luna, just the three of them, a snug little triangle. Papa was slow to come around but is now excited. There have been articles in the *New York Times* about the school and its pioneering spirit. One of his heroes, Dr. Carlson, is a fan. My daughter can study ancient Greek, Papa tells the lawyers and teachers who frequent the store. There is nothing he admires more than education, so that Luna almost wishes she could give it to him as a gift, for while she likes learning, too, she is more focused on other things now: moving to a new neighborhood where she'll have to prove once again that she's not a dimwit and memorize all the potholes, uneven curbs and jagged steps that could do her in; making friends; getting over her own deep resistance, bordering on repugnance, at being lumped in with the halt and lame.

For the photograph, Mother helps arrange her, tucking in her blouse, angling her just so, darting back and forth between Papa behind the camera and Luna sitting on the grass, though with the wind picking up and how hard it is for Luna to stay still, things keep going awry. The pose is designed to disguise Luna's deficits—leg braces removed, a seated position—even though the donors might cough up more for a pity case. "Smile like a movie star," Mother tells her, but it's easy for her to say—she was actually in a movie once in Spain. When Luna first heard the story, she had pressed Mother: "Where is it, can I see it, is it shown in the theater?" "It was nothing, really, just a small film about our community," Mother had said, and then she'd started crying, stunning Luna, who hadn't known she was treading on fragile ground. "If I could find that film, I'd see my father again," Mother had explained as she dried her eyes with her apron. "He's in it, walking, gardening. I'd see him like he's right here in the room."

Papa devotes seven pictures to the photo project for Luna's new school. Six are unusable, but one is acceptable, a slightly blurry girl in the grass, slim-waisted and smiling, though if you look closely, you can see that her head is a little too big for her torso and her legs are hidden and her hair a bit of a mess, with a clump sticking up from her head. "Look," Al crows when he sees the prints. "She has a horn—she's a Jew with a horn!" "Stop it, it's just her hair, what is wrong with you?" Mother snaps, and she slides one copy of the photo into a creamy envelope to send to the school and frames the double so it can join the other family portraits on the stairwell, where Luna, on her way out, finally has a place of pride.

Luna takes the remaining photos and shreds them, using a satisfying combination of her hands and teeth. Years later, she will see a reproduction of Andrew Wyeth's painting *Christina's World*. Another decade will pass before she learns the story behind the image—how Wyeth stuck his young wife Betsy's head and upper torso on his older disabled neighbor Christina's body—but from Luna's first glimpse of the painting, she will understand, as much from the sweep of gold field and faraway house as from the woman's grasshopper legs and tense, twisted pose, that she is looking at someone like herself.

"I'LL MISS YOU," Mother tells Luna plainly on the day in late August when she wraps each ironed skirt and blouse in tissue paper and arranges them in the trunk from Turkey that she's lending Luna for her much shorter migration to the Bronx. Luna believes her, though she also knows that if it came down to kicking out David and Al or kicking her out (as, in a certain way, it has), Mother would eject her in a flash. Mother's hands pleating the tissue paper are like her hands on the phyllo dough, patting, smoothing, flipping, tucking, and Luna feels a sudden wave of homesickness, though Nona and Rachel will make the same *filikas*, and she's not going far. Even as Mother's hands keep working, she is watching Luna. Something must happen. What's the expression? *Meet me halfway.*

Luna returns her gaze, then looks away. "I'll miss you, too," she says.

Leaving Papa is the hardest thing. Luna worries about him now, for he seems older lately and more tired. Someone painted a red swastika on the sidewalk in front of the store, which made Mother want to file a police report and close the store until they caught the culprit, but Papa said no, that would be bad for business and make us look scared; some people are ignorant, pay no attention, just move on. Instead, he scrubbed the sidewalk, applied gray paint and did drive-by check-ins in the middle of the night as his vision of America began to fray.

Now Luna is leaving him, scuttling away, a thief clutching a secret. He still doesn't know what happened in the basement, Luna, Mother, David and Al united in a silent, if uneasy, pact to keep it among themselves. When Papa drops her off at Rachel and Nona's (just him, at her request, with breakfast on the way at a diner) he cannot find the words to say goodbye. "I'll find your schoolbooks in the library," he says gruffly as he turns to go. "I'll read along with you"—though they both know that she has already outpaced him, and he won't have the time.

Cambria Heights, 1944

Our Mother of Blessed Memory is Dead STOP She fell down stairs nobody home STOP No better woman walked this earth STOP Please tell Corinne STOP Your Loving Brother Josef

THIS, *M'IJIKA*, IS HOW TO CLEAN my body, with lukewarm water and a soft cloth, the way you'd sponge a baby—thoroughly, gently, without squeamishness or shyness, as I cleaned you, as we cleaned yours. Get behind the ears, along the neck crease. Wash behind my knees, my tired feet, then rub them in almond oil. Forgive me the condition of my nails.

I can't do it, Mama—I'm too far.

I'm your mother, you're allowed to draw close.

I'm a *kohen*, it's against the rules.

I'm your mother. You're *obliged* to draw close. Circle my wrist stained with tarnish from the cuff bracelet your papa got me at the Grand Bazaar. Take off the bracelet, my earrings, my ring, that I may leave this life unadorned, the way I entered it. Put them away, three gifts for three daughters. Now prepare the shroud. You'll find it in the box under my bed.

Where are my sisters? My brothers?

They come and go, but don't worry, I'm never alone. Keep the threads loose, without any knots.

David is at war, Mama. Al—Berto—will go soon. The world is in flames, I can't be here without you.

I'm tired, *mi alma*. Please sing me to sleep.

Did you hear what I said? Are you listening to me?

Close your eyes, close my eyes. Now cover my face. That's it, that's good. *Grasyas*. Now sing.

THREE MONTHS AFTER her mother's death on the spiral marble staircase outside Elsa's third-floor apartment in the L'Eixample neighborhood of Barcelona, Rebecca receives a certified letter from the Spanish consulate saying that her mother's entry to the United States has finally been approved. Later still, she learns from Josef that for obscure reasons related to the war, Sultana could not be buried next to Alberto in the Jewish section of the Cementiri de les Corts but was instead interred in an unmarked grave in a different cemetery called Sant Andreu, in a section reserved for non-Catholics and infants.

Five years will go by before the name of Sultana Camayor Cohen, of blessed memory, is carved into a memorial stone at Sant Andreu. Sultana will share the stone with other Jewish women—Fortuna, Augusta, Raquel, Miriam, Sarah—who might have been strangers to her or might have been friends, but who all shared the fate of dying during wartime, far from home.

its hands-on, technical nature and the feeling of camaraderie and shared goals, just as he likes to teach the newer crewmen how to stay calm in a crisis and, by repetition and focusing the mind, perform under stress.

Because he refuses to brownnose his superiors, he sometimes gets stuck with the crap jobs when he's not at the guns—being lowered in a harness to hose off the side of the ship with diesel oil (a task that brings back memories of being forced to oil the floor at Pops's store) or scrub duty or hauling trash, but even this he accepts, having found, through actual distance from home, a kind of inner distance: The world is big and he is small, just one of 3,500 people on the ship. It's too late to save Avuela, gone almost a year, but he is nonetheless important; the fate of the world, of the Jews, depends partly on him. At the same time, he's a cog in a wheel, necessary but useless on his own. His ready supply of anger, with him since he left Spain, if not before, finally has a target. It's good to be angry here. Useful. They're shown films full of severed heads and skeletons at the Rape of Nanking and given colorful posters—*Death Trap for the Jap!*—to fan their rage.

At almost 7:00 a.m., he is still topside, biding time before returning to the chow line below deck. If you ignore the time difference, it's his mother's birthday. He didn't manage to send a card, but he whistles "Happy Birthday to You" into the salt breeze and thinks of her—how she sings, how she smells: of floral perfume and garlic and onions from her cooking, and a skin scent, full of light but also soil, hers alone. More than most mothers with grown sons, she still touches him, massaging his back, cupping his face in her hands. When he joined the Navy, he was still seventeen so she'd had to sign the papers. She'd resisted mightily at first, but he'd already dropped out of high school to go to work as a newspaper copy boy at the *New York Times*, and over many months, with Sam's support, he'd convinced her that this war had a higher moral purpose. She didn't hug him the day he left; she was shaking too hard. "I'm sorry," she'd said, grabbing his sleeve. "I'm very sorry, I'm not feeling well. May El Dyo be with you. If you die, I'll kill you. Now go, before I lose my mind."

It's chilly out, maybe in the low fifties, with a rising wind and choppy sea. David's scalp itches and his stomach growls. Big Ben—their nickname for the ship—starts to ease her blunt nose in the direction of the wind and speed up, preparing for the next group of planes to take off.

The explosion lands near the center of the flight deck, followed by another closer to the stern, enveloping David in black diesel oil and the sugary smell of high-octane gasoline. He'd heard nothing to warn him, seen nothing drop from the sky. Not far from the catwalk where he stands, flames start shooting out. His first thought is that the explosion is the result of some problem with the planes docked too close together, slamming into each other and rupturing a fuel line, or maybe a rocket wasn't secured and took off. But as he squints into the murk, more explosions and fires tunnel in several different directions, and it occurs to him with the bright irreality of a comic book that, with no prior warning or call to General Quarters, they've been bombed.

What to do? What to do? His teeth have started violently chattering, and he feels like he might piss his pants. He can't go to his station—his guns may as well be on another planet ringed in flame—but he could help put out fires or drag the wounded to safety. The boatswain's mate is nowhere to be found, but David needs no command to know that turning away is an act of cowardice and abandoning ship a crime. But if you're already dead meat? If it's a lost cause? If you can't see beyond your nose and the whole world is ending? If you're a ready-to-shit-yourself sorry excuse for an eighteen-year-old boy, or an insect scrabbling for its life?

He moves one foot, then the other, extending his hands like a sleepwalker, and takes a few cautious steps away from the flames. With the hard toe of his boot, he locates the base of a 20-millimeter gun and edges past it, hoping to find a life preserver left on deck. Then he'll help, he tells himself. Then he'll turn around and go back in, knowing that if the ship goes down, at least he'll float. He can hardly see; the air is full of ash. *Step this way, m'ijiko. Put on your life vest.* I don't have it, Ma, I left it at my station. *So find one. Now.*

Later, some survivors will say it was God who took them by the hand. Others will claim they were saved by human heroes: Father Joseph O'Callahan, the ship's Catholic chaplain, who directed firefighting and rescue parties and led men below to dampen magazines threatening to explode, or Lieutenant Junior Grade Donald A. Gary, who discovered three hundred men trapped in a blackened mess compartment and returned several times to guide them out. But David is no hero, nor is he saved by one. He is alone on the catwalk, and after witnessing what happens to his fellow sailors that day and the sheer randomness of how events play out, he will no longer believe in God. *Walk up here a little, to your left—get a move on, don't stop now.* His mother is on deck. After, when he tells her this in a rare moment of disclosure, she'll shrug, pat his head and say, I'm your mother, what did you expect? Of course I came.

He stumbles to the gun shack, where he picks up the sound-powered phone to offer help or ask for it, but there's only static, and then the power fails and the shack, poorly lit in any case, goes dark. The place is used to store ammunition, and while he feels momentarily safe with a roof over his head, he realizes he'd better scram; if the shack is hit, it will explode. He opens the hatch, turns on the sprinkler system and returns to the deck, where he sinks to his knees and crawls, still looking for a life preserver. When he bumps into the railing, he stands, coughs wildly from the smoke, steps away from the bars and stumbles on. There is no one nearby. Scores of men must be caught in the hangar deck and mess hall, now a sickening tower of fire punctuated by exploding rockets. He is breathing in acrid oil, diesel fuel, spitting up black stuff, crap.

Every once in a while, the wind opens up, and he gets a few gulps of fresh air before the smoke returns.

Then a guy pops up, out of the blue, from somewhere along the catwalk. This is how David will recount it later—"a guy popped up, out of the blue"—though there is no blue in sight. The man might be an officer; he's too burned to tell, the air dark from soot and smoke. He tells David that the two bombs on the flight deck blasted through the hangar deck into the mess hall, but we shot down the plane—we got it! He starts walking away. David says, "Wait, where the hell are you going?" "I'm going forward," says the man. "Forward, what do you mean, you can't—there's fire all around!" The officer looks back at him and says, "If I were you, I'd get the hell off this ship, I'd jump." "Why don't you, then?" asks David. "I can't," the man says, "not with these burns—I'd be shark meat in the water, I'll have to take my chances here. But you get the hell off, kid, there's nothing you can do here. Save your skin. I'm telling you to go."

With that, the man disappears. He's just . . . gone. Like a ghost. As David stands there, weak-kneed, coughing, he remembers how he used to horse around with Al about jumping off the ship from Spain, pretending he was about to leap or push his little brother off. Now he won't jump for all the tea in China. The water must be seventy feet down—they're four stories high—and moving fast. He'd be a fool to jump. He'd kill himself.

In basic training in upstate New York, he'd learned to tie knots and build stamina by running around the grinder until his pulse pounded and his vision turned red. He'd spent hours watching filmstrips of the Japanese overrunning villages, raping women, leaving trails of dead. In Navy Ordnance School in Maryland, he'd learned how to fashion a life preserver from his own clothes and jump from a twenty-foot diving board. To avoid doing serious damage, you tucked your chin, locked your knees and ankles and gripped the fabric of your trousers with straight arms. As a boy at the public pool in Astoria, before his mother got scared of polio, he learned to swim when a bigger boy snatched the rubber tube keeping him afloat and he went under in a churning, breathless thrash, then somehow worked his arms and legs and tunneled up to fill his lungs with air, swimming several yards of flailing doggy paddle before Pops appeared to fish him out and thump his back.

Now, when the breeze comes up and the air clears a little, he makes out an opening in the railing. In the distance, screams, the sound of worlds collapsing. His hands are empty. He has no time to fashion a life preserver from his clothes. He fumbles to open the chain, then takes off his helmet and makes himself stiff and straight like a knife, tucking in his chin. It all comes back to him, what to do, as if someone were reading the instructions in his head.

He jumps. Into air, into space, eyes squeezed shut. Leaping from so high, he is thrust deep into the water. He can hear the thumping of the screws, four huge propellers that move the ship, each one the size of a room. You get caught in that and you're minced meat. Does he open his eyes to the churning salt sting? Curse, beg, barter, pray, ask forgiveness from his captain or the ship? The words he says to himself imprint indelibly in his mind—*I'll be damned if I get trapped down here like a drowning rat*—and he swims like hell to get back up.

When he clears the surface, his vision is limited, the sea choppy and cold, but he has the presence of mind to register three things: (1) There must be other people with him in the water, survivors or dead bodies, (2) there are Allied boats close by but also surely enemies and sharks and (3) he's got to get away from the burning tinderbox of a ship.

Time drains of meaning, then. Space, too. He swims, his whole self a forward-thrashing muscle or the trace memory of movement, like the shimmering trails left by the snails in the garden at

Provença, when he went snail hunting with Josef after dark. He is hardly a body, just a pulsing vector in the sea, an eel or jellyfish. Maybe he passes by floating or sinking rubble or a drowned man. Maybe he brushes something sharp or soft, yields with a foot or fingertip, grabs hold. Somehow he takes off his heavy Navy-issued lace-up shoes and lets them sink. For a long time, no one speaks to him. No one—not even his mother, not even God—offers to save him, and no one asks him to be saved. His eyes are mostly shut, his ears clogged with water. If he thinks in any language, it's the first one, Spanyol, from his childhood, but he's not really thinking. Later, he will describe this time to a friend as a rebirth. "Did you become a Christian?" his buddy will ask, and David will guffaw. "Me? Ha! Not a chance, but something happened—I, I dunno, I realized I've got one life, that's all, to use or piss away."

Finally, he hears shouting in the distance. He swims toward it, and it turns out to be a pilot floating with a yellow Mae West life preserver. "Am I ever glad to see you," David gasps when he reaches the pilot, who says, "I'm glad to see you, too, it's lonely out here, where's your life jacket?" David tells him he jumped off the ship without one, and the pilot says to grab on to his, then grimaces. "Listen," he says, "I think I was blown off deck—my legs are all messed up." He'd been standing near the elevator on the port side, waiting to hear the order, Man Your Planes. The elevator got blown up in the explosion, and he was flipped high into the air over the edge of the ship, his ankles snapped from the force of the push.

If David hadn't come along, the pilot would have soon been dead in the water, not being mobile. His life jacket is visible and might attract help; David can hold on to it and rest. "I guess we better stick together for a while," David says as he grabs on to the pilot, holding tight as a swell lifts them, fills their mouths with water, then sets them down. They seem to float together indefinitely before they hear shouting. Summoning his strength, or what remains of it, David starts to tow the pilot toward the noise.

In the distance, he makes out a large floating device, a rope and cork raft loaded with sailors who jumped or were thrown or blown off the ship. As they draw closer, he sees that some of the boys are weeping, crying for their mothers, and gasping and coughing as if still underwater. Seeing them so filled with terror makes him calmer for some reason. He exits his self, floating above the scene with the dawning knowledge that he might actually survive this day and live to tell the tale. He can see the top of his own soaked, stubborn skull, and it's the damnedest thing—he's still a kid, only eighteen—but the figure he sees is bald and old, or maybe bald and new, a baby just come into the world.

David gets as close to the raft as he can, and at a certain point, he says to the pilot, "Look, I'm really sorry, pal, but I'm losing steam, I can't sustain my energy to get to that raft with you, but I'll have them pull you in the rest of the way—don't worry, I won't leave you in the drink." The pilot says, "Go ahead, good luck to you." David leaves him behind to swim toward the raft, and he just about reaches it—he's so close, maybe four feet away—but as he raises his hand to touch it, he finds he can't move. He's made it all this way, but he is done. They come toward him. He's dead in the water, but somebody reaches down, grabs him by the collar and hauls him up.

A sailor jumps off the raft, swims out and tows the pilot the rest of the way. Does David sleep then? Shiver? Dream? Later, he will remember all the bare toes on the boat, rows of them, curled and cold, and lying pressed up against two strangers. The sea is calm so they only rock a little, and the pilot flaps and bucks like a fish out of water—his legs must hurt like hell—and David's eyelashes, when he half opens his eyes, are coated in salt, the new world rimmed in lacy white.

Who knows how long they're on that life raft before a destroyer, the USS Marshall, comes along. On deck, David is given warm broth, wrapped in a wool blanket and led to crew's quarters, where a clock reveals that he was in the water for five or six hours—the longest and most timeless hours of his life. The pilot is taken to officers' quarters. David, who just knows that the man's name is Tom and that they probably saved each other, will never see him again, though years later, he'll try, unsuccessfully, to track him down.

The USS Marshall picks up some two hundred men that day. Their families are told only that the ship was bombed, the men MIA. For security reasons, neither the sailors' location nor their status as survivors can be shared. Other ships pick up other sailors. At first, the Franklin survivors are held in confinement to be court-martialed for desertion. Captain Gehres—Asshole First Class, David calls him—gives orders for this, even for the men who were literally blown off the ship, but the captains of the other ships say this is a travesty, these boys were in an inferno fighting for their lives. The survivors—nobody calls them heroes—are terrified to look back and terrified to look ahead, as the fate of Gehres's court-martial is unclear, and they know a successful trial ends with life imprisonment or death.

Is it then, as fear of court-martial circulates from cot to cot, or later, when they're allowed, under strict supervision, onto the gutted, listing Franklin to look for possessions (David finds none), that he recalls a spectral figure stepping out of the smoke, a man, an officer, burned and raw, advising him, *telling* him, to jump? David invents the story of the burned man without quite meaning to, as an alibi for future use or a companion for his own racked conscience because a captain goes down with his ship and a loyal crew should, too, and while part of him knows that saving himself was the only real option, the rest of him isn't so sure. Some of the crewmen made a braver choice that day, heading into the inferno, running hoses to put out the fire, trying to save the sailors and the ship.

The accused deserters are not allowed to stay on the Franklin as she is towed from Japanese waters and then, her boilers miraculously repaired, travels on her own steam to Pearl Harbor and later to the Brooklyn Navy Yard, where she is rebuilt, and then to Bayonne, New Jersey, where she lies mothballed until she is sold for scrap in 1966 and, rumor has it, eventually repurposed by the Japanese.

Even after the court-martial charges are dropped (it turns out that Gehres screwed up by not calling General Quarters, despite having received an alert about approaching Japanese planes), David holds on to the story of the spectral officer, repeating it—*with all these burns, the guy said he'd be shark meat!*—until it takes on the burnished patina of fact. He remembers, even mourns, the burned man, how raw he was, how red, a body with no envelope, a skinless hunk of meat. How, despite his condition, the man paused to offer advice to a lost boy on the catwalk: you better get the hell off.

In time, David comes to regret the fabrication and repetition of the burned man story, and his mother steps in to take the officer's place. This is the truer story: She was with him on the catwalk when he jumped. Does that explain why she wouldn't accept that he was almost surely dead at sea, why she covered her ears when the radio was on and stopped reading the news, and they all thought she'd gone *loka*, grief-crazed, unable to accept the tragic truth? El Dyo, she kept saying, wouldn't take my firstborn child on my birthday. Stop worrying, everyone, stop tearing your hair out, he'll be back. Then one morning, some weeks after the bombing, with David still MIA, she set about making his favorite food: *borekas* and flans, *tishpishti* cake, and that afternoon they got word that David was alive but with no details, it was all still secret. She said see, what did I tell you, he'll be home soon, and invited the neighbors over to share the feast.

The day David actually came home, she prepared all the same dishes. Sam closed the store and got Luna from the Bronx, and Jack, Suzanne and Frank stayed home from school so that everyone was there but Al, who was on an army base in Virginia. David was too fragile, too tired, too jumpy to eat or celebrate, so Rebecca lay down with him on his childhood bed and held him as he trembled. She did not interrogate him or comment on his ragged state or try to clean his clothes. She held him. She'd gained weight in his absence and had new crow's-feet around her eyes, but she smelled like herself—of flowery perfume, lemons and the garlic she'd been chopping for the feast, and that other smell, the one he couldn't name until he was far away and missing her, of light and soil.

"*M'ijiko,*" she murmured. "Nobody believed me, but I knew you'd come home."

"A man told me to jump," he said into her hair.

"Of course he did," she said.

Cambria Heights, 1950

THIS, THE BEAUTIFUL TIME. It turns out that there can be more than one in a lifetime, and if mostly they are viewed as such in hindsight and when funneled through the soft, distorting lens of nostalgia, sometimes you can catch a moment as it happens, and you are deep inside your life and it is unremarkable because lacking (*ojo malo*) tumult, and remarkable because steeped in joy and full of nothing but itself.

Rebecca dances. Rebecca sings, acts and twirls a parasol she trimmed with beads, kicking up her legs like a showgirl in a Broadway musical, threading her arms around the pillowy waists of the other middle-aged ladies of the Beth Shalom Cambria Heights Jewish Center, where she is an active member because she is devoted to its mission and because there's nothing like a variety show, rummage sale, Purim shpiel or square dance to fire her up and distract her from a growing sense of her own invisibility, which might be what happens when your parents are dead and your people have been slaughtered, or it might just be from getting older, for though she's not yet fifty, her monthly blood has grown sporadic—prompted, she's convinced, by the loss of her mother—and white strands salt her curls. She still enjoys pretty clothes and believes in greeting the world with a smile no matter your mood, but when she looks in the mirror, she feels strangely distant from the aging woman staring back and sometimes gets a clammy feeling, as if she were putting lipstick on a ghost.

David is in college in Chicago. Al lives in Brooklyn near his job as an X-ray technician, a skill he picked up in the army. At her school in the Bronx, Luna found friends and a boyfriend, Eugene, with a limp and palsy, quick brain, rich brown eyes, and developed a plan, cut short by marriage to Gene, to go to college to become a translator in the courts. Now she and Gene live near Rachel and work at municipal jobs.

Never one to mope and relieved to be done with the labor of raising a brood of small children, Rebecca has converted the finished basement room into a sewing station and joined forces with Sam to sell homemade chocolates and custom-decorated cakes at the store. She has expanded her garden into every available corner, sunflowers nodding by the front stoop and snap peas scaling the picket fence that divides her wild plot from Essie's groomed one. In winter, she hangs a bird feeder from the pear tree and ties Christmas ribbons to the railings on the stoop to add a splash of color. Random plants pop up from the spent bouquets she tosses into the yard, and if her father—a regular if fleeting presence in her garden, like the hummingbirds that light on the bee balm—is critical of her approach, he does not say.

I'm doing fine over here, Rebecca writes to Elsa in Barcelona and to Josef and Isidoro, who recently moved to Israel (Elsa would have joined them, but she won't abandon Marko in Spain), and it is true. She has made a good home in America, raised good children on their way to becoming functioning adults. She still loves her husband, as he loves her, even if their sex life has slowed. She has, between hot flashes, great surges of desire, so sometimes she's the one who starts things up. Afterward, they lie in bed talking, despite the late hour, occasionally about big things—God and evil, fate, luck—but usually about immediate concerns: the wounded sparrow she found and nursed to health in a shoebox, Sam's exchanges with local characters in the store, picket fencing on sale, the children's friendships, until one of them—usually Sam, who still gets up at dawn—says I need my sleep, and they turn away from each other, toward separate walls and separate dreams.

Their sons made it home from the war; they all have roofs over their heads. The store had a few burglaries and one terrifying holdup when the thugs took Sam away in a car and left him bound and gagged by the side of a highway. After that, Rebecca asked Corinne if Israel would hire Sam as a floor manager at their undergarments factory, but Corinne hemmed and hawed and finally blurted out that managers had, at the very least, high school degrees, which enraged Rebecca (and wasn't even always true) and humiliated Sam ("Truth to tell, my husband is smarter than the two of you put together," Rebecca flung back at Corinne). So it was back to the store, with a security grille and alarm system, and then the locksmith next door went under, so they expanded, and now they're doing well enough to hire a part-time baker and Sam is studying for a real estate license so they can get out of the business when all the children are grown.

Rebecca is *fine*, even lucky, but while she would never say it to her siblings, whose struggles in Spain dwarfed her own, her disappointments are many. She isn't rich or even well-to-do, though she was born to be, and spends too much time clipping coupons, stretching meals (more lentils, more onions) and scrounging for bargains, which depresses her, despite her knack for it. She is not surrounded by family and has a perpetual sense of being not quite at home, no matter how many bulbs she plants and her pear tree growing taller every year. English has never become her language, even as her Ladino and French have dimmed, and she often feels thick-tongued, (something she shares with Luna), without recourse to the present or the past. More than anything, she is often lonely, wanting more chatter, more cuddling, more laughter and especially—is it odd for a woman her age, a mother of six?—more play.

Enter the Center. Who would have thought that a modest congregation filled with Ashkenazi Jews, Hebrew mispronunciations and a set of rituals just different enough to get under her skin would become for her a second (fourth? Fifth?) home? The Cambria Heights Jewish Center has, in part because of the Sisterhood's fundraising efforts, recently moved from a storefront on Linden Boulevard to a freestanding building on 222nd Street, where it boasts two stained-glass windows featuring Magen Davids and twining vines, along with oak pews bought secondhand from a church and a large multipurpose room with a stage. The structure is a vast improvement over the storefront, and if it's not nearly as elegant as the Ahrida synagogue of Rebecca's childhood, neither must it stay hidden like the oratory at Carrer de Provença, though within two months of the Center's opening, someone threw a rock through one of the stained-glass windows, splintering a curled green leaf. Random mischief or anti-Semitism? The perpetrator remains uncaught, and the rabbi warns them not to assume, though they all do.

REBECCA SINGS. She has a small but devoted following and is known for her unusual repertoire of Spanish, Hebrew and Ladino songs. This time, it's a variety show, the "222nd Street Revue." Entrance tickets and donations will go toward the purchase of more coffee urns and chafing dishes, and to the charity fund for refugees in need. It's mid-May, always an emotional time for her—spring with its hopeful sprouts and blooms, but also her mother's *meldado*, with her father's following in June. When Lillian Katz, who is directing the show and thinks Rebecca is exotic, first asked her to perform a solo ("Maybe something in Spanish, to add pizzazz!"), she was happy to oblige but hesitated long enough to have a bargaining chip in the form of a request: "For Sultana Camayor Cohen, of blessed memory" beside her name in the program.

Al comes in from Brooklyn the night before the show, always game for freshly washed sheets and a home-cooked meal. Luna first accepts Rebecca's invitation and then declines, saying she's not feeling well, and then, at the last minute, calls to accept again, throwing a wrench in the plans, because now Sam has to drop everything to drive to the Bronx to pick up her and Gene, who do not drive. This means that Rebecca, due at the Center an hour before showtime, must walk there herself, hauling a bag with her costumes and props, arriving sweaty and frazzled, and that the rest of the children—everyone but David, in Chicago—have to get there on their own, with Suzanne in charge of wrangling Frank. They manage to arrive on time, but Sam, Luna and Gene cause a disruption by walking in a good fifteen minutes after showtime in the middle of a Yiddish comedy sketch, and they can't sit with the family, so that when Rebecca steps onstage for her solo a cappella number, the evening's grand finale, she feels scattered and doesn't know where to look.

Ija mia mi kerida,
aman, aman, aman.
No te eches a la mar,
ke la mar esta enfortuna,
mira ke te va yevar.

My daughter, my dear, *aman, aman, aman*. Don't throw yourself into the sea, for the sea is stormy and will carry you away.

The song is from her childhood, and while the words are bleak, the melody is cheerful, with a dance-like tempo. Sam and Suzanne have painstakingly translated the lyrics into English for the printed program, getting tripped up on *aman*, which Sam thought meant something like love, or maybe Haman, the Purim villain, or maybe amen. At the public library, the two of them discovered that it meant woe is me in Turkish and Greek, safety in Arabic and something akin to believe in Hebrew, but when they came home and told Rebecca, she rolled her eyes and said just let it be, it means *aman,* so they left it untranslated. At home, the family mostly speaks English now, and the American-born children's Ladino is of the kitchen variety, but Rebecca's still comes out for singing, fighting and lovemaking and remains the burnished language of her dreams.

The daughter answers:

Ke me yeve i me traiga,
aman, aman, aman.
Siete puntas de ondor
ke m'engluta peshe preto,
para salvar de l'amor.

May it take me, may it pull me down, *aman, aman, aman*. Seven fathoms deep may a black fish swallow me to save me from love.

Rebecca delivers the song with her eyes shut and hands in fists at her sides, entering into it with her fullest voice and heart. She sings to her mother and father, to El Dyo, to the oceans she's crossed and people she's lost, good souls she met along the way, never to see again. She sings to Rahelika, of blessed memory, and to her brother Marko, who is still alive but has lost his mind; to Josef, Isidoro and Elsa, far away; even to Corinne, who was invited to the show but didn't come—there's a frostiness between them, this the most corrosive sort of sorrow, the nearby faraway. She sings to her children, to protect and instruct them but also to lift their spirits high, for while the lyrics are somber, the melody offers an upbeat counterpoint.

When she finishes, she makes a spontaneous decision to begin again, but this time, she opens her hands and eyes, looks out. Squinting past the lights, she sees many familiar faces, along with a few unknown to her. Some people have lost sons and husbands to the war or had family murdered in the camps, though they rarely speak of it and it's considered taboo to bring it up. A few—Sylvia Berger's German cousin; Gloria Michnik's Polish nephew and his skinny, silent wife; an elegant couple said to have come by way of French Switzerland (in time, they will become Rebecca's and Sam's closest friends)—are refugees. Rebecca sings for their heartache and the ones they lost, and against the evil in the world.

As she rides the melody, she abandons the words and begins to hum the song in nobody's language, which is everyone's.

"Sing with me," she says into the microphone, and Jeannette Matz steps up to the upright piano to plink out the tune, and the audience joins in while Rebecca sways, having become an instrument like her father's hollow ney flute—a channel for the voice, he claimed (though her mother thought it hubris), of God.

Then it is over. There's a moment of silence, followed by a great wave of applause. Rebecca gulps for breath and tries to curtsy, awkward, even shy, the armpits of the rose silk dress she sewed for the occasion damp with sweat. "*Mersi muncho, grasyas,* thank you. You are kind!" she says. She is proud and happy, filled with love for the people in the room, even as part of her is pulled back to her childhood, and she is standing at the ark of the pink Ahrida synagogue with her father, who is not supposed to bring her up here but does so anyway because this is his home and she his little girl who loves to sing.

SHE HEARS a disruption, something happening in the audience. There's a noise, a weird yelp. Heads turn toward the sound. The clapping stops, replaced by a murmur. Is someone sick? Could an animal have crept into the room? (A few raccoons got in once, creating a mess.)

But no, it's Luna, rising from a folding chair at the end of an aisle, stumbling, righting herself, making tapping noises on the parquet floor with her cane. It is Luna; does she need to use the bathroom? Sam gets up and reaches toward her, but she uses her stick to wave him away, and he sits back down. She is heading for the stage, clutching something bundled—it's flowers—saying *CONGRAH CONGROO* (my god), *Congratulations, Mother!* Thank you, Luna, very nice, but why not later in the lobby? The show isn't quite over. Backstage, behind the green velvet curtain that Rebecca made from two sets of rummage sale drapes, Lillian Katz is preparing to step out to make a plea for donations, after which the cast will assemble for a final bow.

By now Luna is halfway down the aisle, walking toward the stage with her lurching gait. Some members of the audience must recognize her from when she still lived at home, or because she comes occasionally to services. Her ninth grade classmate Lisa Bergman, now Lisa Minsky, is here, a swaddled infant on her lap, but the space is full, and there are people who won't know who Luna is. Rebecca sees that she is wearing an unfamiliar navy-blue dress with gold sailor buttons, paired with a blue pillbox hat with a coy little net, and that she has on deep red lipstick, one might even say expertly applied.

Up Luna goes, navigating the steps to the stage, approaching Rebecca with a bouquet of carnations and baby's breath bound by a silky red ribbon, and *thank you, thank you, darling*—Rebecca leans to kiss her on the cheek. Luna is whispering in her ear, saying something—*sorrylatesicktomystomachsomethingtotellyoulater*—and as Rebecca grabs her bare, warm forearm, she grasps Luna's meaning and whispers oh my god, are you, do you mean you're—? And Luna laughs, a quick, delighted peel that the microphone turns into a high-pitched bell, and says yes she is. *I am.*

The news lands in Rebecca in a great, shocked undoing. Everyone is watching. As if on cue, Lisa Minsky's baby wakes up and starts crying lustily. There is something untoward about Luna delivering flowers to the stage as if it's about Rebecca when it's (always) about Luna, then dangling such intimate news. Rebecca could guide the child off except that Luna is no child—she's a married woman. An old, tired anger washes over her. Luna has always had it out for her, for not being her mother or being too much her mother, for dividing Sam's love, for mending but not fixing her, for being able to stand before an audience and sing. But then she catches Luna's hand resting on her stomach—does she detect a swell?—and meets Luna's eyes, which are damp with happy tears.

Luna is pregnant. They said she couldn't walk and (with Rebecca's help) she walked, and then they said she couldn't go to school and (with Rebecca's help) she went to school, and then they said—it was implied—that she would never marry, but Rebecca had her sew items for her dowry because it was good for her hands and because (so said the nuns) even the least among us deserve to hope, and Luna met Gene. Now this.

Rebecca tries to summon her public self, shiny, almost laminated, but she is unsteady on her feet, still processing the news: the joy—a new life, a baby to hold—but also the worry because Rahelika wasn't built for birth, her pelvis too narrow, and Luna might not be either, and even if mother and baby survive, raising a child will be a daily struggle for someone like Luna, and Rebecca is done with all that and cannot (should not) step in to save the day. Did Dr. Carlson give Luna the go-ahead, or is she risking her life and that of the child's, as Lika did, told after her first failed pregnancy not to bear more children?

Rebecca takes a wobbly step, stumbling in her kitten heels, and as she does, Luna reaches for her hand with her bent one, as small as a child's and so deeply familiar that it might be Rebecca's own. Rebecca nudges them toward the top of the stairs, where they stand gripping each other's hands. At Luna's touch, she feels a settling, almost a correction: Push me hard but not too hard, follow my spark, love me (love yourself) through the ugliness, my own and your own. *Deshame entrar, y me azere lugar.* Let me enter, and I'll make a place for myself. Celebrate my one and only life.

It is not the first time that Luna has served as her teacher, nor will it be the last, though Rebecca is—will always be—a reluctant student as far as Luna is concerned, as Luna also is (will always be) with her, though they'll bond for a time over the child, to be born a healthy boy named Carl, after Dr. Carlson.

The audience is loud now, even as Jeannette has started a light jazzy number on the piano, as if to suggest an intentional interlude or signal that Luna and Rebecca (Laurel and Hardy?) are preparing for a final act. Some people stand to let Lisa Minsky leave the hall with her screaming baby, then shuffle back to their seats. Lillian Katz has come out from backstage with a straw sombrero to pass around and is shooting looks at Rebecca. This would be the moment to step offstage, but Rebecca has a premonition that to do so would bring bad luck and that Luna and the baby need a blessing, a welcoming.

"Should I share your news with them?" she whispers to Luna in Ladino. "Has it been long enough, *ojo malo*?"

Luna blanches and says no, then laughs and says actually sure, go ahead, why not, it's three months today. Because whether she knows it or not, this is what she wanted from the start, as early as when she said yes, I'll come to your show, and then sorry, I won't, and actually, I will; when she pinned the blue hat to her head and applied the lipstick; when she came up with the bouquet, stealing Rebecca's thunder. To be celebrated (a pity Lisa Minsky left the room), to be seen.

Rebecca guides Luna carefully toward center stage. "Friends," she says into the microphone. "I ask you for your quiet. I have something to tell you, with my daughter's permission."

Jeannette stops playing the piano. Rebecca scans the chairs. She can make out Sam and Gene whispering, heads bent close, and Al doubled over with what looks to be laughter, and Suzanne with her face in her hands, humiliated beyond measure at the scene.

"Ladies and gentlemen," Rebecca says with a flourish worthy of Barnum's. "My daughter has told to me some very big news! God willing, she'll be a mother in the fall! Please, everybody, clap for her!"

She passes Luna the flowers to free up her hands and start the applause. A few people join in, a weak smattering of sound, as Luna, red-faced, squirming, fixes on her shoes.

"Hello? I can't hear you!" Rebecca cups her ear. "My beautiful daughter, Mrs. Luna Leshefsky, and her husband, Gene, are expecting a baby! Come fall, *mashallah*, I'll be a grandmother!"

~

A PAUSE, AND SOMEONE rises from his seat. It is Al, quickly followed from across the room by Sam, who stands tall, clapping and clapping, he who usually stays on the sidelines at the temple and doesn't serve on committees or play poker with the other men.

"Look up," Rebecca hisses at Luna. "That's your papa clapping for you! Look out at him. Be proud."

Luna lifts her head as Gene stands, too, with some effort, swinging a hand in the air in a kind of royal wave. Jack and Frank get up and start to clap. Suzanne rises now, though with shoulders hunched, and Essie Zimmerman and her husband, followed by the ladies from the Sisterhood. Then Rabbi Schevelowitz, a wet blanket if you ever saw one, and soon the whole audience is standing and clapping as Rebecca retrieves the flowers, takes Luna by the arm—be careful on the stairs!—and prepares to escort her off the stage.

ACKNOWLEDGMENTS

Although I wrote *Kantika* as a novel, I played with the line between fact and fiction and drew on the experiences of some real people, most centrally my maternal grandmother, Rebecca (née Cohen) Baruch Levy (1902–1991). I used real names for several characters, including Rebecca, and made use of historical details, family stories and photographs, even as I changed facts to suit the story, imagined inner lives and invented liberally at every turn.

In 1985, when I was twenty-one, I visited my grandmother Rebecca in central Florida, where she and my grandfather Sam had retired, and recorded her telling stories. The two microcassettes that hold her voice are the seeds that, decades later, grew into this book. More recently, I interviewed my uncle David Baruch (1926–2021) about his childhood in Barcelona and New York and his experiences on the USS Franklin during World War II. From his deathbed, the day before he died on December 10, 2021, David told me over FaceTime that he'd like me to use his real name in my book. My uncle Albert Baruch (1928–2015) did not live to see this novel completed, but I interviewed him in 2013, and this project is the richer for his stories. In her retirement, my aunt Luna Levy Leshefsky Liebowitz (1927–2006) wrote both informally and for a column in the Fort Lauderdale *Sun Sentinel* about the disability community, art, culture, Judaism and her life as a bright, ambitious girl with cerebral palsy in the 1930s and '40s. Luna died before I began this project, but we connected over writing and much else, and I'm grateful for her many gifts.

My uncle Franklyn Levy shared vivid memories of the past. The photograph at the end of this book, of Rebecca feeding the birds, was taken by my uncle Jack Levy (1935–2011). My great-aunt Elsa's daughter, Silvia Lissitza Camayor, welcomed me to Barcelona and took me to the site of the former synagogue on Carrer de Provença and to visit my great-grandfather Alberto Cohen's grave in the Cementiri de les Corts. Hal Behl, son-in-law of Rebecca's sister Corinne, shared oral histories and Corinne's sketch of the family's house in Istanbul. My cousins Rachel Baruch Yackley and Jonathan Baruch shared family documents and photos.

My mother, Suzanne Levy Graver, has been a steadfast companion, guide, reader and inspiration throughout my life and during the writing of this book. In 1995, she took me on my first trip to Turkey, where we were warmly welcomed by my grandfather's cousin Sait Asseo and his wife, Nanette. In 2014, my mother traveled to Barcelona with me for a research trip. My sister, Ruth Graver, was often my first reader, offering astute insights and encouragement and exploring Astoria with me. My father, Lawrence Graver, died before I began this project, but I drew on his rich library of Jewish American literature and felt him cheering me on. My husband, Jimmy Pingeon, and our daughters, Chloe and Sylvie Graver Pingeon, provided companionship, adventure, feedback, peace and quiet, patience, laughter and boundless love.

Many people opened doors for me on my travels and research forays. In Istanbul, I am grateful to Lorans Tanatar Baruh at SALT Galata archives, as well as to Mirey Derkazez, Izak Eskanazi, Abdulkerim Golkap, Saadet Özen and Suzan Sevgi. Burhan Kaya, Nick Ozick and Esther Messing led the Boston College faculty travel seminar in Turkey, where some of my colleagues traipsed with me to the site of my grandmother's childhood home and musicologist Ann Lucas led us to a ney workshop. At Istanbul's Oryom Old Age Home, Rachel Calderon and Estella Mizrahi Estella shared memories with me; Violet Aroyo arranged that visit. Rifat Sonsino, Tony Hananel and my relatives Yosi and Peggy Asseo offered advice before my research trip to Turkey. Aline Gandillon McGowan flew from Paris to Istanbul to tag along on several quests and talk late into the night.

In Barcelona, Lucía Conte Aguilar, Teresa Nandin and Dominique Tomasov Blinder were knowledgeable guides to past and present Jewish Spain. My trip to Cuba and my understanding of the Jewish community there were aided by Maritza Corrales, Armando Montalvo Costa, Yuri Sasson, Judy Schiller, Esther Jequin Savariego and Tim Weed, and by the lively companionship of my daughter Chloe. In Cambria Heights, Queens, Adima and Omar Mohammed welcomed my mother, my daughter Sylvie and me into my mother's childhood home during Ramadan, shared their own migration stories and sent us off with peppers and basil from their garden because, in Omar's words, "We're all from Abraham."

Several scholars responded generously to my out-of-the-blue queries. Aron Rodrigue, at Stanford University, offered invaluable help with regard to both Judeo-Spanish (otherwise known as Ladino, Spanyol, Muestro Spanyol) and Jewish life in early twentieth-century Istanbul. His impressive scholarship informs this project. Gloria Ascher welcomed me into her Ladino class at Tufts University, where I learned a great deal from her and from Matilda Koén-Sarano's book *Kurso de Djudeo-Espanyol.* Bryan Kirschen, at SUNY Binghamton, shared his Ladino expertise. Recordings of Ladino songs by Sarah Aroeste and Janet and Jak Esim brought them alive for me. I have also benefited from the expertise of Martine Berthelot, Dina Danon, Rita Ender, Michal Friedman, Allyson Gonzalez, Lori Harrison-Kahan, Maite

Ojeda-Mata, Devi Mays, Isaac Jack Levy and Rosemary Levy Zumwalt. Sarah Abrevaya Stein's essay about the herb rue, or *rudu* in Ladino, "The Queen of Herbs: A Plant's-Eye View of the Sephardic Diaspora," was a last-minute gift to this book. Thanks also to Sharon Pucker Rivo, Lisa Rivo and Richard Pontius at the National Center for Jewish Film, which granted me permission to reproduce two images from Ernesto Giménez Caballero's 1929 film, *Los judíos de patria española*, after I found, to my astonishment, that the film contained (unattributed) images of my family at the synagogue in Barcelona.

This book would never have found its shape without the gifts of intellectual and artistic friendship. Alexandra Chasin, Sharon Jacobs and Gish Jen were vital early readers. Molly Antopol, Suzanne Matson, Tova Mirvis and Bridgette Sheridan read multiple drafts and offered invaluable suggestions and encouragement. Darcy Frey helped me think about excerpts.

Ralph Savarese, with his groundbreaking work in disability studies, provided a nuanced reading of my manuscript. Dr. Earl Carlson's memoir, *Born Like That*, recounts his childhood with cerebral palsy and subsequent work as a pioneering doctor who founded a clinic at Columbia Presbyterian Hospital. I know from interviewing my grandmother that Luna was treated by a gifted doctor in a wheelchair at a special clinic at Columbia Presbyterian, a detail that, along with the dates lining up, led me to name Luna's doctor in *Kantika* after Dr. Carlson. The historical setting of the novel has led me to include language around disability that, while problematic, is nonetheless true to the period. I welcome how that language has changed over time.

Fellowships at Brandeis University's Hadassah-Brandeis Institute (HBI), Wellesley College's Suzy Newhouse Center for the Humanities, the Corporation of Yaddo and Marble House Project allowed me to dive deep in congenial settings. Special thanks to the Newhouse Center's director, Eve Zimmerman, as well as to Lauren Cote and my fellow Newhouse fellows—John Plotz, Keith Vincent and Kelly Mee Rich—and to Shulamit Reinharz, Debby Olins and Lisa Fishbayn Joffe at the HBI. Wide-ranging conversations and Sephardic cooking sessions with Sam Coates-Finke and Genevieve DeLeon at Marble House Project nourished me during the three weeks in June 2021 when I wrote the final chapter of this book. I am grateful to Boston College for research grants and leaves and to my English Department colleagues, especially Lynne Anderson and Laura Tanner, for their inspiration and friendship. Zachary Frank, Connor Pendray, Kristen Laracuenta and Michal Miller were meticulous, hardworking undergraduate research assistants. Christopher Soldt created digital images from old photographs.

My former literary agent, Richard Parks, is retired now, but his friendship remains a gift. Henry Dunow, my current literary agent, has been an astute reader and patient friend to this project. Riva Hocherman, my editor at Metropolitan Books, saw the soul of this story and drew it out with her keen edits. At Metropolitan Books/Henry Holt & Co., I am also grateful to Marian Brown, Sonja Flancher, Brian Lax, Morgan Mitchell, Shelly Perron, Lulu Shmieta and Allysa Weinberg, as well as to Karen Horton and Christopher Sergio for the gorgeous cover design.

In a 2013 interview in the *Atlantic*, Haitian American writer Edwidge Danticat talks about how all immigrants are artists. "You begin with nothing," she says, "but stroke by stroke you build a life. This process requires everything great art requires—risk-tasking, hope, a great deal of imagination, all the qualities that are the building blocks of art. You must be able to dream something nearly impossible and toil to bring it into existence." My grandmother Rebecca's life journey was infinitely more challenging than the literary one I took to write this book, but her grit, creativity and perpetual refashionings are stitched into every word.

Grasyas, all.

ABOUT THE AUTHOR

ELIZABETH GRAVER's novel *The End of the Point* was long-listed for the 2013 National Book Award for Fiction. Her other novels are *Awake*, *The Honey Thief* and *Unravelling*. Her story collection, *Have You Seen Me?*, won the 1991 Drue Heinz Literature Prize. Her work has appeared in *The Best American Short Stories*, *The Best American Essays*, *Prize Stories: The O. Henry Award* and *The Pushcart Prize Anthology*. She teaches at Boston College.

elizabethgraver.com